MARTIN MARTIN'S ON THE
OTHER SIDE

Mark Wyndham lives and works in Norwich.
This is his first novel.

MARK WERNHAM

Martin Martin's on the Other Side

VINTAGE BOOKS
London

Published by Vintage 2009

2 4 6 8 10 9 7 5 3 1

First published in Great Britain in 2008 by Jonathan Cape

Vintage
Random House, 20 Vauxhall Bridge Road,
London SW1V 2SA

www.vintage-books.co.uk

Addresses for companies within The Random House Group
Limited can be found at: www.randomhouse.co.uk/offices.htm

The Random House Group Limited Reg. No. 954009

A CIP catalogue record for this book
is available from the British Library

ISBN 9780099516026

The Random House Group Limited supports The Forest
Stewardship Council (FSC), the leading international forest
certification organisation. All our titles that are printed on
Greenpeace approved FSC certified paper carry the FSC logo.
Our paper procurement policy can be found at
www.rbooks.co.uk/environment

For Kaoru and Hana

Prologue

Part 1

Fontainebleau Forest, France,
Wednesday 15 November 1944, 11.43 p.m.

THERE IS a strange light deep in the forest. It flickers and makes the trees appear as if they are swaying, dancing even. There is a smell too. The smell is burning petrol, rubber, wood, tarpaulin and human flesh. The light and the smell both come from the same source: an army truck. The truck is a Bedford S Type, 4x4 general service vehicle, used by the British Army for transporting both personnel and equipment.

At a bend, the truck has swerved off the narrow, dark road, which is flanked on either side by the seemingly endless darkness of the forest, and hit a large tree. The tree bisects the front of the truck. The truck's bulbous, friendly face has caved in and the engine block has been pushed back into the truck's cab. There are two bodies in the cab. The passenger is slumped forward, his head between his knees, his arms hanging down, knuckles dragging on the floor of the cab. The driver is pinned to the back of the cab by the steering column, which has penetrated his chest, like a butterfly in a specimen case. His head hangs back and his hands lie limply in his lap. Each man has a single bullet wound to the head. In a little while, they will both be reduced to barely recognisable blackened meat by the ferocious blaze which is consuming the truck. The truck itself will be reduced to its steel skeleton, while the surrounding trees will bear their charcoal wounds for some years.

There is another dead body nearby, 400 metres back up the road from where the truck burns. The body has been hastily buried in the peaty ground of a clearing a few metres into the forest. The back of his head has been smashed like the shell of a boiled egg bashed with a spoon, and the blood in his body is still warm. In the cold night, barely visible wisps of steam emerge from the shallow grave. The man in the grave was called Emile Henderson.

A man is walking on the road. He is heading back towards Paris. It will take him many hours. He is smoking a cigarette and he is swearing to himself under his breath. He has smears of blood on his uniform, and his hands are caked with mud and blood. But this is wartime, and it is not unusual to see a soldier covered in the blood and filth of combat during wartime. The man's name is Edward Jackson, known to his army buddies as Jack Jackson.

Prologue

Part 2

Flat 6, Spa House, Rouel Road, London SE16
Wednesday 15 October 2008, 7.04 p.m.

THE FLAT has two bedrooms, a bathroom, a living room and a small kitchen. The kitchen is reached via the living room. In the living room, the television is quietly flickering. The remote control is on a large green sofa, where it was absent-mindedly thrown by the flat's owner after she'd switched the TV on when she came home from work.

Her returning-home-from-work ritual, which she herself does not even notice, and certainly wouldn't agree was any kind of 'ritual', starts as she leaves Bermondsey tube station on Jamaica Road. She turns left out of the station and walks along the road a short way to the newsagent's shop. Most nights, she goes in and picks up a carton of milk. She often buys a bottle of red wine too. She calls the shop a newsagent, but, in the four years she has lived in the area, the shop has gradually expanded from a modest newsagent, selling tobacco, wine, newspapers, sweets, fizzy drinks, crisps and a large selection of specialist pornographic magazines, into a fully-fledged mini-supermarket with shelves stacked with tinned food, toilet rolls, bread, cold meats, breakfast cereal and anything else the local populace might need to survive between 7 a.m. and 11 p.m., seven days a week.

Once out of the shop, she carries on along Jamaica Road, ignoring the noisy traffic that fills this main route in and out of south-east London, and heads for her flat. The flat is in a low-level new-build, a block of six. Flat 6, her flat, is on the second floor, the top floor. She lives there alone. She walks up the two flights of communal stairs, opens her front door, hangs her coat on the stand in the hall, puts her keys and her mobile phone on the shelf under the mirror and walks into the front room. She picks up the remote control from the arm of the large green sofa, presses the button and her television flicks into life. She throws the remote on to the sofa and goes into the kitchen where she uncorks the bottle of wine and leaves it to breathe on the surface next to the microwave oven. She then takes a frozen lasagne from Waitrose from the freezer. She removes the lasagne's cardboard slip case and places the container in the microwave, sets the dial to eight minutes and then reaches into the fridge's salad crisper and pulls out a bag of pre-washed mixed lettuce leaves. She then takes a plate from one of the cupboards and places it next to the bottle of wine. A knife and a fork and a wine glass soon join the the plate and the bottle.

She then turns her attention to the dishwasher. This morning, before she went to work, she set it to clean several days' worth of dirty plates and cutlery. She begins emptying it and putting everything away in its place.

Meanwhile, on the television in the front room, a chat show has started. A middle-aged woman with an air of authority about her is smiling at the camera. The studio audience is applauding. The programme is being broadcast live, as it is three nights a week. The light from the television illuminates the empty room, the bright television colours flash off the ceiling and walls. The applause dies down.

'Good evening and you're very welcome,' says the woman on the television. In the kitchen, the drone of the microwave and the clattering of the plates and cutlery as they're transferred from the dishwasher to their various drawers and cupboards render the television inaudible.

'Tonight,' continues the woman on the unwatched television, 'my guests include explorer and television-documentary maker Ralph Jellings, just back from an arduous expedition to the South Pole, where he lost three toes to frostbite.'

The audience applauds again, this time briefly and desultorily.

'Also on the show is the leader of what he claims will be a new force in British politics, the Democratic Union Party, Sir Geoffrey Perkins.'

There is even less applause at this announcement.

In the kitchen, microwaves continue to agitate the molecules of the lasagne. The digital readout on the front of the microwave oven reads 6:58. The lasagne has been cooking for one minute and two seconds.

'We have the latest indie sensations from New York playing live, Man, Controller of the Universe,' says the woman on the television.

The woman finishes emptying the dishwasher and helps herself to a generous slug of red wine.

The microwave oven's timer pings. The steaming and dangerously hot contents of the container are quickly sliced and slopped on to the plate alongside some lettuce leaves. On the television, Barbara James is talking to her first guest.

The woman carries her meal into the living room and heads for the sofa. She sets her plate down on the coffee table between the sofa and the television, switches on a floor lamp and focuses on the television.

On the television, a man is sitting on a brightly coloured couch; he is rocking backwards and forwards. He is sweating, his mouth is hanging open in a drooping grin, a mischievous-idiot grin suggesting an imminent act of rebellion. Under his eyes, beneath the television make-up, are the dark crescents of sleep-deprivation or mental illness. The television interviewer looks at him with concern on her face. Several moments of uncomfortable television silence pass.

'She's dead,' says the ill man on the television. 'A man killed her,' he suddenly says. 'Arthur Penroody. 38 Pilmer House, Neckinger Estate, London, SE16. She's still there. He's still there.'

Then the woman sitting on her sofa, about to tuck into her Waitrose lasagne and bagged salad, witnesses four seconds of the conventions of television being abandoned. The image cuts several times in quick succession: the shocked face of the woman presenting the chat show, the haunted face of her guest, Martin Martin; a fast and blurred panning shot of the audience, some of whom are looking horrified; the presenter's face again, looking off-camera, bewildered. The sound is scrambled, as if the sound engineer in the BBC control room is punching buttons and pushing faders up and down at random. There is some shouting. Then the television screen goes blank. A few moments pass, and then a vacuously cheerful voice suddenly fills the void.

'Well, we appear to have lost transmission of *The Barbara James*

Show,' it says, 'but stay tuned for *All in the Family*, which will start in a few moments.'

'Oh,' says the woman in the flat, out loud. She then shrugs and reaches for her food and waits for *All in the Family* to begin.

Later that night, in bed, the woman wakes suddenly. She has been dreaming. She has been dreaming about the strange man on the television. His pale, sickly face, sweating and drooling, had been looming into her mind, in and out like an image in a funhouse mirror.

'She's dead,' the face kept saying.

The woman is delirious. Waking up, she realises she is sick, poisoned. Maybe it was the lasagne, but more likely the crayfish sandwich she'd grabbed at lunchtime that day. She can taste it at the back of her throat. She burps gently, putting her hand up to her mouth. She realises she is going to vomit, throws her bedclothes back and rushes as fast as she can to the bathroom. She spends the rest of the night vomiting. She vomits until she is weak, her body wracked by spasms even when there is nothing left to eject. Eventually, too drained to even grasp the edges of the toilet, she stays in bed, leaning over a bowl on the floor, roaring at it when the waves of nausea and gastric contractions can't be staved off any longer, producing only saliva and a few drips of dark bile. Eventually, she falls asleep.

She awakes again, confused and uncertain of the time. Having been awake most of the night, she has slept through the day, and the evening is fast approaching. She feels better. Her head is throbbing and she is weak, but she is tearfully grateful that her ordeal is over.

She was once told by a student doctor at a party that the best curative for a bout of food poisoning is a fizzy drink, preferably 7-Up. With a raging thirst, the woman gets out of bed, washes, throws on some clothes and heads out of the flat to undertake the four-minute walk to the newsagent.

There is a strange atmosphere on the streets. She can detect a whiff of burning in the air, but it doesn't really register in her distracted mind. If she'd been more aware, less concerned with her pounding head, her sore stomach and her outrageous thirst, she would have realised that it was not the healthy bonfire type of smoke she was smelling, but the acrid tang of man-made products going up in flames, giving off toxic fumes and billowing clouds of dense black smoke. It is the smell of cars burning on the nearby estate, mixed with the petrol-assisted conflagration of a flat occupied by a man suspected by many of the local residents of being a pervert of some sort. If it wasn't for the noise of the traffic on Jamaica Road, she would have heard people shouting and laughing and the sound of breaking glass.

The police sirens don't alert her to anything being out of the ordinary, nor does the thundering whir of a helicopter overhead. They are as familiar and unremarkable to her as the constant rumble of the traffic of London – part of the ambient bedrock of her life.

Before she gets to the newsagent to buy her 7-Up, her mobile phone trills in her coat pocket. Flustered, she scrabbles for her phone, but she misses the call. Annoyed, she throws the phone back into her pocket, deciding to wait until she gets back home, when she'll feel less harassed, to listen to the message, if there is one. She continues on her way to the newsagent. When she pushes open the door of the shop, a man barges past her, nearly knocking her to the ground. She is too shocked to take any action and walks into the shop. But when she reaches for a can of 7-Up, she notices that her hand is shaking, and her brain suddenly processes what has just happened.

'Bloody hell! Did you see . . . ?' she says to the shopkeeper, but the shopkeeper isn't standing behind the counter, where he normally is. He is lying on the floor behind the counter. He has been knocked unconscious by the man who has just fled the shop. Without warning, the man used a torch made of steel to hit the shopkeeper around the side of the head and then robbed the till. He has got away with £320 in tens and twenties and a handful of scratch cards, which he grabbed and tugged from their dispenser like toilet paper.

The woman, a sensible and pragmatic person, calls the police and an ambulance, and puts the newsagent in the recovery position while she waits for them to arrive, her own sickness forgotten in the light of this more pressing medical emergency. The paramedics bundle the newsagent off to hospital, where he spends one night under observation and has his head wound stitched up. He is allowed home the next day, and ordered to take it easy for a week. The woman tells the police officers who arrive what she saw (which is very little: she can't even tell them what colour skin the robber had), gives them her address and, eventually, about an hour later, she gets home.

Excited and disturbed by the evening's events, she fishes her mobile phone from her coat pocket and flops on to her green sofa with the intention of calling her best friend to tell her all about what has happened. She needs to talk to a friendly voice to calm herself down and to screech with laughter at the madness of it all, otherwise she will brood about it and become anxious. She is about to dial when she remembers the call she missed earlier. She dials the message-service number and waits the couple of seconds it takes for the recorded voice to tell her that she has one message.

She continues listening, impatient to take the message so she can get on with calling her friend. The message starts with a few moments of hiss and then a voice that she dimly recognises says:

'My name is Martin Martin. Listen to me. Call the police. The newsagent is being robbed.'

Then the line goes dead.

One

OI OI! Heads up! Jensen Interceptor here. And here is what I have to tell you: my fucking story. All the ins and outs and everything. Believe or don't, I don't give one either way, cos me, I'm going places, yeah? On the ladder, on the way. A grade two man, yeah, not a numb-nuts grade-oner like the boy you're about to meet. The boy I was, once upon a time.

What you're about to read is all tru. The incomplete truth is tru, innit? Geddit? Ha ha ha. So, this is the tru bio of Jensen Interceptor and his adventures with all the Martin Martin thing and how I came to be what I am today. But then, like, after all what I've been through and everything, I've learned that really there's no such thing as the truth. Just different versions or angles, like when you're watching *Porn Disco* and you want to change which girl's skirt you're looking up, so you press the button on the remote. What you see is still the same disco in Brazil or El A or wherever, but what you see is totally different. Do you get my meaning?

Let's get right into it, then, yeah?

Fucking great.

Two

So, to get you up to speed and in the groove, here's a typical day at the inter-department refectory, the place where I was working when it all kicked off. Not in the refectory. I wasn't making food and rubbish. What I mean is, I wasn't fucking working in the fucking refectory, yeah? I just ate there at lunchtime.

Anyway, everyone's in a right fucking tizz about security leaks. Everyone's all gibbering on about it, and there's a load of civil-service drones in shit suits from the Ministry of Peace who are well under suspicion, and they're all, like, totally paranoid and blaming each other and shouting all the time, all, like, giving it argy-bargy and chesting each other about in the refectory, calling each other cunts and that. The trouble is that all this is getting in the news, and the headlines don't look good, which makes the Department of Media and Culture, which is who I work for (in the Social Studies Section), really fucking uptight.

Me, I'm minding my own, thinking about how things went totally monster the night before. I'd just received my first DP (Debt Payment) after a month working at the Social Studies Section. My first job after graduating first class from Study Centre 16. A bunch of us from the old college who all started working on the same day (and so received our first DP on the same day too) got together for a night on the fuck. We started the evening off at the Pepso Tavern, where we had three grammes of boris each before heading off to Starfucks. My mate Fyodor came too.

I wasn't as bad as Fyodor. He can't really take his boris that well and he ended up in the Roman room, and we all know what goes on there, yeah?

Fyodor's fucking funny. He doesn't say 'Starfucks', he says 'Tsarfucks'. It's a Russian thing. Fyodor's Russian, yeah? But like English too.

I stuck to the main room for some hot action and some killer boris. Fucking great. Anyway, to cut a long story short, I forgot to take any Anvil when I got home, which is why I feel so monged on this day, and all the shouting about who's doing the security leaks is doing my head proper in.

With all the row going on, I'm reminding myself that the job I've got is all right. I am serving the community. If I stick at the department, in five years I can expect to be a team leader, and in ten perhaps I'll be a governmental advisor in the D Notice Building. Daddy big bollocks. Fucking great. Working for any of the government departments is totally better than most other jobs. For a start, your initial Life Debt is reduced by five per cent immediately. Mine is 994,000 cos I got seventy years expectancy off the genome comparison scan, and I know people who are the same age as me who have gone into retail whose LD is well over the 1 million mark. I get 1,380 a month, but in five years that'll go up to 1,500, and if I get to be a GA in the D Notice Building, it'll be 2,000. The way I work it out is that once I've got ten years' service under my belt, it'll only be another thirty-four years before my LD is paid off and then I'm home and dry. For now, though, I have a monthly allocation of thirty hours at the Pepso Tavern and thirty hours at Starfucks to keep me all funned up. You get more stuff like that the longer you stay at the department. The older guys like skateboards and getting all boozed and fighting, but us youngsters go for the boris and all the other fun powders and pills and preparations, and orgies. I suppose it's natural, just the way we humans are. It's all about freedom of choice.

I was a student of media relations at Study Centre 16. It was a course module designed specifically for joining the Social Studies Section at the Department of Media and Culture, and so here I am. Fyodor went into the International Media Section, what with him being Russian and being able to speak the lingo. He can speak all the Chineses too. He's a total fucking linguist. It helps when dealing with other governments who haven't got their shit together and learned how to speak the Chineses or English.

The Department of Media and Culture shares a building with the Archive Facility, where Fyodor does extra filing work on weekends like a twat cos he wants to get his Life Debt sorted early. He's always off his choppers after a night at Starfucks when he's wheeling papers up and down the Archive Facility's corridors. He's probably put all the wrong papers in all the wrong places, but he doesn't give a fuck. He says he spends most of his time there kipped out in some far-flung corner where no one ever goes. They leave him to it, he says. No one cares down there anyway. All those smelly old papers about boring gov shit from years back – stick it all in a hole in the ground and burn it, I'm always saying to Fyodor, just to wind him up really. It's a laugh winding Fyodor up.

This is a typical day, so as usual it starts at about seven. I wake up and take a shower straight away. My fucking neat Dermo Shower. You walk in and the water just comes out. You don't have to set it or anything. They clean themselves while you're at work too. I'd sorted myself a spank Dermo Shower as soon as they came out. Fucking great.

The building I live in is the Rotherhithe Sky Tower. It looks out all over London, north and south and west and east. Out of my bedroom window, I can see down on to the flat roof of the next building, what is called the Old Bank. It was never a bank or nothing, they just called it that to make it sound cool. The Old Bank is an all right building, not as tall as the Rotherhithe Sky Tower, but smart flats in there. And sometimes on hot days the girls who live there come out and sunbathe up on their roof, and they get their titties and asses and minges out and lay there all covered in lotion, glistening and juicy. Once, I saw two of them going at it lesbo-style for laughs. Nothing I couldn't see ten times over any night in Starfucks, but when it's happening, like, for real in front of you, where it probably shouldn't be happening, well, it's a laugh, innit? Adds a bit extra to the normal day.

Another time this girl with a totally fucking spank pair of chumblies saw me bogging at her from my bedroom window, and she stood up and did a little dance for me, hanging off the big palm tree they've got growing right on the middle of the roof, where they've got a nice gardeny bit. Fucking great. Then she beckoned me to come over. It looked near enough to jump, but you know, it's like twenty-nine floors down from my bedroom window. I might have enjoyed a bit of roof-tumble action with the girl with the great chumblies, but the risk of jumping it seemed a bit too much just for a squeeze. And by the time I'd have gone down the twenty-nine floors, across to the bottom floor of her building, got in the lift and got up to whatever floor is the top one, she'd probably have buggered off anyway.

Sometimes, the naked girls hide behind the wall that goes around the edge of the building. It's only three-feet high, just to stop people accidentally wandering off the edge, but it's big enough that if they get down next to it, like they often do, I can't see a thing. And that really bums me out.

In the shower, I watch the waterproof screen I had put in with my Dermo, see what's going on. Being a government employee, I get the full set of shows, so I can pick and choose whatever I want. Fucking great. Sometimes I get a porn show, full size, in the shower. Gets me off to a nice start. Fucking great. A bit off-putting when the PM's bit breaks in on the half-hour, but that's what you get, I suppose. When the Prime Minister comes on, there's that little blast of music and his logo and he just quickly runs through the latest business. He's usually sat at his desk. Sometimes he talks about what's going on in the world and where we stand, but mostly he just cracks a funny. Once, all he did was turn to the camera and wink, and you could see over his shoulder that he was watching a porn show – it was the same one I was watching when he broke in! Fucking funny.

I was well into the *Porn Disco* shows. They've got a dance club in every time zone in the world, with a dancefloor made of glass, and under that there's all these cameras. So you flick on *Porn Disco* and you're looking up all the girls' skirts. They get in for free if they don't wear knickers. It's always live, so you never know what you're going to get, but you can change the camera angle or switch to another camera. I'd watch that when I was in bed on the visuals in the ceiling. Feels like you're there, innit?

Anyway, the job I'm doing this day is assisting in focus groups. We get tasks from the Special Media Research Unit and we go out into the community and ask them questions about what they're into and that. We do a group every day, in the morning, and we write up the report in the afternoon, and it gets sent off to the Special Media Research Unit, and then they know what sort of shows people want to see, which ones are working and which ones are crap. We'd done porn shows (which was fucking great, what with it being my speciality and everything), food shows: all sorts.

Now you know all about me and my world and the normal boring shit that goes on, let's move on. Let's get into it.

Three

IT WAS the day the new art was put up. I really liked the one in Piccadilly Circus. It's fucking funny. The PM is standing up, nice suit, shaking hands with a banana. It's even bigger than the one that was there before.

I'd started on food and history recognition for a FG. There wasn't so much work this time, the Special Media Research Unit had done it all. Normally we'd have to do a bunch of research and come up with the initiative concepts ourselves and have them OK'd by the Special Media Research Unit and then go out in the field and use our own material in the focus groups. This time they'd supplied us with all the questions and the structure of the groups. All we had to do was organise them, ask the questions, and send the info straight back. No analysis, no reports, nothing. They just wanted the raw data. It's an annual thing and quite intensive. The real bummer of it was that this time, instead of just going around the usual communities, we had to get loads of info from the D and E grades too. Usually nobody gives a flying fuck what they think about anything, and we just talk to the As, Bs and C1s and C2s. The Ds and Es all live in really shitty places in north London. You never see them about, but we were having to go and find them and get them to join the focus groups.

The morning I'm talking about here, I'd had a real laugh at work. I found myself in the lift with the boss of the whole department, Brock. Brock has a smart suntan, nice watch, decent suit. I was on my way up to the fortieth floor to pick up the stuff from the Special Media Research Unit and Brock was probably heading for his office on the forty-fifth floor. He must be three-quarters of the way through his LD and it shows. It was just me and him in the lift and I goes:

'Nice suntan, Brock.'

And he goes, 'Yeah, thanks, son. Fucking great.'

And I go, 'Yeah, fucking great.'

And he goes, 'Where do you work?' So I told him and I said that we were starting on the Ds and Es next week and he says:

'Not that bunch of cunts,' which really cracked me up, and he starts laughing too and goes, 'You're all right, you are. What's your name?'

So I tells him and then it's the fortieth floor, where I got out.

Anyway, everyone back in the office was really impressed that I'd had a laugh in the lift with Brock.

At lunch, me and Fyodor went to the Starfucks in Charing Cross. I just stuck to coffee and watched all the sex while he went off back to the Roman room for some more torture. Fucking funny.

In the afternoon it's time for the FG for food and history recognition for the food shows and the raw data for the annual Ds and Es. You hear about the Ds and Es and the sort of conditions they insist on living in, but when you see it for yourself, well, it's enough to make you gag. I mean, you know. And they're so suspicious. You're in there to help, being useful to society, making the machinery of the nation tick along nicely, and they're all resentful and weird with you. I'm sure if it wasn't compulsory to attend focus groups they wouldn't even bother. It was a real effort to get them to shut up and, you know, like, focus. It's called a focus group, after all. I'm, like, '*hello*?'

So there we were, us from the Dept. of Social Studies, running the Special Media Research Unit's FGs in this big old boomy hall, sat at crappy old tables made of fucking wood, with hundreds of povos and twats all milling around, waiting to be asked the questions so they can piss off and get back to whatever bollocks it was that they were up to before we arrived.

The first part of the questionnaire was simple enough. I was dealing with this bloke called Reg. He must have been about sixty and was red-faced and looked stupid with all nasty thoughts in his head. He didn't say anything or try to look eager when I read him the FG Declaration ('Under statute forty-five, sub-section six, of the Consumers Act, you are required by the state to answer all and any questions an agent asks you. Any information you give may be used to alter conditions and products and may be passed on to pre-approved third parties blah, blah, blah, and any information which is deemed at a later date to have security implications may result in you being recalled for further interview at the pleasure of the state blah, blah, blah, please sign here' – I can say it in my fucking sleep).

My conversation with Reg went like this:

'Reg, I'm going to ask you some questions about your experience of life. You may find some questions don't mean anything to you, but try to answer them anyway. Do you understand?'

'Yes,' he says.

'How many 15+ meals do you eat in a week?'

Reg blinks and leans forward. 'What in the name of Herbert,' he goes, 'is a 15+ meal?'

'I'll put "none", then, shall I?'

'None. I would have thought so, yes,' says Reg.

'How could we improve the quality of your 15+ meal experience?' I ask. It's question two on the list.

'You couldn't improve my 15+ experience.'

'Right! Fucking great!' I say encouragingly. This is good, I'm thinking to myself, they always like positive feedback at the department.

Question three, then.

'Do you prefer the taste of Pepso Nouveau over old Pepso?'

'No.'

'Really?' I ask. 'Pepso Nouveau is so much better. It's new.' Which it is. Stands to reason. It's totally fucking great.

'I don't know what Pepso Nouveau is,' says this Reg.

'So you prefer old Pepso?'

'OK, put that,' says Reg, not really interested, I can tell. Not taking it fucking serious, which he fucking should, cos it fucking is. By this point I could see why the older geezers at the department dread doing the annual D and E FGs. I tick the box next to Pepso.

Anyway, then we go on to the history bit, and I'm bored with it, not knowing why they need to ask questions about history, thinking that it's all dead and buried and totally shit. We never done history at Study Centre 16. They only do it at Study Centre 1, and even there only five students are taken on each year. Fyodor had a mate who knew someone who went into the History Department, and the Mate said that after a week he never saw the bloke again. They go off into a special restricted department and you never hear of them again. Like mystery men.

The history bit goes like a game. You say words to them and they answer you with whatever comes into their head. I tried it with Fyodor the night before and it was fucking funny. It went like this:

'OK, Fyodor. I want you to say whatever comes into your head when I say a word to you. Don't worry, don't think about it too much. OK?'

'OK,' goes Fyodor.

'PM,' I says.

'Unity and Success,' says Fyodor, quick as quick.

'EU.'

'Euthanasia.'

'Fucking great,' I says, because that's when you have to say it, to keep encouraging the interviewee that they're doing very well.

'Totally fucking great!' says Fyodor, and laughs, excited.

'AIDS.'

'Recovery from mongover. Ha! Ha! Ha!'

Me: 'A Dolf Hitler.'

Fyodor: 'Googleplex?' he shrugs.

'Vietnam,' I carry on, all professional.

'China.'

'Korea.'

'China.'

'Japan.'

'China.'

'India.'

'China.'

'Russia.'

'China. How am I doing?' asks Fyodor.

'Fucking great,' I go. And then the next bit: 'Osama Bin Laden.'

'Widdly doot woodoo,' says Fyodor, doing an impersonation of me. Fucking funny. We both crack up.

'Martin Martin.'

'Martin Martin *Martin*,' he cackles.

'Al-Qaida.'

'Starfucks.'

'The Berlin Wall.'

'Let's go to Tsarfucks.'

'Witch-hunt.'

'I'm totally bored. Let's go to Tsarfucks,' goes Fyodor, looking out the window.

And so we did.

But when I played the history game with Reg, it went different. I don't know. I couldn't put my finger on it, but there was just a bad vibe coming off him. He took too long to answer each question, like he was thinking about what my reaction would be if he said certain things. He kept saying words like 'evil' when I said 'A Dolf Hitler' and 'yurp' when I asked him 'EU'.

Like, when I did the test with Fyodor he was all just having fun and saying the first thing that popped into his little tiny peanut brain. But Reg, he got too serious for my liking; kept swallowing too, like he was thirsty. So I mark him down in the column marked 'suspect'. That's where you put people who aren't good consumers and who piss you off. Twats and idiots get a sus mark. Once they've got a sus mark next to their name off one of our FGs, they don't get no special offers or coupons or three-for-one surprises, ever.

Four

NEXT UP, then, is a call. A call a few days later from Brock's office. So I goes up to see him and I'm feeling well sick and nervous in the lift as I go to the forty-fifth, all the way asking myself, 'What is it he wants to see me for? What have I done wrong?' I thought over everything I'd been working on and couldn't think of anything I'd got wrong. I'd met all my project deadlines on the last Strategic Information Initiative and filed everything just as I'd been told, and I was working on the new set of FGs, which was all going well and according to plan, so I thought I was in the clear all right.

But still.

Brock's got a spright office on the forty-fifth. Totally fucking great, with a smart view and a hot-piece-of-ass secretary who gets me to sit down and wait while Brock finishes off some other meeting. I'm sat there all thump-thump with a dry mouth when Brock pops his head around the door of his office – like the inner sanctum – and goes 'Come in, come in, sorry for the delay and all', putting me at ease as I walk in and take a seat in front of his desk.

'Now then,' he goes, 'Jensen, isn't it?'

'Yup,' I says.

'How long you been with us, Jensen?' he asks.

'A few months,' I says.

'Like it?' he says.

'Yeah,' I says.

'Good,' he says. Then he looks at his internal-info screen and flicks a few things around on the page. I'm thinking this meeting's going pretty fucking well by now. I'm relaxing.

'You was working on the history-recognition FG in Islington last week, yeah?' he says. My mind rushes back a week and I remember and nod.

'And you conducted the interview with Reginald Rankin, yeah?'

'Erm,' I goes, cos I can never remember their names and I'd totally forgotten about Reg cos I'd been to Starfucks after I did his FG and got totally messed up off of some top-bollock boris. Brock turned the info screen around so I could see it, and there was a picture of Reg.

'Yep,' I says, confident, 'I done him, yeah.'

'Was he a cunt?' asks Brock.

'He was a bit, yeah.'

Brock nodded and tapped a few things in on the info screen.

'Thing is,' he goes, 'he's been marked out. Some of his responses have, like, ticked some of the wrong boxes. Know what I mean?'

'Yeah, hmmm . . .' I goes, remembering how I'd put the sus mark next to his name cos he pissed me off and was acting like a tosser. I frowned like Brock and looked serious like he was.

'Listen, Jensen,' he says after a few moments. 'This might call for you to go on SP. Up for it?'

Special project! Working in the field on your own, keeping your own hours. A big deal, yeah? Like a trust thing. Good for promo.

'Fucking great!' I says.

'Fucking great!' goes Brock, and tells me that he'll meet me at the Security Building A19, which is on the Westway, about grid 14, first thing in the morning.

*

The Security Building is totally hardcore. The whole X-ray thing. And the pics they've got of the PM up on the walls aren't funny or anything. Brock was there in the foyer bit, sitting on a big expensive seat, a tagger with his pic on it hanging from his smart jacket. Made him look dead important, which I suppose he is. I'd already banged five dresdens just after breakfast, and their little particles were flying around my veins, making me feel cool and hard and tough and like I could cope with anything. The thing with dresdens, though, is that sometimes you start seeing things, like little specks and bits buzzing around in the air, and that can make you a bit flinchy-winchy, like you're about to get hit in the eye by one of these little darty specs of shit.

'Hey-ho, Jensen,' goes Brock when he sees me. 'Ready?' he asks.

'Yeah,' says I, trying not to duck and jerk my head about too much off of the dresdens and staring at him to prove that I'm in control and not fucked up. I'm not that fucked up, cos that's not what dresdens are s'posed to do, but I am a bit fucked up, cos the dresdens on top of the boris can be a bit of a headfuck, know what I mean? But no worries, I can fucking handle it, totally.

Brock signs me in with the receptionist, who fluttered her eyes at me like she wanted some. I'll do some more work on her on my way out, I thinks to myself, but I actually forgot, as it goes. Too fucking boshed off, I suppose, pumped off the dresdens and the boris and the adrenaline of the scene.

Me and Brock get in the lift, and now we're both wearing the security taggers and I'm feeling pretty cool. Like I've stepped up in the world. I've got a tagger. Fucking great. I want to shout and punch the air, but I keep my fucking lid on. I'm not a fucking prick.

So we goes up to the twelfth, the lift doors swish open and the lift voice comes out of the speakers: 'Brock, Interceptor – clearance three,' and we're stood in a big office which looks so totally boring that I nearly fall asleep on the spot. Just loads of desks and clerks and that dull low buzz of people tippy-tap-typing away on their machines and putting bits of paper in places and having serious chats, but quietly. No one's having a laugh. Real grown-ups' place. I puff my chest out with the tagger on it as we walk through the office and make our way to this bloke who's got his own room. We're going to talk to him about Reg and everything.

This bloke's office is crappy. Nowhere near as smart as Brock's in our building. There's no air, and all the furniture is made out of dark wood. There are filing cabinets lining the wall, the sort that you only see in shows about the old days, and the plastic glass between his office and the main office is yellow cos it's so old; it rattles in the door cos it doesn't fit properly. It even smells old. Dusty old papers and a pongy old-man smell. But Brock seems to think this bloke we're talking to is more important than him.

'Hello, Brock,' he goes.

'Hello, Miskin,' says Brock. 'This is Jensen Interceptor from Social Studies. He's the one what done the FG with Rankin.'

'All right, mate,' I goes, really cheery and polite and sticking my hand out for a shake. Miskin ignores my hand, which sort of hangs there in the air for a few seconds until Brock puts his on top of it and pushes it back down. I reckon Miskin's a right tosser, but I keep it to myself and stay smiling and looking bright and eager and buzzing off of the dresdens. After a few more moments of silence, Miskin sits back in his chair. His hair is thin and grey, and on the shoulders of his old, worn-out suit are flakes of white off his dirty old head. He slaps his hand on a fat file on his desk. It's got 'Rankin, Reginald' written on it. He looks into my eyes. His are blue and cold. He still doesn't say anything, and I feel his eyes are trying to look inside me.

'What we do here, Jensen,' says Miskin at last, 'is serious. It's important that you understand this.' His voice is whispery and higher than I'd expected. Posh too.

'I can see that, sir,' I says. And I can too. The Security Building gives off a stink of serious. Like, in our office, we've got really smart furniture designed in Italy in bright colours, and you can play table tennis or a guitar while you're having a break. All the inventives spend all their time with their feet up in the communal café area, joking about, thinking up new ideas for shows. They're not serious at all, it's like they're on playtime. But here in Miskin's office, there are no fun things, just grey steel cabinets and shabby old desks piled up with secret papers. The room seems to be eating up any light that comes into it. Gobbling it up greedy so no one else can have any. Despite that, and even though Miskin isn't wearing a smart suit with top-notch cufflinks on his shirt like what Brock does, a sparky exciting sense of power comes off him as much as the scary vibe he's dishing out.

'Our job, Jensen,' he says, 'is cleaning up after people.'

'Right you are,' I says, breezy.

'But if we can, we like to clean up before things get too messy. Good housekeeping, Jensen, you understand?'

'Yes, sir, Miskin, sir,' I goes. 'If you leave things without tidying them, it'll only be a lot worse when you get round to it, and it'll take a lot longer too. It's like totally better to keep things clean and tidy. I hate mess, me. Fucking straight up. I'm all for cleaning up.'

Miskin seems impressed by this, and he leans forward on his desk with his fingers making a pointed arch which he presses against his lips before he carries on speaking.

'There are two types of people in our society, Jensen,' goes Miskin. 'There are clean people, like us, and there are dirty people. If there weren't any dirty people making a mess, we could all get on with things and there'd be no need for the Security Department. But, alas, there are always dirty people around, and they will always make a mess. They can't help it, but they can make life difficult for the rest of us who are just trying to get on with things. Like if you have a leaking toilet. You need to mend the leak, yes?' says Miskin, and he looks at Brock before looking back at me.

'Yes, sir, that's right. Like Reg, eh, Miskin?' and then I thought maybe I'd been bit too familiar saying 'Miskin' like that, so I says 'sir' again.

'Mess isn't always the same sort of thing, Jensen, is it?' asks Miskin.

'No, sir,' I says. 'A leaky toilet gives you piss all over the fucking floor, and that's different from not cleaning when it gets dusty.'

'Quite,' says Miskin. 'But sometimes people can get into a mess with the way they think. They lack clarity and simplicity. They become confused and start doing the wrong things, and that can make them dangerous. That is where we come in. We like to keep an eye on situations, monitor people so they don't make the wrong choices, so they don't start making a mess of things. We like to make sure everything is OK for everyone. It's for their own good, you understand. We need to be reassured that just because someone is a bit confused, they're not going to pose a threat to society.'

'Yes. Reg could be a threat cos he's, like, not into 15+ meals and Quad and Pepso and stuff. That's like not joining in. I saw that. I noticed.'

'Yes, Jensen, that's right,' goes Miskin, smiling like when they smiled at me in the Duncan-Smith Infant Unit when I'd done something really skill when I was, like, seven years old.

'So now we need you to check up on Reg,' Miskin goes on. 'Just collect some information. We need to know what he's up to. We doubt it's anything serious, but, if we have you assigned to him, we can all relax, knowing that he's protected and has someone looking out for him, making sure he doesn't stray too far from the path. Can you do that, Jensen? Can you protect Reg for us? Take care of him?'

'Course I fucking can!' I goes. 'Lean on me, Miskin, I'll do it!', and I'm totally fucking buzzing cos this is the word from Mr Big, here's me getting assigned a special project.

'OK, Jensen,' says Miskin, smiling some more. 'You'll report for training and we'll see how it goes. If this goes well, Jensen, you could soon have a caseload of fifteen or twenty, and you'll be keeping an eye on all of them for us. You'll be like a shepherd taking care of his flock. And you can be sure that you're helping the Project, and the Project will help you in return.'

The Project. It's all about policy and implementation. The drive for Unity and Success. It's on all the posters and the art. It's etched into the sculpture of the PM at the Elephant and Castle, the one where he's naked with muscles: 'Unity and Success'. They told us about it at the Duncan-Smith Infant Unit. It's like a catchphrase, I suppose. Something to make you remember to feel good. Unity and Success, I mean, who'd be against that?

'Remember,' says Miskin, 'ours is a very important and a very big job. We here at the Security Department take care of a very great many people indeed.'

As he says these words, I can feel that it's all sort of coming clear to me now. How everything works, I mean. It's about how we all fit in and make things work. Keeping things tidy. Mending leaky bogs. Fucking serious work. Proper stuff and shit. He keeps talking, but I'm not really taking it all in. I'm seeing the way things work, and I'm seeing me walking around all, like, in charge and on my SP, like I've stepped up in the world and I'm trusted and not just the green fuck-weed kiddie. Fucking great.

So anyway, I flip out of my ace daydream as Miskin starts telling me that I have to attend a grade-one-protection training course. If I pass the course and do a good job, I'll get promo and a couple of thousand or more sliced off my LD, he says. Which would be fucking great.

'Yeah!' I says, 'that'll be fucking great!' and Miskin sort of shoos me out of his office by waggling his hand at me, going, 'Yes, very good, Jensen.'

I leave the Security Department with Brock at my side, thinking Miskin's a fucking great bloke, with my teeth gritted really, really hard, and my arms stiff down by my sides with my fists clenched against my thighs cos of the dresdens and the boris. And in my brain are all these mad colours whizzing past my eyes, flashing and spinning and tumbling and there's buzzing and whizzing in my ears and I can't hear a fucking thing Brock's going on about cos of my little private firework show.

Fucking great.

Five

TRAINING TO get my certificate in basic skills (protection) was all right, actually. Well, mostly. I had to get the certificate before I could go out on my SP and protect Reg, so there was no choice. I'd rather have just got on with it, got out there and starting keeping an eye on Reg, but the government-quotas system and the International Training Initiative Programme means that pretty much everyone has to get trained up before they can do anything. Anyway, I told myself as I moped along to the first day of the course at Study Centre 1200, it's only a four-day course.

The first day was just sitting in a classroom with about six other trainee protectors listening to all the induction stuff about health and safety and best practice. They're all dull, dull, dull, except maybe a bloke called Gibson, who's fucking funny and cracks gags all the time. I'm used to all the health-and-safety shit from my training at Study Centre 16. Back then, I sort of didn't pay attention and looked out of the window most of the time. But here they made me try harder than when I took my departmental entrance exams at the old Study Centre 16. That was like a course module and it took two years and all the tutors helped you and made sure you passed. Only total mongs didn't pass, and they were usually dumped out of the study centre well before any exam action got going. They were put into the special centres, where they either stayed for good or came out after a few years to be dirties, cleaning around the arse-end of buildings or working the power hoses on the streets at night-times.

At the end of day one, we all had to do a written test about what we'd learned during the day. It was a multiple-guess exam, so I did

OK. Got sixty per cent. But it did make me realise that maybe I should try a bit harder on the rest of the course if I wanted to pass and get my special project and get the promo and the privileges. The thing is, once Miskin told me all about life working for the Security Department, I'd kind of just fallen right into thinking that I was already a registered protector, living the lifestyle in my head, thinking about the LD getting paid off early and me walking about with the status and everything. So the pressure was on to pass cos I really wanted it.

The training thing improved on day two. I walked into the classroom feeling sleepy cos I, like, was. The smell of the room – wood from the floor and the funky ming of smelly bodies from yesterday – made me feel even more sleepy. I was trying to fight it off, forcing myself to fucking get into it, when Gibson comes up to me, a bit sneaky.

'Hoy, hoy! Jensen Interceptor!' he goes. 'Fancy a go on this?'

He hands me a baggie.

'What is it?' I ask Gibson.

'Fucking hype! A big bag of hype! I'm going to try it out, see if it does the trick.'

I'd heard of hype, but I never done it. Apparently, it was all the rage in the study centres, keeping students awake and making their brain tubes open up and gobble all the info being chucked at them like fat greedy jellyfish.

'Oh yeah, all right then, go on!' I says, all surprised, and I dig a spoonie in and snurfle it up my nodge. Gibson does the same. He looks at me and I look at him, sniffing, like we're both waiting for the hype to do something spectacular in our brains, but nothing comes. I shrug.

'Maybe nothing happens,' I say.

Gibson looks disappointed.

'Fucking shit rubbish,' he says. 'Let's do all of it.'

So we do, one spoonie after another goes up the nodge until we've done the lot.

I reckon it did the trick, and, thanks to Gibson, I learn all about making reports to your superior officer in the department, how to word the stuff that you present to the department, how often you have to report and the sorts of things they want you to make reports about. I learn about using initiative, about how you have to be creative when you're out in the field, how to mix in and not stand out, how to be invisible and ordinary. The tutor tells us how a secure society works, about how everyone keeps an eye on everyone, and how this becomes a self-perpetuating system of security, how lack of trust leads to complete trust. He discusses the relationship between paranoia and security, and shows us how they operate together, in harmony. Security without paranoia isn't security, he says. It's ignorance, he says, and while ignorance in individuals is OK, society cannot afford ignorance. Fucking right.

The teacher tells us about how the most difficult type of protection work, the sort that comes after a year or two, when you've got a larger caseload, is about being subtle, 'emphasising your banality', he calls it. But all of us who are going out into the field initially, he says, we'll be doing the easier stuff with obvious targets, where the dividing line between protector and target is clear. This line, he says, can get more blurred the deeper you go, the further into the craft of protection you go. But we don't need to learn that for basic skills, he says. So I don't.

But I do learn everything he says we need for basic skills, and I do much better when we have the exam at the end of the day. I get ninety-two per cent. Spot bollock! That gives me a running average of seventy-six per cent.

Day three is easily the best day, cos we're out the classroom and on to the study centre's environment simulator. This is where we learn about hiding around corners and how to do all the really smart spy stuff. How to blend in, be invisible.

It's a top laugh, walking behind hologram people, keeping the right distance behind them and sliding in to pretend doorways when they stop or turn around. I managed to follow my target for the full twelve-minute programme, from a shop to another building, and on the way I noted everything about it. I clocked the clothes he was wearing (herringbone-pattern God of Fuck coat – nice), I knew what brand of fag he stopped to light, I remembered the door numbers he stopped at, the name of the shop he started out from, and the tutor said my description of the building he arrived at was 'perfect'.

Gibson was fucking useless at it. He didn't take it serious and was just mucking about to make everyone laugh. The tutor didn't really mind too much, cos he knew that Gibson only needed an attendance credit, and he let him be silly and make us laugh. He made so many mistakes that it showed us exactly what not to do. Having a twat on the course kind of helped, cos it made the rest of us see ourselves as more serious and superior to soppy Gibson. At one point he went right up to the hologram bloke and put his arm over his shoulder and asked him the way to the spy school! That was towards the end of his simulation. It was fucking funny. Gibson's fucking funny.

By the end of the day, we all felt like we were professionals (except Gibson, of course), and there was no exam, just a tutor assessment of our performance over the day. I got ninety-four per cent! So my course pass was eighty-two per cent. It made me wish I'd tried harder on the first day, cos then I might have got ninety per cent overall, and then I'd have got a pass with honours. I was glad Gibson had turned up and nudged me to do better. Without him there, and his bag of hype, I might even have failed.

But then came the final day, the day of review and respond. I'd sort of forgotten about it, really. I'd read about the day in the course notes and it just seemed to be the sort of thing that you could sleep through without any fucker caring or noticing. And it didn't have any impact on the result of your grading for the previous three days, so I took it easy. Well, sort of. Actually, I wasn't that fucking easy at all.

It was Gibson's fault.

I'm in the toilets on the morning of the last day. I'm doing my hair and making sure I look fucking way cool when in walks Gibson. He looks a right old mess, like he's been out all night up some crack or three at Starfucks.

'Ooh, fucking hell, Jensen!' he says when he spots me. He comes up and stands next to me and looks at himself in the mirror. I look all spick and span and fucking cool, and he looks like a dirty, old trampy with white stuff at the corners of his mouth. His hair's all over the place and I see crusty bogeys in his eyes, and under his nails it's all dirty.

'You dirty fucker!' I says to Gibson. 'The fucking state of you!'

'Oh, don't, Jensen,' he says. But you can tell he's sort of proud of his filthy mess, like it's evidence. He's waiting for me to ask what happened.

'All right, you smelly tramp,' I says, and he grins at me. His teeth have got all bits stuck between them, food jammed in there. 'Where have you been?'

As I suspected, it was a night of extremes at Starfucks. Too much fucking boris, too much sex drug, too much crack. He got himself chucked out, which is fucking hard to do, and ended up sleeping on a bench in the park. And in the park he met a trampy, a fucking proper trampy (I didn't fucking ask where the bollocks all this happened), and the trampy shared his bottle of booze with Gibson. And so the pair of them spent the rest of the night drinking horrible old booze made in a tin barrel in some fucking shed somewhere, the sort of fucking booze that messes you right the fuck up for ever, permanent, if you drink enough of it, like, makes you blind and shit. Singing songs and fucking fighting. What a mad fucker!

All the while he's telling me this, he's washing his face. He takes his shirt off and stands there half naked and washes his pits. Then he drops his trousers and does under his wotsits too, and all the while he's looking at me in the mirror and telling me about his mad night and about how fucking dreadful he's feeling.

'But it's all right!' he says when he's got his kit back on. 'I've got this stuff . . .'

Fucking Gibson, he's even more experimental than me with the old pharmaceuticals. He slaps two baggies down on the flat surface in front of the mirror. One of the baggies is full of a brownish powder, the other has about eight vials of a clear liquid in it.

'That,' he says, pointing at the powder, 'is klear haze, and that,' he says, pointing at the vials, 'is klear-haze accelerate.'

I nod, interested.

'You do the powder – nice – then, if you fancy a bit more grunt in the engine, if you know what I mean, you snap a vial, drink it, and it bonds with the powder and kind of doubles everything up.'

'What's it actually do?' I ask.

'Makes you see clearly. With a K. Klearly! Ha ha!' says Gibson. 'It's the top fucking chemo for insight and suss – just what we'll be needing today on the review-and-respond shit, yeah?'

He's already cutting two fat lines of the klear-haze powder as he explains this to me. When he's done, he nods at one of the lines.

'There you go. Bombs away!' he says. So I honk it. Refreshing, it is, sparkles around the lights, everything looks cleaner. A high-pitched whistle starts up in my left ear and travels across to my right ear. Gibson leans down and sucks his line up with a loud farty sort of sniff, like he's hocking a phlegm bullet. He straightens up and looks at himself in the mirror with his eyes wide open.

'Right,' he goes, and pulls out a couple of the vials of clear liquid and hands one to me. He snaps the top off his and sips the liquid down. I do the same.

As soon as I feel it going down my throat, I can feel the effect. It's like someone switched on a fucking big turbine inside me. I can feel the whoosh coming up my throat. I gasp for air.

'Oh fuck!' I say, cos I know I'm in trouble.

'Hang on to your veins, Jensen!' laughs Gibson, and he's out the door. The sound of it slamming behind him crashes around my brain like a bomb exploding in an aircraft hangar. I hang on to the sink as the floor seems to tip away from me, but it's no good. Like on a ship in a storm, I'm being tossed about in this little room. I look in the mirror, and my face is getting bigger and bigger. My eyes look mad, little burning holes in circles of black, I'm sweating, I can see the sweat dripping down my forehead.

'Fuck!' I'm thinking to myself, watching my mad face swell and recede in the mirror while I cling on to the sink, trying to stay on my feet. 'I've been fucking had, Gibson's fucked me over! He's trying to get me!' I try to shout. 'Gibson! You cunt!' But no words come out. As the room jerks around like a box being thrown down a mountain, I get all these flashbacks through my brain, images of fucking Gibson mucking about and not passing his tests but not caring, and I see the fucking tutor not caring either, like the whole thing was just a show put on to trick me, like it's a massive fucking wind-up. I'm trying to work out why anyone would do this to me, why they'd wind me up, when suddenly my face is right in front of my face, if you get my drift, in the mirror, I mean. Then there's a cracking noise, and a whole lot of pain, then cold and white like an avalanche, then darkness.

When I wake up, the lead tutor is leaning over me. I'm on my back in the bog. Over the tutor's shoulder I can see Gibson. He looks well worried. 'Sorry,' he mouths at me and shrugs his shoulders in that way that means 'I had no idea!'

My face is wet. I reach up and touch it. It's blood.

'Jensen,' says the tutor, 'you appear to have head-butted the mirror. Was there any particular reason for this?'

'I must have slipped,' says I, quick-witted despite the shock. 'On some soap. Gibson was splashing around in here just before it happened.'

'Yeah, that's true, actually,' says Gibson. 'Sorry, mate.'

I get to my feet with the tutor holding me up under one arm.

'Feeling OK?' he says.

'Yeah,' I says, feeling sheepish.

'It doesn't look like there's any serious damage. Get yourself along to the nurse and she'll patch you up.'

And so I spent the rest of my final day with a bandage around my bonce, wincing with pain every time I moved my head. I thought about whether Gibson had fucked me up on purpose, but he seemed so apologetic about the whole incident that I soon relaxed about that. Just bad drugs, yeah? Sometimes they agree with you, sometimes they don't. Sometimes the same drug does someone else in, and makes you feel fucking great. Weird shit. It's just the way things are.

So there I was, a qualified grade-one agent for the Security Department, with a SP waiting for me to get started on and a fucking bad headache.

Fucking great.

Six

AFTER THE last day of the course, I met up with Fyodor to go to a
Bammer Rhymes show. I hadn't seen Bammer Rhymes since his first
solo show after the Trinity Rhymes broke up, and there was a total big
buzz about what this show was going to be like, cos like this was a really
fucking important tour for Bammer. There had been word that Bammer
was totally over, especially since he'd started doing the acting. He'd
gone soft, they reckoned, and wasn't the great philosopher he once was.
Me and Fyodor didn't reckon them that was dissing Bammer knew what
they was banging on about. They was just looking to say controversial shit to stir it up and make a name for themselves. Wankers. As far
as we were concerned, Bammer still had it.

Outside the venue the crowd was heaving. There were about 20,000
people, all milling around, chanting Bammer's name. The police kept
having to pull girls who were fainting out of the crowd. When one
fainted, a load more would go all around the first one. Then, after a
while, the boys started fainting too. The teenies really love the fainting.
It's like a craze. There's a fucking magazine about it that comes out
every month. They starve themselves and don't drink enough so they're
weak and feeble, so when it gets hot and they get overexcited, they all
keel over. And it spreads like fire. It's a laugh when it really kicks off,
cos suddenly you can have like 3,000 teenies all suddenly swooning,
and the coppers are all running around trying to gather them up.

Me and Fyodor get inside the venue and stock up on Squeezers and
do a massive belt of boris to get us in the mood. Fyodor decides to
supplement his boris with a new snorting liquid he brought along. I
take a bash off that too. It's not half-bad, kind of tweaks the boris into

a more violent feel, but with a menthol vibe to it so your head's really clear and you can breathe well easily.

By the time Bammer actually comes on stage, the place is so pumped up that it feels like it'll explode, like all the noise and energy will make the roof lift off like a cork launching out of a champagne bottle at Starfucks. I'm really hyped myself cos I've popped my stardust caps when Fyodor wasn't looking and it's making me laugh and laugh and I can't stop.

'Are you ready?' goes a big booming voice, and the crowd all shout back, like, 'Fucking yeah!' which is Bammer's catchphrase. Then the beat starts and everyone is going 'Fucking yeah!' in time with it, and then on comes Bammer, looking really cool in his new chain-mail look. He does three numbers from the first stuff he did after the Trinity Rhymes broke up – all the hits – and then he does the Trinity Rhymes' biggest hit, 'Your Love Face Baby For Me', and there are all these images from the glory days of the Trinity Rhymes up on the big screens: the Trinity Rhymes arriving in Shanghai and meeting the Empremier, the Trinity Rhymes oiling each other up, the Trinity Rhymes playing live on Rock Island, and there are all like snippets what no one's seen before of when Jerking Rhymes was in the big accident – the one when the Scram Jet went up in flames on the runway at JFK – and he's all bashed up in hospital, and Spotter Rhymes and Bammer Rhymes are by his bedside on a vigil until he gets better. When they took the bandages off, Jerking Rhymes was a bit of a fucking uggo cos of what the flames did to his face. Bammer left the group after that and went solo.

Bammer's total genius. He's totally still got it. The place fell silent when he did his philosophy. It was totally awesome.

'You know,' he said, his voice bouncing around the big hall out of the speakers, 'people say to me, "Bammer, how come you're so genius?", and I laugh, and I look down at the floor. And I tell them that it's not about who's genius or who's not genius, is it? It's not that what's important. There are loads of important things in the world, yeah? And they're the things we should be thinking about. About those other important things all over the world. And we can help with those important things. It's down to us; we're the ones who can do it. We can make it happen. But if we just do nothing, then nothing will happen. But together, if we unite, and work together like a team, like the biggest team in the whole wide fucking world, then we can achieve success. Only we have to be together and like a team. It's so important. Just look around, look at you all. You're beautiful. We're all here together, yeah? What a team! Can we unite? Can we get it together? Can we?'

And everyone goes 'Fucking yeah!'

And Bammer just looks around and nods, he doesn't need to say anything. He's fucking amazing. The crowd goes crazy with screaming and shouting and stamping their feet. It's a terrific noise. I can see that Fyodor even has tears in his eyes. It's fucking intense.

After the concert, we go to the Starfucks in Hyde Park. We've been there about ten minutes, just settling down and talking over how great the Bammer show had been when there's a right old commotion by the main entrance. We look over, and it's fucking Bammer, still in his chain mail. He looks totally cool. And there are his helpers and entourage all around him and they are going around smiling and handing out little baggies of Bammer boris with his logo on. I know the Bammer-boris baggies will be collector's items, so I stash mine away. Fyodor just nebs his straight down without any thought at all, so then I do too. But I hung on to mine longer than he did, so I win. It's really fucking great. What a great fucking night.

*

The next morning, I was at a bit of a loose end. The Bammer concert had vibed me right up, all that talk about being together, like in a team, and getting things done. It reminded me of my SP and how I was going to be helping to make the world a better place. I got a bit impatient cos I hadn't received any orders. I didn't have to report to the department any more so I didn't have anything to do, except wait for orders. So I thought I'd get a head start. Get some preliminary work done. Show willing. I wanted to get things going. I decided I'd try to track Reg down.

I thought I'd start with the address that Reg gave when we got him in for the FG. It's in Islington, well north. Fucking hate going well north. But when you're working for the Security Department, you have to go where you have to go. Even if it involves taking the Jubilee line to London Bridge and then the fucking Northern line to the fucking

Angel. But off I went, clackety-clack on the tube, braving the nastiness north of the river. It felt good, being on a secret special project, felt like I was helping pull together as a team, just like Bammer said. And when I looked at the other passengers on the train, I felt totally fucking superior, cos I was doing something so cool and serious and important, and they were just droning around, doing all their normal boring shit.

When I got out at the Angel, I headed towards the address that Reg had given. I had a look around the area. Dingy. None of the buildings had got much in the way of windows or things that shine. Where I live everything shines. It makes it look new. Which it is. When it rains where I live, all the reflections wobble around in the water and it's as bright and fresh-looking on the pavements as it is when you look up. Around here the ground doesn't reflect things and the rain sits there all brown with scum floating on it. There are no surveillance cameras around here neither. They have them where the nice areas start, further south. They're more to keep undesirables out when they do venture down our way. They don't have the under-floor lighting like we do. That's why it's dangerous in the D and E districts. No cameras, no lighting, people can lurk around, hiding. Around my way, you can see everyone's face easily. They're all lit like on a glamour show all the time, looking beautiful and healthy. But there's no point in putting in any decent amenities in the rough areas. They won't appreciate them. They'll only break them. And the thing is, they don't fucking deserve them neither. They've got nothing cos they're fucking lazy, yeah? Like, when I wanted the new Dermo Shower in my spank pad at the Rotherhithe Sky Tower, I put the work in. Well, I mean, I will put the work in. You're allowed to add another five years on to your work life to pay for all the extra shit you want. Happy credit! I signed the paper that said I'd do another six days of work, and bish-bash-bosh, there you are; Jensen has a new Dermo Shower and feels fucking great about it. I work hard, I get my smart stuff. So anyone who doesn't have smart stuff is just a lazy nob.

But, you know, while all the grimy dinginess around here is depressing and a reminder of how some people just won't get on board to help the Project, it is good for spy/protection work. Plenty of hidey-holes for an ace government spy who was wearing a natty tagger just the other day and hanging with Brock and Miskin like we're all mates on the same side, on the lookout for people. Fucking great.

I walked up the street a bit, kicking old newspapers and tin cans out of the way as I went, trying not to let the smell make me feel pukey. It's a rot smell, like old veggies left out for too long; the armpitty sort of reek that everyone gives off around these parts. Not nice, you know? Each of the buildings has a small set of steps leading up to the door with all weeds sprouting up in cracks in the concrete or brick or whatever they're made of. And below the steps are little windows with feeble yellow light coming out, and people actually live in there – almost under the ground, in basements, like cave-dwellers – the dad in a vest with his ugly hairs sprouting out the sides, like some kind of ape with his vermin all running around going 'Dad, Dad, Dad' and him shouting 'Fuck off you little shits' and 'You fucking ugly old bitch' to his wife.

I sneaked into a little hidey-hole behind one of the sets of steps and kept a lookout at the door to Reg's building.

Exciting.

Every now and then someone would walk past, shuffling through all the rubbish. They'd be all mad, fucking mumbling to themselves, and sometimes they'd be all violent in the head and punching out at things that weren't there and shouting 'Fucker'. Fucking funny. It was like they'd got all boozed up, only instead of doing it just the once, they'd been doing it all the time and they'd grown wormholes in their brains cos of it, so that even if they're not actually boozed, they are. Permanently boozed. Booze is no good. It's not like the boris. The boris focuses you in, makes everything snap into shape and sharpens it around the edges. You feel your brain revving up and taking everything in at fat speed. Booze isn't like that. Booze swills around and eats into your brain like acid and it makes you puff up in the belly and the eyes. Why would people do that to themselves?

Seeing all the drunk fucks made me think about having a sharpening toot on my boris baggie, just to widen the gap between me and them. I conked a noseful and felt a lot better and really enjoyed the feeling of the warm air coming out of my innards through my mouth and into the cold air, where it clouded up and zoomed around when the wind caught it. Fucking great, especially when I breathed out through my nostrils and my mouth at the same time and got a sort of triple blast of fresh cloud going on – one out of each nostril and a big one out of my gob.

I'd been triple blasting for quite a few minutes when I saw a girl walking towards Reg's door. Nice-looking. Tasty, even. I suddenly realised that I'd not been watching Reg's door properly cos the triple-blast thing had got my attention for quite a while and, what with that and the screaming stained hairies in the basement flat and the boris, I'd sort of forgotten what I was doing there. I was just, you know, hanging out and not, like, spying.

Whatever.

This girl trotting up to Reg's had her shoulders all hunched up and was in a hurry. She looked dead suspicious. If she'd been swaying all over the place and muttering loony things under her breath as bold as you like, she'd have blended right in like a part of the scenery. But there was something different about her and that made her stand out from all the losers around this place. She looked, you know, kind of sorted. Not mental, and not like someone who'd accepted that they'd never make anything of themselves and had given up. She looked like she was going somewhere, like she had something to do, which meant she wasn't really just another bit of the rubbish being kicked around on the floor, but like a real person. She took care of herself, I could see that. Her clothes were neat. The way she dressed made sense. The shoes were shabby and the overcoat was a bit stringy, but she was wearing them like she thought it mattered what people saw when they looked at her, unlike everyone else around here and not like the family of losers in their basement cave by my feet.

Now I was really concentrating on it. I couldn't let Brock and Miskin down, and I thought about the cool meet we'd had. I thought about my training, and it made me get determined and lose the silly smile I'd had on my face because of the nose-blast thing. No time for that, Jensen, oh no, this is the real world now, and you've got an important part to play in it, to protect it and everything.

The attractive girl in the shabby shoes had disappeared. Shitholes! I'd missed her getting let in to the house. I'd been thinking about

Miskin and Brock and all that cool Security Building stuff with the tagger and that. But now when I looked out in the street, I could see several more people who seemed to be moving towards Reg's house. They were trying to do the whole nonchalant thing and didn't look at each other. One of them, a bloke in a long mac with a hat pulled over his eyes, even pretended to be interested in a different house as he walked past it, making like he was just going there and that nothing unusual was going on, but then he appeared to change his mind, like doing a big act, checking his watch and shaking his head as if he was thinking, 'Oh no, I was going to go in here, but the time is wrong so's I'd better walk about a bit more and I'll come back later,' but then all he did was suddenly skip up the steps outside Reg's, where the door swung open and he slipped inside. Well weird, eh? Something going on here, I thought to myself. All these D and E freaks doing amateur spy stuff, trying not to be seen, and all the time they've got a real spy just along the road a bit clocking the whole thing. A professional, yeah?

All in all, I saw eight of them go into Reg's place. Each time the door opened just wide enough for them to slide through. I waited another ten minutes or so, trying not to start getting into the triple-blast thing, and then I formulated a plan.

Opposite Reg's gaff, on the other side of the road, there was a little shop. The shop was closed. It sold all kinds of stuff second hand – the sort of stuff I would have thrown away like totally five fucking years ago; mainly old clothes, totally out of fashion, that have been worn for years already. Between the shop and the building next to it was a dark alley where they put all their stinky bins. And next to the bins was a sort of network of drainpipes running down the side of the shop. Little drainpipes under little windows came out of the wall and joined a larger drainpipe. I reckoned I could get up on to the bin, and from there I'd be able to sneaky up the drainpipe and get a good look into Reg's window and see what was going on in there. It looked like it might be quite a way off the ground, a bit scarifying, but you have to take these risks when you're a gov spy. OK, it was a bit beyond my initial idea of doing a bit of preparation work for my SP, but I'm eager. I want to do well, yeah?

With a heartbeat as loud as the kick drum at Starfucks during party-music hour – buh-buff, buh-buff, buh-buff – in my head, I left my little hidey-hole above the peasants' nasty cave and strolled along the pavement towards the side alley. I was giggling a bit as I walked, and I felt jelly at the knees with all the tummy flips and the buh-buffs, but the boris kept it all in check with an electric feeling of buzz all around my body which makes you want to shake with pleasure and shout and twitch. I suppose as I walked along, a bit jerky and uneven on the old pins, giggling with nervy excitement, I must have looked like one of the old drunk fucks. When I realised that, I sort of exaggerated it a bit and threw an arm out and shouted 'Grah!' all of a sudden. It made me feel better and even more spy-like, cos it was like I was putting on a big act and fooling everyone that I was just another loon from around these parts, even though it wasn't so much of a big act to start with, just twitchy off the boris, and then just going for it. Fucking really great!

There was no one around, just me in the dark grotty old alley, standing in front of this stinky bin with my climbing frame of drainpipes, and I'm twitching and gurgling a bit and giggling and I'm really psyched about this climb I'm about to do. No time like now, I thought to myself lurching forward and gripping the old drainpipe in my hands. It smelled bad, and rusty and flaky old green paint came off in my hands in sharp lumps that made my hands sore. It was then that I wished I'd brought some gloves. Everyone knows that spies need gloves, but it hadn't really occurred to me when I got dressed earlier. I suppose I was still thinking too much about me and Miskin and Brock and the whole, like, glamour of the situation, and how you can wake up one morning and everything is the same as normal, then after a couple of meetings and walking about wearing a tagger, your life goes upside down. And there's no thoughts in your head about no gloves.

Anyway, with one foot levered against the wall and both hands wrapped around the creaking drainpipe, I started my climb. Getting up high enough so I could see into the window where Reg and his gang had gathered wasn't too tricky. A few shimmies and leaps and I was there. I wasn't really sure how I managed it, actually. I guess when you start climbing, the old monkey in you comes out and it just flows pretty natural, you just seem to know where to put your legs and how much strength you need in your arms to hoick yourself where you want to be going.

When I peered through the window of the first floor, I could see an old lady sitting in a stinky old seater, one with about a hundred different arse-stinks in it. She was talking to a bird in a cage, going all 'Coo-ee, coo-ee' and 'Who's a pretty boy then' and this bird just cocked its head to one side and sidled up and down its perch, not making a sound and looking at her like she was potty. She had no idea that she had a government spy/protector looking in on her. I don't think she would have noticed me even if she'd looked out the window, cos it was pretty dark in my alley and she was probably half-blind anyway. They all are, aren't they? Old people, I mean. Especially poor old people.

So, Reg's flat was the next one up, meaning that it was all about to get a bit more dangerous. Looking down on the alley below, I could see that I was safely out of view, and that there was no one around anyway, so I had a bit of a relax and another parp on the boris to fix me up for the big bold climb. I grabbed the drainpipe again and climbed up. There was dust and bits of cobweb and little lumps of brick crumbling away as I climbed, and the creaking noise of the drainpipe was getting worse. Every time I pulled up a few inches, the drainpipe groaned and moved ever so slightly, then there would be a little avalanche of shite from above. I had to screw my eyes shut and blow raspberries to get it away from my mouth.

It was, like, really difficult.

Getting up higher was totally more difficult and tricky and everything than the first part. Maybe you get heavier the further from the ground you go? It seemed like it took me ages to get up high enough to see into the next window up. Out of the corner of my eyes, I could see mad shapes swirling around, and darts of light came across my vision, probably cos all of the boz I'd been hooting. By that point, it wasn't the nerves making my heart pump-a-thump any more, it was the exertion. It was cold on the outside, but I was boiling up, sweat pouring down my head and my back, and all the shitty-gritty falling from the drainpipe was sticking to me and dusting my hair. A really big flake of the thick green paint came floating down like a leaf in autumn, flip-flapping down until it splatted on to my cheek and stuck there. I couldn't take my hands off the drainpipe to wipe any of this muck off me, cos there was no platform for me to rest on or anything. All I could do was hang there, one foot stretched out on to a little ledge, the other wedged behind the drainpipe, both hands wrapped around it like it had done me wrong and I was strangling it to death.

From this angle, high up, with only the hard concrete below to break any fall, I could see what I wanted to see: Reg and his gang in his flat. The carpet had flowers on it and was all gone to thread from the door to the seater, like a path cut through. The glass in the windows was all cracked. I could see Reg, and I could see the attractive girl. She was sitting opposite the window, on the floor with her knees up. The shabby old coat had gone, and underneath she was wearing a cutesy little skirt in purple. Which was absolutely fucking great cos I could see her knicks. It was just like *Porn Disco*, but with the added thrill of me being a secret spy and her being, like, a possible subversive, but me protecting her and saving her from Reg and his mad club or whatever it is, and her being all grateful and me being all, like, in charge and cool and spy-like, and then we do it. Ace! With *Porn Disco* it's kind of not real and you're just looking and not involved. This felt much better, even though I didn't get to see as much as with the shows.

The girl's knicks were very distracting, but I knew I had to concentrate on Reg, and take it all in so I could tell them all about it at my first report meeting, whenever that might be.

Reg was talking, waving his arms around, smacking a fist into a palm, putting his arms out like he was weighing melons; the group of eight all sat around in a circle. Then the nice girl did a bit of talking, looked at another member of the little secret group, and that person started talking. Then they stopped saying stuff, and then Reg started talking again, but not with the arms waving this time. Everyone just looked at Reg as if they was looking at Bammer Rhymes off of that show all the girls are going crazy about, where Bammer is a doctor and goes around making girls better and saving them from death all the time. Girls love that. And they all love Bammer. If only the girls knew what Bammer gets up to at Starfucks, they'd think again about going all dreamy when they see him being the good doctor. Heh, heh. Good old Bammer. He's so cool. Still, the nice girl obviously didn't know that stuff about Bammer Rhymes. Come to think of it, she probably doesn't even know who Bammer Rhymes is. Reg is her Bammer Rhymes. When you don't watch the shows and can't afford to buy all the smart mags with the pictures of the famous people, you must sort of lose touch with what's going on in the real world, and then you find your heroes in people like Reg and worship them like they're Bammer Rhymes. It's tragic, really. As if Reg is as cool as Bammer. Reg is totally poor and doesn't even know what Jizz Factor or Purploids are! How can she be impressed with that? Fucking Reg.

I couldn't hear what was being said. All I could do was see. And what I could see was not enough for me to be able to make a big deal about when I next see Brock or Miskin. Unless I can hear what they're on about, what they're planning or what sort of mess they're about to make, all this effort and drainpipe dingle-dangle will have been a waste of time.

Feeling brave, I decided to get closer to the action. I dropped down off my drainpipe, on to the bin and then on to the ground, being sneaky quiet, quiet, quiet all the time. Then I walked across to the building where Reg's flat is. As I made my way across the road, I sussed where the building's drainpipe was. Feeling something like a bit of a drain-pipe-climbing total fucking expert, I had worked out how to get up to the window where Reg and everyone was by the time I reached the bottom of the building.

I grab the pipe as high as I can with both hands, get my feet planted against the wall, and then start grappling my way up, feet shuffling against the brickwork, my arms taking all the strain. It's even more fucking difficult than climbing the other drainpipe, and that was fucking difficult enough. I squint my eyes shut with the effort and I see angry red swishing behind my lids, and a hissy roaring noise comes in my ears. I keep shuffling up, and it feels like my arms are just going to pop out of my shoulders, leaving me to fall to the hard ground below with my arms still hanging on to the drainpipe. I'm making little noises, like 'Erg, erf', as I climb, and I try to think about positive things to keep me going. I'm thinking about all the smart stuff I'll be able to buy when I get promoted and how everyone'll think I'm so fucking cool and ace and that. With each heave up the drainpipe, I'm going 'Yeah!' and

'Fucking A!', like every time I manage to get my hands another few inches up the drainpipe, I've achieved something totally skill. I'm really into this positive-thinking vibe, but the pain in my shoulders is getting worse, and the angry red behind my tight-shut eyes is swimming around and darkening into a filthy brown with blobs in. I'm going 'Yeah! Yeah! Yeah!', rhythmic and intense, like soldiers on assault courses.

It seems like I've been climbing for ages when I finally dare to open my eyes. I really want to see the bit of drainpipe sticking out at a right angle from the main one I'm climbing, cos I know that I'll be able to haul myself up and get a foot on to it. Then I'll be able to relax and get my breath back and start my sneaky-peaky.

But I don't get no chance to relax or nothing, cos I hear the rattle sound of an old wooden window being thrown open. I look up, above me is the window of Reg's flat, and leaning out of it are three heads; not Reg and not the girl, but three blokes.

'Oi!' goes one. 'What do you think you're playing at?'

'Fuck!' I says. 'I'm erm, I'm . . .' I stutter, trying to think of an excuse, some really fucking good reason why I'm halfway up a drain-pipe outside this here house, but nothing's coming into my brain, which is overloaded with like far too much fucking info.

I've got two choices, either I get down from this drainpipe fast by letting go and falling to the hard ground below – probably breaking my legs and geting seen by Reg – or I shin up another few feet, up on the roof, over the back and take my chances.

All this I think in the space of not even a second, less than that. And before I know it, I'm off. Up I go, my feet somehow finding the bits they need to and me zipping up past the three heads like a monkey on a pole.

'Oi! You! Stop that!' the heads shout, but I just fucking go for it, hard and fast. I kick at the hands that come grabbing at my ankles and they don't stand a chance. I want to get away a million more times than they want to catch me. After all, what would they do if they did manage to grab my legs? Yank me off the drainpipe so I'd fall to the ground and crack my skull open and all my brains goo out on to the pavement? They don't want that to happen, do they? That would be fucking murder.

I hear Reg shouting from inside the room, 'Well, what's happening?' really loud, but my top half is already on the roof. The gutter, which is chock-a with mouldy old leaves and trapped rainwater, digs into my stomach and makes me all wet, but with my hands on the slates of the roof and my feet pushing up against the house, I manage to get all of me on to the roof. Its slope is shallow enough for me to stand up, so I try to do a floaty run over the roof, making myself as light as I can, and I run up over the pointy part, past the old chimney stack and down the slope on the other side.

Up there I could see the moon in the sky and all the rooftops reflecting it. I could see right across London, back to civilisation around where I live, where all the buildings are high, high, high and lit like they're all sculpture, which they so are. As I ran across the roofs, I felt like I could fly, like if I spread my arms I would take off and soar into the sky where I could look down on the streets and see everything that was happening, where I could breathe clean cold air, drink it down and have my blood pump crimson with it. I was so happy and fucking vibe-pumped strong from my escape and totally fucking zizzed off the boris. It was the best feeling I'd ever had.

Seven

THE NEXT morning, when I woke up back in my spank pad, the electric-fuzz excito-vibe of my night-time adventures had worn out and I felt fucking shithole. The boris and the dresdens (and the three Mucky Sleeps I'd taken to help me come down) had fucked me right over, and I woke up feeling like all my blood had seeped down into my legs, and that my face was made of rusty old metal, and that if you could unscrew it and take it off, throw it away and put on a new one, I'd be well happy. My brain felt like it was coughing and hacking, snot dribbling out of it. And through all the pain and aches and shite, memories of the night before appeared in my snotty brain and it became clear in my head that I'd well fucked up. Everything was shit. I'd felt fucking great as I danced across the rooftops from the clutches of the Reg gang cos I was off my flaps. But all I'd done was take a massive risk and come away with nothing. No info about what Reg was up to with his little band of secret people having a secret meeting in his horrible crappy flat. I lay there thinking about how I'd totally fucking blown it. They must have seen me climbing up the drainpipe. It was so fucking noisy as I scrabbled up there, and I'd been going 'Yeah!' and making all those positive noises on the way up too.

I looked at the clock. It was ten in the morning. I got out of bed and walked into the shower. Not even the Dermo Shower could cheer me up, although it really is a fucking bang-on shower. The pounding water just made my head clatter, every drop of water a thump on my bonce, reminding me what a bobbins nob-up I'd made of my spy/protection work.

After the shower, I got dry and put my clothes on. I wasn't hungry, and I was still misery guts, so I had a look in the medi-cab to see what I could rustle up to sort out my bad feelings. Obviously, it's always tempting to go for the old boris. It's the blast that satisfies, after all, but when you've neglected some of the other goodies available for a while, they sort of come back into fashion when you see them in front of you. Like the dresdens. I'd got to thinking that dresdens were maybe too cranky, too full-on. Fine for when you want to munch the inside of your mouth or if there's violence in the air, cos they're good for bravery, but, all in all, I thought they was too brutal. But last night, popping them on top of the boris was a revelation of thriller-diller fun, fun, fun. But I must try to keep a lid on it, cos the combo of the dresdens and the boris made me lose my marbles and do mad shit.

I eventually settled on some stabilisers out of the medi-cab. I like the way they make a veil come down between you and the world without you even noticing, and before you know it you're feeling like there's nothing wrong and you're all settled and chilled and shit. They've got a rep as being a bit lame, cos it's what they give kiddies. They gave me fucking loads of them when I was in the Duncan-Smith Infant Unit. They made me munch them like sweeties, and if that didn't work it'd be the fucking needle and night-night Jensen. But I've got full-strength stabilisers, the ones with the red and green dayglo packaging that you can only get from proper dispensaries from geezers in white lab coats who ask you questions about how you're feeling and log your ID before they sell them to you.

The stabilisers did OK, but they couldn't get rid of the nag, nag, nag at the back of my mind that there was something wrong. I sort of couldn't remember what it was that was wrong, and I'd watch some cartoon shows and I'd be laughing and then I'd suddenly hear my own laugh echoing around the flat and I'd stop laughing, and there'd be a little lump of darkness floating around, just outside my consciousness, but it would be enough to bum me the fuck totally out for like three minutes.

After a couple of hours of this, I was right adged off. I figured what I needed was some company and some distraction. I was getting myself into a spiral of bum, and I needed to get out of it. So I called Fyodor and we organised to meet at the Rotherhithe Starfucks for a late lunch.

I got dressed, honked some boris ('Ah, the old faithful,' I thought to myself) and went on my way. I met Fyodor at the entrance to Starfucks.

'Oi! Oi! Jensen!' he goes when he sees me, and ruffles my hair and punches me on the arm. He's grinning away, like always. He turns towards the entrance of Starfucks and rubs his hands together in anticipation.

'Right-oh! Right-oh!' he says. 'Let's have some, then.'

He doesn't notice that I'm a bit low. I don't say nothing. I just make weak smiles and follow him in to Starfucks. The Rotherhithe one is a little Starfucks, and quite old too. They've stuck to the traditional vibe with wood everywhere and the girls and boys all wearing little satin shorts and tight T-shirts with 'Starfucks' written on them. The atmos isn't really Fyodor's bag these days, what with him having got into the whole Roman vibe lately (something not on offer here at Rotherhithe), and I'm not bothered, so we just sit around eating a few bits of food and drinking coffees and that and having a chit-chat; although I'm not being very conversationalist cos I'm still bothered by my spying failures. Eventually Fyodor notices my mood (he'd been banging on about some new gear he was hoping to get hold of later that night, some patch that you stick to your arm and it releases its active ingredients into your bloodstream so you feel like you've got menthol for blood. It's like being hot and cold at the same time, says Fyodor, and he can't wait to try it out).

'All right then, Jensen,' goes Fyodor, eyeing me impatiently. 'What the fuck's up with you, you twattage? Here's me all giving it this and giving it that and doing all the chit-chat and you're just giving it all the sighs and the heavy shoulders and looking at the ground. What's up, innit? For fuck's sake.'

'Oh, nothing,' I say.

'Oh, nothing,' goes Fyodor, in a funny voice, wagging his head from side to side, copying me, making it sound like I'm a whingey mental.

So I tell him. I tell him about how I've been, like, working for Brock, and how I went to Islington and how I saw Reg's flat and all his little secret pals having a fucking secret little meeting. I tell him how I was doing really well, but then how I fucked it by climbing the drainpipe and how I nearly got fucking caught and how I scarpered. All through the story, Fyodor's all 'Yeah?' and 'Wow!', 'Fucking hell!' and 'No!', and it's quite a lot of fun telling him all about it. When I tell him about how I was climbing the drainpipe up to Reg's window and how I opened my eyes to see his gang looking at me, he laughs and laughs and I end up laughing too. It's fucking funny, as it goes.

When I've finished, Fyodor is wiping his eyes and going 'Oh, oh, oh', like he's nearly crying with it all. Then he gets his boris out, cuts two fat lines right there and we do one each, still giggling about my nightmare night.

When we've calmed from the giggling and the first rush of the boris has passed, I start talking again.

'No, but seriously, Fyodor, it's not fucking funny, cos I've really fucked it all up, yeah? I really wanted to show Brock and Miskin that I'm totally fucking on it and that, that they can trust me and that I've got, you know, initiative and that, but all I've done is fucked it up. I wanted to have something to show Brock, so he'd be all impressed, but instead all I've done is nearly get caught.'

Fyodor listens to me and then puts his arm over my shoulder.

'Now you listen here, Jensen,' he goes, 'there's no need to worry. Something'll turn up, won't it? Remember what Bammer said the other night? You've got to, like, keep it together and be united like a team and everything, innit? I'm sure something will come along that will help you out.'

He was right about Bammer. He did say that. You've got to be united like a team.

I was well cheered up by now, and so I decided to go back to my place and catch up with the *Monster Trucks* shows that have been piling up unwatched in the last few days. Cos I've been so busy and distracted, I've totally been neglecting my *Monster Trucks*. I said goodbye to Fyodor at the door of Starfucks and we went our separate ways home.

'Don't fucking worry,' said Fyodor as he wandered off.

And while I was watching *Monster Trucks* later that night, I did just that; I forgot all about my worries.

Eight

THE NEXT morning I woke up and I didn't feel too bad. I hadn't been up too late giving it loads at Starfucks or anything like that. I'd come home early, having been well happied up by good old Fyodor, got stuck into some fucking top-bollock *Monster Trucks* action and was in bed by two. I hardly did any boris once I got home neither, so I was quite clear in the head while I was getting some coffee and food together and starting to wonder what the day might have in store for me.

On my journeys between the kitchen and the front room fixing breakfast and coffee, I must have walked past the brown envelope that was sticking under the front door at least a dozen times. But I didn't notice it. I don't know what made me notice it when I finally did notice it. I just suddenly did. It was just there, like someone had slid it in. I went and picked it up. There was no writing on it, no stamp, nothing. I even opened my front door and looked up and down the corridor, in case postie was there, or some secret weird postie who goes around slipping unmarked envelopes under doors and then runs away.

I went back into my flat and sat on my seater in the front room. I put the envelope on the coffee table, next to the cup of steamy coffee. I sipped the coffee a few times and looked at the envelope. It felt like whatever was in this envelope was important and I wasn't sure I wanted to open it.

I have a little think about what medication to use before I open the envelope, and I decide to drop some jingle bells. They're a bit like a cross between boris and stabilisers, with a little bit of colour enhancement thrown in for a laugh. Fyodor says they're for grandads, but I find they're just the thing for a gentle start to the day. They're only little tiny pills, and a handful goes down easy with a sip of coffee. I figure that if the brown envelope has got some bad news inside that bums me out, the jingle bells should kick in and level me out.

I give it five minutes and then I open the envelope.

Inside, there are pieces of A4 paper, some stapled together to look like a magazine. There's one bit of paper not stapled, in there by accident by the looks of it. All mad medical shit:

GOVERNMENT RESEARCH STUDY P11/95504392
RESULT 5/19
DIENCEPHALONIC EXPERIMENT 7995:
LIMBIC SYSTEM MANIPULATION: ALTERATION OF AMYGDALAE PROCESSES AND ITS EFFECT ON MEMORY CONSOLIDATION, DEVELOPMENT OF BELIEF SYSTEMS, RETROCOGNITION AND POSTCOGNITION
Research study into the action of drugs combined with controlled environmental stimuli on the VENTROMEDIAL HYPO-THALAMUS via controlled sexualised environments and B-19 (RIS) molecule compounds.

None of it makes any fucking sense to me. Not even fucking English, half of it. The only bit of it I understand is stamped across the top of the page in red. It says:

Duncan-Smith Infant Unit/Lab School 53

Like, I went to the Duncan-Smith Infant Unit and Lab School 53. I look on the other side of this bit of medical nonsense, but there's nothing written there. Load of fucking rubbish, yeah? The other document's much more interesting, the bits of paper what are all fucking stapled together. In wobbly writing on the cover it says:

The MM Society
The Transcript Excerpt
With an introduction by Reginald Rankin.

Right-oh, then. Reg the writer, is it? Mad Reg with his secret meetings. He's all 'Reginald' when he's writing.

On the next page is a short bit of writing, like a letter or something:

Dear friend,

We only have this excerpt. It was discovered after the fire at the old Ministry of Defence archive at Kew. For days after the blaze, ashes and partially burned papers continued to blow around the streets of Kew, mounting up in corners or lying in gutters. Most were collected and disposed of. A dredger was commissioned to clean the river of several tonnes of papers. Some, however, survived, and were picked up by souvenir hunters and saved as mementoes.

These particular pages were found by an antiques dealer during a house clearance many years after the fire. The antiques dealer, personally known to me, had purchased the contents of a small flat behind King's Cross station. He took several pieces of furniture from the flat to his shop in Chelsea, including a Victorian chest of drawers. While restoring the chest of drawers, he discovered the following transcript. When he questioned the elderly man who had lived at the flat about the document, the man confirmed that the document had indeed been found in the streets near the Kew archive facility on the day of the fire by the man himself, who was then a boy of fifteen. He thought the document looked interesting and squirrelled it away.

The argument for the authenticity of the document is, therefore, compelling.

The following is a facsimile of the original document. You will notice that the transcript, while slightly fire-damaged, appears to be a complete document. Whoever commissioned this transcript was only interested in this part of the proceedings. With good reason too, as we now know.

Because this document was lodged at the MoD Archive Facility, plus the fact that it was marked secret and stamped with catalogue codes known to be associated with the secret services, we can surmise that it represents a part of the secret government enquiry into the death of Martin Martin. This suggests that Martin Martin was of the utmost importance to the government and not, as the deniers would have it, some petty conman. This transcript, this tantalising excerpt, is where Martin Martin starts his rapid journey towards his ascension.

SECRET – NOT FOR RELEASE
TRANSCRIPT EXCERPT
44/55/655/66/082/21
EMERGENCY STUDY DOCUMENT 10
TRANSCRIPTION FROM CONTINUOUS VIDEO FOOTAGE
'MARTIN MARTIN'S ON THE OTHER SIDE' (SPANKING FILMS LTD, SOHO)
RECORDED 10/10/08
SEASON I #2
FOR THE PURPOSE OF THE ENQUIRY, THIS TRANSCRIPTION EXCERPT COMMENCES 91 MINUTES AND 31 SECONDS INTO RECORDING

MARTIN MARTIN (MM): Can we retake?
(studio-audience laughter)
UNIDENTIFIED AUDIENCE MEMBER: Sorry, sorry. I was just surprised.
(studio-audience laughter)
MARTIN MARTIN: Don't worry about it. Can we . . . *(unintelligible)* OK. Here we go again. You OK? *(unintelligible control-room crosstalk)* There's something here. *(five-second pause)* Do you know the name Emile?
UNIDENTIFIED AUDIENCE MEMBER: I don't . . .
MARTIN MARTIN: It's definitely Emile. No? OK, I understand. I will. Is there a 'J' name here? A Jack, a Jackson? He's looking for a Jackson. Is there a Jackson here? Anyone have a connection to that name? *(twelve-second pause)* You, madam? There's a strong feeling here. Jackson: what does that name mean to you?
WOMAN IN AUDIENCE (AMY JACKSON): *(laughing)* It's my surname. Our surname, I mean.

MARTIN MARTIN: Ah, and who is this?

AMY JACKSON: My grandad.

MARTIN MARTIN: And they called you Jack Jackson, didn't they? He's telling me they called you Jack. You're Jack.

EDWARD 'JACK' JACKSON: Who? Who's telling you that?

MARTIN MARTIN: Emile. It's a man called Emile.

EDWARD 'JACK' JACKSON: I don't know no Emile, mate. I'm sorry.

MARTIN MARTIN: Yes, yes you do. He's rather afraid that you do. *(studio-audience laughter)* He's saying there were problems there, and you set out to resolve them, didn't you, Jack?

EDWARD 'JACK' JACKSON: You're barking up the wrong tree, mate.

MARTIN MARTIN: Problems over a truck? A long time ago. A green truck.

EDWARD 'JACK' JACKSON: Now listen here, pal, I don't know nothing about no truck. Mumbo-jumbo, ain't it?

MARTIN MARTIN: I'll tell you what fucking happened, pal. *(gasps from audience)*

EDWARD 'JACK' JACKSON: What did you say? Did he swear? Did he say what I thought he said?

MARTIN MARTIN: France, November 1944. You and me, Jackson.

EDWARD 'JACK' JACKSON: I don't have to listen to this.

MARTIN MARTIN: *(shouting)* An army truck loaded with enough goodies to keep the pair of us on easy street once the war had finished. Our little pension plan, you called it. Full to the brim with loot. Dig a big hole and bury the lot. Shoot the truck up, torch it. Make it look like the Jerries had ambushed us. We'd have to slap each other about a bit to make it look believable. We had that Luger, and one of us was going to take a bullet in the side. Toss for it, you said. And I won the toss. So we buried the loot, and after that we were going to drive the truck into a tree and torch it. Then I was going to use the Luger and give you a little nick with it. *(shouting intensely)* I was having a fucking ciggie and you caved my fucking head in, you fucking cunt. I see you. I see

55

what you did. I know you, Jack fucking Jackson. And this is where you get yours, you little prick.

AMY JACKSON: Grandad? What's . . .

EDWARD 'JACK' JACKSON: Don't listen. It's all rubbish. I'll sue you, you know. You can't do this. It's not decent. What? What's he doing now?

MARTIN MARTIN: *(shouting)* Murderer! Murderer! He's a murderer!

(screaming from audience)

EDWARD 'JACK' JACKSON: He's sick, that's what it is. Oh God, look . . . see. Oh God, that's disgusting.

(Martin Martin vomits and collapses to the floor)

DEVLIN WILLIAMS: Could everybody please stay calm. Is there a doctor in the house? Please, stay calm. There's no need to panic, ladies and gentlemen. Please make your way to the bar upstairs, where complimentary drinks will be served and you will find a running buffet. Oh God . . . Martin, what the fuck are you playing at? No, he's really ill. He's gone white. Is he breathing? Tell me he's breathing. Is that blood? Is he puking blood? Oh, for fuck's sake . . . Call an ambulance.

MARTIN MARTIN: You fucking murderer! Murderer!

DEVLIN WILLIAMS: Martin, shut the fuck up!

MARTIN MARTIN: Murderer! Murder! With a fucking spade! When I wasn't looking!

DEVLIN WILLIAMS: How's he doing that? Someone stop him bleeding. Where's that blood coming from? Oh my God. Jesus fucking wept. Why won't he shut up?

END OF EXCERPT

I put the pages back into the envelope and rest my head back on my comfy seater. The jingle bells have kicked in and I feel like I'm covered in soft. The warm soft gently presses against me, all over, and supports my head and my legs and my arms and everything. I close my eyes and I feel like I am floating, and in my head I see images of this bloke Martin Martin rolling around on the floor with all spew and blood, and

Devlin Williams slipping about in it, going 'Agh!' and 'Oh no!' and going panicky nutbags.

But then the words just stop and the images in my head stop too. It makes me want to know what happened next, and what was going on in the first place, and how it all ends up. Like, does Martin Martin die on the floor with his blood all over people and dripping down the seats, with people all going, 'Urgh! Urgh! I am all covered in blood! Urgh!' And what about that Jackson feller? Does he get all violent about whether he mashed in someone's head once? Does everyone turn on Devlin Williams and duff him over? And what's the connection between all this and Reg and his little gang? Why are they so interested in this Martin Martin? And who put the brown envelope with all this info under my door? I'm trying to make connections between all this stuff, but it's like I can only make little, thin spider-threads to join them up, and they get broken, like, by little puffs of wind.

The effort of trying to put it all together makes me sleepy. I doze off and I can feel my body go paralysed, and my mouth is open and dry and I need a piss, but there's nothing I can do about it. I'm stuck there, on my seater, asleep, but not asleep caught halfway in between.

In my half-on, half-off brain, I'm thinking that now I have something to talk to Brock about. I can go and see him and fucking well large it and be Daddy Big Bollocks.

I am fucking great at spying.

There is dribble on my face.

Nine

W HEN I get to the office to see Brock, I'm still a bit thick in the head off the jingle bells and my dribbly sleep of paralysis. Falling asleep in the middle of the day really does you in, especially when you're locked into some hi-res jingle bells dreams about Martin Martin and his puking, shouting, bloody mess.

I'd only been away from the office for a few days, but when I walked back in to get up to Brock's mint office on the forty-fifth floor, it looked really different to me. I hadn't been in the flow, I'd been missing out on what had been going on, so I felt all a bit out of sorts as I walked over the glass tiling, like I'd done a million times before, on my way to the lift. Before, it was all automatic. I knew where I was going and what it was I'd be doing when I got there. Now, it's the same building, yeah, but what I do in it is different. I'm here for something else, something far more important and, like, fucking totally serious. Like, before, when me and Fyodor came in to work – him off to the International Department on the twenty-third and me off the Dept of Social Studies on the fifteenth – when we went past the PM's portrait, the famous one they have in all the government buildings and post offices and those kinds of places, the one where he's pulling a fucking awesome ollie on his board, me and Fyodor would go 'Wotcha, mate!' to it. You know, we were joking about a bit, I suppose, making light of the whole PM thing, like it wasn't much to think about or be serious about. But this time, on my way to see Brock, with secrets to tell him and a serious duty given me by Miskin, who's probably mates with the PM like I'm mates with Fyodor, well, suddenly it seemed so much more real. So when I saw the portrait, instead of my usual 'Wotcha, mate!', I just looked at it, and I raised my eyebrows. Like, 'Yeah, I'm working with you now, PM. Unity and Success.'

Also, I'd done an enormous crank of boris before I left my flat to shake off the jingle bells, maybe that had something to do with the way I was feeling all different about everything. But it wasn't just that. I felt so fucking cool cos I like *was* totally fucking cool. It was like I was born to be a spy/protector. My destiny. I was feeling so fucking cool it was unbelievable.

I stepped into the lift and said 'forty-five' and listened to the music and looked at myself in the mirror as I boxed it to the forty-fifth. It was weird. There was me, in my nice suit in the nice surroundings of the lift – with its complimentary box of choccies and tissues and music – with the secure feeling you get after having walked across the glass floor and eyed up the receptionists sitting in a row with their uniforms and their mouthpieces and those huge screens behind them, everything clean, everything in its place and organised; then there's me, who, only the other night, had been spying it up in a place where none of this happens, where there's no under-street lighting or huge screens or nice flats with self-cleaning Dermo Showers. Nothing's sorted out up there where Reg lives. It's like a savage place where people haven't evolved, they're still hairy. But there was something about it that was making what had seemed normal to me before, i.e. the Social Studies building, seem not so normal any more. Deffo. Fucking weird. Maybe it's the jingle bells and the boris.

When the lift reached forty-five, the doors de-opaqued and I stepped out where I'd been only days before, when I was still the insignificant child fresh from Study Centre 16, having only just celebrated my first payday and having just met Reg in a routine boring FG, all nervy cos Brock had called me in and I thought I was in the shit.

But now, all is different. I'm on a special project. I've met Miskin and he gave me a job to do, and I've been doing that job.

Yes I have.

I took risks.

I could have been killed, but I did it. I did it for the department, for Brock, for Miskin, for the PM, for the country. I did it for Unity and Success. Really fucking great.

Then I realise why everything seemed so different and out of sorts when I came in the building. It's because I am looking at everything from a different place. Me, I've moved up in the world, and everyone knows it. That puts me in a better place. I'm higher. Higher, like when I felt I could fly on Reg's roof. As I thought these thoughts, I walked with more hardness towards Brock's office and got taller and braver.

Brock let me into his office and I looked at his hot-piece-of-ass secretary again. I don't think she recognised me, but that's OK cos now I'm a new person anyway.

Here is the new Jensen Interceptor, the spy/protector.

'Jensen,' says Brock, in that way that means 'hello'.

'Brock,' I says, with a serious little nod of the head.

'How's it been going?' Brock goes, getting back around his desk and falling back into his big comfy seater, sticking his hands behind his head.

'I found Reg,' I says. Dramatic.

'What?' says Brock. 'But you've not had any orders yet.'

'Yeah, I know, but I thought I'd use some initiative,' I says.

'You prick, Jensen,' goes Brock. He sighs and looks at me like I'm a nobhead, shaking his head.

Bastard! He calls me a prick for using my initiative.

Then he says, 'OK, what did you find out?'

'Well, I found out where he lives, for starters.'

'And?' says Brock.

'He's got a little gang. They meet at his flat.'

'Who's in the gang? Names? Addresses?' says Brock, like he knows that I'm not going to be able to give him names and addresses. I'm not sure what to say.

'I'll be following that up,' I says. It sounds clever.

'"Following it up,"' says Brock, taking the piss proper now, doing my voice in a sing-song way, like a mental, like when Fyodor is having a pop at me.

Thinking that I need to rescue this situation, I pull the envelope out of my case and push it across the desk. I need something to impress Brock, or I'll get bumped off my SP and I'll be back doing FGs.

Brock opens up the envelope and pulls the papers out, the papers with Reg's writing on and all the Martin-Martin-puking-blood stuff.

As he looks at the paper, I say, 'It's to do with Martin Martin.'

Brock reads the document and says nothing for a while. He is concentrating and frowning.

'All right, Jensen,' says Brock, 'you might be on to something here after all. Where did this come from?' He waggles the document around.

I don't know how to answer this question, cos saying that it just appeared under the door at my flat doesn't seem to be the best thing to come out with. But I can't think of anything else, so out it comes:

'It just appeared in my flat, sir.' I shrug.

Brock tilts his head to one side and looks stern.

'"It just appeared in my flat, sir,"' he says, imitating me again, but less angry this time. Then, after he looks at the papers a bit more, he says, 'All right, Jensen, I understand. You're close to something. Don't want to tell me too much, right? You're worried that if you tell me where it came from I'll set another team on it. Don't want your delicate little investigation getting trampled over by the big boys in their big boots? Ambitious little fucker, aren't you?'

'Well, you know,' I say, shrugging again. There's a few moments of silence while Brock looks at the document again.

'Martin Martinists,' he goes, nodding.

'Right,' I says.

'Haven't heard from them in a while,' says Brock.

'No,' I says, agreeing.

'How much do you know about the Martin Martinists, Jensen?' says Brock.

'Not much,' I admit.

'They're a cult,' says Brock. 'Wankers.'

'Cult wankers?' says I.

'They've not been active for some time, or at least we didn't think they were. We've been more occupied by the fucking Prophets of Doom lately.'

Yeah, I'd heard of the Prophets of Doom. They're like an organisation of loons and crackpots who keep threatening to put poison in the water supply and shit like that. It's all to do with the environment or something. They're against it, so they say they're going to fuck it up. Nothing's ever happened, but they keep threatening. Sales of bottled water have gone through the roof since the Prophets of Doom came out.

'Martin Martinists sprout up from time to time,' Brock continues. 'Little cells of them, like fucking cancer. Stamp it out in one place and sooner or later it pops up somewhere else. Each and every one of them is a fucking nutter. They know it's not allowed. It's fucking illegal, Jensen, being a Martin Martinist, you know. We got fucking laws against it and everything.'

'Fucking right,' I goes, 'you need laws against things like that. Stands to fucking reason.'

'Spot bollock, Jensen, spot bollock,' says Brock, really into what we're talking about and how we're agreeing so much. I'm feeling totally better already, back to new Jensen again and not the Jensen Brock just called a prick.

Brock looks out of the window and waits a bit before he tells me more.

'They're religious nutters. They believe that some dead bloke is going to come back to life and go around making everything better.'

'I see,' I say, even though I don't.

'It's just some story, Jensen, out of an old book,' says Brock.

'A story out of a book?' I goes, thinking about the books I've read like *A Guide to Your Life* and the *We Think It's Great* series.

'Yeah, yeah,' says Brock. 'They say that Martin Martin was this bloke who lived in olden times and that he could read minds and see into the future and talk to the dead – all that old rubbish. And they reckon that he was killed by the king or someone because Martin was going to teach everyone in the world how to be like him, how to do all the seeing into future stuff. He had his fans before he was killed, and this lot, Reg and his mates, they're carrying on the fight. They believe that Martin Martin is the real king, the king of kings, number one, above the PM even.'

'But that's mental!' I says. Which it is.

'It's a myth,' says Brock. 'It's all trees and flowers and bubbles cack. You know what these soppy spiritual types are like. They took it too serious because they don't fit into society the way everyone else does.

You and me, Jensen, we got our shit together, haven't we? We play our part. We are contributing. But these Martinists just fart about and cause trouble.'

'Trouble?' I say.

'Oh, you can be sure that when a cell of Martin Martinists appears, car bombs won't be far behind.'

'Fucking car bombs?' I goes. 'That's what the Martin Martinists are into, is it?'

'Yes, it is. They're a bloodthirsty lot,' says Brock.

This means that the other night, when I was looking in on Reg and his pals, and up that girl's skirt at her white knicks, thinking that I was just keeping an eye on them and protecting them and making sure everything was OK, all the time they're people who make bombs out of cars and drink blood? It's all a bit too much to take in. Like, what a fucking huge fuckload, yeah?

'You must remember, Jensen, they're nutters,' says Brock. 'Proper out of it in a really bad way. They're not like us. They've messed up their lives so they want to mess up ours.'

'But that's so not fair!' I goes, and Brock nods.

'I know, Jensen, it sucks ass. Which is why we need to keep an eye on them, so we can move if they start to threaten our security. Don't forget, we're here to protect society. And if we can't protect them from car bombs, then what can we do?'

'And blood drinkers!' I goes, all whipped up with horror. 'I mean, that's just disgusting!' Brock frowns slightly. We're so on the same wavelength, me and him.

'We should kill them!' I shouts. 'I know where they meet! We should go around there and shoot them up.'

And while I was saying this, I was also thinking that maybe I could make sure the nice-looking girl wouldn't be around that night. It didn't seem right to off her in a spray of bullets when she's so pretty and I've seen her knicks. I can't believe *she's* a blood-drinking car-bomber.

'All right, Jensen. Your enthusiasm is noted,' says Brock, trying to totally bum my excitement the fuck out. 'We have to gather evidence that they're plotting to do something, then we can arrest them, try them in a court of law, put them away and throw away the fucking key. That's the way we stop car bombs. All above board. Reported on the news and supported by the people of the nation. It's democratic. Unity and Success!'

'Unity and Success!' I reply, sort of automatically, but with feeling.

'They might not be plotting anything,' says Brock. 'But still, they're Martin Martinists and they're illegal. But if we wade in and arrest them straight off, we might miss out on getting them on a more serious conspiracy charge. If we bang them up on Martinist charges, they'll become heroes to other Martin Martinists, and that's more fucking bother than it's worth. Before you know it, we'll have bombs going off all over the place and decent citizens getting mangled up on their way to work, and we don't want that.'

No, we don't want that. No way.

'So,' I asks Brock, 'what do I do next?'

'We'll go and see Miskin,' says Brock.

And we did. About three hours later.

Ten

ON THE way to the Security Building to see Miskin – in one of the swish Department of Social Studies motors – I thought some more about this Martin Martin. It's like he's a ghost or a spook or a legend, but the way the paper I got tells it, it's like he was ordinary enough, except he was like on some kind of show. His mate Devlin Williams didn't seem to think he was anything special. He's all telling Martin Martin off for spewing and shouting.

Martin Martin's just a bloke who's ruined a show recording. It doesn't seem much to base your life on. And certainly not worth car-bombing for. And so what if the king got him done in? It must have been at least a hundred years ago, and back then that sort of thing happened all the time anyway, so, like, who cares? And he probably asked for it anyway.

By the time the staff motor pulled up outside the Security Department, I was well worked up about the Martin Martinists and their stupid beliefs and their car-bombing. I wanted to go up to Reg and go and explain how it's all silly stuff he's preaching, that they ought to pack it in. At his age. Believing in stories. And taking young people and influencing them in a totally bad way. Like the nice girl. He's probably seen her knicks too and thought that he could talk her into the whole Martin Martin thing and take advantage.

Fucking Reg.

The others, they're all losers. You can see that, it's really obvious. Old hags with nothing to look forward to, or just retarded twats, like the lads who are after the girl's knicks, just like Reg. But she's not like them. I can just tell. She doesn't belong with the Martin Martinists. I'll have to sort it out.

That's where I'm at in my head when we get out the motor and go into the Security Building. Miskin's going to tell me what I do next.

We went through the whole hardcore Security Building X-ray procedure again, but this time it went faster, and in no time at all I was feeling like the top dog once more, with my tagger hanging off my chest giving me special security clearance to see Miskin.

Me and Brock, suits and taggers. Important.

Miskin's horrible little office on the twelfth was just the same, all the people in their grey, concentrating and moving papers around, and Miskin sat in his separate room at an old desk made of wood, looking at papers in files which were all over his desk, like big floppy towers about to fall down. It makes me feel a bit unwell, all this grey and all this crappy old furniture. It's funny though, the old stuff and the grey gives the place the feeling of proper seriousness. Like Miskin said before, what he does is serious. He's not mucking about making shows or porno. He's not laughing all the time. I can't imagine a night on the fuck at Starfucks in Miskin's company, for example. Miskin's really different from what I'm used to. Being here, I'm getting a peek at a different world, an old secret one that I'm not normally allowed to see. And that makes it feel exciting. Even though it's dull. If you get my drift.

'Brock,' says Miskin almost as soon as we get into his room, 'could I have a moment alone with Jensen?' Brock doesn't even say anything and just backs out the door and closes it after him. I sit down and Miskin looks at me like I'm not Jensen but something to look at, like a sculpture or something, like when you look at a statue and think, 'Oh, they've done that hand really well, it looks really real, aren't they clever?' On his desk is the envelope with Reg's papers inside.

Then Miskin says something. He says:

'Looks like your little friend might be causing us some problems, then, Jensen?'

'He's no friend of mine!' I splutter. Like, Reg a friend of mine? Dream on! I've met him once, and that was only cos I was working and I had to talk to him for that fucking focus group.

'I'm glad to hear it,' says Miskin. 'Leaking toilets, eh, Jensen?'

'Yeah,' I say. 'Piss all over the floor, yeah?'

'Quite so. Still. Not to worry. I think we all know what's going on. We'll deal with it from here on. No need for you to worry.'

'But sir!' I says, 'I've done all the work so far. It's not fair! I've really taken fucking risks and everything! It's my job, innit? I've shown initiative. Let me take care of it! I've come this far, it's only fair! Don't be a cunt!'

Miskin looks surprised, but I think my outburst has impressed him.

'I suppose we could do with some more evidence,' he says, sort of to himself.

'Yeah!' I says. 'And I can get it. Leave it to me! I'll get loads!'

'We'll need you to be friendly, Jensen. Draw him in.'

'I can do it, Miskin!' I says. 'I'm well friendly!'

'Any health problems, Jensen?' asks Miskin.

'Nothing wrong with me, Miskin, sir,' I says.

'No, I didn't think so, Jensen,' he says. 'But all the same, I'm not sure you're up to it.'

'I am, sir, I am up to it,' I says, feeling this is the moment I lose my SP, the one where I get sent back to the Social Studies Section, back to FGs about soap and shows, and have to forget about having the tagger on my chest and the spying work and all the excitement. It felt really bad. Miskin carries on looking at me.

'You may not be ready for this, yet,' says Miskin. 'I'm not sure you're mature enough. After all, you have joined the Social Studies Section fresh out of school.'

'I am ready for it, Miskin, sir! I'm bang up for it! I've already done loads for the SP and I want to do more!'

Miskin says nothing and carries on looking at me like I'm a piece of art or an advert about something he's only half-interested in. Eventually he starts to talk:

'Jensen, do you understand what it is we do here?'

'Yes! You look out for people and clean up when they make a mess! You told me before! I understand!' say I, eager.

Miskin nods slowly.

'You may have to go deeper, Jensen. Are you prepared for that?' says Miskin.

'I am, sir,' I says. 'I'll go as deep as you like. I'd go down the deepest mine in the empire, sir. For the Project. For Unity and Success.'

'All right Jensen. I'll assess your files and discuss it with your line manager. We'll let you know tomorrow.'

'What?' I says.

'Go home, Jensen. Take a night off. Have some fun. We'll let you know what to do tomorrow.'

I sat there for a few moments, not sure quite what to do, until Miskin nodded at the door, saying 'Clear off, then' without words, so I left. As I walked out the door, Brock went in without speaking to me.

So that's me, then.

They'll let me know what to do tomorrow; have a night off, he said, have some fun. So that's what I do.

I go home and I call Fyodor and tell him that I've been told by a superior to have fun, which means that me and him are off to Starfucks. He's well up for it. He always is, Fyodor.

Eleven

I REALLY, totally went for it at Starfucks. I had this feeling that it might be a long time before I'd be going again, what with the new orders that Miskin was going to give me, so I thought I'd best fill my boots. We went to the new Starfucks, the flagship one on Wardour Street, and Fyodor was all 'Fucking hell! Fucking hell!' as we walked up to the door, cos he's seen all the stuff on the news about it and, like, everyone's talking about it and it's so hard to get into.

The interior was designed by Melons Fabulous, who did the PM's gym, and they are like so hot right now, and as soon as you go in you can see their touch. The cushions are all by Tunc. When I look at the stuff they do, like their beds and their cutlery, I sometimes wish I hadn't gone to Study Centre 16 but to Study Centre 3, where all the designers come from. But if I had gone to Study Centre 3, then right now I'd be sitting at a desk trying to come up with a new type of coffee pot or something instead of flashing my Security Department tagger to get into Starfucks, where I'll be sitting on their Tunc cushions and having a laugh.

You can tell it's the flagship Starfucks. Aside from the Melons Fabulous interior, you get treated really, really well. Like, at some of the Starfuckses, you can see that the interiors are starting to get a bit dated and shabby round the edges, and the staff are kind of bored and can't be as bothered like they used to be. Like the Rotherhithe Starfucks. But you sort of get used to bad service, don't you? You don't notice the bit of wood coming loose here and there, or the fact that the floor needs redoing. Or that behind the plastic there is black mould that's been growing for years, clinging to the plaster and stinking. So you just keep going to the same place for weeks and months, until you go somewhere else and you realise how crappy the old Starfuckses are.

So Fyodor is gurgling and giggling as we sit down and check out the flagship menu. Everyone was there: Kurt Beast, Marcel Auxere, Bammer Rhymes, Theydon Bois (with her arse already out, as usual), Tinker Tailor, Smart Reckons and David Licence. Me and Fyodor gakked a hatful of the finest boris the house had to offer and set off on our little adventures.

Fyodor went straight off to the Roman room, which I thought was kind of boring of him, never wanting to try anything new. Me, that's a different story. I like the new things, the innovations. I see it as a sign of progress and the general improvement of things.

The house boris really did the trick; the night went by so fast, blurred and cut-up with bits in the wrong places. I can remember seeing Fyodor come out of the Roman room and starting to make a big speech about grapes, and then he fell down the stairs all tangled in his toga and when he hit the bottom, he rolled out straight on to the ice (they've got a great North Pole room for people who like that kind of thing) and knocked down a bloke dressed as a mountaineer, who was headed for the blue igloo. I was at the top of the stairs and saw him go. Graceful, it was. And all around me were the girls from the Roman room who'd come out to see Fyodor the Great make his big speech about grapes, and we all stood there together, me warm from their naked bodies all, like, cuddling me and fondling me, and we all giggled as Fyodor slid across the ice. We could see the direction he was going in and that he was going to hit the mountaineer, and that made us all laugh even more.

I put my arms around the girls and they carried me, still giggling, into the Roman room. I could see why Fyodor loves it in here so much. Fucking great. You don't have to go in for all the old Roman torture (although that's always where you'll find Fyodor, going 'Ow! Ow!' as he gets thwacked by a big naked girl who's going, 'You love it, you bitch!' over and over). If you stay in the main room, you can just sit around watching shows, eating, doing it, looking at other people doing it, or getting all loved over with a massage next to the hot pool.

Fyodor came back into the room, and the girls gave him a new toga, cos the one he'd been wearing had got all wet off the ice and was making him cold. We stayed there for the rest of the night, getting as much boris down us as we could and having a really top time with the girls, singing and chasing each other and eating cake.

I sort of passed out with my head on the belly of one of the girls with her big boobies resting on my face. Very comforting. I could hear her blood running around her belly in pumps, rhythmical and soft. Everything at the right temperature. It made me feel safe and happy.

Twelve

I CAN'T really remember getting home, but we must have done, cos when I woke up I was in my bed and I could smell the perfume of the girl whose belly I'd fallen asleep on all over me. I stretched out and hit something with my hand. It was warm and soft and solid. When I opened my eyes I saw that it was Fyodor. Fyodor snoozing gently next to me with a silly soft face and his hair all straggled over his face, him sort of curled up like a little furry creature from the forest. I sneaked out of bed to get my shit together.

I was in the kitchen, making coffee and watching a news show about the new fruits they were launching (the spherenana looked really good), and suddenly all the speakers in the flat started making this nasty noise like the alarm test they do every Monday afternoon across the city. When you've just woken up after a night like the one me and Fyodor had, that is a really fucking bad noise to have in your flat. I nearly fell over, and if I'd been holding a cup of coffee, I'd have thrown it all over my own head.

The noise only blasted out for about two seconds, then all the screens in the flat turned on and went blue. Then up came the logo of the Security Department and under it were the words 'Message for Jensen Interceptor: five minutes.'

With the two cups of coffee I'd just made, I went into the front room, the one with the comfiest seaters, and sat and waited for my message. Fyodor came out of the bedroom, his eyes all squinty with goo stuck to the lashes, trying to cover his nads with a tiny towel with kittens on and looking grumpy cos he'd been shouted awake by the alarm sound.

72

Fyodor sits down next to me and I hands him his coffee. We both sit there looking at the screen.

'Message for Jensen Interceptor: four minutes.'

'Is this your orders, do you reckon?' asks Fyodor, slurping his coffee – too fucking loud for my liking.

'Yeah,' I says. 'Dunno why they're coming through like this, though.'

'Oh yeah, Jensen,' says Fyodor. 'This is always how they do it. They always issue orders to workers this way.'

'I've never had any like this before,' I says. Cos I ain't.

'Yeah, well, that's cos you've not done much work, innit? And you've been doing like donkey-grunt work. Them orders don't come through to your home cos it's all just bollix. Only more important stuff, like what I do and what you're now doing, comes this way.'

'Oh, right,' I say.

'Yeah!' goes Fyodor, getting excited cos he's telling me something I don't know. 'I know what I'm talking about. Issuing orders through the screens, it's, like, to keep you up to speed. You know, they need to let you know that your nice flat and your spank system with the flat wall-speakers and all your cool shit, it's all there cos the gov put it there for you. It's all about Unity and Success. Orders through screens are way cool.'

'Right-oh,' I says.

'You'd better get dressed,' he goes. Now, I'm not sat there naked or anything. I'm not all meat and two veg (unlike Fyodor, who cannot cover himself properly with the tiny towel with kittens on).

'Uh, yeah. Like I can be fucking bothered,' I says.

And he goes, 'Suit yourself, it's your loss, don't blame me if they . . .' and blah, blah, blah, as he stomps back to the bedroom and starts clomping around in there.

Up on all the screens it says, 'Message for Jensen Interceptor: three minutes.'

Fyodor comes back out of the bedroom and he's dressed.

'Right, I'm off,' he says.

'No breakfast?' I says.

'I'll pick something up on the way to work. And besides, I don't want your boss seeing me in your flat. He'll be really, like, angry, cos what he's going to tell you is supposed to be secret orders and if there's someone else in the place, he'll go spare.' And Fyodor leaves, flipping me off with his new middle-finger sign as he goes.

'Wanker!' I shouts and I hear him down the corridor, even through the walls, shouting 'Wanker!' back at me.

Fucking funny.

And then it says 'Message for Jensen Interceptor: two minutes' on the screens.

I look around the place. It's in a bit of a mess. Me and Fyodor must have carried on partying when we got back, cos there's stuff all over the place. Old food in the boxes they were delivered in, socks, tissues, choccies – all just scattered around like we were throwing them at each other. Which, come to think of it, we was.

Then I remember about how I told Miskin how much I hate mess, and that I like things to be tidy, and how that was part of me managing to talk him into thinking I was up to the job and that he should count me in on the whole thing and I wouldn't let him down.

And here I am, not even twenty-four hours later, in my pants in a room with all mess in it.

Then the screen says, out loud, 'Message for Jensen Interceptor: one minute . . . fifty-nine seconds . . . fifty-eight seconds . . .' and I'm like, 'No! No! No!' cos now I'm totally freaking that when Miskin sees the state of my fucking place, and the state of his new spy/protector in his pants with all rubbish around him in his flat, he'll think I'm just mongy Jensen, who just sits staring at the screen, tugging one off for hours on end, all numbed out off of whizz, eyes all fucking bloodshot, and he'll dump me off my bliss special project. And then I'd be back doing the focus groups, and I'd probably bump into Brock who'd just look at me like I was an arsehole and Fyodor'd go, 'I fucking told you so!' and that would be fucking totally, like, shit.

I run into the bedroom and put my suit on real quick and then I try to hide all the cartons and mess by kicking them behind the seater, all the while the screens going, 'Forty-two seconds . . . forty-one seconds . . .', adding to the whole freak-out of the situation. By the time the countdown has got to 'Ten . . . nine . . . eight . . .', I'm kind of sorted and sat on the seater, trying to look casual yet professional.

'Three . . . two . . . one . . .' says the screen; then the Security Department tune plays before the department's logo vanishes. Then the Security Department face appears, the one that's on all the posters and warnings, the Friendly Face.

'Interceptor,' it says. Very formal. 'Jensen Interceptor, you are now in the employ of the Security Department. We will shortly issue you with your start-up orders, which have come directly from Vladimir Miskin, Head of Laboratory Operatives, Security Department.'

'Right you are,' I says.

'You will continue reporting to Shane E. Brock on a daily basis. He will instruct you on procedure as the operation continues.' So, I'm actually still working for Brock.

'Continue covert surveillance of established target,' says the friendly face. 'Log significant movements. Collect further security information. Maintain daily contact with Brock.'

As far as I can make out, they're asking for me to tell them who all the other members of Reg's little secret gang are. Makes sense. Stage one of the operation: find out who they all are.

'Meanwhile, in order to facilitate your surveillance of the Reginald Rankin group, you will shortly be visited by Makeover Team. Please allow them to complete their duties without hindrance.'

Makeover Team?

'Don't let us down,' says the Friendly Face.

'I won't. Promise,' I go, and then the screens all flick off. And if you're thinking what I'm thinking, then you know that I'm thinking about whether Miskin was lurking behind that face, having a good deckers at me in my flat, checking me out, spying a bit. But I don't have long to think about it.

The doorbell goes. There's a serious-looking bloke with long hair at the door when I open it. Behind him are three other serious boys with long hair. They're all carrying little metal boxes and they smell nice. The boys, I mean, not the boxes.

'Jensen Interceptor,' says the leader. 'We are the Makeover Team.'

I let them in and they troop into the front room, where I've just been taking my orders. They put their boxes on the floor. The leader makes me sit down and he sits opposite me. He takes out a gizmo with wires coming out of it, which he sticks to my fingers; one wire for each finger. He looks at me very fierce in the eye. Really scary. A really scary face. Then he looks at his gizmo thing attached to my fingers by wires, nods to himself, takes the wires off my fingers and puts his gizmo back in his box.

Then Scary Face tells his mates that they can proceed.

'Proceed,' he says.

They open their metal boxes. Scissors, mirrors, make-up – little bottles of it, tons of them – and suddenly my front room is a salon with me as the only customer and three stylists all at it all over me, doing my hair, make-up, twanging my eyebrows and painting gloop on my ears. Normally, a fucking great situation, but I'm still trying to work out what's going on and I'm confused. Like, I was asleep about ten minutes ago, and Fyodor left only about five minutes ago.

'Now I know why you're called the Makeover Team,' I goes to Scary Face, leaning around the stylist who's yanking my hair and snip-snipping away.

'Yes, Jensen Interceptor. Now you know why we're called the Makeover Team,' says Scary Face. He's not the conversationalist type. So I sit a while and let them do what it is they are doing.

'Is this, like, a disguise, then?' I asks one of the snippers.

'Yes, Jensen Interceptor, this is, like, a disguise,' he goes.

'Right-oh,' says I. Then I think, like, how about a nice cuppa for everyone, that might cheer everyone up.

'So, how about a nice cuppa for everyone?' I says. 'It might, like, cheer everyone up, yeah?'

Scary Face looks at me. Then he nods to one of his underlings. The underling goes off to the kitchen and starts banging about in there, making a nice cuppa for everyone. After a few minutes, he comes out with a steamy hot mug of tea. Just the one. He sets it down next to me.

'Don't anyone else fancy a cuppa, then?' I says.

'No,' says Scary Face, and that's that.

Then, just as I was about to reach over and grab my cuppa to take a nice big sip, one of the fucking underlings pulls my hand towards him. He says, 'Look at me, Jensen Interceptor,' so I do. I look straight in his face. Then there's this sharp pain in my arm, right above the wrist, and a kind of flash, and then, for a moment, a really odd sort of darkness, like when the light bulbs break and they go bang and then everything's fucking dark until you sort out another bulb.

'Ow!' I goes. 'What the fuck was that?' And there's this nasty taste in my mouth. My gob has gone all gooey and there's like treacle in there, and I'm dribbling some of it out.

'What was what?' says Scary Face. His underlings all sit back and look at me, heads cocked to one side like I'm a fucking painting or screen or something like that. The one who held my arm isn't holding my arm any more.

I reach for the steamy cuppa, cos I want to get rid of the nasty taste and all the fucking treacly shit in my fucking gob. But when I take a big old glug, it's fucking cold.

'Oi,' I says, 'this tea's fucking cold!' And then I feel this itch in my head and I reach up to scratch at it.

'Leave that alone for a few moments,' says Scary Face. He says it so loud and sort of commanding that I do what he says. He nods to one of the underlings again, and he stands up and fiddles about under my hair, putting some more stuff out of another bottle up there.

'What's going on?' says I. I'm all fucking confused, cos it feels like I've been asleep. The tea's cold and everything, like when someone's made you a cuppa when you've just woken up and left it next to your bed, and you see it there, and then you fall asleep and wake up, and you have a drink, but the fucker's all fucking cold and horrid.

'The tea's all fucking cold and horrid and it's like I've been asleep.'

'No, you haven't been asleep,' says one of the underlings.

'Yes, asleep,' says another, at the same time.

'Which is it, then?' I go, feeling like these makeover freaks are like a pack of loons all talking shite and being totally, like, fucking mad.

'You fell asleep, Jensen Interceptor,' says Scary Face. 'You must have been very tired. We didn't want to embarrass you about it. We waited until you woke up again. But nothing else has happened. Everything is OK. Perhaps it is the effect of the makeover treatment. It can be very disorientating.'

Another nod from Scary Face and they start packing up their cases.

While they pack away, gathering all their little bottles, Scary Face talks to me.

'If you need the makeover removing, contact us here.' He gives me a card with a number on it. It says 'Gervais: Beauty and Hair'.

'We can have you back to your old self in under thirty minutes,' he says. 'If you then need disguising again, we can do that in under thirty minutes too. If you need us to be discreet – if there is someone else in the room when you are contacting us, for example – use the code word 'strawberries'. The disguise is water-resistant, but try not to go swimming or throw yourself into any waterfalls. You may experience some psychological discomfort if you look in the mirror. If you do, take these, they will help.'

He hands me a small bottle of pills. They are called dislocators. I know this cos that's what it says on the label.

'The pills engender a mild sense of dislocation, which should help you adapt to your changed appearance,' says Scary Face as I look at the bottle.

'Dislocation?'

'They help to disconnect your sense of self from your appearance. To put it simply, it won't disturb you if you don't recognise yourself in the mirror.'

And then the Makeover Team disappear as quickly as they arrived.

And then all is calm. It's like nothing has happened. The screens are silent and dark, the flat is empty and quiet, and I'm sitting down in my suit and in front of me are two cups of coffee and a cup of tea. They're all cold. If someone walked in, it would be really difficult to explain to them what's happened, and they wouldn't believe it. But it happened.

I look in the mirror. I nearly fall over.

Like Scary Face said, I don't recognise my own face. It's well a shock and makes my mouth go dry and my heart beat fast. I have to grab on to the towel rail to steady myself on my wobbly knees.

My skin's somehow different, but still the same. And my eyes are no longer blue, but brown. My ears are bigger and my hair is cut shaggy and messy, black in colour, making me look like I've just got out of bed. Which I had, I know, but my hair never looks like I've just got out of bed, even when I've just got out of bed. Now I look like I might be a bit dangerous. I sneer into the mirror and this face sneers back at me, and, like, I'm convinced. A ruffian is looking at me in the mirror. Someone up to no good, make no mistake. I even look over my shoulder, thinking this face I see is lurking around behind me – it's that fucking clever. I look like I belong up in the crappy areas where Reg and his pals all hang out. All this they did to me in less than thirty minutes. Real professionals. And now I'm looking at me in the mirror, a new version of me.

Me, but not me.

A new me.

And now that I'm all disguised up I can go to Reg's and feel like I fit in around there, find out more without getting caught or having to leg it up drainpipes with Reg's gang clawing away at my heels and nearly catching me.

I take six dislocators, just in case of the psychologicals.

Thirteen

I SPENT the rest of the day in the silent flat. I didn't watch no shows, not even *Porn Disco*. I just looked out of the window and thought.

I thought about how stuff can change so quickly, like out of nowhere. And I kept looking at myself in the mirror and touching the new face and talking to myself. It was well weird, seeing someone I didn't really recognise in the mirror. I didn't know what to say to this new face, except things like 'Hello' and 'Is that you?' Eventually, I got sort of embarrassed, especially when the face in the mirror seemed to be, like, taking the piss out of me. Sometimes I would glance quickly in a mirror and it was like the person I saw there was someone who'd been looking at me and thinking bad thoughts about me. Just watching me and judging me. Horrible feeling. It made dark clouds come inside my head and everything go murky and wet like when a storm comes. Then I would sort of get over it. I'd do something normal, like make a cup of tea, and I'd calm down. But then I'd catch my reflection and the shock would come over me again and make me shout out in surprise, and then I'd start moaning. And then came this itch in my head, right deep in, a hot little itch. It got so bad that I began crawling around the flat on my hands and knees, crying, and all the while trying to avoid the reflections which just made everything way worse with like fucking bells on.

After a couple of hours of this suffering, I decided to get right with some decent boris and a load more dislocators. I also bombed a purple, which I keep for special occasions cos they're so fucking pricey. I had to plan what I was going to do next and get over my wah-wah reaction to having a new face, and a purple was the only thing I could think of that would deffo get me up and running and maybe calm the brain itch. The purple really fried me up and got me dashing around the flat, going 'Yeah! All right! Well, all right!', like Bammer Rhymes when he does his big concerts. I was well worked up and really keen to get going. The more boris I honked, the more I felt like a proper spy/protector, so I was waiting for it to get dark, I was like fucking totally raring to go and get out there and actually do some spying.

Eventually, it got dark. I left the flat.

I ate three Squeezers, so I wouldn't be getting hungry. And then, cos I was nervous, I tanked another big hit of boz (after I'd put some in my coat pocket for later) and gulped a couple more dislocators, just to be on the safe side.

When I got down to the street and headed towards the tube, I seemed to be moving at twice the speed of everyone else, with my jacket lapels up around my new face and a great spy-hat on my head that I found in the wheelie thing under the bed. It was like I was gliding while everyone else was stuck to the floor and having to lift their feet out of mud or something to take another step.

I had a plan for my night's spying and protection work, and I was really fired up about it cos now I was the real thing, a real spy, working for the Security Department. I'd had my special orders straight from Miskin and got the full makeover treatment off of the Makeover Team. Even Fyodor wouldn't have recognised me if he walked past at that moment.

I was feeling so fucking ace that not even the stink of the tube bummed me out. Three stops to London Bridge on the Jubilee line, then the change onto the fucking Northern line for the Angel, and on the train there are too many povos and their stinky feet.

But I was feeling sharp and cool and fucking great, so the mental bag-collectors and shuffly stinkers with their depressed faces couldn't bring me down. There's nothing like a mission to keep you apart from all that shit.

When I came up to the surface at the Angel, I needed some time to feel my way back into the whole Reg-district vibe with its shabby gaffs and crumbled people, alkie loons and the like. The last twenty-four hours had been a bit too chock-a-block with all different kinds of action for me to just switch back into the Reg vibe.

So, I'm, like, getting into it, walking along, heading for a street near

Reg's, but not too near, taking deep breaths and shaking my arms around to sort of relax myself. Like off the shows for keeping fit. Feeling pretty fucking cool. I know my spot now, from the other night. Right near the flat where the basement hairies live. The same spot I stood and watched the comings and goings around Reg's. That's where I'm headed when I hear this voice:

'Gizza kwid.'

I look around and there's this geezer coming out of a doorway holding his hand out. He's well grimy and there's a piece of string holding his trousers up, and his cock's hanging out.

'Gizza kwid,' he says again, and he's sort of in front of me, getting in the way so I can't get past.

'Fuck off!' says I.

'You fuck off!' says the geezer.

'Get out my fucking way!' I says. ' You fucking trampy twat.'

'You get out my fucking way and gizza kwid!' he says.

So I push him, just to get him out the way. He stumbles back a bit, bent over. Then he comes at me. He's got a bottle in his hand and he's waving it about like he's going to bash me with it.

'Oi!' I shouts at this ghastly monster, 'don't bash me with a bottle, you bloody fucker!'

'Gizza kwid!' he shouts and bloody fucking bashes me on the head with his bottle. Not so hard that it breaks, nor so hard that it makes me go unconscious, but it fucking hurts.

'Agh!' I go. 'That hurt!'

So I smack him one on his nose. And he gets a boot in the bollocks too.

'Oof!' comes out of him, and he folds over. I clobber him on the back of his head. He goes down making noises like 'Oh!' and 'Argh!'

While he's lying there on the floor, all 'Oof!' and that, I get my Security Department card out and shove it under his stupid bleeding nose.

'You're fucking lucky I don't run you in, pal,' I say. I'm all totally angry with this stupid old bastard and I want to show him who's boss and that he shouldn't go around bashing people, especially me, on the bonce with his bottle.

'Ooh! Argh!' goes the stupid trampy. 'I'm sorry, feller, so I am, I had no idea! Ooh! Argh! Don't run me in! I beg you!' and all crap like that.

'Yeah well, just watch it. And piss off,' I says.

I look around, but there doesn't seem to be anyone taking notice, so I scarper up the road a bit, rubbing the bit of my head where the bottle hit. It totally hurts, but there's no blood. I'm feeling well dizzy, though. And there's that funny taste in my mouth again.

Once I'm out of sight of that fucking bloody old trampy, I duck into a doorway to get a breather. My chest hurts cos of the scarpering and the fighting, and my noggin well hurts cos of the bashing it just got, and I'm like in a bit of shock. My mouth is dry and tastes like I've been eating metal, and it hurts to swallow. Once my chest has stopped heaving up and down quite so much, I decide to have another bash on the boris to set me straight. I do a bigger hit than normal, and it's soon having its lovely FX. I start to giggle about all what's just happened, and I feel excited about all the real danger that I'm facing being a spy/protector.

Then time starts to really drag. I'm standing about, looking innocent, but it's really cold and after a while I notice that my knees are really aching and my feet hurt. And the pain in my head is getting bigger and making me squint with it. I can feel a big hard lump coming up on my bonce. The boris is keeping the worst of it off, but it's getting really unpleasant, standing around, gazing up at Reg's dark flat.

Waiting and waiting, but fucking fuck all's going on.

People walk past. They go into the dimly lit little shops and come out with paper bags full of the sort of crap they eat.

Then, just as I'm thinking of packing it in, cos the cold and hurt in the head is getting too much and I'm seeing nothing going on at Reg's flat, I see this person walking up the street right towards me.

It's a girl.

It's the girl whose knicks I'd seen when I'd been peeping in on Reg's meet the other night.

She's coming right at me, not really paying attention or anything. I'm sort of stuck where I am with nowhere to go to get out of her way. If I scarper, she'll definitely spot me, and it'll look really weird and she might tell Reg. If I walk towards her, she might see me, and I can't really handle that idea. I'm supposed to be discreet, so walking right into the face of one of my, like, spy targets on the first night of my mission seems like something I should avoid.

So I lean up against a railing outside a house and hop about a little bit, like I'm trying to tie a shoelace. And she walks straight past me. I don't look up, so I don't know if she looked at me or not. But there was no way she could have seen my face. I'm dead crafty, yeah? She goes round a corner, and after a few seconds I stop my hopping shoelace act and go after her, staying close to the darkness of the walls and not even bothering if there are puddles under my feet, walking straight through them, staying in the shadows.

And all the time there's no one else around. It's just me and the girl, me still gliding like I'm on hovercraft shoes, and her clip-clopping along, brisk and echoing all around. It's so gloomy it's like in black and white. Still cold too. No decent places warming the street up with their shiny signs and electric buzz and people flocking in and out to buy things or to eat. No fun kiosks or machines. No Starfuckses. Just miserable old houses, leaning over like they just can't take it any more, filled with peasants and half-wits like the family of hairies I'd seen the other night in their basement, and surrounded by weeds and old rubbish, and shit shops for vegetables with dim lights and signs they've made themselves out of wood and paint.

I stay behind the girl at a distance, acting casual, remembering the simulator on my basic skills (protection) course, and she stops outside a big window and looks in for a moment. Then she walks in. I hear a little bell go 'tinkle-tinkle' and her heels make a dragging sound on the doorstep as she goes inside.

I walk along the filthy street on the other side of the road so I can take a look at this place she's just gone into. As I walk along, I'm almost too nervous to look over, just in case.

But I do.

Through the big window I see a few tables with candles on them and people sitting down, eating and drinking in the gloom. A restaurant! Just what you'd expect around here. All cracked plates and glasses which they use over and over again, probably smeared with germs, crappy broken old furniture from the dark ages, cheap food made in some nasty kitchen out the back. Peasant food for peasants who like the taste of unhygenic things and who don't eat decent food like the Squeezers sitting nicely in my tum.

When I make my first pass on the other side of the road, I can't see the girl, so I carry on a while and decide to cross the road and come back on the same side as the restaurant so I can take a closer look. A risky strategy, for sure, passing so close to a target, but, I mean, this is a stroke of luck when you think about it. I could have spent fucking days wandering around trying to track down Reg's Martin Martinist gang of mentalist tosspots. Who knows how much time I might have had to spend keeping an eye on Reg's place before he had another meeting? I might have been there for a week, listening to the hairy peasants shouting, freezing my arse off, getting bashed by fucking old trampies. Maybe even longer. But here, on my first night, I locate a target. So I have to check her out and that. I'm thinking that this stroke of luck is probably down to my natural spy abilities spotted by Miskin and Brock, and so it isn't a stroke of luck at all, but just my, like, total fucking spy talent.

As I head towards the restaurant for my second looksie, I hear the tinkle-tinkle of the bell over the door again. Then there are voices, lots of them, all laughing and talking extra loud to each other, and then there are suddenly people on the street, a load of them. Just as I arrive at the door of the restaurant, they all pile out, full and happy and drunk and saying 'Night, then!' and 'Thank you!' and 'Ha ha ha!' There are so many of them that they block the way and somehow I find myself in the doorway of the restaurant, with the door being held open by the owner of the place, who was going, 'Come back soon, ha ha ha!' and stuff. He just steps aside to welcome me in, just like any other customer.

I look over my shoulder, thinking I could just turn around and go back the way I came, ignore the restaurant owner and get going. But stumbling up behind me, singing a stupid song to himself and with blood dried on his face, is the bloody fucking Gizza Kwid trampy what I'd had the dust-up with earlier.

I look past the owner into his smelly little place and I see the girl sat on her own at a table for four, sipping at a glass and reading a book.

The crowd is still milling about, laughing and happy, and the drunk old trampy fuck is getting closer.

Now the owner's all 'Ha ha ha!' to me, and I'm going 'Ha ha ha!' too, fitting in with the good laugh everyone's having, but inside I'm panicking that the drunk tramp bastard is going to see me and start going on about me being Security Department or something, and maybe tell everyone that I gave him a proper kicking earlier. Then I'd be screwed.

'Well,' I thinks to myself, 'here goes', and I steps inside the restaurant. The owner pats me on the back as I walk in and starts saying things in a language I don't know. It's like we're old mates now. I walk into the place. It's small. The table where the crowd of six have just left is all filthy with plates and glasses and cups. There are three other tables in there. Two of the tables have couples sitting at them, gazing into each other's eyes over a candle. The only place I can go is the table where the girl is sitting. The restaurant owner has still got his hand on my back and is manoeuvring me towards the girl's table, still talking away in his language. There I am, stood at the table for four where the girl's sat, deep into her book and her glass of red booze.

The owner pulls out a chair, which makes the girl look up. She lets off a little smile which means 'Hello' and 'Oh no' at the same time. So I do one back at her and sit down. I really need to sit down. My heart is hammering and my head throbs with every thump, like I'm getting hit with that bloody fucking stupid trampy twat's bottle again with every pump of my hot innards' juice. It's dark in here, and warm too. I hadn't realised how cold and uncomfortable I'd got outside. It feels nice to be inside and sat down and warm.

Once I'm actually sat there with the girl, the whole situation changes. Being a spy and just peeking in on people without them knowing feels nervy and weird, but when you're just a few inches away and properly in their space, then something else takes over and the spying part fades away a bit and a normal feeling comes over you. This is the emphasising-your-banality bit that they taught me on my protection course. It gets easier, which isn't what I'd expected. I thought it would be more difficult when I came face-to-face with my prey. Or, rather, my object of protection. But then I remembered about how this lot are probably doing car bombs, and that yesterday I was wanting to shoot them all up with guns, and how Reg must be an evil madman and how they drink blood like Miskin said.

When I look at the girl, though, now back into her book, in a world of her own, I can't believe that she would drink blood or car-bomb. She seems too pretty for that. If you're pretty there's no need for car bombs, is there? Everyone likes you if you're pretty.

The warm of the restaurant and my head pain are making me feel light-headed. There's a rushing noise in my ears and my eyes keep fluttering like they're going to close. I'm feeling sleepy and woozy. I'm well trouble-fucked.

I hear some far-away noise. I'm looking down at a menu on the table, not thinking about anything, just swaying around ever so slightly, trying to keep my eyes open, but really wanting to doze off and have a little kip, like I'd feel a lot better after a little kip.

The noise in my head carries on, and then there's a hand on my shoulder, which jerks me out of my sleepy cocoon. The girl is looking right at me, and the noise in my head suddenly sharpens. It's the restaurant owner. It's his hand on my shoulder.

'What you want to eat, friend?' he's saying.

'Oh, I don't. I mean, I'm not sure, sorry; I was just dozing off. I'm, it's . . . I've had a long day . . .' I burble.

There's no point in asking for a 15+ meal, cos a) they wouldn't have any 15+ Meals and b) if I asked for one, it would blow my cover by making it obvious that I didn't belong. It was a worrying moment, cos I had to order some food so I wouldn't look suspicious, but whatever I ordered would be a nasty gloopy mess that smelled bad and which I'd have to eat. And I'd already eaten those three Squeezers earlier. Plus the fucking whack to the head I'd got off Gizza Kwid is not only making my skull go clangy like bashing a big old ship when it's not in the water, but there's also a kind of gutty pukey nausea coming on, like a close relative of the dizziness. Being, like, knowledgeable about these eating places seems pretty important if you want to make like everything's just as normal and you always eat in these places cos you're from around these parts.

'Erm . . .' I goes to the owner, who's stood over me holding a pencil at the ready.

'The bolly naze is good,' says the girl.

'Is it?' I says.

'This is the best little Italian for miles,' she says, smiling at the bloke holding the pencil, and he smiles back at her, his fat cheeks almost covering his eyes.

I look at the bloke holding the pencil.

'Is he?' I says.

'*Sì, signore*. Provengo da Napoli,' he says, making a big bow like an actor when the audience starts clapping.

'Right you are,' I says. 'I'll have the bolly naze, then. Yum, yum, eh?'

I thought that last bit, the 'yum, yum', would sort of make everything go along nicely. Sure enough, the girl giggles and the bloke with the pencil smiles again, looking at both of us in a weird sort of way, like he knows something's going on between us. Young lovers. All that.

The girl puts her book down.

'I haven't seen you around here before,' she says.

'No. I don't suppose you have,' I says. 'But I've seen you.' Then I, like, kick myself mentally. What am I saying? I mean, what was coming next out of my mouth?

'What I mean,' I says, cos I can see her eyebrows going up which means she's surprised and probably wanting me to explain where and when I'd seen her before, 'is that I saw you in there. Here, I mean. When I walked past. Just now. Then I felt hungry. So I came in. And there you were. Again. I'm not following you or nothing.'

My throat's getting dry, there's a lump in it, and I can feel all sweat starting to form down my back and under my arms, just like when I was climbing up the drainpipe to spy on Reg. Why the fuck did I say that I wasn't following her? Like, who needs to be introducing the idea of anyone following anyone else? Under my new black shaggy hair, my head feels very hot and wet.

The pretty girl reaches for her glass and sips some red booze.

'You're not from around here, are you?' she goes.

'Erm. No,' I says, having to think double fast, but all I can think of is that I'm from the Security Building, via the Duncan-Smith Infant Unit, then Lab School and then Study Centre 16, and that I was supposed to be just, like, keeping an eye on Reg and his gang to find out where they lived and that kind of thing, and not chit-chatting to one of them. Like, I'm in really deep.

Fucking arsepiece.

Seriously.

But it's too late to worry about that. Here I am, and I have to do the do and keep it all together, so it's, like, all together.

'I've got to go to the, er . . .' I says, half-standing as I say it. It's a ploy. I'm employing a ploy to buy me some time to come up with answers to possible questions this girl might ask me, and I also need a chance to chop out some fat boris to stave off all this nausea and brainache.

'It's over there,' she says, pointing to a door at the back of the room.

'Oh, right. I won't be a sec,' I goes, and I trundle off, through a swing door at the back of the restaurant, down a little corridor where there are big tins of cooking oil and crates of onions and stuff stacked up, past the door where the kitchen is to another door where the toilet is.

When I get in there, I sit on the loo and try to breathe slowly, trying to calm myself down. Then I get my baggie of boris out and give myself a right old seeing to with it. The electric buzz comes on strong, really strong, and sends my hands shaky.

I splash my face with water and look at myself in the mirror. I get another shock at seeing the work the Makeover Team have done, despite all the dislocators what I've necked.

I take a few deep breaths and remind myself not to freak out or anything mad like that. I don't want the pressure of the situation to get to me. Just act natural, I tell myself. She doesn't know I'm a spy, so don't go around acting like one and saying things like, 'I'm not a spy or anything,' which I did think about saying once or twice when I was feeling a bit tense earlier on. I suppose I was hoping she'd say, 'I didn't think you were a spy,' so I could relax a bit more, cos then I'd know that she didn't suspect that I was a spy, but then there's me putting ideas in her mind about spies, which was probably the last thing she was thinking about. Once the word 'spy' had been used, she'd start thinking, 'Why'd he say that thing about spies?'

Fuck.

No talking about spies, then, Jensen. Act natural, be yourself. Not the spy-yourself, but the regular Jensen-yourself. Probably best not to talk about Starfucks or Fyodor either. And try not to think too much about how you were up the drainpipe that time, looking in on their Martin Martinist meeting and how you saw her knicks.

I wouldn't mind seeing them again, as it goes.

And with that thought, I take another deep and calming breath, let the boris zizz around the circuits for a moment or two, shake myself down and then go back into the restaurant.

She's gazing out the window when I get back to the table, but her eyes aren't looking at anything, like there's thick glass between her and the outside world. When I arrive back at the table, the scraping of the chair when I pull it back makes her return to the real world with Jensen and bolly naze and the little Italian.

As soon as I sit down, the little Italian turns up with my bolly naze, sticks it on the table and says 'Enjoy.'

It's steaming, brown stuff and red stuff on yellow tubes or string. There's yellow powder on it that smells like puke. I starts to neck it, thinking that if I get it down me fast enough, I won't have to taste it. Halfway through I stop for a drink and to catch my breath. I grab the glass of red booze, gulp it down, and carry on with the bolly naze. When I finish, I look up, and the girl's staring at me with a smile at the corners of her mouth. I feel bloody awful, but I manage a weak grin.

'Delicious,' I says, but it comes out feeble, cos I'm feeling well rough. All that nasty gobble on top of the boris and the dislocators and the booze – and the whole tension of this scenario – isn't making me feel too fucking clever.

'Were you hungry?' asks the girl.

'Oh, er, yeah, I was. Well, no, I wasn't. I mean, sort of, yeah,' I goes, not very convincing.

'What I mean is that I'm not, like a poor person,' I says, trying to think what the best thing to say might be, but then forgetting how I should be behaving. Like, do they think of themselves as poor around here? In which case, should I say that I am a poor person too? But if I said I was poor, it might put her off. She might not like poor people.

'What I mean,' I says, all these bits of info about who's poor and who's not poor and who should be poor and whether that's me and her (being poor together, I mean, and so like, therefore being automatically pals), running around in my head and bumping into each other and falling over. My mouth keeps opening and saying words before I am, like, really ready. 'I mean to say . . .'

'Don't worry. I understand. You're just hungry, right?' she goes, her eyes with that glow of understanding in them that you see in the PM's when he is holding a baby or shaking hands with a mong from a special centre on the news shows. It's a look that makes you feel warm and safe.

'So,' says the girl, a bit more businesslike now, but still friendly, the sympathy bit now disguised behind a speaking-with-equals look she is giving me and little shakes of the head, 'where did you say you were from?'

'Oh, er, well I didn't, I don't think. Did I?' I says, thinking to myself, I hope I didn't. The boris is all crackling around my tubes and it's making me clench my teeth tight so they hurt.

'No, you didn't,' she says.

'Right,' I says, relieved. A few moments pass.

'So?' she goes, all question-faced, waiting for me to tell her where I'm from.

'Norfolk!' I says.

I don't know why.

Don't ask me. It might have had something to do with a show I'd seen once about mongs who live outside of London. I remember seeing some blokes lurching around all covered with mud and without all their teeth and going 'Ooh arrr' and talking about farming. They seemed like the kind of people the girl would think were all right. I knew that she wouldn't like people like me who work for the government and have spank pads in the Rotherhithe Sky Tower.

'Wow!' she says, which was encouraging. 'Very good!' she says, and giggles.

'Yeah,' I goes, 'I'm like totally fucking oppressed and everything,' I says, smiling too, enjoying her giggles, thinking I've totally cracked it. In the fucking bag, yeah?

'I understand,' says the girl, and then she goes: 'What's your name?'

It's about now when I realise that there are some holes in my planning. Not that I'd had any kind of plan at all. It had all gone wrong from the very minute I'd arrived here in Reg's run-down part of the world. All I'd meant to do was keep an eye out. But before I had time to think, I found myself getting into a proper biffter with fucking Gizza Kwid, and the next thing I know I'm sitting with the girl in the restaurant talking shit and feeling like I'm all fucked up cos I've done too much boris and been bashed about the head and eaten too much bolly naze and drunken too much red booze.

So, I thinks to myself, I can't tell her my name is Jensen Interceptor, cos that's like a totally fucking cool and modern name and totally means that I'm in with the Project and the PM and all that, you know? The only name I can think of that would fit in around here is Reg, but I can't tell her my name's Reg, cos that would be really confusing, as if things aren't fucking confused enough already, yeah? We don't need two Regs. So then I start thinking about the mong from Norfolk on the show, and I try to remember what he was called, and all that's going around in my head is, like, 'Norfolk, Norfolk, Norfolk' and my lips are moving around sort of quietly saying it while I'm thinking, and all the time the girl is looking at me, really closely, like urging me on to say my name, and then I suddenly hear her say something.

'Norfolk?' she goes. 'Your *name* is Norfolk?'

I must have said it out loud. Like a twat I'd said 'Norfolk'. She'd asked me my name, and I'd said Norfolk. Like a twat.

'Is that a nickname?' she asks.

'Yeah,' I says, 'it is. That's what they call me. Norfolk. Cos, like, I'm from Norfolk. Makes sense, doesn't it? I mean, it's fair enough, yeah? Norfolk. It's as good a name as any, yeah?'

And I pour myself another large slug of the red booze and drink it, trying to cover my face with the glass while I drink, the inside of the glass getting all steamy with my breath, cos I could feel my face going red with the embarrassment of the situation and my heart is booming in my ears, all squelchy and sick-sounding, moist and slippy.

'Well, Norfolk,' says the girl, 'my name is –'

She doesn't finish what she has to say, cos at that moment, I suddenly feel very, very ill. Not half-ill, like a bit fucking peculiar, but total biology-ill. Like when you're going to shut down and let loose, and there's going to be puke and shit and wizz and the whole fucking works – screeching in the head like an alarm going off. It must have been the bolly naze and the red booze and the boz and the whole stress of everything. The girl's voice goes distant and small, and a roaring noise like a jet engine comes up in my ears, and the shadows in the restaurant from the candle light suddenly grow and grow like a great scarifying beast about to leap out and gnaw on my bones.

I hear a thump, and then the sound of cutlery rattling, then there's a sensation like pain on my head, in a different place from where Gizza Kwid smacked me. It's not really painful.

Then there's nothing.

Fourteen

THESE WORDS I hear next:

'Norfolk! Norfolk!'

They're sung, gentle and soothing.

I was dreaming – a bad dream – dreaming that I was tumbling around in, like, a big drum, with screens all smashing up and falling apart in the drum, and big sharp spikes of glass coming at me, going straight into my eyes, and the lumps of glass have still got pictures from shows on them, and they go right into my skull, and into my soft brain, and the images off the broken bits of glass slip into my squishy brain, where they all jumble up and stay, and actors shouting bits off shows all cut with someone making a recipe and *Monster Trucks*.

Then I'm not so asleep any more, and I realise that this horror of smashing glass and all my bones getting busted up is just a dream, and I'm thinking maybe I'd fallen asleep on a train or something, and that I'd woke up cos the voice on the speakers was telling all us dozy travellers that we'd, like, arrived in Norfolk: 'Next stop, Norfolk.' I feel like I should be jumping up and grabbing my bags from the compartment above our heads, getting all ready to get off the train at Norfolk, elbowing other travellers out the way so's I can get to the door first and escape the train when the platform comes up. Then I'm wondering why they would call a train station Norfolk, cos, like, Norfolk is big, a county or something, not a place as such – not a place that would have a train station named after it. And I'm confused and wanting to go back to London and start saying, 'No, I want to go back to London. To old Rotherhithe,' but my head's hurting like bastards and my face is swollen and numb and all I can do is blow air between my crispy lips: 'Pffffffff, ffffffffff, perfffffffffff'.

'Wake up, Norfolk,' goes the voice again, and it's only then I sussed what you've already well sussed reading this. It's the girl. She thinks my name is Norfolk. I told her Norfolk's my name, and so she's calling me Norfolk. And I'm feeling well bad. I mean, like, fucking totally not great with the head inflated like a rubber balloon and my brain rattling about inside like a hard little pea. And my mouth tastes like the powder off the top of the bolly naze.

'Here's a glass of water,' says the girl as I try to open my eyes, which feel like they're sealed with like slimy sleep gloo and bits.

'Ergh,' I says, and it's just about all I can do to hold the glass and bring it up to my mouth. I can't see much and I don't know where I am.

So I ask.

Turns out I'd yagged a gutful all over the place in the restaurant, bashed my noggin against the table and passed out on the floor. No wonder my head feels the way it does. The little Italian helped the girl get me outside and into a cab which whisked us back to her place. So here I am, dark outside, in the girl's little flat, lying on a seater with the balloon head, the sour reek of spew all over me.

Fuck!

At least that's what's in my head as the full, like, fucking uncool enormity of this situation really hits me and I sit up. It's all gone totally, like, Harry Bollox. And my stomach is knotting and gurning like it's going to blow again. And I don't know which end it's going to come from. And I'm shaking. And my head is tight like the rubber balloon and the pea brain. And like, you know, I'm like a fucking old tramp here. Some stupid fucking old tramp who's got himself all smacked around the head loads and fucked up off of booze and bad food. Like fucking Gizza Kwid. I'm feeling well sorry for myself, just imagining what Miskin and Brock are going to have to say to me about all this. And I can't help it, but it all comes out cos I'm feeling so terrible and bad about having made such a giant fucking toss-up over the whole spying thing.

'I'm like some stupid fucking old tramp!' I goes, and it comes out all whining and like a kiddiewinkle noise, me gulping for air so the last bit is like 'Tr-uh-tra-uh-uh-tr-uh-uh-amp', and I'm fucking totally crying and everything.

'There, there,' says the girl. She's sat next to me now, and she puts her arm around me. Even though I'm damp with red puke, she doesn't mind touching me.

And this makes me cry even more, so I'm really like full pelt with words coming out my mouth like spew, out of control.

'Wah! It's the government what's done this to me! They made me like this! Wah! Wah! They totally fucking done me in and made everything really shit! Wah! Wah! I hate them! I hate them! It's like I've got no choice! Wah! I was happy before, you know, but then they came along and they really fucking messed everything up for me! Wah! Why don't they leave me alone! They can stick their Project right up their arse! Wah! Wah!'

And the thing is, what with the tears and all, I'm actually meaning what I'm weeping about. Like, in a way, that's how I'm feeling. In my mind are all pictures of me and Fyodor at Starfucks having a laugh, with Fyodor falling down the stairs and me and the Starfucks girls all stood at the top of the stairs chuckling at silly old Fyodor as he goes sliding across the ice and all that. And I'm thinking about how I didn't have any cares at all and it was all so smart and ace and easy. But, like, now I'm suddenly all serious and a spy, and I've even got a new face, and I'm confused and want to be at happy Rotherhithe Sky Tower, checking out *Porn Disco* on my bed, going 'Ha ha ha!' at the different girls' knicks. Instead I'm all covered in puke in the middle of fucking nowhere in some crappy old flat, with misery Miskin and Brock breathing down my neck wanting, like, results, and I've messed the whole thing up. It's a really bad scene.

But of course, while what I'm crying about is the stuff I've just outlined, what the girl thinks I'm crying about is something different.

'Don't worry, calm down, Norfolk,' she keeps saying, stroking my head. 'It's OK. We'll soon have you cleaned up. You were just tired, that's all. It was all a bit much for you,' and each word coming out of her mouth seems to stroke me on the inside, like the stroking on my head, and, after a bit, I get calmer and start feeling a bit better, like all is not lost after all, and I start breathing properly and not all jerky. The girl rests her hand on my head and looks at me in a really deep way, her eyes are lasering into my brain and it's like she can see things there (not me and Fyodor all off our choppers having a laugh at Starfucks, but all the sadness stuff), and she says:

'You've had a hard time, haven't you? Don't worry: There, there.'

She asks if I want to take a bath, and I just nod, sat there sniffing snot, looking at the floor.

She goes off and I hear the roaring and bubbling of the bath filling, it reminds me of the noise in my head before I passed out. Then she comes back, gives me a big red towel and a robe and points at a door.

'It's all ready, just through there, first door on the right. Leave your clothes outside the door and I'll pop them in the wash.'

Still sniffing and bleary with tears, I head off in the direction she's pointing and take the first door on the right and let myself into the bathroom, which is all steamy and sweet-smelling. I strip off, open the door a crack, and put my old stinky clothes in a little heap just outside and climb into the bath.

The warm water feels good, and I close my eyes and let everything just soak out of me, including the vommy smell, and I start to feel, like, loads better and warm and cosy even. My tum's calming down as I lie there, and the water's holding me up, making me almost float, and the steam coming off it is making my face wet and taking all the stress of the day away.

I start to think that maybe everything's OK after all and that when I see Miskin and/or Brock, they'll be pleased, cos it'll be like I've been really brave and everything. By going in this deep, all like undercover, I'll be able to get some hardcore spying done. These things take time, yeah? You don't just hide behind dustbins and climb up drainpipes for a couple of minutes and then report back and go, 'Ooh, ooh, Mr Miskin, sir, I've, like, been behind a fucking dustbin and up a drainpipe and, like, I saw some stuff, but I'm not really sure what's going on or anything.'

What good's that? That's not spying. That's not being effective. That's no help to the Project or anything. That's no fucking use to anyone, is it? That's just pissing about. You don't stop car-bombers and blood drinking by pissing about. Even I could see that, and there's me all, like, totally fucking fresh to the whole spying malarkey. No, what you do is go in deep. You win the trust of the people you're spying on. Or protecting. And then they tell you loads more by accident. The girl, for example, she's washing my clothes and totally thinks my name's Norfolk. She's all, like, looking after me and everything, and I'm in her flat. She'd never let the police in her flat, would she? She wouldn't just tell them what Reg and his Martin Martinists are up to, would she? But she might tell poor old Norfolk, old trampy Norfolk, who's so, like, I don't know, stressed and ill and repressed that he went all sick and yagged up his bolly naze and his red booze by accident in public like that.

Yeah, Jensen, it's OK. Everything's OK. It's going to be all right.

And I'm thinking of when I finally see Miskin and Brock and I can tell them about what I've been through and how totally fucking committed I've been to my special project, and how sweet the meet should go. I remind myself that I should be pretty cool and, like, professional and not get all carried away when I tell them what I know.

'Yeah,' I imagine myself saying, in Miskin's crappy old office in the Security Building, the security tagger with Jensen Interceptor written on it dangly off my spank new suit (I'm thinking that I'll get a fucking totally aced-out new suit from Spinoza or Vincelli or somewhere like that when all this is over), 'Reg is, like, totally a cunt about stuff, and here's the proof!' Or, even: 'Yeah, well, actually, I went pretty fucking deep and, you know, Reg is nothing. He's just an old nonce arsing around. Nothing for us to be worried about.' I like how I say the word 'us' there. Like we're a team. All in it together. Me, Miskin and Brock. Me and the gov. Us.

But then I think that if I say Reg is just nothing, then I won't look so good. So I erase that bit, pretend I didn't think it and go back to the bit where I present Miskin with a ton of evidence, evidence that I'll get once I'm out of this bath and back to normal, evidence about Reg's involvement with car-bombings and his dangerous Martin Martinist beliefs, and how the gang is, like, really fucking dangerous and planning something really big and how I thwarted it somehow.

And then there's me getting introduced to the PM at Number 10 and he's like really fucking serious, and he shakes my hand and gives me a medal and says, 'Fucking Jensen Interceptor, you are the bollocks.' Or something. Then we go out and get all messed up together at Starfucks and we become, like, mates, and we hang out all the time and that. And Bammer Rhymes is there too.

Yeah. Fucking great.

And by the time I've thought all that, I'm brought back into what's going on in the here and now, so to speak, i.e. the girl's bathroom, cos there's a timid little knock on door and she goes, 'Are you all right in there?' and I'm suddenly all, 'Oh, uh, yeah, just coming!' and I stand up with that loud whoosh noise you get when you suddenly stand up in a bath.

'Coming!' I goes. 'I feel loads better! Thanks!' And I'm all sing-songy like her.

When I'm dried, I pop the robe on and I go back into the room, where only a while earlier I'd been wailing and feeling rotten, and everything is so different. I'm clean and relaxed, I don't feel sick any more, and I've straightened everything out with Miskin and Brock in my head.

The girl's little flat looks nice now. I mean, don't get me wrong, it's like a total shithole from the nineteenth century or something, and everything in it is shitty and old, all made of wood and worn old fabrics and somehow crappy and shabby, nothing like my pad with its sharp lines and ace gear and System-8 screens with SurroundScape and smart stuff like that, but you know, she's made it as nice as she can. It's kind of warm, I suppose. There are a few candles burning and the lights are low and yellow. On a little table in front of the seater I was conked out on before are a couple of steamy mugs.

'I thought you might like a cup of tea,' she goes, nodding at the table. And next to the mugs, piled up all neat, is all the stuff I had in my pockets. She'd taken it all out when she'd put my clothes in the machine to wash them. I swallow pretty hard when I see the stuff, cos of course the evidence of my real identity and everything is there. Like my ID what I shoved under the nose of Gizza Kwid after delivering unto him his proper kicking. But my cards and all that giveaway stuff that would tell her my name was not Norfolk but Jensen Interceptor, and that I was on an SP for the government, all that stuff is inside my wallet, zipped up.

I looks at the girl, and she looks at me. She's looking pretty serious and I'm thinking 'Oh-oh . . .'

But then I'm thinking that she doesn't look like she knows who I am. She's not looked inside the wallet, cos that would be the sort of thing I'd do, and not the sort of thing she'd do, cos I can tell that she's, you know, nice. She's innocent and trusting and good. She wouldn't look inside poor old trampy Norfolk's wallet. She might not even get sus when she sees that poor old trampy Norfolk has got a Ho Chi Minh retro-special wallet, cos she wouldn't know a Ho Chi Minh retro-special wallet if she saw one, and so she wouldn't know how much a Ho Chi Minh retro-special wallet costs. But on top of the wallet is my baggie of boris.

Whoops.

'Listen, Norfolk,' she goes. 'I don't want you to get the wrong idea, but I don't approve of drugs.'

'Yeah, no. Me neither,' I goes, nodding, but I'm grabbing my top lip with my bottom teeth, which shows I'm fibbing.

'They don't really help, you know?' she says.

'Yeah, that's right,' I says, not really thinking, just eager to agree with her.

And then I goes, 'Don't they?' Cos, like, well, you know, don't they?

'They're just a crutch,' she says.

'Really?' I says.

'I've got nothing against the odd glass of red wine, but these things,' and she picks up my baggie and waggles it around, 'they're just a chemical cosh, Norfolk. You said earlier you were oppressed, didn't you?'

'Oh yeah, I am, totally,' I goes, remembering that pretending I was an oppressed peasant from Norfolk called Norfolk had got me into this situation.

'Well, these drugs are just another way of oppressing you, Norfolk. You've seen the people around here. You've seen the ones that are lost to drugs, haven't you? They can create psychosis in the most balanced of individuals. And you're not telling me that you haven't seen it all before where you come from, are you? You know what I'm talking about.'

I wasn't about to tell her anything about what I'd seen up in Norfolk, cos I'd never been there so I didn't have a fucking clue. I knew what she was talking about, though: all the shouty headcases roaming about the place with piss in their pants, like Gizza Kwid. But I thought that was the booze. Not the drugs. I was about to, like, point this out and say, 'Yeah, but, right, it's not the drugs that make the people all messed, it's the booze. I read about it in the reports and it's on the shows quite a lot too. Even the PM says so.'

But that's not exactly the wise way to go, considering I'm a spy and not here to defend drugs or the modern way of life and big up the Project or anything. That's the thing with the spying thing – you have to keep quiet about what you know to be true and sit inside the head of someone who thinks that the opposite is true.

'Right,' I goes. And then I say a smart thing: 'I suppose I've got a lot to learn.'

The girl smiles.

'Maybe you've come to the right place, then,' she says, her telling-off voice gone and the nice soft one back.

Fucking bingo!

And then we sit quiet a while, supping our teas. And as we're supping and sitting something gets sort of heavy in the atmosphere. I can hear her breathing. When I look at her, I can see her chest moving up and down. She keeps swallowing. She shifts herself on the seater, and her leg touches my leg. And now it's my turn to swallow and start breathing in a different way as I get a feeling in my own chest, under the ribs, like when I was up the drainpipe, but not quite the same. Like nerves and excitement at the same time, making my mouth sticky – like when you've gobbed a whole pack of Peanut Pogues and there's no drink to wash them all down.

'Your clothes aren't going to be dry until the morning,' she goes, and she sounds different from before. Her voice is deeper and there's something a bit threatening about the way she says it. 'You can stay here,' she says.

So here's a situation I hadn't planned for. I'm naked under my robe, my clothes are in the wash, it's late and I've been Mr Vomit. Although I'm feeling better, I'm not giving it a hundred and ten per cent, and I'm pretty fucking tired. I don't even know where I am right now. I was passed out, yeah? What are the chances of me going out there into Crap Town and finding myself a cab to take me home at this hour? And anyway, I'm sort of remembering the sight of the girl's knicks and I can feel her leg pressed against mine accidentally-on-purpose, and really I'd just like to slip into her bed and maybe have a little kip right there and perhaps a cuddle or something like that. I'm not thinking of the full-on Starfucks reverse-double-bang action or anything. Nothing like that. No, I'm just after some rest and some niceness. It's been, like, a really fucking hard day, you know?

The silence since she said I could stay has been going on a while, with me thinking it all through ('Should I stay? Would it be unspy-like? Unprofessional? Nah, it'll be OK,' etc.). So I goes:

'Yeah, I'd like to stay and that, actually.'

'Well,' she says, 'I might have a blanket somewhere, but if you don't mind sharing, you can sleep in the bed. With me. I don't normally . . . this isn't something I make a habit of –'

'Yeah, with you,' I goes, decisive now, cutting her off. 'I want to sleep with you,' and she giggles.

And so we go to bed. And her bed smells nice, of her. It's fresh and the pillow is deep. Me naked, her naked (she gets in and slips off her clothes under the covers).

The light goes off and I lie there on my back for a while, feeling drowsy and nice, and then I feel her warm little hand on my chest, then her head goes where my armpit is. I sort of automatically put my arm around her and my hand goes on her side. It's soft. She just sighs deep and adjusts herself against me. I can feel her whole body pressed against mine – one boobie resting just above my belly, the tuft between her legs brushing against my leg. My head goes empty and sleep starts to come.

I know what you're thinking.

You're thinking, 'Come on, Jensen! Did you give it her, or what?' And I understand, really I do. What with all the looking-up-her-skirt stuff, it sort of seems like it was on the cards. But really, I was too tired for all of that, and anyway, it was a different scene, yeah? If you want all the gang-bang action, then it's Starfucks all the way, yeah? And don't get me wrong, you know I'm as up for it as the next bloke. But right there, in the girl's bed, after the day I'd had, it was like my life had changed, and all that had gone before was different. And when it came down to it, all I wanted was to sleep and to feel warm and safe. And somehow the girl seemed to make me feel that way.

It was, like before, no one had ever really cared about me. Not even me. But now, the girl was caring. So if you don't mind, there'll be no action-packed double feature here. You'll have to make do with what's come before on the subject.

Anyway, it's kind of nice, isn't it? Better, perhaps, than *Porn Disco*. Although *Porn Disco* is way fucking cool.

Fifteen

AMAZING WHAT a good night's kip can do for you. When all you can see is darkness, and you're just left to make horrible guesses as to what might be out there in the shadows, just wait until the sun comes up, have another look and see how it feels.

I am rested and feeling good. Sharper than before. My head still aches a bit from where I got the whack off Gizza Kwid, and from when I smacked it against the table in the restaurant. But it's not too bad. I don't feel like crying no more.

There is sun peeping around the curtains in the girl's bedroom. The girl isn't in the bed, but I can hear her voice somewhere in the flat. She's talking to someone. She's on the blower.

I can't hear everything what's going on. I sit up and try to listen, but the swishing of the bedclothes blots out her voice. I can just about hear her muffled talking, then the conversation stops.

She walks into the room and she's dressed just in a pair of white knicks and a vest. she's scrubbed and happy-looking. She perches on the edge of the bed.

'How are you feeling, Norfolk?' she goes.

'Oh, tickety-boo!' I says. 'Great night's kip and everything, ta!' I look at the window where the sun is trying to yank the curtains apart so it can get in and do its business and think that I don't even know her name yet. I can't just ask her. It's too late for that. It's a bit awkward.

'It's a nice day,' says the girl, following where my eyes are looking. She gets up to open the curtains and, sure enough, the room is filled with the warm sun.

While her back is turned, she says, sort of casual. 'A friend just called, he might drop in later. I think you might like to meet him.'

I'm just gazing at her bottom, the way the white knicks stretch over it and how perfect it looks. She's lovely.

'Who's this friend, then? Your boyf, is it?' I say, in a bit of a grumpy voice, and I'm all squinty cos of the sunlight.

She laughs. It comes out easy.

'Reg? My boyfriend? No!' and she giggles.

The giggle she does is like tinkle bells. I really like it and want to say things that make it come out more. But I'm not quite sure what it is I say that makes the giggles come. Like, when I said about this friend being her boyf, I was like proper feeling pissed off and sounded it, but she giggles at it. Which makes me smile and not pissed off any more. Fucking weird, what's happening here. I'm starting to do my own head in.

But hold on – I missed something there.

'*Reg*?' I say.

'Yes, Reg. That's right,' she says. 'He's an old friend. Literally!' She laughs here again, but I just sit in the bed still squinty. 'I was just talking to him. He's a nice guy. A bit mixed up, but you two might have things in common.'

'This Reg, is he coming here?'

'Yes.'

'This Reg, is he, erm, who is he?'

'Oh, he's someone I sort of work with. I help him out from time to time. He's a good man. He's devoted his life to fighting poverty and helping the underdog. He's quite a character. You'll really like him.'

'Is he coming here soon?' I say, frowning.

'Soonish. This afternoon. Don't worry. You've got time to have a shower and get dressed. We'll have some breakfast. It's a nice morning. We should go for a walk. I've got a few errands to run. You can come with me, if you like. Relax, Norfolk. Everything's going to be OK now.'

Shit! Me and Reg. Face to face. The last time I was near Reg was when I was on his roof and legging it with him and his lot going 'Oi!'

after me. The time before that we'd met when I was doing a focus group about food and history recognition. Only a few weeks ago, that was. If that. When I was talking to Reg back then, he was just another bloke. Didn't mean much to me, except that he was being a bit of a tosser about it all. Now look where it's got me. Here we are, eh? Me and the girl and my new identity. It's enough to make your fucking head pop.

I'll be testing the work of the Makeover Team to the full when Reg comes over to the girl's and we have a nice chit-chat. I'm a bit shit-pants that he'll see through my disguise and remember who I am and where I'm from. But this time I decide to think ahead and so I'm ready for anything. The plan is, if he goes, 'Oi! You're not from Norfolk! You're bloody that bloke from the FG and you work for the government, which is the bloody enemy! Oi!' or something along those lines, I'll be double clever and confess all.

'Yes, yes, that's me!' I'll say. And then comes the clever bit: 'But I've, like, switched.' Then I'll say, 'The government is totally oppressive and bad and stuff, so I've come over to your side to help you out against the Project, cos they've, like, treated me really badly and I want to get my own back, and so we should be pals.'

That should do the trick.

But before all that, there's a morning with the girl. That'll be nice and easy. She's banging around in the kitchen, so I get up and have a shower. It's like standing under a leak in a drainpipe compared to my Dermo Shower back at Rotherhithe, but the water is hot and steamy. It gives me a few minutes to think myself back into where I'm at. After a night of sleep, it's easy to be confused about who you are. Come to think of it, it's difficult when you're tired out too. When you're being more than one person, and you've munched loads of dislocators, it's just plain difficult to remember which one you are, or even who you were to fucking start with.

'I am Norfolk from Norfolk,' I say to myself, in my head, while the steamy water rumbles against the bottom of the plastic bath I'm standing in.

'I am a renegade anti-gov bloke who has escaped some sugar-beet-processing factory up in Norfolk and is in the big city trying to disappear among the povos and the trampies.'

As a cover story, it covers everything, I think. I'm just another runaway in London town, seeking refuge by hiding out in the dark streets, where no one decent ever goes. I'm just lucky that I bumped into the girl and that she's looking after me.

I get dressed, my clothes are all clean and folded – no trace of spew – and I wander out to find the girl. She's in the kitchen, where there's a little table. She's still dressed in just the white knicks – tight across her botty – and the little vest.

'Take a seat, Norfolk,' she says. She stretches up to get a couple of plates out of a cupboard above her head, straining on one leg to reach, and the vest lifts up, showing her naked waist and the arch of her back. I feel a special stirring downstairs and a big smile comes over my face. She gets the plates and turns around to put them on the table. She sees my big smile and smiles too.

'What?' she says. 'What is it?'

'Oh, nothing,' I say, not able to stop the smile.

'Come on, Norfolk,' she says, 'don't keep secrets. What is it?'

When she says not to keep secrets, I suddenly remember that I am keeping a big fuck-off secret, and that if she knew the secret, she'd hate me. That wipes the smile off my face.

'It's just that,' I say, looking down, feeling embarrassed now.

'What? What is it, Norfolk?' she says, cocking her head to try to get eye contact with me.

'I was just thinking that you're, like, really pretty and that,' I mumble, flicking a knife on the table with my finger so it spins around.

'That's very sweet,' she says quietly. 'Thank you. I think you're very nice too.'

And then she coughs. I look up and she's gone red in the face. She starts getting the food together and although she's got her back to me, I can tell she's still red in the face and that she's smiling.

The food she makes is all totally lush, actually. Normally, I'd have a couple of Brekko Bars and a tin of coffee from the vendo in the hallway on my way out, and I'd be out the flat in a few minutes, but she's laid out a whole spread of things on her little table. It's all totally old-fashioned food that you just don't bother with these days. Toast, scrambled eggs, bacon, orange juice and old fruits like apples and bananas. You'd think that apples and bananas are really boring wouldn't you? But not these; they taste fucking great. And there's marmalade and butter and jam and ham. All stuff I never had before.

After my night of vommo and head-bang, I'm well starved and I tuck right in, stuffing my face. I try not to down it like I did the bolly naze last night. That was a bit too quick, and that was probably what made me puke it up again. By the time we're finished, we're both totally stuffed and sitting back in our chairs rubbing our bellies.

'That was fucking lovely!' I say.

'Well, thanks, Norfolk. It wasn't anything special, but I'm glad you liked it. It's nice to have someone to look after. It's nice to be appreciated.'

'Yeah, well, I do totally appreciate you,' I says. And I totally do. She's really, really fucking nice. And it's really, really fucking great just sitting here with her, having a lovely bite for brekky, and her with her smooth legs and her white knicks and her shoulders and the way the nibblets of her peaks show through her vest ever so slightly, and the sun coming through the window. It's totally better than staring at stupid Fyodor's face after he's kipped over at my place again cos we've been caning it something rotten at Starfucks, and him calling me a wanker and picking his nose and farting and stinking boris breath.

I feel something against my leg under the table, something warm and alive. I look under the table. It's a puss cat.

'There's a puss cat!' I say.

'Oh, don't mind him. Charlie, come here!' she says, and Charlie runs towards her with his tail in the air and rubs around her legs instead of mine. 'I rescued him,' she says. 'He'd been abandoned. I started feeding him and that was it. He just moved in, and we've been together ever since.' She bends down and starts to scratch Charlie behind his ears. He closes his eyes and purrs.

'Haven't we, Charlie?' she says to him. She picks him up and Charlie gazes at me and I look at him.

'He was in a terrible state. He was all scabby and his coat was ratty.

He had fleas and he was violent too,' says the girl. 'But now he's all soft and lovely and a very happy cat.'

'Lucky Charlie,' I say.

Sixteen

GOING FOR a walk around this strange enemy territory doesn't sound like a great idea to me. But she wants to go out. The sun is shining and she wants to get out of the flat.

'Come on, Norfolk,' she says. 'Don't worry. Everything'll be OK.' It's like she picks up on my nervousness and understands it. But she's not going to let it get on top of me. Of course, she thinks I'm nervous about going out cos I'm a daft yokel freshly scarpered from the countryside, and that I'm worried some gov snatch squad is going to round me up, haul me back up to Norfolk and dump me in an agri-factory to work in chains until I die. But that's not the worry, is it? No, I'm worried that I'll get caught out for being what I am: a gov spy/protector. What if that fucking Gizza Kwid trampy twat is out there, howling and scrounging? What if he sees me and starts up again? He might fancy some seconds, start shouting the odds about me giving him a right duffing and about me being from the Security Department. I'd have a proper situation on my hands then. An angry mob might gather and tear my legs and arms off. But the girl makes it seem like everything'll be all right.

'Come on, Norfolk. Nothing bad's going to happen while I'm with you,' she says. And I believe her.

So out we go.

She puts her arm through mine as we start walking along the street. That makes me feel better. The sun too. That helps.

Walking around here is OK, actually. In the daytime and in the sun, the area doesn't look so bad. OK, it's not all fucking well smart with aced-out shops for buying all the latest hot shit. There aren't any Starfuckses. There aren't any big screens showing clips and ads. There's no under-floor lighting, so nothing's lit up and the buildings don't change colour. I don't see any places to get clothes from. No accessory outlets. No sell machines and no auto-fun booths for when you're shit out of ideas as to how to have a laugh. No one gives you free shit when you're out for a walk around here. No girls in the little skirts with the big smiles and bubblies bursting out their tops handing out caps of a new boz that they're testing. (One time, in Peckham, I was out and I got pulled in by this girl with a blue-satin bodysuit and the biggest bumpers you ever saw for a random market research on a new sort of boz they were going to call harry. I did one blast and was off my nut for two days and saw bats and birds flapping around my head for a fucking week.) And there are no chip-responsive locator boards. No towers made of glass. No environment-enhanced mood zones.

Here, under your feet, the slabs are cracked and wonky. If you don't look properly, you could easily trip on them and fall on your face. There are railings made of metal that's gone rusty. There are houses with their front doors right on the street. You walk past the windows looking into their little stinky holes and you can see the people in there, sitting around eating food off of plates on their knees or sipping on old cups full of tea. They're wearing slippers or just a dressing gown. Sometimes there are steps going up to the houses' front doors, and they are made of stone, but they don't have nice sharp edges, they are worn and rounded and look like they might be soft. Nothing is new. It's all old and worn. It's a total ghetto shithole, full of povos and twats who can't get it together. But it's not so bad, walking around with the nice girl on this nice day with her holding on to me. It gets me to wondering why. If this place is a shithole cos the people around here are shit, what about this nice girl. She's not shit, is she?

On the pavement outside one section of houses there are chalky drawings. Badly drawn animals, badly drawn people and wonky boxes with numbers inside them.

'What are they?' I say.

'Hops kotch,' says the girl. 'Didn't you play hops kotch when you were a kid?' she says.

'No,' I says. 'Never heard of it. We never had no hops kotch at the

Duncan-Smith Infant – erm . . .' I remember not to tell too much about the real Jensen, not to mention the infant unit or anything like that. So I just say, 'We never had no hops kotch.'

'Well, that's sad,' says the girl. And as she says that a little girl, about five years old, appears. She's sort of shy, but she is interested in us looking at the hops-kotch squares on the ground and is hanging around to see what we're going to do. I've never met any little kids before. I don't know what to say. But the girl does. She kneels down so the little girl can see her face.

'Hello, do you remember me? My name's Claire,' she says to the little girl. And when she says this, she looks up at me and smiles. Claire! That's her name. And she's just told me. She told the little girl so she could tell me. That's so . . . she's just so fucking great! Claire!

'My name is Rose,' goes the girl, smiling and twirling a bit of her long hair between her fingers, and she's sort of swivelling her body around, balancing on one foot, gently rocking herself.

'I know your name is Rose!' chuckles Claire. 'Are these your hops-kotch squares?' Claire asks the little girl.

'Yeah,' says the little girl, still shy. And then suddenly she loses the shyness and blurts, 'I done them myself with chalks that Danny gave me. And the numbers too. I done them too. I did. I live here and there's a cat comes around here. He's black and white with a fluffy tail and he's called Pongo. He's mad. Have you got a cat?' All through this she's pointing all over the place: at a battered old front door painted green, at the corner of the street further away, down at the gutter. It's quite comical and makes me laugh. Claire laughs too. And then, seeing me and Claire laugh, the little girl Rose starts giggling.

'My cat's called Charlie,' says Claire. 'And I think you've done very well, Rose,' she says. 'You're a very clever little girl. Can you show us how to play hops kotch? My friend here has never played hops kotch and he'd like to see how it's done.'

The little girl looks up at me, scrunching her eyes up cos the sun is behind me. I shrug.

'It's true, I ain't never heard of no fucking hops kotch,' I says. Claire frowns at me suddenly.

'Norfolk!' she says sharply.

'Yeah,' I says, looking at Claire and then at the little girl, not sure why Claire is getting in telling-off mode. I think maybe I'm not being enthusiastic enough for Claire.

'Yeah,' I says to the little girl, trying to really fucking get into the hops-kotch thing, 'it's a real shitter that I never played no hops kotch when I was kid, cos it looks fucking top bollock.'

The little girl turns around to the hops-kotch squares, throws a pebble into one of the squares and starts skipping into them, balancing on one foot when there's just one square and stomping both feet down when there are two squares.

'Norfolk!' says Claire again. 'That's terrible!'

'What?' says I, all wounded innocent.

'I don't know how you talk to children where you come from, but we don't use language like that around children here.'

Rose ignores me getting bollocked.

'Oh right,' I say, not too sure what I've said that's wrong. 'Soz and everything, then.'

'I don't know, Norfolk. You are a one, aren't you?' says Claire, but she's smiling now.

'Yeah, I'm a one,' I say.

We watch Rose doing her rhythmic skipping. She starts chanting:

'One for sorrow, two for joy, three for a girl and four for a boy, five for silver, six for gold, seven for a secret never to be told.'

We both chuckle some more at this cute little Rose skipping over her hops-kotch squares. She's engrossed in her playing now, forgotten us. Claire stands up and puts her arm back into mine and we move on. As we leave, I can hear her chanting still:

'Cinderella, dressed in yellow, went upstairs to kiss a fellow, made a mistake, kissed a snake, how many doctors did it take?'

After our little walkie, we're back at Claire's flat, and I'm feeling pretty confident about everything when the doorbell goes ding-dong and she gets up to answer it. I'd almost forgot. This will be Reg. I'd been getting into the calm vibe of just hanging around with Claire, eating and drinking tea and watching little girls do hops kotch so much, that I'd not thought much about Reg and all that business.

I can't lie, it is a bit of a tense scenario. I try to act cool as Reg comes in the room and I try to hide the fact that I totally recognise him when I see him. There he is. The same Reg who nearly caught me outside his window. It's like meeting someone famous that you've only seen on shows. I'm well nervous.

I sort of think I ought to be a little bit shifty with him at first. Like, if I really was Norfolk the Innocent, I'd be suspicious of who this Reg is and why it is that the girl wants me to meet him and all. So I can afford to be a bit agitated at first. Which is just as well, cos I am agitated.

I hear Claire and Reg talking low by the doorway. Then they both come in, the girl first, extra-big smiling, putting on the nothing-to-worry-about face that I like so much, then Reg, looking sort of dad-like. He's got this pressed together smile, like not too big a smile, but a serious smile. It seems to be saying, 'Hello, Norfolk, I know you've had a tough time and about all your oppression, cos Claire's told me all about it, but I can help you. It won't be easy, but you can trust me. It's OK, I'm here now. Straight up.'

He walks straight up to me and says, 'Hello, Norfolk, my name is Reg,' and puts his hand out for a shake. Which is more than what Miskin did when I first met him, yeah? I try to look a bit sus and that, but I shake his hand.

'Hello, then,' I say, which seems to give out the right amount of wounded-animal, sort of guarded vibe. Reg nods slightly and sits down opposite where I've been sitting.

'How are you feeling, old boy?'

'Oh, well, you know,' I say, hoping that he'd fill in the gaps for me. He nods again, all sympathy.

'Claire tells me you're a bit troubled.'

'Maybe I am, Reg,' I say. 'But what's it to you?' That last bit I threw in to keep up the suspicious vibe, which I think Reg has been expecting and is almost pleased to see. He makes a friendly sigh.

'You're not alone, Norfolk,' says Reg.

'Yeah?' I says, a little bit aggressive, but with half a note of interest in there too, cos this is like, here-we-go time, this is Reg about to tell me stuff that I can pass on to Miskin. Here comes a bit of evidence. But then Reg changes the subject.

'Are you going to be in town for a while?'

'Well, yeah, s'pose.'

'A few of us are getting together later this evening to chat. Why don't you pop along? It's informal, nothing to worry about. We'll be having some drinks. It's more a social gathering, really. A few like-minded individuals gathering together for some mutual support and to knock around a few thoughts. What d'you say?'

I look up at Claire who's stood by the doorway looking eager. She smiles and nods at me.

'I'm going, Norfolk. We can go together. It'll be fun,' she says. I nod. I want to be where she's at.

I sit there while Reg stands up and says things like, 'Good, that's settled then, I'll see you later,' and bustles about as he leaves Claire's flat, but I'm not listening to him. I'm looking at the floor, trying to think. I'm wondering what it is I'm here for. I want to be where Claire is, but I'm a spy. Maybe I should be concentrating more on the spying and perhaps try to think less about Claire and everything. But it gets cloudy when you're in the thick of it, you know? Big thick clouds in the head, like black cotton wool.

If you're going to convince other people that you're simple old trampy Norfolk, who's nothing to be afraid of, then you've got to almost convince yourself too.

Seventeen

REG'S FLAT. On the way over, when Claire wasn't looking, I necked the last boz cap I had. Boz caps are pretty hardcore. They sort you proper out for a full session, like even ten hours sometimes. They variegate the release so your synapses don't implode and fry your brain's CPU, and you just keep rolling along on the vibe with ups and downs, but without having to find your stash and honk some every time you need an upsy. It's, like, efficient, but it's all out of your control. I think it was designed for, like, truck drivers or something. If you do lines on top of a cap, you can really get into orbit. I'd been saving it for a monster night out with Fyodor at Starfucks, when all this Jensen-the-spy thing was over, but I was feeling a bit too flutter to cope with the Martin Martinist meeting at Reg's without extra chemical assistance, so I thought I'd drop the tab. You're not supposed to mix them with other drugs, but the way I see it, I've got so many in my system already, what harm's some more going to do?

I hardly notice the walk to Reg's. I feel like I'm in a big bubble, and the big bubble's making everything soft; the hard stone under my feet, the air coming into me when I breath. Everything's soft. Soft.

Suddenly, it seems, we arrive. I walk into the room, Claire stands to one side and sort of wafts me in with her hand, all a big smile (every time she looks at me, it's like I can hear her saying, 'Don't worry, this is OK, everything's OK,' in my head). Reg's place looks different from the inside. I try not to look at the window I was nearly caught at the other night. But I can't help it. I sort of stare at it for a few moments, vacant in the head, my mouth half-open, catching flies. I'm dosed up good and fucking proper.

Also in the room is Reg's faithful flock. I think back to when I was hanging around outside, staring in on Reg's cosy front room filled with car-bombers and ciggie smoke. There are three smoking boys, holding their fags between dainty thumb and finger, each with their little pinkies sticking out. I can feel them tighten up when they see me, shooting looks at me and Claire, sniffing for clues, suspicious and jealous. They think I'm some bit of old rough, giving it to Claire hard from behind, then spuffing into her face before moving on to another, like a porn-show actor. But I'm not. There's been no spuffing. Just kipping and relaxing. Poncy fucking smoking-boy fuckwads with their ciggies.

The room goes quiet. My arrival has created a pause. I'm like a big walking question mark what needs an answer from Reg. I need to remember to be Norfolk the old tramp from Norfolk, oppressed and a new convert to the Martin Martinist cause, and not give away that I'm Jensen Interceptor, ace gov spy. The two lady Martin Martinists (the two older, not-buff ladies) peer over their glasses at Reg. Reg looks my way, smiles in a comradely sort of way, and says for us – me and Claire – to sit down, if we can find space, ha ha ha, and would we like a tea or something?

No tea for us. Let's get on with it.

'Hello everyone,' says Reg, taking his place on his chair, sort of looming over all of us. Now it seems clear to me that he's the boss, we're here to learn from Reg. He's going to tell us what's what. The smoking three have stubbed their ciggies out. The two old lezzers have stopped peering over their glasses in that o-lipped suspicious way and are focused on Reg. Me and Claire are on the floor, close and together. The other blokes, two of them, they don't seem to care one way or the other about me. They must be the hard men, the group's muscle. The three ponces and the lezzers are the intellectuals. I don't know what all this makes Claire. She's the one who shouldn't be here. She's in the wrong place and thinks it's the right place. Me, I'm in the right place, but that's cos I have a job to do, I'm a professional, yeah? But this isn't the right place for a decent member of society. That much is obvious. And Reg? Reg is the leader. The ringleader. The car-bomber. Blood drinker.

'You're all probably wondering who our new friend is,' says Reg. He means me.

'They call him Norfolk,' Reg continues. 'Norfolk comes to us thanks to Claire. He's escaped from the food factories in East Anglia and has rolled up down here in London.'

And he looks at me, with his eyes all warm again.

'Isn't that right, Norfolk?' he says.

'Food factories. Yeah. Sugar beet and all that kind of shit.' I say, thinking back to the show I'd seen, the one where I'd got the idea to tell Claire I was from Norfolk, the one with two toothless old ooh-arrs in it, and I remember that they worked in the food factories. Just about everyone in Norfolk works in the food factories. That's all there is to do up there. The show was one of those ones where they reveal how different people in the country live, and how they all contribute, and how Norfolk produces loads of sugar beet, and how the sugar beet is made into sugar in big factories and how it then goes all over the world and ends up in cups of tea and cakes and sweeties and stuff everywhere from London to Shanghai to Moscow to Bangalore and Kabul. And Tokyo and Mogadishu.

'In our struggle,' Reg says, now addressing the whole group and waking me up from my memories of the Norfolk food-factory show (which was totally fucking boring, by the way, and lasted less than three minutes on my screen before I switched over, and two minutes fifty seconds of that was only cos I was trying to find the remote, shouting, 'Fuck! Fuck! Where is the fucking remote!' – weird the things you remember sometimes), 'we tend to focus on what's happening here in London. We have our own problems here in the cities, Norfolk. Only a few nights ago, we chased a boy away from this very building. One of our own. They burgle so they can buy drugs. We've seen the cultural apartheid that's been imposed on us here, how the gulf between the have and have-nots has broadened, and how that process has been successfully blamed on the very people who suffer the most because of it. And the same process has divided all of our once-great cities.'

Reg goes on and on about how the agri-factories in the countryside are like big machines which chew people up and spit them out like they was pips in fruit and how the workers have to live in the factories in big dormitories with earth floors and no heating, and how they start work when it gets light and how they work into the darkness under the glare of huge arc-lighting which follows them across the fields, and how they die early cos of how hard it all is, especially in Norfolk, cos that's where they farm all the sugar beet, and the sugar-beet season is the winter, when it's harsh out there on the flat land with the snow and the bitter cold from the east, like Russia and Scandanavia and that.

Then I feel a hand on my shoulder. I turn around. It's one of the soppy smokers.

He says, 'Poor you.'

And I go, 'Yeah, poor fucking me,' and turn around to look at Reg again, pulling my eyes as wide as I can get them, so as not to nod off into my full-strength boz-cap trip while Reg drones on.

'Norfolk knows the evil this government is capable of. He has suffered. And now he is with us, and he wants to join us and to learn. Isn't that right, Norfolk?'

'Reg . . .' says Claire, sounding like she did when I was telling the girl Rose about me not having never played no fucking hops kotch and she didn't want me talking that way to no kiddies.

'Yes, Reg, teach me all about it,' I goes, wondering where all this is heading. Reg smiles at me again. My mouth is dry from the boz cap and my eyes are heavy, heavy, heavy.

'Today,' Reg goes on, talking to the whole group and not just me, 'we'll be doing things a little differently. We will attempt to commune shortly, but first, I think I should recap. For Norfolk's benefit, but for all of us too. We all need to remind ourselves why we are doing what we do, and who it is that supports us through all our endeavours: our leader, our saviour.'

'Oh, Reg . . .' says Claire. I can't tell if she's excited or disappointed.

'Who is it, Reg?' I goes, sort of forgetting myself. Reg looks at me and smiles again, and he says the name I know has been coming.

'His name is Martin Martin. His kingdom is not of this world. His kingdom is from another place. He was born to testify to the truth, and everyone on the side of truth will listen to him. Are you on the side of truth, Norfolk?'

I look around the room, and they're all gazing at Reg like their brains have short-circuited and left them stuck with a dopey grin on their faces.

It's like when the shows freeze up sometimes, and for a second or two everyone's face looks mad.

'Norfolk, you don't have to,' says Claire. But I want to look like I'm on the right side, yeah?

'Yes, Reg, I am on the side of truth,' I goes, enthusiastic. Reg grins. There's a light flickering on and off in the back of his eyes when he talks about Martin Martin. It makes him look like a cartoon robot, and his voice goes all deep and boomy.

'Reg,' says Claire, 'perhaps this isn't the appropriate time to discuss this.'

'Martin Martin was just a man, Norfolk, like you or me,' says Reg, ignoring Claire and talking straight to me again, but the way his face is, and the way the others are, it comes over like what he's saying is for everyone, and not just everyone in the room, but everyone in London, in the old UK, perhaps even all the people in the whole world.

'But he was mankind's prophet of truth, and because he told the truth, he was persecuted and murdered by a government bent on denying the truth. A government whose power resides in lies and disinformation.'

'Reg, who is Martin Martin?' I say. It just comes out my mouth without me thinking.

Reg doesn't answer me. He stands up, and puts a hand on my head. It's like he's completing an electric circuit. He looks up at the ceiling.

'Martin Martin,' says Reg, loud and boomy again, like he's talking to the whole world, or at least some different place where you have to speak all loud and boomy and not like a normal person.

'Martin Martin,' he repeats, 'we beseech you, we are your servants, we shall do as you bid, please come among us.'

Suddenly, I feel cold, like someone's opened a window. It gives me the creepies, so I have a look around. The window is shut, but I'm well feeling chilly. There's no one there. Of course there isn't. I'm the one doing the spying here. So I close my eyes, and I start to think about Martin Martin. I don't know much about him. All I know is written on that bit of paper.

With my eyes closed and Reg trying to call Martin Martin over and over ('Please come among us, show us the way, teach us how to harness the human gift, blah, blah, blah . . .'), I start to sort of go off on one. I feel sleepy. The light in the room is low, so it's sort of half-dark. Reg's chanting and Claire's warm hand holding tight to mine are soothing. I close my eyes, and my head starts to spin around cos of the boris. But once I close them, I can't open them, and it's like I can see Reg's words swirling around like wisps of glowing smoke, darting around the room fast, and then gathering together to make a big fucking globe of flying glowing words around my head. The sound of Reg's voice becomes just a pulsing drone, and the the word-globe gets denser and throbs in time with the regular rhythm of Reg's voice, just like the fucking lump on my head from all the bashings, all fucking throbby cos of the blood inside it wanting to spray out. That's how I feel, like my brains want to spurt out of my head like a fucking volcano or a great big fucking spot. I want to squeeze my head and burst the insides all over the place to relieve the pressure that's building up in there. I hold my head and start squeezing and probably moaning a bit, like 'Ohh! Ohh!' and that.

And this next bit might seem well out of fucking order and weirdy-woo and fucked up, right? But I can see Martin Martin. I can see MM right there like he's below me and in front of me at the same time, like I'm floating around above his head. What I'm seeing isn't like on a screen, it's like full-colour 3D. I've spun right out of this world and into MM's world and I can smell it and feel it and see it. My throbbing head is hot and my eyes are half-closed, like when you're just coming around from the biggest bingey night of fuckery you ever had at Star-fucks. Total brain-mash headfuck.

Here next is what it was like. It's fucking well cool. Check it totally the fuck out.

Eighteen

THERE'S AN open window and I am totally floating outside it, like I'm flying, or I'm wafting like a big fucking underwater weed flapping about in the big, big ocean. I can see through the window. I can see Martin Martin. There he is, as large as you fucking like. Real life. I can see his mate Devlin Williams. I know it's them. It's fucking them coming alive off the pages that were slid under my door that morning, yeah? Somehow I know this is what I'm seeing, it's in my fucking brain, like sure-as-shit knowledge. I can see a studio with an audience of old biddies. I can see all these big machines – cameras – moving up and down and along the floor, like they're dancing. I can see lights up in the ceiling hanging down from metal poles and making everything extra bright. And I can hear voices. And I can actually see Martin Martin talking. He's in front of an audience, talking to them, and he is being filmed. And there is Devlin Williams standing behind one of the cameras, to one side, with a pair of headphones on his head, and attached to the headphones is a little microphone which sits just in front of Devlin Williams' mouth.

The window just melts away and I tumble slowly into the studio, unnoticed by anyone, like a fly or a bit of fluff or dust. Fucking head-fuck, yeah?

'Can we retake?' says Martin Martin, holding the bridge of his nose between his fingers like he's about to get a big old pain deep in his bonce. Some people in the audience laugh a bit. Devlin Williams looks around and smiles. He looks back at Martin Martin and gives him the thumbs up. He's well fucking happy with how it's all tickling along.

'Sorry, sorry. I was just surprised,' says a voice from somewhere in the audience. I can't see who says this, but I can see a microphone hanging off a long pole which is being held by a man wearing head-phones. It's aimed at a woman who's all smiles and silly chops. A camera points at her too.

'Don't worry about it,' says Martin Martin to the woman. 'Can we retake from where we left off there? Is that OK?' He puts a finger to his ear, and I notice there's a curly lead coming from his ear and going down his back. Some kind of earplug thing through which people can speak to him, I suppose. Some old-school audio shite.

I feel sick, but nice, as I float around, watching all the action.

'OK,' says Martin Martin to the voice he can hear through his earplug. 'Here we go again.' And he looks across to the woman in the audience.

'You OK?' he says to her. She nods her head eagerly.

Then Devlin Williams puts his hand up to his little microphone and says, 'Don't bother with the woman, Martin. She's boring. Try for someone else.' And then, in a different voice, louder, obviously not just for Martin Martin, he says, 'OK, action!' Martin Martin looks at the floor with his hands on his hips. He stands like that for a few seconds. All this I can totally fucking hear like it's for my benefit, in my ears only.

'There's something here,' he says. Then he goes quiet again.

'Do you know the name Emile?' Martin Martin asks the woman in the audience who's still got the camera and the microphone pointing at her. There's something in his voice, serious, which stops her from being all silly-old-slag chops like she was before.

'I don't,' she says, and shrugs up her shoulders. And now Martin Martin has got himself into a totally different vibe, like he's about to find something important.

'It's definitely Emile. No?' he says to the woman, who shakes her head again.

And then Martin Martin says, 'OK, I understand. I will,' like he's talking to someone in his head. And then: 'Is there a 'J' name here? A Jack, a Jackson? He's looking for a Jackson.' When he says that, Devlin whispers into his microphone again and three of the big machine cameras swing around and search the audience, as if they're following Martin Martin's eyes as he looks for someone who might be Jackson.

'Is there a Jackson here? Anyone have a connection to that name?'

I look at the faces in the audience, some of them are staring at Martin Martin in the same way that the Martin Martinists gazed at Reg, like with their brains switched-off, like a load of monghead fuckwit twats. Some look around the audience, craning their necks, following where the cameras are pointing. Then the cameras seem to settle; there's a little commotion there, which Martin Martin notices. He walks towards where the cameras have settled, and there's a middle-aged woman. She's sat next to an old geezer, older than Reg even. He's got his arms folded on his chest and looks not at all happy at all the attention he's suddenly getting. The woman is excited, though. Her hair is long but it's all pulled off her face in a pony tail. She's dressed like for sports or something. Like you see the athletes before they strip off down to the tight stuff and run around really fast.

'You, madam?' says Martin Martin. 'There's a strong feeling here. Jackson: what does that name mean to you?' The woman starts to laugh.

'It's my surname,' she says. 'Our surname, I mean.' And she nudges the old grumpy geezer next to her.

'Ah, and who is this?' says Martin Martin, a smile on his face that he probably uses for dealing with total stoating stupids, which this woman obviously is.

'My grandad.' she says, with a stupid's proud voice, mixed up with the sort of whiney voice you'd expect to hear from a ten-year-old, like there's all snot blocking up her ugly nose and she can only breath through her fucking mouth.

Martin Martin takes a look at the stupid's grandad, whose expression hasn't changed from before, like he doesn't want to be there and doesn't want Martin Martin talking to him. But Martin Martin talks to him anyway. He won't be put off.

'And they called you Jack Jackson, didn't they? He's telling me they called you Jack. You're Jack.'

The old geezer, this Jack, unfolds his arms and says:

'Who? Who's telling you that?'

'Emile. It's a man called Emile,' says Martin Martin. The old geezer looks very unhappy when Martin Martin says this. Shocked almost.

'I don't know no Emile, mate. I'm sorry,' he says.

'Yes, yes you do. He's rather afraid that you do,' says Martin. Some people in the audience laugh again. The old geezer isn't playing along, and it's been making the audience feel a bit nervous and uppity. But now Martin Martin shows everyone who's boss, and the audience is relieved about that and shows it with quiet giggles – 'Arf, arf, aha, ha' and all that kind of shit – but I can tell they won't be fucking laughing in a minute.

Martin Martin goes on: 'He's saying there were problems there, and you set out to resolve them, didn't you, Jack?'

'You're barking up the wrong tree, mate,' says Jack. Jack's having none of it.

'Problems over a truck? A long time ago. A green truck.'

'Now listen here, pal,' says old Jack, proper stern, 'I don't know nothing about no truck. Mumbo-jumbo, ain't it?' he says, looking around, trying to get some support from others in the audience, but they're giving him none. They want to know what Jack did. They believe in Martin Martin, that he's talking to someone called Emile. They don't believe Jack, cos now it looks and sounds like Jack is hiding something, and Martin Martin isn't going to let it go. They're thinking that Jack is a fucker who's hiding something and that Martin Martin is going to fucking winkle it out. The audience has stopped the giggles and shuffling around and is really interested to see how all this is going to turn out. I scan the faces in the audience, and one or two of them are talking to one another, quiet, behind wrinkly old hands with loads of rings on them. I see one old lady's face change, from looking like she's having a right old good time, to suddenly looking worried. Her eyebrows turn down in the middle, her mouth drops open and she nudges her pal next to her, another oldie, and the pal nods as if to say, 'Yep, look, this is getting serious.'

I look back at Martin Martin, and he's looking very fucking peculiar. Ill. And he says, sounding strained and not natural:

'I'll tell you what fucking happened, pal.'

Everyone in the audience does a big gasp at this. Maybe it's cos his voice suddenly changed. It went from Martin Martin's voice, which sounds all average, even a bit soft, to a sort of rough voice. He's talking with someone else's voice, is Martin Martin. Another man's voice is coming out of his gob, all loud and spraying spit and shit.

The old bloke, the Jack Jackson who's not been at all impressed with anything Martin Martin has said so far, looks pretty surprised too, like he's seen a ghost. He's gone pale and his mouth is lolling open and he stares at Martin Martin like that for a moment.

'What did you say? Did he swear? Did he say what I thought he said?' says Jackson, looking around the people sat near him.

Then Martin Martin again, who by now is looking well dodgepot with his eyes rolled up in his head and white: 'France, November 1944. You and me, Jackson.'

'I don't have to listen to this,' says Jackson. He looks like he's wants to get up and walk out, perhaps even give old Martin Martin a right kick in his goolies, but he can't. Devlin Williams is stood there with his mouth open, holding on to his little microphone, but not saying anything into Martin Martin's ear. And then Martin Martin starts shouting, really, really totally fucking loud:

'An army truck loaded with enough goodies to keep the pair of us on easy street once the war had finished. Our little pension plan, you called it. Full to the brim with loot. Dig a big hole and bury the lot. Shoot the truck up, torch it. Make it look like the Jerries had ambushed us. We'd have to slap each other about a bit to make it look believable. We had that Luger, and one of us was going to take a bullet in the side. Toss for it, you said. And I won the toss. So we buried the loot, and after that we were going to drive the truck into a tree and torch it. Then I was going to use the Luger and give you a little nick with it.'

Then Martin Martin really loses his rag, like what came before was just a fucking warm-up, and he starts shouting at really fucking full volume, off the fucking dial, yeah, like this: 'I was having a fucking ciggie and you caved my fucking head in, you fucking cunt,' he screams. 'I see you. I see what you did. I know you, Jack fucking Jackson. And this is where you get yours, you little prick.'

As Martin Martin says all this, he's jerking about, his neck is wobbling, and his head rolls about, all out of control. There's gob and spit and stuff coming out of his mouth too. Bogeys out of his nose, his eyes are bulging out. He looks like a right fucking mental, not like MM no more, but like some horror monster off of that show about when the mental bins all blew up and all the freaky scary binners escaped and went all over old London and started eating people, their fucking brains and all that. Devlin Williams starts walking towards him as the old biddies in the audience really start freaking out. They're not liking any of what they're seeing, because, like I said, it's like it's turned into some kind of horror show, and these old biddies don't want to see any more. They don't want to see no horror-zombie binner eating brains or whatever's about to fucking happen. They just came along to see a nice show, and suddenly it's all brains and goo and spit and shouting and shit. Jackson is all out of sorts too. His stupid snot-voiced granddaughter goes, 'Grandad? What's . . .' but she doesn't get to finish what she starts saying, cos Jackson cuts her off, real angry now.

'Don't listen. It's all rubbish,' he says. Then he stands up, at last, and the old biddies all go 'Oh my!' and 'Dear oh dear!' and stuff like that.

'I'll sue you, you know,' shouts Jackson, pointing at Martin Martin. Then he spots Devlin Williams, who has made it on to the stage, where Martin Martin is.

'You can't do this. It's not decent,' goes Jackson, He's afraid now, really shitting it, covering up with the big fucking angry, but MM don't give a shit.

Then Jackson goes, 'What? What's he doing now?' and his voice is real panicky and Martin Martin is shouting at the top of his gob, 'Murderer! Murderer! He's a murderer!' and this is too much for some of the old biddies. The shouting and the dribble spraying out everywhere and the word 'murder' sets them off screaming, proper loud. 'Eeee! Eeee!' they go, and it's all getting totally, like, out of hand as loads of them all stand up and try to get out of the way. Some are trying to pick bags up from under their seats, but they get pushed over. All you can hear is 'Eeee! Eeee!' and the bashing of seats and the stamping of feet as a hundred people all try to escape at the same time.

Jackson is standing up and he's trying to get people on his side.

'He's sick, that's what it is!' he shouts, and then Martin Martin does a huge spew, real projectile, and it splashes all over the the front row of escaping biddies and makes them scream loads more, and Jackson –

he's now got the proper fucking fear in his eyes – shouts, 'Oh God, look . . . see. Oh God, that's disgusting.'

By now, Devlin Williams is standing over Martin Martin, who is on the floor with more spew coming out of his gob, like when the drains overflow in a storm, and he tries to stop everything getting totally bang out of order. He's a bit bloody late, though.

'Could everybody please stay calm.' he says. 'Is there a doctor in the house? Please, stay calm. There's no need to panic, ladies and gentlemen.' But no one's listening to him. They're storming out in a hurry, pushing and shoving and stomping.

'Please make your way to the bar upstairs, where complimentary drinks will be served and you will find a running buffet,' says Devlin Williams, his voice getting smaller in the noisy racket of the panic, like a little lifeboat on a huge angry ocean.

'Oh God . . . Martin, what the fuck are you playing at?' says Devlin, kneeling down to look at floppy MM on the floor. He's lying there, sort of growling like a doggie as all the spew comes out, his eyes staring out but not seeing anything.

'No, he's really ill,' says Devlin to no one. 'He's gone white. Is he breathing? Tell me he's breathing. Is that blood? Is he puking blood? Oh, for fuck's sake . . . Call an ambulance.'

Martin Martin, meanwhile, props himself up on an elbow. His eyes are still rolling around in his head, dead, like a pair of greasy white marbles, and the spew is dripping off his lips.

'You fucking murderer! Murderer!' he moans, which sends poor old Devlin Williams over the edge.

'Martin, shut the fuck up!' he says.

But Martin Martin won't shut up. 'Murderer! Murder!' he goes, trying to stand up, but slipping in the pools of vom, his head wobbling around like there aren't any muscles in his neck. 'With a fucking spade! When I wasn't looking!' he goes.

Devlin Williams looks like he's on the verge of boo-hoo tears. The audience is streaming out of the doors, Jackson and his stupid grand-daughter with them. She's crying and he's looking like he wants to hurt someone, grabbing old ladies who are in his way and pushing them to one side where they stumble and fall on the floor.

Martin Martin collapses again and just lies there gurgling. Now there's blood coming from his mouth and his nose.

'How's he doing that?' says Devlin Williams. He sounds sad and frightened and angry and desperate all at the same time. His voice is trembly. 'Someone stop him bleeding. Where's that blood coming from? Oh my God. Jesus fucking wept. Why won't he shut up?'

I look out across the audience of panicky oldsters. I can see Claire. Fucking Claire! She is sitting there with her legs drawn up on the seat, and I can see her knicks. She's staring at Martin Martin, her eyes wide, wide, wide, ignoring all the mayhem around her, not reacting when she gets shoved and knocked by the people trying to escape. As the place empties out, I see others who are not moving; there are the smoking boys, sat together, and the lezzers. There is Reg too, standing up at the back of the place, his arms outstretched and his eyes closed.

And then I become aware of some more violence happening behind the scenes. It's Fyodor, he's running away, bashing into things as he runs and nearly falling over, but he keeps on running, like he don't feel the pain. Fucking Fyodor and Claire! And chasing him are Brock and Miskin. Brock and fucking Miskin! No one else seems to notice them. Devlin is still hunched over MM, trying to get him to wake up and stop sicking up blood.

I look back to see if I can see Claire, but she's not there any more. Neither is Reg. The smoking boys and the lezzers have disappeared too. I look back to see how Fyodor is doing, and he's bouncing a football off his head, real skilful. Brock and Miskin are watching him. Then Fyodor nods the ball on to Miskin's right foot, and Miskin catches it there, balancing the ball on his foot. He flips the ball up to his knee and then on to his chest, then back down to his foot, which kicks it up in the air. Miskin gets under the ball and it lands on his head. Miskin balances the ball on his head for a second or two, and then it falls to the floor and bounces away. Then the three of them laugh and clap each other.

I mean, what the fuck is all that about, eh?

And then, right, I feel myself lift up into the air, and I float slowly out of the studio, over the heads of the oldsters who are pushing and shoving as they make their way out up the stairs. I can smell piss and old clothes as I fly over the tops of their heads, and I can see their wrinkled faces all squished and screwed up with panic and confusion. But I just float over them without any effort at all. Up the stairs, I float through the door where there's just enough room for me above the heads of the shouting smelly oldsters. I feel like there's a big light in my brain and that when it flashes the light comes out my fucking eyes, and I can fly and I feel all sort of fucking calm, like a big fucking flying lighthouse or something.

The doorway opens on to a large bar, where startled-looking bar staff dressed in white shirts and black waistcoats stand around, looking at the babbling, panicking crowd, which bursts out through the doors like a dumpster letting its load off at the shitheap. The crowd fills the place with shouting and the rumbling sound of feet trying to run, all the energy of what's just happened in the studio in the basement.

Me, I float out of the building, and the sound of the crowd gets quieter as I float even higher. Soon I can see the whole building below me, and all I can hear is the calming white noise of the breeze. Far below me, around the back of the building, I see Devlin Williams come staggering out of a doorway, he's holding Martin Martin's legs. Someone else is holding him under his armpits. They look like hectic little ants down there. Together, they stuff Martin Martin into the back of a van thing with aerials on its roof. Devlin jumps in the driving seat and the van screeches out of the car park.

I follow the van from high up, as high as a fucking airplane. Down there, Devlin must be driving well fast, honking his horn and shouting as he tries to get through the traffic. But from where I am, all is silent, apart from the odd tweeting bird and the sound of wind. I feel that, if I close my eyes, I will fall asleep for, like, fucking ever, so I try to keep them open. I try to check out the details. I try to remember that I'm a spy and that I need to be taking notes or something, then I can tell Miskin and Brock all about it. But as I look down at the cars below, all scooting about like stupid little toys, and at the buildings, which all look so old and filthy, like the people never get up on the roofs to clean the shite off, I wonder whether I can really tell them about this. There's something in my mind which is letting me know that what I'm seeing isn't for Miskin and Brock and the Security Department. It's like I'm being allowed a sneaky-peaky of something important. Info for me only, a show for an audience of one.

I watch Devlin Williams' van dart through the busy streets of London, and eventually it pulls up outside a big fuck-off building, a hospital. He parks on the pavement, jumps out and people come out of the hospital to help him. I dive down and, as I get closer, I see that the bonnet of the van is almost inside the hospital. The doors have been left open. By the time I get down to it, the van is empty, the engine pinging and ticking as it cools down after its mad dash through London. The back of the van is like a little studio, with screens and wires and bits in there. Inside the hospital, nurses have already got Martin Martin on to a bed with wheels on and are starting to push him through corridors beyond the reception area.

The next thing I see is Martin Martin in a hospital bed, and Devlin Williams is sitting next to him, eating grapes. I float into the room, and I sit down opposite Devlin Williams. Martin Martin, clean now, but not looking very well, jerks his head in my direction.

'Burrrrp! Jensen Interceptor!' says Martin Martin. He looks like he's dead, white face, eyes sunk.

'Martin Martin,' I says.

'Who. The fuck. Are you?' says Devlin Williams, looking at me, a squashed grape between his thumb and finger.

Martin Martin's head, wobbly still, turns to Devlin Williams. He belches again and syrupy drool dangles from his bottom lip. Devlin Williams looks at me. I look at him. Martin Martin looks at Devlin Williams and burps again.

'Arrrrrp!' he goes, and then breathes through his nose very heavily. 'It's – barrrrp! – Jensen Interceptor,' he says.

Devlin turns to face Martin Martin.

'Well, that fucking clears that up, then,' he says, really sarcastic.

'Yes,' says Martin Martin. And then his head flops forward on his chest. He starts to snore. Devlin Williams stares at him, then at me, then back at Martin Martin. Then he notices the squashed grape he's holding and throws it in a bin next to the bed, shaking his fingers like it had been a lit match burning his fingers. It looks like Devlin Williams isn't having a great day. And come to think of it, I'm not so fucking sure whether things are going that well for me either. I feel so tired. I try to speak to Devlin Williams, but my mouth feels slow, full of stinky fucking mud. When I breathe in, the air seems heavy, like water and it makes my fucking chest hurt, like it's getting stomped on by a load of bastards in big boots, the cunts.

'How is he?' I try to say, but it comes out blurred, all distorted, like a long, slow groan.

Devlin Williams stares back at me. He is still. Like a statue. A tiny stream of bubbles comes out the corner of his mouth, like in a fish tank. I feel like I'm underwater, but I can breathe, and there are little fishes all different colours darting about, and Devlin Williams is like a craggy old statue that's been there for centuries, covered in barnacles, like a big lump of coral. In my ears there's a comforting pressure and I'm all floaty again. I take off, lifting from the seat. Below me Devlin Williams is covered in tiny shells. Fish flash around and nibble at him. I do a couple of underwater somersaults, in slo-mo, and it's all totally fucking special FX, more than real. I feel like an athlete with big muscles, powerful but relaxed. Fucking Jensen Interceptor: underwater fucking submarine-lighthouse thing with a fucking great light bulb for a brain, breathing like a fucking fish or shark or whale or fucking squid.

Then I see that a window is open, and bits of paper are floating out of it and joining a strong flow, like an underwater river, and this flow is tugging at me. I tumble out of the window, leaving Devlin Williams and Martin Martin behind, and there are pots and pans and bits of stuff and crap all tumbling along with me as I join the flow of the underwater river. Below me, the streets are empty and the doors of the buildings flap open and closed, like the gaping mouths of the fish. The water seems well fucking deep. I can't even see the fucking surface, and it's cleaned all the streets. All the old rubbish – beer bottles and newspapers and all that old cobblers that you'd normally see all over the streets around here – is gone, lifted up and floating around. They look almost beautiful, like they're dancing with me, spinning around like they're in outer space.

I wonder where all the water has come from. Perhaps the Thames has puffed up and taken over, joining north and south, making a new London with new rules and some sort of crackpot new geography.

You'd need a new kind of map to get around this new London. It would have to be a fucking 3D map with height and streams as well as streets; the Thames would have to be mapped down to its sludgy stinking bottom, cos there's no difference any more between being on the land and being on the water.

I speed along the underwater current, and I try to gain some height, to see where the surface is, but I still can't get out of the fucking stream I'm in. It's flowing really fast, like a moving pavement, and I'm locked in, going faster and faster, and I feel double cool, shooting along like an underwater-bullet submarine lighthouse squid, right over the Old Street gyratory, past the old City with all the crumbling tower blocks where they used to make money by moving money around and selling it to people who'd move it around and sell it again. And it all looks so fucking clean and beautiful, untouched by the headcases and drunks who dirty this place up with their piss and shit and their scaly human skin, scabs all shedding off them. It's like all this water has flushed all them cunts all away.

Then, suddenly, I'm at the river and I take a lurch to the left. Although below me the river is now just a little stream inside a huge great wad of water, it's still flowing hard and fast enough to spurt me towards Tower Bridge. Ahead there's the Rotherhithe Sky Tower, sticking up all proud, and I feel a happy warmth come up inside me, cos all of a sudden I'm so tired and I want my bed and I don't to be wet and underwater any more. I don't want to be no fucking special lighthouse squid no more. I go straight over the top of Rotherhithe and look at the streets below me, and I can see the shape of Rotherhithe, like a pert boobie. I imagine being able to suck milk from it, all warm mum-milk, and I laugh bubbles.

The next thing I feel is a huge slap, all over my body, and I'm pinned against the window of a tall, tall tower block. My tower block! The water is pressing me against the floor-to-ceiling window of my own front room. I can see all the rubbish I'd kicked behind the furniture from when I got my orders from the Security Department. It feels great to see it. Fucking great! It reminds me that I've been out for just one night of spying since my orders came through. It seems weird that it was only yesterday. Or was it only yesterday that I was here? It makes my eyelids heavy trying to think about it, so I give up.

The force of the water slows and I'm able to lift off the window a bit. And there I am, floating loose outside my front window, on the twenty-ninth floor, eighty metres above the ground. But that measurement don't count, does it? I am where I am, and below me is only depth. I'm not up high, just at a certain depth, but I don't know what it is cos I don't know where the fucking surface is.

I get my fingers around the window's edge and slide it open. With a huge gush of water I get catapulted into my living room and fall to the floor with a sloppy bang, not underwater any more, but with the new fucking mad Thames pouring into my place in a big glassy lump which is shattering all over my nice floor, all my fucking sharp stuff getting wet. But I slide the window shut, and it stops.

I get up and take a look at myself in a mirror. I'm all sunburn-faced and my eyes are like tight sacs of black ink, but I feel OK. Tired, but OK. I decide to clean up in the morning, and I fall on my seater for a dark deep sleep.

Nineteen

'FUCKING HELL, Jensen! Jensen?'

This is Brock, being all totally fucking surprised when he sees me.
I'm in a suit and I'm in Brock's neato office up on the forty-fifth floor.
I've got my security tagger on, but it doesn't feel so special any more.
I hardly even look at Brock's hot-piece-of-ass secretary as I walk past
her and into Brock's place, even though she's wearing a really tight top
with the buttons straining to keep it closed over her huge boobies –
between the gaps you can see a bit of bra and squeezed boob.

It's the face what's got Brock all shockered. My new Makeover Team
face. The face that survived last night's underwater tumble from Reg's
flat to my flat without any damage.

Yeah, about that, actually . . .

When I woke up this morning, I felt a jaggy stab in my innards as
I remembered everything that had happened and everything I was
supposed to be doing. Being back home in my familiar surroundings
with all my smart stuff and everything, the place where I'd woken up
every morning for months and years, it kind of brought me back into
reality.

At first, when I woke up, I thought everything was OK. In my
sleeping, I had forgotten everything that happened. But then I remembered all that water that had poured into the flat when I opened the
window, and I sat up and looked around, but there was no water. I
patted the floor with my hands. It was as dry as sand.

I looked out the window. There was London, sunny, the river down
below, where it should be, twinkling. Not underwater. Everything
normal.

Except it fucking isn't.

Everything is very much not fucking normal, is it?

Everything has gone fucking wonkified.

My head still hurts and there's sickness in my belly. I am in a bad mongover. I decide to have a shower. I strip off, and in my bathroom I spray myself with KleenIt: The Self-Lathering Miracle Body Wash (with polished-oak fragrance, which is rarer than fucking rose or lemon cos it's a totally limited edition; I bought another one and kept it in its box, mint condition). But when I walk into my ace Dermo Shower, the refreshing jets of water don't come. There's just the sound of a little motor, trying to rev up with, like, a feeble little mosquito sound. Then there's a louder noise, a noise that sounds like something breaking deep inside the Dermo Shower's innards. A little piss of steaming rusty-brown water spurts out the nozzles and dribbles down my chest, burning as it goes. Then the fucking KleenIt starts self-lathering and I'm suddenly covered in foam but with no water to wash it off. I step outside the shower and the noise stops. I am naked and I badly want to have a shower to clear my head and help me think and clean me up so I can go and report to Brock. But my fucking Dermo Shower has fucking packed up. I step back inside the enclosure and the clattering noise of bust cogs and shit starts up again. So I get out the shower, try to wipe off the lather with a towel, put a robe on and stomp around in a huge fucking radge.

I mean, fucking hell, yeah? My fucking Dermo Shower packs in and it's not even six months old. Nothing packs in after six months. A year maybe, but not six poxy months. You expect most stuff to go shithole after a year, cos by then it's rubbish and boring anyway and you want the new one. But something serious like a shower, that should give you the full year. I mean, even my JonToldMeEverything LightBox lasted twelve months.

And that's when I cranked some uppers and some boris and a few of the dislocators, put the suit on and headed off to the office to see Brock. I packed a load of purples and some fucking dresdens too. I had a feeling I was going to need them.

I smell. I feel awful. All the way to the office, the voices on the tube are going, 'Service on the River line is excellent,' and 'Please mind the gap,' and 'Please avoid the Northern line western extension this morning,' and 'Please be vigilant; is your neighbour a bomber?', and as the advert songs about Quad and the government tunes are playing, I keep thinking about how radged up I am about my Dermo Shower packing in. It's like the icing on the cake. Shit icing on a shit cake. I think about how Claire hasn't got a Dermo Shower, and how happy I was in her old bath, floating around.

I catch my reflection in the window opposite, the tunnel rushing by in the dark with all its wires and soot and shit blurred by the speed, and I see my mad new face there again, and I see that I am rocking backwards and forwards in my seat. I look around the carriage. It's pretty full, but the seaters either side of me are empty. No one wants to sit next to Jensen. Not when he smells and is rocking backwards and forwards with the face and hair of a bad boy, mumbling like a mental.

I feel like there are little lights going off in my head, glowing and flashing. Weird new thoughts are popping up in there. Like, if the gov is so great, how come half of London is a total shithole with broken old buildings and no modern stuff like what it's like in south London? And if everything's so fucking great where everything is fucking modern and cool and shit, how come my Dermo Shower's bust? And if it's so fucking great around here, and so fucking rubbish where Reg and Claire and little Rose live, how come I felt all right and happy when I was there with Claire, and how come I feel so shit and adge and hyped and wankered now I'm back home, where I suppose I'm supposed to be. If you see what I mean. And if the MMists are like the enemy and one car-bombing blood drinkers and all that, how come Claire's so nice?

The only way I can get answers to my questions is by getting into the Archive Facility, where the gov keep all the info about everything they know about everything and everyone and that. And I realise that I want to know about Claire as much as I want to know about Martin Martin. I want to know if the gov know about her, cos if they don't, maybe I can save her from the MM stuff before it's too late.

By the time I get to the office, I'm off my fucking head with it all. I get a burning feeling in my eyes and a fucking monster headache that makes me squint.

It's still going over and over in my noggin as Brock stares at me. I'm in his office, hanging on to the doorknob, leaning back against the door I've just closed behind me. I'm sweating and aching and my Gizza Kwid headlump is throbbing.

'Fucking hell, Jensen!' he goes. 'That's fucking amazing. Your face, I mean. Did it, like, hurt?' And he's looking at me with funniness in his eyes. He's between laughter and awe, and it's making me feel like a bit of a twat.

'No. It didn't fucking hurt, Brock, all right?' I say, a bit testy, mouth dry, his voice coming through all echoes and distorto.

'All right, Jensen, cool your jets. Sit down,' says Brock, realising that he's made me pissed off. 'Tea?'

'No,' I goes, stroppy.

Brock, now sat back over on his side of the desk, me on the other, starts looking at his info screen and says, 'Fire away, Jensen. Anything to report?'

I look at him and I can see that he's not really that interested. He's not bothered that I didn't report yesterday either. He's not expecting anything.

I watch Brock (still sniffing and swallowing from a honkful of management-grade Formula 3 boz, I reckon) flicking pages on his info screen, and I get to thinking. I don't want to tell him much at all about what's gone on, yeah? Like, arseholes to it and him.

Brock looks up at me, cos I've been silent for more than ten seconds.

'Come on,' Brock goes, 'anything to tell me?'

'My fucking Dermo Shower's broken,' I say, shrugging.

'What?' says Brock.

'My fucking Dermo Shower's broken. It makes this weird noise and no fucking water comes out. It's shithole. I've only had it about six months.'

'What model is it?' asks Brock.

'DS 166-89,' I say.

'Why d'you get the 89? Should have got the 90B, it's loads better. The plastic motor thing in the 89 usually breaks after six months of operation.'

'What?' I say. 'But it's supposed to last at least a year, yeah?'

'Yep,' says Brock. 'You'd have thought so, wouldn't you? But they don't. The plastic rotor snaps after six months. It's an early warning that the whole motor needs replacing. They'll do the whole lot when they fix it: the motor, the influx and reflux piping, the heat interchange, the turbos. It'll cost a fucking load too. The 90B lasts two years before anything packs in. It's well fucking cool.'

'Yeah, well, it's shithole,' I say.

'That's as may be, but the shower engineers need work, don't they, Jensen?' he says, like he's telling an idiot something really fucking obvious. 'If showers don't break, Jensen, what would the shower engineers do? Think about it.'

I can't hardly think about it at all for the pounding in my brain off of my double-bad mongover.

'Anyway, never mind about fucking Dermo Showers, Jensen. I'll get a couple of people from the department to go over and sort it out in a few days. Security Department privilege and all that. Have you got anything to tell me?'

'Nah, not much,' I goes, trying to pull myself together. 'I reckon I might have a few things to go on. There's been no activity. I need a few more days.'

'Right-oh,' says Brock, now looking back at his screen, bored.

And suddenly it's like I'm seeing Brock for what he really is: a worker who knows nothing. He's just doing as he's told until his LD's paid off and he can go and live in a cottage in the country, cut roses and wait to die. And until then he's sticking to the boris to get him through the dullness of his job.

'I reckon I need more info, Brock,' I says, playing it cool and cagey.

'Yeah,' goes Brock, nodding like a toy, but not really like he's heard what I've said.

'I think I need to do some research,' I says.

'Yeah,' says Brock again, glazed-over with the boris and whatever it is he's looking at on his info screen.

'So I need authorisation for the Archive Facility, yeah?' I goes. The sort of info I'm after you don't get in the normal libraries. They're all just full of buttons and buzzers and pretty pics of celebs and all that common stuff that people like. I need real info – history info, innit? And that kind of info is kept all locked up in the Archive Facility.

Brock stops looking at his screen and looks at me again.

'Ah, now this *is* interesting,' he says. 'You'll have to go to Miskin for Archive Facility access, and he'll only tell you to fuck off. Maybe there are other ways to get what you need? Hmm?' He says all this brightly, drumming his fingers together and looking at me with a smile on his face.

'Other ways?' I say. 'Like what?'

'Like how you got your other information?' says Brock.

'What other information?' I ask.

'Oh for fuck's sake, Jensen, you really are too dense. The envelope? About Martin Martin? Your secret source?'

'Oh, that,' I say, flatly, thinking to myself, 'Actually, where the fuck *did* that come from?'

'All right,' I says, getting up to leave, 'I'll have a think about that. See what I can do.'

'You do that, Jensen. Let's get our leaky toilets and broken showers fixed, eh?' he says, and he's not smiling.

'Yeah, let's,' I say.

Twenty

'Oi!'

This is me talking to Fyodor. I've come out of my meet with Brock and I'm straight away formulating my plan of action, moving ahead, getting on with it, no fucking mucking about. Calling Fyodor. Getting it together.

'Wot?'

This is Fyodor talking back to me. His voice is all like 'Tchoh' and sighs and grumpy-face pet lip. What a ming-mong.

Fyodor works in the Archive Facility, yeah? So it's him I need to speak to about some sneaky-peaky action for the kind of info I'm after. So I called him. And this is me and him talking, me all dizzy and pukey off of my mongover and my mad night floating over London, head throbbing cos of the lump put there by fucking Gizza Kwid and no amount of boris or dresdens are putting a stop to it. He's all grumpy trousers cos I'm being all short with him.

'What you doing for lunch?' I ask Fyodor. It's lunchtime and I have a plan that involves Fyodor, so I need to see him and talk him into it.

'Going to Swirlies with the guys,' says Fyodor.

'From your office?' I says, knowing that 'the guys from the office' is actually just the fat twat Fyodor has to sit opposite, who smells bad cos he never washes his pits, the stinker.

'Yeah,' says Fyodor. He knows what I'm thinking. He's a bit defensive, but he knows.

'Fuck that shit. Swirlies is for twats. Come to Starfucks, the one near the Media Building. There's a monster lunchtime special on today. Fucking great. You'll love it. I'll meet you there. Don't be a twat. I'll see you there in ten.'

'Jensen . . .' he says, about to, like, complain or something about me telling him what to do and when to do it, and how it's like totally bad for me to call his workmate a fat smelly mong. But I cut him off. He'll be at Starfucks in ten. He always does the right thing, does Fyodor. He's fucking great.

Sat in Starfucks, it's all clink-clink and chit-chat and smells of coffee and sounds of machines sloshing and whooshing, making more coffee for all the workers who are streaming in and out to buy it with cakes and bix and stuff. The lunchtime special is a three sausage double-double, but I can't be bothered. Anyway, I haven't got time. I sit on my own, on a stool by the window, waiting for Fyodor to arrive, making a plan to get what I need off of him and how I'm going to talk him into it, cos he won't want to do it.

I'm not able to sit still. I'm just thinking and thinking. All the ideas and things that have happened are swirling around in my brain. They get all mixed up like paint. I'm grinding my teeth and the grinding is making the pain in my noggin sharper.

Then the door of Starfucks goes again – bing-bong! And for some reason, I look up this time. It's gone bing-bong a hundred times while I've been sat there, holding my coffee and staring at its frothy surface, and I hadn't even budged. But this time I look up. It's Fyodor.

'All right, wanker?' I go, and I'm, like, saying 'Wanker!' in the special voice we do to each other. It's fucking funny. I'm laughing and feeling happy. He's barged in on my teethy-grind mood and it goes in a puff of smoke.

He looks at me, confused, and goes, 'Who the fuck are you? I don't want no fucking trouble but I'll give you a fucking load if you want some, all right?'

It's the face. My new face. He's not recognising me.

'Fyodor,' I go, 'It's me! Jensen!'

Fyodor comes closer and looks more closely at me.

'Fuck me!' he says, with a big grin. And then he says 'Wanker!' back at me and we laugh and piss about. He sits down next to me and orders a Milky Chilly with extra choccie chips off a Starfucks girlie dressed as a sort of cat.

Our laughter dies away like when a jet fighter comes over in the sky:

at first it roars and fills your head, but then it's gone, and, up in the sky, the blue and the clouds go quiet again, but the quiet is different because of the noise that went before. So this quiet is different. I haven't seen Fyodor since he left the flat that morning after the monster night at Starfucks; the morning when I made the two coffees and was waiting for my orders from Miskin. It was only a few days ago. But it seems like years.

'So . . .' says Fyodor with a pause which waits to be filled, 'new face, then?'

'Yeah! It's all part of my work now I'm with the Security Department and that. It's, like, a disguise. I got these to take cos of it,' I say, and I produce the bottle of dislocators that Scary Face gave me.

'Give us a few!' he says. So I do. He gobbles them without even asking what they're for.

'So . . .' says I.

'So . . .' says Fyodor. 'What's been happening, then?'

I shrug. What *has* been happening?

'Fyodor, there's something fucking weird going on, yeah?' This much is true.

And he's like, 'Yeah?', all distracted, looking over his shoulder, trying to see what's happening in the dark of Starfucks' daytime. And then he's like, 'What's the lunchtime special? Three sausage double-double? Boring.'

'Yeah,' I goes. 'Three sausage double-double. How about that, eh?'

'So?' says Fyodor. He's still waiting for me to tell him about the weird stuff that's going on.

My hands are shaking. I can't stop them. Shakes off of the drugs.

Fyodor looks like he can feel something weird about his old mucker Jensen. He's spooked, cos there's a new sort of seriousness in the air.

'You still doing your mongy shelf-stacking at the archive on a Saturday?' I says.

'Yeah,' he says, 'course.'

'Can you get me into the archives?' I says, straight out.

'What!' he goes, coughing into his Milky Chilly. 'No! Not me. No. I can't get you in there. No way. Fucking hell, Jensen . . . I might have sneaked out a copy of that document that Reg did, but I can't get you *in* the fucking place!'

'*You*!' I says, my fucking eyes bulging out of my fucking face. 'That was you? You put that envelope under my door?'

I can hardly fucking believe it.

'Yeah,' says Fyodor, sneering in sort of disbelief that I hadn't worked this out already. 'Course it was me, you twat. Who d'you think it was?'

'Fuck!' I say. 'I didn't really think about it. Well, top bollock, Fyodor, that was fucking well ace. Really handy. Right got me out of a spot, ta and everything, yeah? But what was all that brain stuff about?'

'What brain stuff?' says Fyodor, blank in his face. 'I didn't fucking *read* any of it. I got better things to do than read some old guff out the archive. I just grabbed a load of stuff out of the Martin Martin file, that's all. There's fucking tons of it.'

'Tons of what?'

'Shit about Martin Martin. There's shelves of it. Fucking tons.'

'Fuck,' says I. 'All right, well maybe I don't need to get into the archive, but can you sneak me some more info out, yeah?'

'I don't know, it's well risky. It's not super-easy, you know. They do spot checks and shit,' says Fyodor.

'It's not much. All I need to know is, who the fuck was this bloke called Martin Martin? I've been having some well weird dreams about him, and I want to find out more about him. Just to clear up some confusion. It's no big deal. I've virtually been told by my boss to sort the info for myself. They don't give a fuck.'

I tell Fyodor that it's just some standard low-level kind of thing. Most spy stuff, I say, is pretty much just procedural, just info-gathering. Not really that different from running focus groups, I say. I tell him not to get his knickers in a twist about it or nothing.

'I'm sorry, Jensen, but no can do,' says Fyodor, looking at the floor and pushing an imaginary bit of dirt around with his foot. 'You know how it is and everything.' He's been listening to me going on, trying to talk him into a spot of light sneakiness and calm his freak-out at the same time, but he's resisting.

'You can, Fyodor,' says I, and I say 'can' really long: *caaaaaaan*. Persuasive, you see, like the voice I've heard Fyodor use loads of times when it's like five in the fucking morning and I'm all fucked and ready for bed and I'm saying I can't possibly do any more fucking boris and he's like, 'Course you *caaaaaan*!' so I end up doing a load more and there's no fucking sleep to be had for another twenty-four hours.

'But Jensen,' he says, and he's sort of whiney, like a kid. He doesn't want to do it, but he knows he's going to.

'Look, Fyodor,' I says, 'I'll totally make it worth your while.'

'How?' he says, in a tone of voice that's saying that there can't possibly be anything I can do to make it worth his while.

'You know my signed pic of Sheeba Twosort?'

'Yeah,' says Fyodor, his eyes narrowing. 'What about it?'

'It's yours,' I say.

Fyodor well fancies Sheeba Twosort. She was the top actress in the Age of Glam period, when all the shows went soppy for three months and were about boys rescuing girls off of desert islands and out of castles. It was all the rage last year. And Fyodor was as bang into that as he is into the Roman rooms at Starfucks now. He's like that, is Fyodor. He gets a craze on and that's that. He just loves it.

Anyway, Sheeba Twosort was found with her head chopped off under a bridge in Shanghai. You couldn't switch on a news show for days without seeing images of her headless corpse being moved from the side of the river and into a corpse van by the Chinese military. After that, the Age of Glam shows came to an end. And since then, they've come to be thought of like a classic period of show history.

Fyodor was well upset about her murder. He didn't come out for three days. He's a member of the Sheeba Twosort Society who meet up once a month and are trying to get a Sheeba Twosort monument built in Crystal Palace, where she was born. It just so happens that Sheeba Twosort did a public appearance at the Surrey Quays Hollywood Bowl, right near the Rotherhithe Sky Tower, just before she left for Shanghai. And it also just so happens that Fyodor was out of town that night, but I went along and met Sheeba Twosort and got her to sign a pic what I'd bought. Fyodor was as sick as a fucking parrot when he got back, and I well wound him up about it. And then she was found with her head chopped off, and we both sort of didn't talk about it any more.

I was thinking of giving the pic to him anyway for his stupid birthday or something. But now I'll give it to him for getting me info out of the archives.

All I'm doing is looking at Fyodor, and after a bit he cracks, like I knew he would, and he's like, 'All right, then.'

'That's great, Fyodor,' I say. 'You're really helping a pal out. You're a good bloke, you are. There's one more thing, though.'

'What?' says Fyodor, moody.

'Can you see if there's anything in there about a girl. A girl called Claire.'

'What's her surname?' asks Fyodor.

'I don't know. Just Claire. See if there's any Claire mentioned in any of the Martin Martin stuff. Do the gov know her? Is she, like, a fucking car-bomber or terrorist or anything like that? Find that out for me, yeah? Meet you here, this time tomorrow?'

'Yeah, all right,' sighs Fyodor, and he drinks up his Milky Chilly and stands up.

'I've got to go back to work now,' he says.

'Yeah, see you tomorrow, then. Here, same time, yeah?'

'Yeah,' he says. He hesitates. 'Jensen,' he says.

'Yeah?'

'Take a shower, yeah?'

What a *wanker*, eh?

Twenty-one

HOME.

The journey back from my meet with Fyodor was rough, what with the aching head off of Gizza Kwid's thwacko – and the lump's getting hot now too, burning like sunburn and making me sweat. Plus, I had to keep swallowing, cos I felt like there was liquid on fire coming up my foodpipe, and if I didn't keep a swallow happening all the time, gouts of hot spew would have come flying out my gob and sprayed all my fellow passengers on the tube, just like Martin Martin when he splashed all them old biddies with his stomach contents.

But eventually, I get back home and put the key in the lock. When I step inside, I know there's something wrong straight away. There's an odd smell. A damp sort of a smell. And when I walk into the flat, under my feet doesn't feel right. It's squidgier than usual. I look down and lift a foot, then I put it down again, to test what's there.

Water.

There's fucking water there.

Why is there water there? I take a few steps and there's a squish sound with each step. Is it the water from last night? The water from the Thames that I floated home in last night? The water that splashed into my flat when I prised open the window? The water that was missing when I woke up this morning? Has it showed up while I was out? The front-room carpet is wet too. It's fucking saturated, holding its own weight in water, and it all squelches out when I walk on it. The whole fucking flat is wet. A film of water covers every bit of floor space. Where there's carpet, water has seeped into it, and where there's wood, it sits on top.

I walk into the bathroom, and in here it's the worst. I look into the shower and I suss where my flood has come from. Water is emerging out of the plughole. It's coming up, like the gooey contents of my tum-tum rising up my pipe. But here it's risen up to a gaping plughole, and has spilled out enough to have saturated my flat in the four hours or so I've been out. I can't even tell you how fucking pissed off I am about it. Fucking totally.

There's nothing I can do about it. I put a cup over the plughole to block it, to stop any more fucking water seeping out into my flat and fucking my life up. And then I put a big glass full of water on top of the cup, to keep it there. Then I put, like, a fucking plate on top of that. I can't be arsed to try and clean up. I think I've stopped the water actually coming out, so it shouldn't get any worse. I'm not about to sit around trying to get someone to sort my floors out, not with the way I'm feeling.

So I decide to try to forget about it all and catch up on *Monster Trucks*. I was going to wait until me and Fyodor could settle down for a weekend and watch all the *Monster Trucks* action that's been building up, but there's already four hours to get through, and if I leave it any longer, there'll be six hours, and while we're watching that, there'll be another hour. So it's best to get ahead.

I sit down in front of my big fuck-off screen, set up the SoundScape to the heavy-II setting (that being the recommended setting for *Monster Trucks* and all other racing events), get myself a pack of crisps, lay out a decent spread of pharmaceuticals next to me and start watching.

But I can't get into it. No matter how much I tuck into the boris and everything, there's the claw of death still gripping my insides and twisting them all around, and my throbbing bonce too. I keep at the boris, but none of it stops my mind from chewing over and over what's been going on. I wonder whether my spying caper has been blown, cos I still don't know what happened at Reg's when I floated out the fucking window. I'm really fucking worried about what Claire is thinking. Where is she? What is she doing? For a few minutes, I even consider getting out of my swampy stinky flat and heading over to see her. But I know I should wait for Fyodor to get me my info before I do that. My once-spank pad now feels total shithole and broken, and my memory of

Claire's place is of all warm fuzziness and niceness, and I could well do with some of that right now. Her old shower might be rubbish, a feeble tumble of water that would get blown away by a little puff of wind, but at least it works. And it doesn't make her flat into a fucking dripping mess. I'd like Claire to stroke my hair and say, 'There, there,' and all that. Maybe we could go to sleep again. I liked that.

I keep piling the dislocators down my gullet, on top of purples and dresdens and a couple of philips too. The philips are for sleeping. *Monster Trucks* is booming and throbbing away on the screen, all bright flashing colours and shouting off the blokes commentating.

Eventually the noise dies away, and I'm in some kind of stupor. I can't sleep, but I can't stay alert either. Droopy on the seater, eyes and body. I just sit there like a saggy lump of old rubbish, a bin bag full of adge and pills, desperate for sleep, but with none coming.

I think about Miskin and Brock, about how I never done the gov no wrong before. I'd always behaved and stuck by the rules. I'd never even thought of not sticking by the rules. No point. Before, to my mind, it was only the fuckwits in their nasty hovels over where Reg lives who broke the rules. Them and stupids, like politicians who get caught with their hand in the kitty, and really that's just a laugh for the news shows. But now I'm breaking the rules, and I know that Claire isn't a fuckwit, but she lives among the fuckwits and their nasty hovels. And Fyodor, he's breaking the rules now too. I hope he is, anyway. I drift into oblivion with these thoughts all torturing me as I go.

Then there's this fucking brain-shrivelling loud moaning in the flat. The noise of it punctures my head, making me realise that I've kipped out. My head is about as far back as it can get without snapping off. I lift my head and, with a sticky gob and muzzy eyes, I look at the screen. *Monster Trucks* has finished, and now there's all porn up there. Slippy-slappy and yelling. I've no idea how long I've been passed out. I stand up and my eyes scan around trying to find something with the time on it. It takes a few moments for my body to realise I've woken up.

It's time to meet Fyodor again. It's like the last twenty-four hours have passed in twenty minutes. Not enough time to do anything.

I've cricked my neck, falling asleep like that, not going to bed all comfy. I haven't showered. I'm wearing the same suit I've had on for, like, fucking days now. The pain in my head is now a hot buzz, like someone's jammed a fork in my skull and snapped the long bit off.

I get to Starfucks. Fyodor is already there, supping away happily at a Milky Chilly. When he spots me, he stares with his cup stalled halfway to his mouth. He's wearing sunglasses and he's turned the lapels of his coat up around his face. He looks like a spy out of a show where they show spies having secret meetings in coffee shops.

'Fucking nobwaz, Fyodor! What the fuck do you look like?' I whisper angrily as I sit down next to him. I try to glance around to see if anyone's looking at us, but it hurts my neck too much, so I turn back to Fyodor.

'What?' says Fyodor, innocent.

'You totally look like you're guilty of doing bad things, with your sunglasses on and your coat up around your face like that! Are you trying to fuck this up, or what?'

'*Me*! *I* look guilty?' says Fyodor, his voice all rising amazement. 'Have you looked at yourself recently? You look like a fucking trampy twat!' He sniffs the air around me. 'And you smell like one,' he says.

'Yeah, well, my fucking shower's bust, yeah?' I say, giving up on the argument cos there's no fucking point in it.

'Have you got me anything, then?' I ask.

'Have you got my signed pic of Sheeba Twosort?' he asks straight back.

I'd forgotten it. I hadn't given it even one second's thought since I mentioned it. I don't even know where it is.

'Fucking hell, Fyodor, who gives a shit about a pic of Sheeba Twosort? That's not what's important right now, is it? What's well fucking important is some info about you know who. Did you get anything for me?' This comes out a bit loud, and I look around again, in case anyone is looking, and again I'm reminded not to move my head around cos it makes my neck ache, all the wrenched muscles in there. I have to hunch my shoulders up until they're nearly touching my fucking ears cos of the pain of it.

'Actually, *I* give a fuck about a pic of Sheeba Twosort,' says Fyodor. 'And anyway, I thought you said this was just procedural and, like, not very fucking important.'

'Yeah, all right, Fyodor, I'm sorry. I'm just a bit tired. Been up all night. Fucking shower's fucking conked out. I'm a bit testy, yeah?'

'I'd fucking say you were. Well fucking testy. Do you know how fucking risky it is sneaking shit out the Archive Facility?' says Fyodor.

'Well, it can't be that hard can it? I mean, if you just swiped that stuff you shoved under my door, how difficult can it be?' I say.

'Oh well,' goes Fyodor, his head wobbling from side to side with indignation, 'if it's not very fucking hard, maybe you should go in there yourself and nick your own fucking stupid info.'

'All right! I'm sorry, sorry, really. Tense, yeah? Off my tits with it. Sorry. I know it's well risky, what you done. You done good, helped me out. I'm totally fucking grateful and everything, yeah?'

'Yeah, well,' says Fyodor, moody, and we settle down, calm.

'When do I get my Sheeba Twosort pic, then?' says Fyodor after a minute of slurping his drink.

'Will you stop going on about the fucking pic of Sheeba Twosort, Fyodor!' I nearly shout this, cos I really am at the end of my tether, all strung out and fucked up in pain, with no proper relaxing-bed sleep and my own awful stink. Fyodor sinks into his coat, pulling his lapel up higher around his face and goes quiet. He stares out the window.

'Fyodor?' I say. He's ignoring me.

'Fucking *Fyodor*!' I say again, and poke him in the side with my finger, jabby. 'Stop giving me the silent and hand me the stuff you got!'

Still he ignores me.

'Oh for fuck's sake,' I sigh. '*Please*, Fyodor. I'm sorry I snapped at you. I was out of order. Really. I'm sorry. I am.'

Fyodor says, like, 'Humph' and he leans down to the leather bag he's got leaning up against one leg of his chair. He pulls out a plastic wallet and hands it to me.

'I couldn't find anything about no Claire being in with Martin Martinists, but like I said, there's fucking tons of shite about your mate Martin Martin. This is all I could get my hands on,' he says as I take it from him.

At that moment, I've got the wallet in my hands and I'm not looking at Fyodor. I hear a deep voice – a commanding, bossy voice.

'Fyodor Belinsky,' says this voice.

I still don't see anything, cos next I get a whack to the side of my face. It's enough to knock me off my stool and sprawling across the floor.

'After him!' the deep voice orders and, accompanied by the sound of clattering coffee-shop furniture and the surprised shouts of the other customers, I see two men trying to wrestle Fyodor to the ground in the doorway. I've still got the wallet in my hands, so I stuff it down my trousers and cover it with my shirt. Then I run. I shove the two men wrestling with Fyodor as hard as I can. One of them falls over. I scarper. I don't look back.

Twenty-two

I'VE SCARPERED and I've got the wallet of papers. I run for as long as I can before I feel like I am going to puke, and then I slow to a fast walk. There's no one after me. I've escaped. The wallet is stuffed half up my oompah-oompah-stick-it-up-me-jumpah and half down my trousers. It's making me walk strangely. And the bottom of it keeps digging into my cock. I'm trying to walk normal and look calm, so no one thinks I'm a mental and calls the cops.

In my head is still the noise of what happened in Starfucks, and the face of Fyodor being biffed about by them two fucking blokes. They must have been Security Department, busting him for nicking stuff out of the Archive Facility. My heart is still beating hard and fast; bish-bash, bish-bash. Feels like it's going to leap out my mouth. It's all my fault. Poor old Fyodor. He only did what he did as a favour to me, and now he'll be trussed up down the cop shop, getting his kidneys bashed by gov thugs who think he's a baddie. And I'm a baddie now, well on the other side. They'll be after me too. I got away in the confusion, but it won't be long before there are agents tracking me down, like with fucking dogs and that probably.

The boris is churning around me, making me clamp my mouth shut. I'm trying to get the oxygen I need through my nostrils. There's not enough getting in that way, but I can't open my mouth. If I open my mouth, I'll start gulping like a fishy snagged out of the water and my eyes will bulge out.

I just keep walking and walking. I'm in like a dream, a dream of pain and panic. It's cold, but my body is hot and sweating. The faster I walk, the hotter I get, and the harder my heart beats, and the louder my breathing through my nose becomes. No one looks at me on the streets, but they all give me the fear, every one of them. People who before looked normal and OK in nice gear and carrying shit-hot accessories, like Bongo Leather Goods bags and all that, now they look like enemies. They're all stern-faced and not wanting little shits like me breaking the law and stuff, finding out all of society's nasty little secrets from the Archive Facility. They don't even want to know society's got any nasty little secrets. They'd kill me dead if they knew what I had down my trousers; they'd corner me and point me out to the cops, or they'd just start on me, kicking and punching and throwing rocks at my head until I got bashed in bad with too much blood pouring out of me to stay alive.

Eventually, as I keep walking and walking, there are less people, and the bright shiny streets of south London give way to one of the tunnels under the Thames. On the other side there are the dark brick buildings from the olden days. And I find myself getting deeper and deeper into parts of London I've never been, the no-go zones where once bullets and bombs were flying around, blowing people all up to fuck, until the gov came in with bulldozers and crushed the buildings and got rid of all the mad bombers for our security. I was only a kiddiewinkle when all that happened.

I can smell the river. It's like an off sort of smell. Damp, mouldy, slimy, a bit like how my flat's gone since my fucking shithole shower packed the fuck up like the piece of shit it is. As I get nearer to the river, the roads just peter out and the buildings get more rotten and decayed until they become just rubble and wasteland, with horrible little stunted trees sprouting up out of piles of old bricks. It gets more difficult to walk, and I keep losing my footing on the shifting piles of old buildings what have fallen down and just been fucking left there.

Mixed in with the river's rotting-weed stink is a sharper pong of animal piss and the fruity heavy smell of shite too. Maybe it's the smell of human shite, cos there's evidence of human life down here. There are old bits of paper, newspapers with smeary shite stains on them, abandoned old food boxes, stinking old mattresses surrounded by empty booze tinnies. This is the sort of place you find mad old trampies like Gizza Kwid, staggering around where no one'll bother them. Here they can sleep and piss themselves and no one'll drag them off to prison or even kick their heads in or nothing. They live here, where the city has fallen apart, in holes in dead buildings with no roofs or water or heat or fucking nothing.

I see an opening, like a tunnel. It's made of old bricks and is dark. I can't see into it, so I keep walking, stumbling over the rubbish and crap under my feet, until I get to the opening. There's an old seater in there. I feel very tired, the aching from all my escapology suddenly becomes very strong, and my arms feel like heavy bits of lead swinging around, pulling at my shoulders. My head feels too big and is sagging on my neck with its red-raw torn muscles and tubes. My legs, they throb and buzz from all the walking and stumbling, and the plastic wallet up my jumper and down my trousers is hot and sticky from sweat.

I pull out the secret gov papers what Fyodor pinched for me and flop down on the stinky old seater. I'm too tired to care about how filthy it is. The smell of shite is particularly heavy in here, but it's not making me feel pukey or anything. I've got used to it. It's just shite out of a human's bum, a human who needed to get away from people. A human who wanted a bit of privacy for his shite.

I am tired and I ache, but I start to read the papers. They start with this:

CODENAME: 'THE PROJECT'

PUBLIC BEHAVIOUR SYSTEMS: PREDICTION AND CONTAINMENT

WITH REFERENCE TO: IMPACTS OF POST- AND PRE-COGNITIVE DEVELOPMENT IN THE HUMAN BRAIN AND THEIR ROLES IN HUMAN FAITH SYSTEMS

CONTENTS
1) The Sturgis Report
2) Recommendations from the Association of Chief Police Officers
3) Recommendations from the Committee for Public Mental Health
4) Recommendations from the Special Committee for Parapsychology

5) *Report from Dr Brian Greenhalgh on amygdala processes*
6) *Report from the BMA Medical Ethics Committee*
7) *Feasibility study on instigation of 'the Project'*
8) *Lord's report on instigation of 'the Project'*
9) *Time-frame proposal*

The only thing actually in the plastic wallet is the Sturgis Report. None of the other guff. Just Sturgis, whatever or whoever fucking Sturgis was.

The Sturgis Report

Witness statements and transcripts of hearing appearances from:
Britney Jackson
Peter Smack – CEO of LFF TV
Barbara James
Security officer aka Officer A

Witness statement
Britney Jackson

Britney Jackson will say that:

1: *I attended the filming of the television programme* Martin Martin's on the Other Side *with my grandfather, Edward Jackson. My grandfather agreed to come along to keep me company, even though he thought the whole idea to be mumbo-jumbo.*

2: *I had seen Martin Martin on television before, on his previous show,* Spectre vs Rector, *and was an admirer of his.*

3: *I had written off to get free tickets to attend the filming of the new show,* Martin Martin's on the Other Side.

4: *This was the first time I had attended the making of a television show and I was excited to see the inside of a television studio. I* was looking forward to seeing Martin Martin in the flesh, and I was keeping an open mind about his special powers.

5: We arrived at the television studio at 2 p.m. and, after spending about ten minutes in the bar upstairs, we were asked to take our seats in the studio, which was situated in the basement of the Television Building, Cuba Street, London E14. We were told to expect that the filming would take about two hours.

6: Martin Martin appeared normal and gave several psychic readings to people in the audience, which seemed to be quite accurate. After about an hour and a half, there was a short break in the recording and Martin Martin appeared to be gathering himself for what we assumed would be the last reading of the show.

7: Martin Martin asked if the name Jackson meant anything to anyone in the audience. As this is my surname, I put my hand up. I was excited that someone might be coming through from the spirit world for us. My mother died when I was ten years old and I was hoping it might be her. Martin Martin then said that it was my grandfather that the spirit wanted to contact, and that the spirit's name was Emile. My grandfather told Martin Martin that he was mistaken. It was then that Martin Martin began using abusive language and accusing my grandfather of murder. Martin Martin then collapsed and was sick. I heard people scream and my grandfather and I stood up and left the studio with the rest of the audience. We were shocked and upset by what happened and left the building immediately and caught the bus home. My grandfather refused to talk about what had happened and I tried to forget about the incident.

8: Some days later, I saw Martin Martin was due to appear on The Barbara James Show. I called my grandfather to tell him that Martin Martin was appearing on the show, but he wasn't interested. I watched the show and was shocked at Martin Martin's appearance. He looked to me to be drunk or under the influence of drugs. When he made his psychic predictions about the paedophile and the company chairman I was shocked. I assumed that Martin Martin had suffered some sort of a breakdown, or was trying to be controversial in order to make himself more famous. It seemed to me that our encounter with Martin Martin at the television studio had been the start of his breakdown or his attempts to be controversial.

9: The day after his appearance on The Barbara James Show, my grandfather received a telephone call from Martin Martin. I was in the room when the call came through. Later that day my grandfather committed suicide. I don't know what Martin Martin said to my grandfather, but I think Martin Martin was somehow responsible for my grandfather's death and I feel that if we had not gone to the recording of Martin Martin's on the Other Side, none of this would have happened, and my grandfather would still be alive today.

*

Hearing transcripts
Peter Smack (called)
Examined by J.F. Strong QC

STRONG: Mr Smack, would you please tell us your name and your connection to the inquiry.

SMACK: My name is Peter Smack. I am the CEO of LFF TV, the cable-television channel which broadcast Spectre vs Rector. We had commissioned the television show Martin Martin's on the Other Side.

STRONG: Would this mean that Martin Martin was in the employment of your television company?

SMACK: No. The way it works is that we buy programming from independent programme makers. We bought the series Spectre vs Rector from Spanking Films Ltd, so effectively Martin Martin was employed by that company.

STRONG: Who is responsible for commissioning independent programme makers for your television channel?

SMACK: I am.

STRONG: Would you please tell us what form the television programme Spectre vs Rector *took?*

SMACK: Certainly. It was a show aimed at a daytime audience which took a difficult real-life moral dilemma and tried to resolve it.

STRONG: What kind of moral dilemmas would the show attempt to resolve?

SMACK: It was often a marital issue of some sort of another.

STRONG: Yes. I believe there was, for example, a show called 'Should I leave him for my sailor boy?'

SMACK: Yes.

STRONG: And another called 'I love threesomes but he won't join in'.

SMACK: Yes.

STRONG: And am I right in thinking that viewers would send in their own moral dilemmas?

SMACK: Yes. The first part of the show would outline what the moral dilemma was, using interviews with the main protagonists and reconstructions of key events. Then the show would bring the protagonists out in front of a studio audience and our two experts to discuss the issues, hopefully to arrive at a solution.

STRONG: The two experts being?

SMACK: The two experts being the Reverend David Watts and Martin Martin.

STRONG: What was the purpose of the two experts?

SMACK: Well, the Reverend David Watts was there to provide guidance from what you might call a loosely religious perspective, while Martin Martin would use his psychic skills to tell the people involved what advice was coming through from the, ah, spirit world.

STRONG: From the dead relatives of the participants?

SMACK: Sometimes, yes. Sometimes they just seemed to be random dead people showing an interest.

STRONG: And did you believe in Martin Martin's psychic abilities?

SMACK: My beliefs weren't important. The fact is that a lot of people did believe in him and they found what he had to say both entertaining and perceptive. But I did find a lot of what he would say on Spectre vs Rector *quite compelling.*

STRONG: Now then, Spectre vs Rector *was Martin Martin's first television show. Can you explain how* Martin Martin's On The Other Side *came to be made?*

SMACK: Of course. When Spectre vs Rector *came to the end of its series, I had a meeting with Devlin Williams, who wanted to abandon the series and replace it with another which would be a vehicle for Martin Martin.*

STRONG: Devlin Williams thought that Martin Martin had what it would take to be a star?

SMACK: He felt that Spectre vs Rector *had become tired as a format and was more excited about a show which focused more fully on Martin Martin.*

STRONG: Devlin Williams was quite a flamboyant character, was he not?

SMACK: He was well known in the television business and had made several shows which had interested the general public.

STRONG: Homeless, *for example?*

SMACK: Yes.

STRONG: And another called Alone?

SMACK: Yes.

STRONG: The latter being a game show of sorts, where one contestant was placed alone in a small house filled with hidden cameras and subjected to a series of psychological and physical trials over a six-week period for a chance to win £25,000?

SMACK: That's right.

STRONG: And was it the case that the conditions the contestant was subjected to would have contravened the Geneva Convention if had he not willingly participated?

SMACK: That's the whole point. He participated willingly. He was free to leave at any time. That was made very clear to him. He wasn't a prisoner of war. It was just a TV programme.

STRONG: He made it to the end of the six weeks, didn't he?

SMACK: He did. And he won his £25,000.

STRONG: But not before he had stripped naked and started spreading his own faeces on the walls and onto the camera lenses.

SMACK: That was his own decision.

STRONG: Where is the contestant now?

SMACK: I believe he is in prison.

STRONG: For stabbing a man.

SMACK: Yes.

STRONG: In his defence, he claimed diminished responsibility, saying that his experience during the making of Devlin Williams' show had put him under unnatural stress and made him mentally ill.

SMACK: The jury rejected that defence.

STRONG: Quite. And the programme Homeless, subtitled The Dirty Dozen, this was another controversial show, wasn't it?

SMACK: It interested the newspapers, yes.

STRONG: Twelve homeless people were put into a house, again with hidden cameras.

SMACK: They weren't hidden.

STRONG: Each week viewers voted out their least favourite participant until there was one left, who would win the house itself.

SMACK: That's right.

STRONG: There were fights between the contestants every day.

SMACK: There were lively disagreements, yes.

STRONG: And the house was burned to the ground in the fifth week.

SMACK: Yes. No one was hurt, though.

STRONG: And within three weeks, Devlin Williams' company Spanking Films Ltd had released the DVD The Making of Homeless, with forty-five minutes of previously unseen footage.

SMACK: I believe so, yes, but that had nothing to do with LFF TV. Devlin Williams was a freelance producer, and his contracts with us only gave us first broadcast rights for his shows. He was free to sell the format to foreign television stations and to exploit any of his productions in terms of merchandise.

STRONG: When did you first hear about the problems that occurred during the filming of the first episode of Martin Martin's on the Other Side?

SMACK: Within an hour of it happening. Devlin called me from the hospital.

STRONG: What did he say?

SMACK: I can't remember exactly what he said, he was quite agitated, but he said that Martin Martin had collapsed and that he needed to speak to me very urgently.

STRONG: And then what happened?

SMACK: The following morning Devlin Williams came to the office and showed me the tapes from the previous day's recording.

STRONG: And what did you think?

SMACK: Well, I was horrified.

STRONG: It was a disaster?

SMACK: Yes, it looked like it. You don't want the host of your new flagship daytime psychic programme abusing his audience and collapsing.

STRONG: LFF TV had invested heavily in the show?

SMACK: We had a fair amount riding on it, yes.

STRONG: What was Devlin Williams' state of mind when you saw him that day?

SMACK: He was anxious, agitated.

STRONG: Was he excited?

SMACK: He was more nervous.

STRONG: Did he propose a scheme to rescue the situation?

SMACK: I wouldn't put it quite like that.

STRONG: How would you put it?

SMACK: At that stage, all I knew was that the recording of a television show had gone wrong. But Devlin said that something had happened which gave incontrovertible evidence that Martin Martin was able to communicate with the dead, and that he would be able to provide such evidence on demand, on live television. He said that Martin Martin was a saviour. He said that Martin Martin would change the world.

STRONG: Did you believe him?

SMACK: No. I thought he'd gone mad.

STRONG: But you went along with Devlin Williams' scheme?

SMACK: Sort of.

STRONG: And the scheme was . . . ?

SMACK: Devlin said he wanted money to launch Martin Martin into the mainstream. We're just a small cable channel. Audience figures of 400,000 are what we're aiming at. But Devlin thought that Martin

Martin could make it in the real big time. In exchange for fifty per cent of the net profits from the DVD which Devlin was planning, plus a written undertaking that he would record a special for LFF TV, we agreed to pay Devlin's production company £25,000.

STRONG: *Apart from the production costs of the DVD and the television special, what was the money for?*

SMACK: *To hire the right publicist, to groom Martin Martin for stardom and to get him on* The Barbara James Show.

STRONG: *A bribe?*

SMACK: *I wouldn't put it quite like that.*

STRONG: *And then what happened?*

SMACK: *Devlin Williams left my office with a cheque for £10,000.*

STRONG: *Only £10,000?*

SMACK: *The payment of the balance was subject to certain conditions.*

STRONG: *I see. And when did you speak to him again?*

SMACK: *He rang me a few days later to let me know that he had secured a booking for Martin Martin to appear on* The Barbara James Show.

STRONG: *And after that?*

SMACK: *That was the last time I spoke to him.*

STRONG: *Thank you very much, Mr Smack.*

Barbara James (called)
Examined by J.F. Strong QC

STRONG: *For the record, could you tell us your name and what it is that you do?*

JAMES: *My name is Barbara James and I am a television journalist.*

STRONG: *When you say you are a journalist, you mean you had a chat show on the BBC?*

JAMES: *I do. I am a trained journalist. I worked in Fleet Street for fifteen years before I started on television.*

STRONG: *Yes. You had a long and distinguished career with the* Daily Mirror.

JAMES: Thank you.

STRONG: Your show was always broadcast live, was it not?

JAMES: It was.

STRONG: And on the night in question, you had Martin Martin as a guest on your show.

JAMES: That's right.

STRONG: What did you know about Martin Martin before you interviewed him?

JAMES: Not much. I'd watched his showreel and read his bio. That was about it.

STRONG: His 'showreel' and his 'bio'? Would you just clarify what those are for those of us who aren't media insiders?

JAMES: I'm sorry, I mean to say that I had seen the promotional material his agent sent us, which included a disk of Martin Martin's segments from his television show Spectre vs Rector and a brief biography which outlined his particular talents and his career to date.

STRONG: Before seeing this material, were you aware of Martin Martin?

JAMES: Vaguely. I'd seen his name in the TV guides from time to time, but that was about it. I was aware he was a television psychic.

STRONG: So, the first time you met him was when he came on your show?

JAMES: I'd popped my head around the door of his dressing room earlier in the day and said hello, but he was deep in conversation with a man I took to be his agent or manager. So I just introduced myself from around the door.

STRONG: That man was Devlin Williams?

JAMES: Yes. But I didn't know that at the time.

STRONG: How did Martin Martin appear to you when he walked on the set to be interviewed?

JAMES: I thought he was either ill or, more likely, drunk. He was very unsteady on his legs, his eyes were glazed over and he was sweating. I didn't notice it at first, when he walked out on to the set, but when he sat down I could see that he was drooling.

STRONG: And how did the interview go?

JAMES: It was awful. I asked him if it was true that he could communicate with the dead and he actually belched. And when he talked, he sounded like an idiot. I remember asking him how his gift manifested itself, and he said something like, 'It manifests itself by me seeing and hearing people in my head what had died.' I was shocked. I was expecting a television professional, some kind of clever hypnotist oozing charm, but Martin Martin appeared to me to be a drunk stupid person with no social skills whatsoever.

STRONG: So what did you do?

JAMES: There'd been some communication between my office and Martin Martin's people before the show, and we'd agreed a loose structure for the interview. I'd ask him about his psychic abilities – when he'd first realised he had them, how they worked, that kind of thing – and then Martin Martin would give us a live demonstration of his skills. So I cut all the preamble and asked him to give us a demonstration, hoping that we could get it over with as soon as possible and I could get him off the stage and pass the whole thing off as a bit of a light-hearted joke, one of those unpredictable moments that happen on live television every now and then.

STRONG: And so Martin Martin gave his demonstration?

JAMES: He said that there was a man who ran a big corporation who had been lying. The audience all laughed. I think I said something like, 'Oh, they all do that. Tell us something we don't know.' It was all very amusing. He then said that this man had been lying about the figures, that he'd been saying the company had been making huge profits when in fact they were making none.

STRONG: He used an unusual colloquialism, I believe?

JAMES: Yes. He said that although the man was telling everyone that the company was healthy, that actually everything had gone 'tits up'. And then he belched again. I think I said that his prediction was a bit vague, and that's when he said the man's name.

STRONG: Sir Steven Billings?

JAMES: That's right.

STRONG: Which worried you?

JAMES: Oh yes. Either this Martin Martin creature was correct about Sir Steven Billings, or we'd just slandered the chairman of the largest power company in Europe live on the BBC to an audience of around 8 million.

STRONG: Then what happened?

JAMES: Before I had time to stop him, he'd given the name and address of a man he claimed to be a paedophile and a murderer.

STRONG: Arthur Penroody?

JAMES: Yes.

STRONG: And then?

JAMES: And then I heard in my earpiece that they'd cut transmission. Martin Martin stood up and started shouting that he'd been hit in the head with a spade and that it was Jackson who'd done it, that this Jackson was a murderer. I could see that people in the audience were getting upset and a few men were approaching the stage. They looked menacing, as if they wanted to do harm to Martin Martin. Martin Martin was swaying around like a drunkard, waving his fists around. I saw Devlin Williams come running on to the stage and I walked off to my dressing room.

STRONG: And then?

JAMES: I sat in my dressing room and cried. I thought my career was finished.

STRONG: And was it?

JAMES: I still don't know.

STRONG: Thank you, Ms James. You understand that this inquiry isn't here to establish guilt or innocence, merely to establish the chain of events?

JAMES: Yes.

STRONG: However, I can't see any reason why you should be held responsible for any of the appalling incidents which took place after this interview.

JAMES: Thank you. I hope my employers agree with you.

STRONG: So do I, Ms James. Thank you for your evidence.

Officer A (called)
Interviewed by J.F. Strong QC
(Public Interest Immunity Certificate)

STRONG: *Can you please tell us your name and your connection with the matter under investigation?*

OFFICER A: *I'm afraid I cannot give you my name.*

STRONG: *This is because you are in the employ of the United Kingdom's security services?*

OFFICER A: *Yes.*

STRONG: *Can you tell us which department you are attached to?*

OFFICER A: *I'm afraid I can't.*

STRONG: *I understand. However, perhaps you could furnish us with the details of the day you were ordered to pursue a vehicle being driven by Devlin Williams on the M1 motorway.*

OFFICER A: *We received orders at 4 p.m., and we were in the air within five minutes. We located the vehicle fifteen minutes later.*

STRONG: *When you say you were in the air, you mean you were in an army helicopter, is that right?*

OFFICER A: *That is correct.*

STRONG: *Who issued these orders?*

OFFICER A: *May I refer you to the Public Interest Immunity Certificate which has been issued in connection with this inquiry?*

STRONG: *Which means that the Prime Minister is protecting you?*

OFFICER A: *Which means that to answer some of your questions could jeopardise the safety of British agents, as well as the future and ongoing investigations and missions in which they might be deployed.*

STRONG: *Thank you for clarifying the purpose of a Public Interest Immunity Certificate for the inquiry's benefit.*

OFFICER A: *That's quite all right.*

STRONG: *What were your instructions?*

OFFICER A: *To take Devlin Williams and Martin Martin into custody.*

STRONG: *Why were they to be arrested?*

OFFICER A: *Intelligence had been received which suggested they might be involved in terrorist activity.*

STRONG: *Terrorist activity? You were ordered to take into custody a television psychic and his producer on suspicion of terrorism?*

OFFICER A: *We were instructed to carry out an order. We weren't interested in whether they were in television or ran a grocer's.*

STRONG: Is this kind of mission something of which you have experience?

OFFICER A: Yes.

STRONG: Was your mission considered dangerous?

OFFICER A: We were prepared.

STRONG: You were armed?

OFFICER A: Yes.

STRONG: What happened next?

OFFICER A: When we located the vehicle being driven by Devlin Williams, we saw that it was surrounded by many other vehicles. They were travelling at a relatively high speed, perhaps eighty miles per hour. There was another helicopter above the van. We were keeping observation when Williams' van appeared to lose control. It crashed into the barrier separating the north-bound and south-bound carriage-ways and then rolled several times, coming to a halt on its side some way further along the motorway.

STRONG: And what did you do when the van crashed?

OFFICER A: We abandoned our mission.

STRONG: You didn't stop to help?

OFFICER A: The police were already there, on the ground, as were ambulance and fire services. There was no need for us to attend.

STRONG: This crash was convenient, was it not?

OFFICER A: To the contrary, I believe the crash caused considerable traffic-disruption for many hours.

STRONG: What I mean is that the existence and activities of Martin Martin and Devlin Williams had become embarrassing to the government, and this accident abruptly ceased their activities.

OFFICER A: I am not a politician.

STRONG: Are you aware that the autopsy conducted on the driver of the crashed vehicle, Devlin Williams, found that he had been shot in the chest?

OFFICER A: So I understand.

STRONG: Were you also aware that forensic tests have concluded that the bullet came from a high-velocity rifle?

OFFICER A: No.

STRONG: And that the trajectory of the bullet suggests that the

rifle was fired from an angle of 45 degrees above the victim?
OFFICER A: *No.*
STRONG: *Let me ask you outright: were you under orders to assassinate Mr Williams and Mr Martin?*
OFFICER A: *No. There was no order made to assassinate Devlin Williams.*

Twenty-three

I PUT the file down on the stinky old seater. The aching in my bod has moved on a bit. The darkness of the night is coming. The old seater I'm sitting on seems as good a place as any for me to hide out for a while, as vile as it is. I'm tired after all my action. I'm well hungry too. And thirsty. I'm miles from civilisation and I don't want to risk going back to the shiny shops, where I might get spotted.

I get up and emerge from the old wrecked tunnel. I look out across the wasteland. In the approaching gloom, it looks different. The blue of the sky is going black, pressing down on the scene, and the rubble looks like a big fucking mountain range. Now the sun has gone, it's cold, and my breath comes out as clouds. I'm not really prepared for a winter's night out with no food and no comfy bed neither. As I scan the darkening rubble, I spy a little glinty of flickering light. Squinting, I can see that there's smoke coming off the light, wisping up into the twilight sky. It's a small fire. I walk towards it, clumping again over the uneven ground of bricks and crap, my ankles twisting and my body arching backwards and forwards and my arms thrown out like a high-wire artist, trying to stay balanced as I walk, and saying 'Fuck' and 'Bollocks'.

I'm getting nearer to the fire, then, suddenly, out of the dark, a voice shouts.

'I don't want no trouble now, don't you go giving me no trouble!' Then: 'I'll hoy this rock on yer face as soon as look at you! Don't you give me no trouble! I'll do it! I'll smash yer face in, don't think I won't!'

'I'm not after no fucking trouble neither, not me!' I shout back, suddenly rooted to the spot cos this mystery voice with its nasty threat has made me fearful. 'I'm just after some warming by the fire. I can help you keep it going!' I shout again, staring into the dark beyond the fire, trying to make out who it is threatening to bash my chops in with a rock. I can just see a dark figure, darker than the darkness around it. It shifts around like a fucking ghost made of black.

'Come closer, then,' says the voice, quieter now, suspicious sounding, but no longer all fucking hysterical and threatening. I stagger a few paces forward, into the light of the crackling fire. The fire is made of a pile of old bits of wood about knee-high, and the flames are licking up to waist height. They throw a nice orange glow around. I stand there, looking into the fire, grateful for its warmth, and I hold my arms wide, to show that I don't mean no harm.

'I don't mean no harm, mate,' says I. 'I'm just after a warming, and I need to have a fucking think, yeah?'

This geezer on the other side of the fire steps forward into the light. He's a scruffy old trampy, white-whiskered and with teeth missing, his little tongue darting out of his mouth as he peers at me, like he's tasting the air around me, trying to get a flavour of me. On his head is his battered old trampy's hat, and his old raincoat is tied together with string. In his hand he's grasping a bottle of hard booze by the neck. He looks a bit like Gizza Kwid, but he don't look quite as fucking mad.

'Well,' he says, stepping forward a bit more, but sideways, 'a feller needs a warming and time to think. There's no law against that, as far as I can see. Would you want a drop of this?' He's all friendly now, offering me the bottle over the top of the flames.

'Thanks,' says I, and I take the bottle and take a gulp from it. It burns my mouth and throat and makes my nose feel like there are fumes coming out of it, but I swallow hard. As it goes down, it's like I can feel it drip through my ribs, past my heart and down through my innards, drizzling down like liquid fire, until it reaches my stomach, where it releases a deep warmth out from the centre. The old trampy must have seen my face react to this hard booze and he cackles a bit.

'A drop of the good stuff, eh?' he says, taking the bottle back from my outstretched arm. I'm coughing, and he's laughing at me. I start laughing too, and coughing at the same time, my shoulders lurching up and down. I have to sit down, my head is spinning, and I find a log under my bum as I sit.

'Ah, you're all right, feller,' says the old trampy, and comes around my side of the fire and sits next to me. For a while we just sit there staring into the flames, each of us thinking about our own stuff, not bothering the other. Every now and then he hands me the booze, and I take a sip. The flames crackle and puff and whoosh in the light wind, and it gets darker. After a while, the trampy gets up and throws another few bits of wood on the fire, and sparks fly up into the blackness, dancing as they go. After a while, the booze cuts the feelings of hunger out, and I just feel warm and hypnotised by the fire.

'Have you had a good think?' says the trampy.

His voice comes after a long time of silence and makes me jump. I realise that I hadn't been thinking at all. Just staring and being blank in the head. Taking a rest.

'Yeah. Ta,' I say.

'I grew up around here,' says the trampy. 'I used to fish in the river. Eels. Ever had eel?'

'No,' I say. 'There's lot of things I've never had.'

'Ah well, son,' says the trampy, 'you ain't lived till you've eaten eels you've caught yerself out the ol' river.' He stands up and beckons me to follow him. We go back to the side of the fire he was on when I first got here. On top of a pile of bricks, he's got an old frying pan. It's black, fucking totally encrusted with soot. Next to that is a plastic bag. He opens it up and shows me what's in there. There's a wet old sack inside the plastic bag, and inside the wet sack there's a couple of big horrible-looking snake things. They're half-alive, slowly slithering over each other and coiling up.

'I was about to cook them when you turned up and scared the bejesus out of me. Fancy a bit?'

'Are they eels?' I ask.

'Caught 'em earlier today, I did,' he says, nodding. 'I'll fry 'em in oil and chuck some salt and pepper in, a bit of onion, some garlic. A bit of booze, maybe. Delicious.'

I'm well hungry, so I say yes, I'll eat the slimey eels. He puts the frying pan on the fire, and pours some oil into it from a bottle he's got stashed away under some bricks. Then I watch as he cuts up the eels with a knife he produces from his pocket. He starts by sticking a fucking nail right through their fucking heads, just like that.

'That'll kill 'em,' he says. 'Best to keep your eels alive until just before you eat 'em.'

Then he holds the eels up, and slits them from their heads all the way down to their tails, and then he strips the skins off. Then he slices into their raw bodies and pulls out all their innards and bits and shit and hacks them away. Next, he unhooks them and, using an old piece of flat wood as a chopping board, he slices them into lumps. Then he takes out an onion from the same hidey-hole he had the oil in. He slices the onion into lumps, and then he slices up a load of garlic he's found. The whole lot he throws into the frying pan, which spits and sizzles and bubbles like mad. He then takes the bottle of booze, and with his thumb over the bottle's neck, sprinkles booze into the pan. This makes the oil writhe and boil, and explosions of flame burst and disappear over the pan. Then he brings out a salt grinder and a pepper grinder from his secret outdoor-kitchen stash hole, and, with a flourish, he adds salt and pepper to the sizzling pan.

It's like watching a famous cooking-bloke on the big screen, except he's a stinky old toothless mad fucking tramp. It's well fucking impressive. I'm proper impressed.

After this performance, he takes the pan off the fire and hands me a fork. We both tuck into the eel. It tastes good.

After we've eaten, he says, 'Well son, at least now you've eaten eel.'

'Yeah,' I say. 'Ta. I needed to eat something. They were all right, actually.'

My eyes are heavy and he sees me starting to nod off.

'Here, lad,' he goes, 'come in here and have a kip.' And he shows me to a hole in the bricks. I hadn't noticed it before, it was half in the shadows, and just looked like another random gap in the higgledy piles of bricks. He steps into the hole and I follow him. The hole opens up into a large hollow. This trampy feller has made himself a well-comfy little hidey-hole where no one would find him. It's like an igloo you'd see on the shows about the folk who live up where the snow is all time, where they make little houses out of fucking ice or they burrow into the snow. He's burrowed into the broken remains of old London and made his home here.

There are a couple of mattresses, pillows, blankets, there's even a little cupboard with a candle on it, which he lights with a match.

'Get your head down, son,' he says, and I lie down on the mattress he's pointing at.

I like the way he calls me son.

I need sleep like I needed the food, and I am asleep so fast that I can almost feel myself falling into it, like from the top of a tall building, and I cry out after a few minutes, like the sleep has come on too quick, and I'm drowning in it. When I cry out, with a squeaking-grunt sound, I hear the trampy talking, soothing again:

'Don't you worry son, there, there. You sleep. Nothing to worry about,' and although he's toothless and old, and we're in a cave made of collapsed buildings, and I've eaten worms out of the river, it reminds me of how I felt when Claire took care of me and told me not to worry. I feel safe.

I sleep, and in my dreams there are all kinds of visions and plots and chasing and stuff like that. Some of it makes sense, some if it comes from nowhere. But in the dreams are Reg and Claire, and the lezzers and the three smoking boys and the muscle: all the Martin Martinists. And they're all against the gov, running around trying to fuck them up, putting tacks on the road in front of their bicycles, throwing rotten fruit and veggies at gov people. And I'm with them. We're hiding out on top of a building and digging into the supply of rotten old veggies, hurling them. I hit the PM, a squished tomato right on his fucking head, and he looks up, trying to see who it is what done it, and we duck down behind a wall, giggling.

But then it stops being so much fun, cos suddenly there are security guards all tooled up, who are well narked that the PM got hit by a squished tomato, and they want to find out who threw it, and suddenly I'm all dressed up in the smart suit with the tagger and I'm in the Security Building, being hassled really fucking totally badly by Miskin, who's going, 'You are a Martin Martinist. You are a threat to the stability of the Project. You have committed treasonous acts of violence against the state!' and all that kind of thing. And while he's saying these things, making all these well-heavy accusations, he's stripping the skin off of eels that he's got hanging off of hooks on the wall of his office, and there's this horrible ripping noise as he tears the skin from the wriggling eels, and blood comes streaming off them as he tugs at the skin, revealing the flesh. Then he starts eating the raw, skinned eels, blood squirting out from his mouth, and he's grinning and grinning, like a madster, his teeth are all bloody with bits of eel gut caught between them, flopping around inside his mouth and dripping blood everywhere as he grins. Then he presses a button, and through the window comes an assassin all dressed in black and he pulls out his gun and points it at me and it goes 'Blammo! Blammo!' I put my hands up as if I can stop the bullets coming into me. Two bullets go into me, but I don't die. I just feel the pain of them ruining all my insides as they slip though my body making blood spurt up all over Miskin, who's already drooling all the eel blood everywhere. There's fucking blood everywhere, and Miskin's gulping it down, laughing and laughing with handfuls of eel guts.

'Agh!' I shout, and wake up.

Daylight is creeping into our brick igloo. It is morning. All night I have had horrible mixed-up dreams and I sit upright, sweating and panicked.

I decide that I need to go and see Reg. I need to see whether it's Reg I should trust or not, look him in his fucking eyes and check him totally the fuck out. I leave the trampy to his snoozing, and I leave the brick igloo, and I blink in the early-morning light and stumble off towards the river, where I'll be able to get my bearings.

Twenty-four

'NORFOLK!'

I've made it back to Reg's. He's pleased to see me. I feel like a trampy, all covered in brick dust and dirty from my night inside the broken city. It has taken me fucking hours to walk here. All the way I worried about being caught by Security Department thugs, and about the looks I was getting off people. Looks off people who don't have no fucking right to give me looks, know what I mean? Smelly mongs checking me out like I'm the nutbag and they're the fucking all right one. And when I wasn't worrying about all that, I worried about what Reg was going to say when I turned up at his door, cos I didn't know if I'd blown it the other night. I thought all the time that I was just walking into more trouble. It seemed to me, on my long march what made my fucking feet hot and hurt, swelling up inside my shoes, that wherever I went, there was only misery and terrible things in store for poor old Jensen. As I trudged and trudged, my ankles sore with it, I thought to myself that even if Reg was angry with me, at least he couldn't throw me in prison or nothing like that. And I had to see Claire.

'We were a bit worried about you. Is everything OK?' says Reg, guiding me into his flat.

There's just Reg here. And me, of course. It's different from being here with Claire. It's quiet and there's more space cos there aren't any MMists here. Just me and Reg. The two of us. Actually, it's a little bit awkward, cos suddenly all the attention's on me, and it's obvious that I'm here for a reason. Me and Reg together like this, it's like we're going to the next level. In a lift together, like that time when I bumped into Brock in the lift for the first time and it was one of those awkward situations. Press the button. Everything is quiet. Toe-to-toe in a little box with someone you've not talked to before. A little cough – 'ahem' – and then the fresh chit-chat, new to both of us. Suddenly we know who each other is. Anyway, it's like that again, here with Reg. Except we're not in a lift. But we are going to the next level.

Reg is worried cos of my disappearing act the other night. I don't know what really happened there, as you know. The last real thing I can remember is the bit at the meeting, when Reg put his hand on my head. After that it was all potty.

'Yes, Reg,' I says, answering his question from a while back, when he asked me if everything is OK. 'All is fine and dandy. Erm . . .' and I gets a bit stuck as to what to say next, so I decide to go for honest. Well, not the full fucking honest, obviously. Steady on.

'Look, Reg,' I says. 'Something well fucking weird's going on. There's been some mad shit taking place.'

'Has there?' says Reg. 'Yes, I thought so. Something's happening, isn't it, Norfolk? There are forces at work we don't understand. Storm clouds are gathering.'

'Yeah. Sorry about not being around for a day or two, Reg. I am, really. I had some, erm, thing I had to deal with,' I says.

'Well, yes,' says Reg. 'That's what you said when you left the other night. You seemed a little preoccupied. I expect you had things to do.'

Here's me sounding relieved:

'Yeah, that's it, Reg, I had things to, erm, attend to, yeah?'

Then I swallow. More to say:

'Actually Reg, something happened that night . . .'

'Go on,' says Reg.

'Reg, I met Martin Martin.'

Reg smiles slowly and his eyes go wide.

'Did you?' he goes. He doesn't sound like he believes me, but then again he doesn't sound like he doesn't believe me either. He sounds like a doctor asking about your symptoms.

'How was he?' Reg asks.

'He wasn't doing that well, actually,' I says. 'He was on his show, talking to some idiots, and he went sort of mental with all spew coming out his mouth and he fell over. And all the old biddies in the audience all panicked and ran out like fucking cattle. And then, right, I sort of followed him and Devlin Williams to the hospital. They went in a van thing with all screens and aerials in it and on it, really fast, but I could follow them. I was flying up in the air, and then they were in this hospital and I was in the room too.'

So Reg looks proper interested now. So I tell him all the details I can remember, the works. The lot, just like I told you before, with all the descriptions so it makes it feel really real. And I finish up:

'. . . and then Martin Martin says "Hello" to me, and Devlin Williams was there with a grape and he goes, "Who are you?" and he's all totally freaked, and then, well, then I sort of floated away.'

I miss out the bit about floating home to the Rotherhithe Sky Tower.

'I know it sounds mad,' I says, 'but it's true. Reg, what's going on? What's it all about?'

'It was a dream, Norfolk. You've been under a lot of pressure recently,' he says. I knew he was going to say that. It's obvious that he would say that. I'm prepared.

'No, Reg,' I says. 'I knew you'd think that, but it wasn't a fucking dream. It was straight up. It's what happened, yeah? You know that what I saw is actually what happened, don't you? How would I know all that stuff about the studio and the hospital? You never told me. I must have seen it.'

Reg has gone quiet and he's looking at me really intent, cos he does believe me. He is a believer, after all. He already believes in Martin Martin, so he wants to believe what I'm telling him. It doesn't seem mad to him like it might to you, that I've been slipping through these holes in time and Seeing things with a capital S. It's all par for the course with Martin Martin. This is all the stuff the MMists want to hear, it's what they want to be able to do. This is all the skill shit that they think the gov has taken away from them. If they could See things all the time, like they think humans should, like what I've been doing, then there would be no bad things. There'd be no gov with its Life Debts and the Departments that they hate so much. The PM wouldn't be the PM, and there wouldn't be all the shows all the time about how you need to buy the stuff they make and about how the gov are really fucking smart and do all the right things. All the modern ways would be replaced with the old ways, which mean the stinky old seaters and the old cracked cups and mugs and the bolly nazy and eels out the river, not the Quad and Sticky Beans and Schtix. There wouldn't be the agri-factories in Norfolk (like the one Reg thinks I've scarpered from), where they just work and sleep and work and sleep and then die.

It's cos they hate all that so much that they believe in Martin Martin. (Or is it the other way around? I must find out.) It keeps them going. And it's cos Reg does believe, that he believes me. And he should believe me, cos it might not be believable, but it is what happened, believe me. I can hardly believe it myself.

Reg stares into my eyes, like he's looking into a really fucking huge dark, dark cave where he thought he saw something in the corner, like a little piece of gold, something he wants to see again and maybe get his fucking grubbies on before anyone else sees it.

It's a bit embarrassing actually, cos he's gone like when old blokes go all bleary in the eyes when they remember something from the olden days. I just sit there quiet and let him have his smeary-teary memory.

At last he brightens again and starts up, more whispery than before, looking at me like he's trying to look inside my head. Like he's trying to See, with a capital S:

'But you, Norfolk. There's a reason for you being here. You're here to help, aren't you? You're here to . . .' he tails off, still staring into me, trying to get his fucking head together, squinting his moist eyes like he's groping around in the dark with just a candle to light everything. It's all gloomy for Reg. Not clear and bright. Like he needs a good pair of specs for his brain to bring everything into focus.

'Tell me more about meeting Martin Martin,' says Reg. There's a bottle of the red booze on the low table between us and he pours us a glass each.

And so I tell him it all again. All what I told him before, I tell it to him over and over. He stops me and asks for more details every now and then. I miss certain bits out, of course. Like what's happened with Fyodor. And that my name is Jensen Interceptor (gov spy), not Norfolk from Norfolk (trampy). I don't tell him about the brick igloo neither.

And while I'm talking, Reg is getting cheered up and is all like 'Go on' and 'Yes' and 'Why, of course . . .', like the things that I'm telling him are filling in gaps in his head.

Reg's gaps are big. All this Martin Martin stuff happened a long, long time ago. He's guessing at most of it. From what he's been told, from some bits that he's read, he feels like Martin Martin is inside of him. But he has a lot of gaps still. And I know what it's like to have those big gaps. Holes, like in cartoon cheese, that run through your thoughts. Cheese with fucking dirty great big tunnels running through, and you can't see where the tunnels go, cos they bend in the middle, or maybe they meet another hole and go in a different direction altogether. How can you know where those tunnels go without crawling through them?

It's all tunnels, this Martin Martin stuff. Tunnels under tunnels with secret doors to other tunnels and rooms. Rooms with trapdoors in the floors which lead to another room with another secret passage hidden behind a bookshelf or a screen. And we're all like worms, living under the ground, or eels in the mud at the bottom of the river, all burrowing away in our little tubes, eating the fucking mud and thinking that there's nothing else going on – just our little tunnel and our mud and our wriggling. But that's not how it is. There's totally, like, a fucking whole lot more to it. Like, eels, yeah, they're just in the mud at the bottom of the river. They think that's all there is. Until they get grabbed by a hungry trampy, then they discover that there is air and blue sky and the whole world above the river. Then they get stabbed in the head and have their skin stripped off and then they get eaten. To us, the river is just a bit of water, cutting our city in half so we have to build bridges over it and tunnels under it, but to an eel it's their whole world. Our world is bigger and better and cleaner, that's for sure, but we don't see much of it, even though we think we do. We don't see much more than the eel in his mud. Not until we get plucked out for some reason, and we find out there's more to our world. Like being able to fly through time, for example.

'So Reg,' I goes, after I'd told him all about the show with Martin Martin, and what the Jacksons looked like, and what Martin Martin looked like, and how he was in the hospital, and what Devlin Williams was like, what sort of a bloke he seemed to be, and what London looked like, and whether anyone else talked to me other than Martin Martin and Devlin Williams, and whether there were any smells, and how I felt when all this was happening (like it was normal, actually, in case you were wondering too), and what the weather was like, and all other tiny details about everything I saw and did. 'What's it all about, Reg? What's happening?'

And Reg says, 'I think you might be very special, Norfolk. You have seen things which we have only guessed at. I think there's a reason why you've been shown these things, Norfolk.'

'Oh yeah?' says I, 'What's that then? What reason is there for me seeing all this stuff?'

'I think it's a sign, Norfolk.'

'What, like a road sign?' I asks.

'Yes, like a road sign. It's telling us which way to go, warning us what is about to happen. The Return is imminent. We must act.'

'The Return?' I says.

'The Return of Martin Martin. We always knew it would happen, but we never knew when. We knew there would be the Revelation before the Return, and you have been chosen as the channel for the Revelation. The Revelation has begun!'

'So what do we have to do?' I says, feeling half weirded-out by Reg's tone of voice and half excited about the Return and the Revelation and all that, cos the way Reg says it, it sounds important and exciting.

'We must prepare for Martin Martin's return, and for his sharing of the Gift. We have to weaken the state's control of the people. The time for decadence is over, the new dawn is upon us! We are his apostles, Norfolk. And you, you are perhaps the most important.' And he's sweating and rocking backwards and forwards in his seater, staring at me.

Then he suddenly stands and goes, 'There's no time. Tonight. We start tonight.' Reg is excited, adge. 'Plans, Norfolk. I have to make plans.' These words he says in that singing voice he does, and then it drops to casual and he goes, 'Can you come back here later? Say, seven?

Claire will be here.' And then he's back to his moany singing-talking: 'These are very exciting times, Norfolk. Your arrival has changed things. I knew there was a reason why you came to us.'

Twenty-five

So I goes on a walk, around and around while Reg gets his thinking and his planning together. I just walk the streets, saying hello to puss cats and sitting drinking reeking tea in an awful old caff where the woman called me 'duck' and cackled like a bird when I walked in. I must have been looking sad or lonely or something, cos after she poured me a cup of tea into a stinky old mug out of a huge great metal teapot with steam all coming out which covered her in cloud, she says to me:

'You all right, duck?'

I think to myself, 'duck', and wonder why she would call me that. Maybe it's what the Makeover Team have done to my face.

'I'm all right,' I said, shrugging my shoulders.

'You don't look it, luvvy,' she says, and gives me a big smile.

'Yeah, well,' I say, thinking that I need something to say that won't make me sound like a spy. It's like trying out a foreign language sometimes.

'You know,' I say, thinking that there's always one thing to say that people around here would agree with, and one thing I know all about, 'it's the government, yeah?'

'Tchoh!' she goes, popping her eyes upwards. 'Don't talk to me about that lot of liars.'

'They are liars, aren't they?' I say back to her.

This woman in the caff, this caff lady, she's the down-to-earth type. You know what she says comes from experience, not from ideas she baked up in her brain, like Reg. The only things she bakes are pies and potatoes. Her world is stewed tea, fried eggs and a slice, pots and pans and feeding hungry ruffians from around here, not fucking nutty MMist meetings.

I want to hear why she thinks the gov are liars. It would have nothing to do with Martin Martin, I was sure. She wouldn't know or care about any of that. No, she'd hate the gov cos of something they'd done to her. Something real and not mad like all the thoughts and experiences I've been having.

'What did they lie to you about?' I ask, putting the stress on the word 'you', cos then she'd understand that they'd lied to me too.

'Oh, you don't want to hear about my grumbles, duck,' she says. 'I'm sure you've got problems of your own. Drink your tea and take the weight off, darling.'

'Darling' and 'duck'. I like all that.

'Oh, but I do,' I say. 'I mean, if we can't share each other's troubles, they've sort of beaten us, haven't they?' This seems to do the trick.

'Ah well, you're right there, sweetheart,' she sighs. 'Darling' and 'duck' and 'sweetheart'.

But then I feel that I don't need her to tell me why she hates the gov. As I look at her, it's like there's water in my eyes, and there's the swimming feeling in my head, the tiredness. It's like there's a nugget in my brain where her story already exists. All I do is look at her and the nugget cracks open and its contents flow out. I can See why she hates the gov.

It was when she was young like me, when she started to hate the gov. She was young and beautiful with big lush titties and long legs; soft and hard in all the right places. Wearing a skirt with flowers on it and cycling around in the summer with her man. Laughing and pretending to knock each other off their rickety bicycles. Country lanes, but near the city. Maybe up Hampstead way. And the young lush caff lady, giggly and dizzy with the sexy feelings welling up inside her innocent bod, she wants to stop cycling and find somewhere nice, a little nook where they can put down a blanket and eat their picnic and drink the booze they've brought with them. And then maybe they'll do it. Maybe the man will want to do it with her, and this is the first time the lush little caff lady will have done it. It's time for her to do it, she's well ready and looking forward to it. She's been thinking about it for ages. Maybe she'll just squeeze his pole. Maybe she'll give it a lick, but she's hoping it's time for the Big One. She's excited about it and keeps thinking about it.

And so they find somewhere. It's a private little opening in the woods, sunlight dancing around through the leaves in the trees, which sway about in a light breeze. There's grass and flowers. It looks comfy and clean and natural, it's just the right place for her to do it for the first time. In her mind she can see herself remembering this moment for the rest of her life, and she thinks that because it's pretty, the sun is shining, and her man is a nice man, that she will feel warm and happy inside forever when she thinks of the afternoon she did it for the first time. Perfect.

And so they lay their big blanket on the ground. And they take out their bits and pieces of food from the backpack the man is wearing. They pull the plug out of a bottle of red booze. It goes 'thunk!' and they both laugh. They eat bread and cheese and tomatoes. They knock back their red booze. It's warm and cosy in their little nature burrow, surrounded by trees and grass and flowers. Their bicycles lie on the ground a little way away, sort of on top of each other, in a heap, the pedal of one poking through the spokes of the other. It's quiet and peaceful and the red booze is doing the trick, making them at first all giggles, pushing each other and jokey, and then making them more strokey and cuddles and murmurs.

They start to kiss, he with his arm around her shoulder. He strokes her hair with his hand. She gently pushes her chest towards him, her lush boobies hoping for a stroke too. He gets the message and slides his other hand inside her top and feels what she wants him to feel: the softness and the hardness she has in there. She reaches out and finds his spot. It's bulging there, looking painful, but in a good way. She places her four fingers along the hardness so her palm cups the top of it, and she moves it gently, freeing it from the awkward position it had got itself into. He sighs with relief and kisses her harder as she strokes and strokes with long elegant fingers and starts to push her bottom into the ground. She's rocking backwards and forwards, just slightly, but he can feel the movement against his legs and he starts doing it too. It's like a dance, a quiet little sex dance in a shady glade on a sunny day in a little corner of England's big, big city.

But then I can see more. Like before, when I was watching Martin Martin at his mad show-gone-wrong and I could see the oldies all streaming out of the studio, and then I watched from the sky as Devlin Williams drove Martin Martin to hospital. This time, I rise up above the sunny love scene and I can see across the whole area. There're patches of wood and open grassy areas.

But from up there, watching the good loving, I feel something is wrong. A sound, but not a sound. A horrible rumbling maybe, but not like in an earthquake or an avalanche. It's something I feel inside me, this noise, this horror, not something that's happening out there in the love woods or the sexy meadows.

And then I see it. A vehicle. A big black box on wheels, belching smoke from big round pipes, the engine rattling and throbbing like industrial machinery, not smooth and quiet like Devlin Williams' van. It drives up the little lane and stops by the woods where the caff lady and her man are loved up. Two men come out of the van, men wearing black uniforms and visors, holding sticks and with guns dangling off their belts, making them walk funny, with a swagger. They've got big kick-boots on their feet and they clump along. They're like coppers or soldiers. They start walking into the woods.

The coppers or soldiers use their big sticks to whack tree branches and undergrowth out of the way as they advance across the meadow, towards the woods. They look like robots down there, marching along, swishing their sticks in front of them, or like a machine, a harvester scything and hacking, relentless and unstoppable.

They're heading towards the caff lady and her man.

When they hear the copper/soldiers clumping towards them, my caff lady and her man stop kissing and squeezing and look scared. They quickly gather up their blanket and picnic stuff and roughly shove it all in the man's backpack. Then they start towards their bicycles, but it's too late. A copper/soldier crunches in on them.

'Oh dear, Archie,' says one copper/soldier to the caff lady's man. 'Looks like you've run out of luck.'

The caff lady is standing to one side, looking desperate. The copper/soldier pulls out a gun and points it at her man.

'Come on, Archie, time for you to face the music,' says the copper/soldier.

'I've done nothing wrong!' shouts the man.

'Tsk, tsk, Archie,' says the copper/soldier. 'I think harbouring a known terrorist is doing something wrong.'

Suddenly, the man starts to run, and as he runs, the caff lady makes a lunge at the outstretched arm of the copper/soldier. The two of them struggle for a moment, then there's a loud crack – the copper/soldier's gun going off. The caff lady's man, only two paces away, falls face-down on the ground and stops moving. My caff lady screams. The copper/soldier hits her with his stick and she falls to the ground, quiet. There's some blood coming from her head.

And then, after all the violence is over, with blue smoke from the gun drifting in the air, lit up with the bright sun, the copper/soldiers drag the body of the dead man and the unconscious caff lady back to their van.

When she wakes up, she's in prison, and she stays there until she agrees to sign a confession that says that she was plotting against the state, but that it was the man who did it really, and, because she's just a weak woman who was in love with her man, she sort of just got pulled into it. My lush caff lady, now swollen around the face and broken in the head, wouldn't sign. She stayed in the prison for a year, no one knew where she was. I See all this time pass in mere moments. I See it all, everything they did to her. I feel all her pain. They interrogated her every day. They made her stand naked and sprayed cold water at her. They woke her up when she fell asleep. Sometimes they touched her in places and in ways she didn't want to be touched. They beat her until, eventually, she did sign.

When they released her, she had nothing. Her brain was broken by her twelve months of torture and she became homeless. She drank what-ever ghastly booze she could get her hands on and she slept in parks and shouted and pissed in her pants.

For twenty years afterwards, she would wake up screaming every night and walked through each day like she had got shot in the back of the head that sunny day too. She couldn't sleep at night and she was never properly awake during the day.

Then, one day, she changed. She decided it was time to stop being dead-but-alive. It was because a young woman helped her. At first the young woman just talked to her. She would say 'Hello' and smile every time she saw her. And then she asked if the old lady was hungry and brought her some food. Then she offered to bring her some clean clothes. And she brought her into her house and gave her a bath. And I could see that this helpful young girl was Claire. My Claire. Claire, who saved me also, and wiped away my vom and calmed my shouting in my brain and made me into a different person than before.

Now the old lady makes cups of tea and bad food in the caff for the grey and smelly men who suck on ciggies and squint at newspapers in there. She says nice things to them because she knows that the only way to feel good is to be good. She sees all the hurt people around her, and it reminds her of how she was hurt, and she wants to help. So she makes tea and food for them and calls them 'duck' and 'darling' and 'sweetheart', and for five minutes or an hour, when they're in there, everything's OK. These old men, they feel a bit like they did before their old mums died.

'At least they didn't torture him . . .'

This is the caff lady, forty years later, behind a cloud of steam from her big old teapot, talking to Jensen Interceptor, me. She's all mumbles now, lost in the memory I've just been peeking at. My face is wet from tears dripping from my eyes like a leaky gutter. I gaze at the old caff lady and in my chest there is a pain harder than when I ran from Fyodor getting arrested at the coffee place.

And I'm thinking, 'Am I mad? Have I totally lost it?'

But I think, 'No, I've not lost anything.' What all this is, all these visions and nuggets and stuff, it's the truth, more true than anything I took for truth before. I feel like some bloke you see on the news shows, shouting that he's innocent just before the gov take him off to a chamber to get him all killed up cos he did a murder, but then they find out he was innocent after all. The way that man felt before he got executed, how he knew he was innocent, I mean, that certainty, that's how sure I felt about what I Saw. It's not me what's mad. It's everything around me.

Twenty-six

I'D DRANK all the tea I could drink. My time with the caff lady has to come to an end, and so I leave to once more walk the streets. I don't look up as I walk around. In my head are all these clashing ideas, banging into each other and falling over, rubbing their skulls as they sit on their arses, looking at each other as if it's the other's fault that they're in this pickle.

After I've walked for a while, my brain quietens down. The pattern of the pavement's cracks and the different colours of the stones scrolling past under my feet become hypnotising and fill my mind with emptiness. I am thinking of nothing when a new feature suddenly appears. It is white chalk or paint in square shapes. It is the hops-kotch game what me and Claire had seen when we went for a walk and met the little girl called Rose, and I am in the middle of it. I try to remember the rhyme the girl said when she danced around in the squares.

'One for sorrow, two for joy, three for a girl and four for a boy,' I say, almost singing it. And I jump from one square to another, balancing on one foot when there's just one square and landing on two feet when there are two squares next to each other.

'Erm, five for a squirrel and six for beans,' I say, guessing at the next bit cos I can't remember the words. 'Seven for . . . erm . . . a toilet on my shower screen.' This makes me chuckle a bit to myself. 'Eight for a baby and nine for a bike, ten for an eel's head stabbed on a spike –'

'That's not how it goes,' says a little girl's voice. I look up and there's Rose, the girl whose hops-kotch grid this is.

'Hello Rose,' I say, and smile.

'I know you,' says Rose. 'You're Claire's boyfriend.'

'Well, I don't know about that,' I say, feeling a bit embarrassed. You know, like, 'boyfriend'. That's a bit strong, yeah?

'Yeah, you're her boyfriend and she's your girlfriend. You love her. She's nice. She helped my dad when he got out of prison.'

'She helps a lot of people, doesn't she?' I say.

'Yeah,' says Rose. 'That's what she does. She helps people. She's nice. And you love her.'

'She is nice, that's true,' I say. And I wonder whether I love her. Maybe I do. And I'm like all thinking about her knicks and her face and that, and that it's her I need to see, and that if we're at the girl's hops-kotch thing, that means that Claire's place can't be far away.

'Rose,' I say to the little girl, 'I've forgotten where Claire lives. Is it around here? It's near, isn't it?'

'Yeah,' says Rose, she's skipping away on her pavement game, singing her little rhymes to herself.

'Can you take me there?' I ask.

'Yeah,' says Rose, still skipping and rhyming under her breath. I stand and watch her for a few minutes. She's totally into what it is she's doing and has forgotten all about me. I may as well not be here at all.

'Rose?' I say.

'Yeah?' says Rose.

'Claire's?'

'Claire's nice. Has she got a cat? I got a cat called Pongo. He's mad and he goes "Roar!"' she says, bringing her hands up to her face and clenching them like claws.

'Is he an angry cat?' I say, thinking that if Pongo goes around roaring with his claws out, he must be.

'No,' says Rose, like I've just said the most stupid thing in the world. I laugh, and so does Rose.

'Come on, Rose,' I say, 'show me the way to Claire's, please.'

Finally Rose stops her game of hops-kotch and takes my hand. We walk along the street. The little girl's hand in mine feels so soft and tiny, it's hard to believe it's real. Walking along with her like that, this

odd feeling comes up in me. It's as if I'm her fucking dad or something, and we're on the way to see her mum, who is Claire. It feels so
nice that I get hot in the eyes like I'm going to cry again. But not the
crying of pain, a crying of, I dunno, fucking joy, I s'pose.

We arrive at a door.

'Here you are!' she chirps like a little bird and reaches up and presses
the doorbell.

I say, 'You sound like a little bird!' and I make a chirruping noise.
Rose giggles and tries to make the sound I just made.

'No!' I go, laughing. 'It wasn't like that, it was more like this,' and
I make another sound like a bird, only it comes out wrong and sounds
more like a cat.

'That's like Pongo!' screams Rose, delighted, and makes her own
Pongo noise.

We're both making noises like Pongo when Claire opens the door.
She leans against the doorframe and watches us miaowing with a smile
on her lips. Rose is giggling so much she can hardly stand up.

'Oh, hello,' I says to Claire. 'We're doing impersonations of Pongo.'

'I thought so,' says Claire. 'Maybe you should come in for a saucer
of milk.'

'Bye-bye!' says Rose and scarpers off, singing to herself as she
goes. Me and Claire watch her skip off down the street, back to where
her hops-kotch grid is, back to her home and back to Pongo and her
real mum and dad. Then Claire turns around and walks back into her
flat.

'Come on in, Norfolk,' she says. I follow her into the familiar little
place. The smell is exactly the same as it was the last time I was here.
It's not the kind of smell I get back at my place at the Rotherhithe Sky
Tower, and certainly not the smell you get at Fyodor's place, especially
when the fat mong from IT who Fyodor shares with is there, grunting
and leaving his old food bits all over. She smells good, does Claire.
And so does her place.

She's got the kettle on for a cuppa. I join her in the kitchen. She
looks me up and down. I'm in a suit which is dusty with red brick dust
and crumpled up from my night in the brick igloo.

'Oh Norfolk, just *look* at you,' she says, suddenly all concerned. 'I've been worried sick about you.' Now Rose isn't here, she doesn't have to pretend I'm all normal.

'Don't worry about me,' I say. 'I'm all right. It's just that things are getting a bit complicated. There's a lot of things that need organising. Reg is organising things.'

'Yes, I know. He called. He wants us to be at his by seven. He says it's very important.' She sighs and shakes her head. 'I'm very worried about Reg too. He can get quite manic sometimes. It's not good for him. Maybe we can calm him down.'

She wants to save Reg. She saved the caff lady, and she's saving me. Claire totally saves people. Claire's fucking cool.

'Claire . . .' I say, thinking about the caff lady, wanting to ask her all about it, but I can't think how to say it. I shut my mouth.

'Yes?' says Claire.

'Nothing,' I goes.

We drink our tea quietly. It gets dark and rain comes. Thunder rumbles away in the distance and the temperature drops. The rain comes well heavy, snapping against the windows. After a while, I hear the sound of running water, little rivers flowing along the gutters. I think about the rain coming down on the pavements, wiping Rose's hopscotch squares away. I think about the rain falling on to the surface of the Thames, making little circles with each drop. I think about the eels squirming about under the river. I wonder if they can sense it's raining. Can they hear the thunder? And I wonder if Miskin is gazing out of his office window, watching the grey clouds gathering over London's old skyline, wondering where I am. Or has he got his head in a pile of musty-fusty old papers, doing his job, ignoring what's happening outside?

Claire takes me into her bedroom and we do it. She is soft and warm and she smells good. There's no boris-lightning in my head, like when I do it artificial at Starfucks, only the real lightning from the storm outside, and real explosions of thunder from the angry sky. No special FX here. Every time the lightning flashes, Claire holds me a little bit tighter, not relaxing until the thunder has come and gone. She doesn't say anything, but I can feel it – her little grips of fear.

Afterwards, we sleep for a little while. Then we wake up, eat some nice food. We don't say much as we prepare to go to Reg's. It rains still, constant and hard. It's dark with the rain clouds.

All is grimness at Reg's at seven. Serious stuff, this. And no one's more serious now than their newest member, Norfolk from Norfolk, whose head is now full of the feelings from our afternoon of bed-sex love, and also full of images from the lush caff lady's horrible life. It was Claire who saved the caff lady and it is Claire who is saving me too. I came here as Jensen, to spy and to grass them up to the gov, and now I'm Norfolk from Norfolk, and I don't feel that grassing them up is what I want to be doing. Norfolk loves Claire and Claire loves Norfolk. Just like little Rose said.

'Thanks for coming,' says Reg. We all know something's up, and that Reg will soon be issuing orders. It's got all military. We sit around a table. Reg reaches under the table and gets a hold of a floorboard in this ancient room. The section of board is loose. He pulls it up, scrabbly with his nails, and there's a hidey-hole under it. And in the hidey-hole, all covered in dust, is a package. It's wrapped in an old rag. It's about the size of a thick book.

Reg brings the dusty thing up and plonks it on the table in front of us. Then he unwraps it. It is a book. Reg reaches out and opens the book, and we can see that all the pages have been cut out, leaving a hole, but so that it still looks like a book from the outside. And in the hole there is another package, wrapped in another rag. Reg pulls this package out, pushes the book to one side and places the new package on the table. Then he unwraps it. It's a square lump of something grey and soft-looking, sealed in plastic. One of the boys whistles through his teeth when he sees it.

'One kilogramme of unmarked C6,' says Reg, by way of explanation. 'Also known as plastic explosive. Also known as Nortex. It's very unstable. Once the Nortex is armed with P15 accelerant, the slightest thing can set it off.'

Fucking terrorist car-bombing!

'Oh, Reg . . .' says Claire. She sounds sad and angry at the same time.

Reg slices a tiny little pellet of the bomb goo. It's no bigger than half a Midgy Button flavour pill. He rolls it between his finger and thumb.

'If I add some accelerant . . .' he says, taking a bottle of clear liquid from the tin, and pouring a tiny puddle of it on the table, then putting the little pea of bomb goo in the liquid. 'And introduce sufficient heat . . .' continues Reg, lighting a match.

'Reg!' shouts Claire, urgent. 'Don't!'

There's a loud noise, like someone slamming a door in another room, muffled, but really, really, loud, and there's a rank smell of chemistry and burned hair and smoke.

And at that very second, I see someone in the room, over in the corner, behind Reg. Someone lurking in the shadows. Someone there, and then not there. Shifty. I don't move. I glance around the table. No one else has seen the person in the shadows. I say nothing. No one says anything. They're staring at the table, trying to take in what just happened. The figure behind Reg shifts again. Moves a little closer to the table. I can see the person coming nearer, over Reg's shoulder. Still no one else reacts. When I look up again, he's right there. His hand is on Reg's shoulder, he's looking at the bomb goo with a smile on his face. Then he looks at me. I know this face.

It's Martin fucking Martin. He's all bashed up. Bruised and bloody, swollen in the face, his clothes ripped.

The one person Reg wants to meet more than anyone else in the world, and here he is, with his hand on Reg's shoulder. And Reg doesn't know. It's just me who can see him. Just Jensen, who, only a week ago, hadn't even heard of fucking Martin Martin. I've been visiting him, and now he's here visiting me, like we're old fucking pals or something.

'Jensen,' he goes, 'Jensen Interceptor.' Blood comes from his gob when he talks.

'Fuck off!' I says back, thinking that Martin Martin is about to grass me up as a gov spy good and proper to the assembled faithful. I say 'Fuck off!' with my mouth closed and without words, my eyes flipping from Reg, to Claire, to the bomb goo in the book-disguise. And I'm feeling like I did when I was hanging off that drainpipe outside this very flat, spying. I feel like I'm about to be caught. Panicky.

And then Martin Martin goes 'Arrrrrrrrrp!', a huge belch like you'd hear outside the pubs and clubs on a Friday night. It's sloppy and stinky. I look around the room. Everyone is frozen like waxworks. Reg is all glassy-marble eyes. The only sound in the room is Martin Martin's heavy breathing. He's leaning over our secret little meeting, swaying about like an old drunkie, belching like he's going to blow chunks all over Reg's head and the table and the bomb goo.

'Jensen Interceptor. Wanker!' goes Martin Martin, in the voice that me and Fyodor use to call each other wanker. 'Wankaaaaaah!'

And he does the wanker sign at me too. Then he turns around in one move, so he's gone 180 degrees and is facing away from me and Reg, and he starts staggering off towards the door.

He's just turned up, called me a wanker and now he's buggering off.

'Oi!' I goes, but Martin Martin is already leaving, collapsing through the door. I hear a tumble of body against wood, and I wince, expecting everyone to rush to the door. They don't. They haven't heard it. They're motionless still, like they've just stopped, like clockwork dolls run out of tick-tock. Reg's mini-bomb has stunned them.

I can't control what I'm doing: I want to check that Claire is OK, but instead I stand up. I can hear Martin Martin thundering down the stairs, bumping into the walls as he goes. I go after him.

Twenty-seven

ONCE I get outside Reg's, I look up and down the street. I'm hammering hard in my chest and the breath is thick and quick too. I can't hear anything. I don't think that's cos of Reg's stupid mini-bomb or anything, but the street is quiet and cold, like it's dead. Old bin bags lean against lamp posts, some spilling their rotting innards over the pavement. I hear a thump. Then I hear what I think is another belch. It echoes around. It's so loud that I think it can't possibly be a belch. But it is, and it can only be Martin Martin's. I follow the belch. Then I see a figure again, it darts down a side alley, so I starts to run after it, not wanting to lose sight.

'Martin Martin! Stop bloody running away!' I says, but in my head again.

'Jensen Interceptor!' comes the reply, also in my head, then 'Urrrrrp!' again.

'Martin Martin, that is bloody disgusting!' I think as I half-run, half-walk down the alley. The alley's round the back of some squashed old brick houses, and there are little scrappy bits of grass and concrete there, with bright plastic toys for children and all olden-days bicycling contraptions spread all over, all messy and like they're spilling out from the doors of the houses. And there are sheds with cobwebs, smelling of wood. These tiny messy gardens are all next to each other, on top of each other, almost. Under my feet, the alley is made of smooth round stones, which are slippy in the greasy night.

'Sorry. I've still not got the hang of this. Errrrrrchup! Sorry,' comes the voice of MM in my head.

'Where are you?' I goes, I'm looking all over, behind old bins and in doorways and over waist-high walls.

'Near. Keep coming.'

'Where near?'

'Here near.'

And there he is, standing in front of me. I can't believe I didn't see him before. I nearly run straight into him. He's not looking great.

Right there and then, in a moment of, like, totally freaking out, I think to myself, 'Why can't I be a shop assistant, working the tills at God of Fuck, selling T-shirts and cheap trousers to norms?'

'You weren't destined to work at God of Fuck,' says Martin Martin.

'What was I fucking bloody destined to do, then?' says I. 'Run around after you, you belchy nutter?'

The hideous burpy corpse thing that's swaying about in front of me doesn't answer me. There are tears in my eyes. This feels like an important moment.

'Martin Martin's not coming back, Jensen. I thought I'd better let you know. It doesn't seem fair to let you all carry on like this.' And then he goes all 'Buuuurrrrrrp!' again.

'But you are back,' says I. 'I saw you before. I saw you on your show. I came to your place, and now you're around my place. That means you are coming back. You have bloody come back. Here you are! In front of me!'

'It's not that simple,' says he. 'I'm not quite who you think I am.'

'Who the fuck are you, then?' I goes. By now, I'm screaming, but I suppose if you were looking in, like out of your bedroom window in one of these old dark bricky hovels, all you'd have seen would be me stood there, on my own, waving my arms around, making no sound. Like a fucking loonbag.

And then this (it's coming up, after this next bit) comes in to my head, like a flood, all in one go, no gaps, no holes, in no time, like the way warmth spreads through you when the sun hits you. It was like I'd always known it. But I hadn't. Not until I did, if you follow my drift. To me, it became knowledge like a magic trick.

My name is Emile Henderson. I was born in Rotherhithe in 1924. Near where you live, Jensen. From your bedroom window in that big tower you live in, you can see where I was born. You could see the street I used to play in if it was still there. It is still there, but it's buried under your world now. Lived there with my mum. Dad died in an accident. I was nine. He worked on the docks. Everyone in Rotherhithe worked on the docks. He was crushed by a crate of garlic. He wasn't really my dad. Mum got pregnant by another man. His name was Emile. Told her he was French. He wasn't. He was from Stepney. Stepney's on the other side of the river. Other end of the Rotherhithe Tunnel. Emile worked on the docks too.

She told him she was pregnant and he told her he had to go back to France. He lied to her, like he'd lied all along. He just went back to Stepney. Never used the Rotherhithe Tunnel again. Stayed his side of the river. Then I was born, and she called me Emile after him. You can imagine how that went down with the other kids when I was growing up.

In 1939, there was a big war. All the men were sent to the war. When I turned eighteen, I was sent to the war too. I became a soldier. Awful. Saw terrible things. Fought in mud. Fought in forests. Fought in buildings with no windows that smelled bad because people had pissed and shit in the corners like animals. People had died in them too. I saw mates get shot and die, right next to me. Bits of them hit me. My face got sprayed with their brains and blood. Some of it went in my mouth. I was very scared. I'd never seen dead bodies before.

Never enough to eat. We were always cold and dirty. People were trying to kill us. We had to try to kill them.

During the war, I met Jack Jackson. Edward Jackson. In the army, if your name is Jackson, you're called Jack. If your surname is Carson, they'll call you Kit after the cowboy in the films. If your name is White, they'll call you Chalky.

Jackson was older than me. Like an older brother. Told me if I stuck with him, I'd be all right. He had plans.

He was a crook.

We stole food. We stole blankets. From the army. Sold them to the refugees. The Yanks were bringing in stuff twenty-four hours a day. Ammunition, weapons, fuel, cigarettes, rations: the works. Everyone was at it; stealing, selling. So were we.

Jackson heard about a supply train that got stolen in Italy. A whole train. He kept talking about it. He thought it was the best thing he'd ever heard. 'Imagine,' he'd say when we were in our bunks, trying to get some kip, 'stealing a whole train.' It was like his bedtime story, his soothing nursery rhyme. And then he found out about a truck that was due to be arriving in Paris. Loaded with treasure, he said. He'd heard it was a precious load, some of France's most important national treasure. Diamonds, gold, coins, he said. It had been stashed away somewhere earlier in the war, and now the Germans were being pushed back and taking some of it with them. Jackson wanted to steal it. He made a plan. He called the truck 'our Italian train' and 'our pension plan'.

We spent a week preparing. He found out the truck's route. The truck was due to go through Fontainebleau forest. So we went out to the forest and dug a deep hole, ready to hide the gold and the jewels. We set up a fake checkpoint and dressed in MP uniforms. Hid in the forest. Waited.

The truck arrived. It was early evening. Cold. The driver's window was open and he was smoking a fag; he wasn't suspicious. Jackson went up to the truck and chatted to him. They were laughing, the driver and Jackson. Jackson shot the driver in the head. Then he shot the driver's mate too. That was it.

In the back of the truck, there were some wooden boxes and some large square objects covered in tarpaulin. Jackson ripped the tarpaulin off one of them. It was a painting. There were forty more of them there. Our treasure: paintings. Jackson was angry. He kicked them. Kicked the paintings out of the frames, put his boot through every one of them.

Then we opened the wooden boxes. There were four of those. Inside there were coins. Old ones. Probably from a museum. They were in display cases. Not enough for a pension for either of us, but we buried the cases anyway. Left the art in the lorry. Pushed the truck down the hill, where it crashed into a tree.

I went to set fire to the truck. When I got back to the hole we'd dug, no Jackson. I called his name. I decided to have a piss. Then I felt something hard on the back of my head. It was Jackson, hitting me. Hitting me on the back of the head. With a spade. The blow made me bite my own tongue off. And that was the end of Emile. Like killing a fly. Jackson murdered three that day. He murdered another during the war. A French woman. Didn't want to pay her for the sex he'd had. Stabbed her instead.

And he didn't stop killing when the war ended. Back home in London, he started a haulage company. Lorries. He got contracts delivering building materials. He collected bricks from Kent and took them back to London, where they were rebuilding. He took timber from the docks at Rotherhithe up to Coventry. By 1960, he had a fleet of lorries. He still drove a lorry himself. He didn't need to. He had plenty of drivers. Jackson didn't drive one of his own lorries because he liked driving. He used it to pick up prostitutes all over England. He'd rape them, then he'd kill them. That's what he liked to do. He'd got a taste for it during the war.

Jackson had a family. A house. A successful business. He never got caught. Got away with everything he did in the war; he got away with killing those women after the war. He thought he'd got away with killing me. But he never.

After he smashed my head in, there was nothing. Not blackness. Not silence. The spade hit me, then nothing. Then something: Martin Martin. Maybe he was always there. Maybe he came into things before my teeth had clamped together and cut my tongue off in that forest. Or maybe there was nothing for thirty years, or fifty years. It's not really relevant. You've seen how all this works, Jensen. Time isn't the issue. That's how you can be in several places at the same time. That's how you saw Martin Martin on the day he was rushed to hospital. It's how I'm here talking to you now. Wormholes, Jensen. Once you realise they're there, you can slip through them; between now and then, between life and death.

I'm lying under the forest floor, buried, face-down, no tongue, no back of my head, no pain, no sensation. Then I feel a presence near me. It's only when I feel this presence that I realise I've felt nothing before it. A voice is saying, 'Is there anyone there? Can I help? How can I help?'

When I hear the voice, I realise that I need help. So I try to lift a hand, or moan, anything to get the attention of the presence. But I can't. Nothing works, it's all broken. Nothing physical is working. But as this presence goes by, asking if there's anyone there, I start to feel things. I can smell the earth of the French forest. I can taste it. It's packed into my mouth and my nose. But then the presence, the voice, starts moving away, getting more distant, until it's gone. And then there's nothing again. But it's a different kind of nothing. It's a nothingness that I am aware of. It's my nothingness.

But then the voice comes back again, asking the same questions, like there is someone looking for me. It's like they know I'm there, but they *don't know who I am and they can't quite pinpoint where I am. As I become aware of the voice again, the nothingness is gradually replaced by more sensation, stronger this time. Not just whiffs like before, but something I can hold on to, something which will drag me out of the shallow grave, out of the nothingness and into something else, something better. It seems like the place this voice is coming from is somewhere I ought to be. But the voice fades again. I can't grasp it for long enough, but I'm determined that I shouldn't be taken by surprise the next time it comes along. I decide that I will be ready the next time, and when the voice comes, I will answer it.*

But it's still a surprise when the voice says, 'Is there anybody there?' again. This time I reply.

'My name is Emile.'

And then the connection comes. I am connected to another being, like with jump leads. His spark comes into me, and I start to turn over, like an engine. And this other being says, 'What do you want?', and straight away I can feel that I've caught up with Jackson. He is near. The bastard who caved my head in with a spade is there, with the being who has contacted me. I hang on for all I am worth, and the longer I hang on, the stronger I feel and the more clearly I can see.

The image comes into my vision like a photograph developing. I see him. There he is – Edward Jackson. Sitting there. Arms folded. He is old. Bald and fat, grey hair poking out of his ears, a rumpled face of veins and bulges. But it is him. It is Jackson. He sits there, and I can see him. I feel his resistance to what is happening. On the outside he is calm and arrogant, but he can't hide anything from me. I see it all. His evil surrounds him like a horrible fleshy sac. Deep red – poisoned-blood-red – this sac is. It stinks too. When he moves, the sac undulates around him, cushioning everything. But, inside his protective layer, he is scared. He knows it is me.

He tries to brave it out. 'I don't know no Emile, mate,' he says. But this being, the being that has called out to me and has given me the strength to meet Jackson, he is helping me. He puts Jackson on the spot. Gives him some stick while I try to do more. I want to kill Jackson, but I can't. I have no body.

'He's rather afraid you do,' says the being on my behalf, meaning that although Jackson was denying any knowledge, the being feels my anger and

knows it is righteous. This being, it's Martin Martin. He's helping me. He called me, and he's helping me confront my murderer. So I tell Martin Martin about the truck, about how he smacked me in the head with a spade, I tell him like I'm telling you this. To Martin Martin, it comes through all garbled, like radio interference. Martin Martin is trying to lay it on the line to Jackson, but he can't give it to him hard enough. 'Problems over a truck . . .' he says. Then I realise I need to take over, I have to deal with it myself. It is down to me.

So I possessed Martin Martin.

The possession didn't go well. I couldn't control Martin Martin's body. It rebelled against me. I wanted to bash Jackson's head. But all I could make Martin Martin's body do was shout. Martin Martin was elsewhere. He was now where I once was. We swapped. I was determined to stay where I was and finish things with Jackson, but the body failed me. It just collapsed and expelled air and blood and other juices from the inside.

That was what you saw in the television studio.

Now I think it's time for you to take over, Jensen Interceptor. You have to put a stop to the things that are wrong. I think this is your destiny.

I wait. But Martin Martin, or Emile Henderson, gives me no more. He stands there with his chin tucked into his neck, breathing heavily though his mouth, burping – 'Eeerrrrrrrrrp' – long and low. I feel the old tiredness, the scary strange tiredness that seems to mean that Jensen is going to lose it again, and start floating off somewhere, up with the clouds, or under the water, tumbling over and over in slow motion and watching things happen, like the old biddies scarpering out the television studio, or the lush caff lady and her man in the field.

Everything goes boomy and big in the street. I can hear water dripping from a leaky drainpipe like it's the loudest noise there is. With each drip it gets louder, until all I can hear is the dripping. And then there's the lightness. Like my body doesn't weigh anything any more, like I could fall over and all that would happen is that I'd hang in mid-air until a puff of wind starts to push me along. It's like having a dream. Peaceful. And like I'm not connected to anything any more. I close my eyes.

Martin Martin, or Emile, whoever he is, is pointing at me, and I remember where we are: on the street, the spot I chased him to before, behind all the houses with the bins and the gardens, the greasy pebbles stuck to the road under my feet. Emile Henderson/Martin Martin is stood there, a bit wobbly, pointing at me, like a spook out of a ghost show, which is what he sort of actually is.

And then Emile/Martin lets out this fucking enormous burp – 'Eeeeeuuuuurrrrrrp!' – and starts staggering off, like a piss artist again.

'Oi!' I goes, 'I haven't finished with you yet! What happens next?' But Martin Emile Martin is picking up speed now, marching like a mad puppet down the empty street, burping and waving his arms around as if to tell me it's not important.

'Urppp! You'll work it out, Jensen! Baaarrrrp!' he goes.

'Emile!' goes I again, but he's off, staggering and bumping into walls as he goes. He's unsteady but he's fast. So I set off after him, all the while saying, 'Emile! Martin Martin! Whoever the fuck you are! Stop!'

'If you keep coming after me, it'll be you all smashed up with your teeth broken and blood coming out of you! Urrrrrrp! Mark my words!' he goes, still moving fast, with me jogging, trying to catch up.

'Slow down! Where are you going?' I shout, in my head. No matter how fast I run, Emile/Martin keeps ahead of me. I see him disappear around corners, and when I get around the corner myself, he's already fifty metres or more down the next street, like he's jumped forward. This chase I keep up. I will not lose him. I want answers and he's not told me nearly fucking enough by half.

We keep going and going. My legs ache with the pavement-pounding. After an hour, we are at the river. I see him in the distance, his head bobbling around under the lights of Waterloo Bridge. My heart feels like it will tear if I keep running, but I have to keep Emile/Martin in sight. He keeps staggering on at outrageous speed, further south. He takes a left at the other end of the bridge and is barrelling towards the east.

Stamford Street gives way to Southwark Street, where the buildings start to look bad. He keeps on, hurtling down towards London Bridge. My mouth is dry, my tongue sticks to the roof of my mouth. My head is lolling around now, just like Emile/Martin's. I've given up calling out to him. Now I'm just chasing him. When I slow, he slows, but then when I start to get near him, he takes off again. I hear him burp, and then he dashes off, out of earshot.

Every now and then I can't carry on and I stop and put my hands on my knees and gasp for air, like when he turns right on to Tooley Street. When I catch my breath and get on to Tooley Street, he's waiting. As soon I appear, he turns and runs again. We're soon on Jamaica Road, where the streets are polished and fine. This is home territory. Towards the Rotherhithe Tunnel he runs, and I wonder whether he's heading for his old home, the place he grew up before he got sent off to war, before he got his head smashed in.

He suddenly stops. I can fucking see him right there by the opening of Rotherhithe Tunnel. He's waiting for me. I keep expecting him to fucking lurch off again when I get near, but he doesn't, he just stands there.

'One last thing,' he says as I get near enough to hear him.

'Fucking what is it, you mental case?' I says. I'm a bit fucking radged up and puffed out and pained with everything, and my head is throbbing bad.

'I haven't got long. Listen to me. You've got a chip in your head. The government put it there. A tiny electric chip. It's messing about with your brain. They think they've worked out how to get deep inside people's brains and that they can get in there and tinker around, put things in there that weren't there before, and take out things that were there before. They're experimenting on you, Jensen Interceptor. They want to see if they can make you believe in me. Because if they can make you believe in me, they can make you not believe in me too. They can send information straight into your brain. They want to switch you on and off like a light bulb. They want to see what happens when they send information into your electric chip. If it works, they think they'll be able to make you believe what they want you to believe. They don't want you to believe what you want, because you might believe in something that makes it difficult for them, like when people believed in Martin Martin. But what I am telling you is not from the electric chip in your brain. This is me telling you this. I am here to tell you not to believe what the chip is putting in your brain. If they can make you believe in the idea of me, they can make you not believe in me. But the idea of me is all wrong. I am not all wrong, just the idea of me. Do you understand?'

I don't, but I nod anyway.

'This is all real, Jensen, and you must sort it out. It could be you. You could be the one to stop it all. Reg needs sorting out too. There will be a dangerous moment soon with Reg. Be very careful. When the time comes, you must go for the left pocket. That's where the detonator will be. And beware Claire. She is not quite what she appears to be. Don't let the electric chip guide you in the wrong direction. Remember, your limbic system is a mess.'

There is a sudden piercing in my brain and I fall down to the fucking floor, right there in the street. My head hurts really fucking rotten.

'Electric fucking chip?' I think as the sharp fucking bonce pain fades out. I look up, but fucking Emile/Martin-fucking-Martin-Henderson, or whoever the fuck he is, is nowhere to be seen.

I am at the Rotherhithe intersection. One road goes into Rotherhithe, one goes off past Southwark Park, Surrey Quays, then Deptford and Greenwich. The other road heads under the river, through the tunnel, and comes up in Stepney. I sit there, gasping and gasping, having chased Emile/Martin for nearly two hours, I hold my head and feel the bump under my hair. The bump that fucking Gizza Kwid put there with a bottle. And to the left of it is another little itchy scab. Maybe that was put there when I smashed my head on the table in the Italian restaurant. But no, that fucking bump is round the front. Is it from when the gov agents bust in on me and Fyodor in the coffee shop? I got smacked around a bit then. I've had so many biffos to the head, it's a wonder it's fucking still attached to my fucking shoulders. But this little scabby itchy hole in my head I'm feeling isn't to do with any of those fucking incidents. This one was put there way back by the fucking Makeover Team. They must have put the fucking electric chip in my head.

The Rotherhithe Sky Tower flashes its light. Home. At least I can get a good night's fucking kip, even if my flat's fucking flooded and stinking like an old fucking swamp. I'm so tired, and I need to drink water and I need food. I need to let the heat in my head cool off. I can't even think straight. I start to trudge slowly towards the tower, holding my hips like a marathon runner, my face all twisted with the pain my lungs are giving me.

Twenty-eight

MY HEAD hurts as if there's a stone lodged inside it, like when you get a stone in your shoe, only now the stone is in my brain. Only it's not a fucking stone in there, is it? It's this fucking ghostie electric chippie thing what Emile Martin told me about, burning away in my brain, bleep-bleeping its messages at me, fucking me up in the head so I'm, like, all fucked up in the fucking head. I feel like one of them old soldiers with the metal plates in their heads, the ones who pick up radio signals in their brains and messages from aliens telling them to do things like collect rubbish off the streets and save it up in their houses. I'm like one of the old mental headcase fuckwits who stagger around the povo districts all messed off their booze, shouting the odds. Like fucking Gizza Kwid.

All this action that's been happening to me, it's all been bit by bit, one minute here, one minute there, and sometimes these minutes aren't even connected: minutes that happened, like, years apart are happening right next to each other with me, or even at the same time. Like fucking time has split open like a ripe melon, and the pips are all over the place, the fucking pips of time, and my brain is like the ripe watermelon, all smashed up and pulped, and the pips, which should be all orderly and in a nice row, they're all over the fucking place. Pips and fucking electric chips.

So here I am, walking back to the Rotherhithe Sky Tower with all these aches and pains and symptoms of the giddy sickness in my brain. Still, Jensen's a trouper, and I'm on my way back home. I need to pick up some boris and I need to have a serious fucking think about everything. Have I gone totally fucking mental? Is it, like, the fucking pressure? Is what is happening straight up or is it fucking mental bollocks? Have I got a fucking chip in my fucking brain? Is all that's been happening just coming out of the electric chip? Or is it for real? If Emile/Martin is telling me that everything's out of a chip, how do I know he's not out of a chip? Or are they both in my head; is Emile/Martin in there as well as the chip; half truth, half lies?

Fuck. I need to get home, where I can relax and sleep and be myself and not worry about no fucking electric brain chips or having to remember to pretend to be fucking Norfolk all the time. I need to get my head straight. I need to have a look at my fucking head. Take a good fucking butcher's at the scabs and bumps. Maybe I can get an X-ray or something.

And I need to have a big fucking think about Claire, and all that sort of soft stuff I'm feeling. Cos like, after being with Claire, everything else seems so tough and harsh and horrible. It's the way she is and the way she does things and the way she, like, talks and is really understanding. The way she looks into my eyes like there's going to be something there she recognises. All that.

My stomach still aches with the need to go, like cramps, cramps of nerve; my guts trying to tell me something, clenching up in there like a gnarly fist. But I move on anyway, ignoring the flapping and the punching inside me, and I get closer to the old Sky Tower.

Normally, the closer I get to home, the better I feel, looking forward to cranking up the music or flicking the shower on to my favourite up-skirt action and getting some food in and generally have a fucking ace time. But the closer I get this time, the worse I feel. My stomach grinds and goos, making me hold on to it and wince. I walk along the shiny streets, all lit up neon for twenty-four-hour night-time fun action, and full of beautiful people on their nights out, all with things to do. Me, I'm dressed rough, like Norfolk from Norfolk. I'm dirty and sweaty with the ruffian's face given to me by the Makeover Team, holding on to my belly and going 'Oh, argh, oh' under my breath and wincing and puffing.

I get a lot of fucking looks again.

Once in the lift of my tower, heading to the twenty-ninth floor, I feel slightly better, only cos I'm off the streets and no one will look at me funny. Then the doors open and I've only got another six seconds walk to my front door.

As I leave the lift I see the door to my place is open, just a crack. My stomach knots up and my throat goes hard so it's impossible to swallow, but that's all I want to do: 'ack! ack! ack!' Someone's been in my place.

Even though I am a spy, I don't go sneaky to the door, thinking spy thoughts like, 'There might be someone in there.' No. I run towards my flat and don't stop running when I get to the door. I keep running, barging it open with my shoulder, it swinging fast and wild into the wall and making a huge 'Smash!' noise, the handle going through the plaster wall.

Then I hear a thump inside the flat, and as I hear it I realise what I felt as soon as I saw that the door was open: some bastard is robbing my fucking place and he's still in here.

He comes out of the bathroom. His eyes are wide with surprise. Ugly fucker.

I know where my baseball bat is at; leaning against the wall, close to my right hand. He doesn't. He probably didn't even know I had a baseball bat in my flat.

So here's how it goes: as I hear the thump in the bathroom, I'm grabbing for the bat; when I see the figure in black come out of the bathroom, the bat is in my hand and I'm swinging it as hard as I fucking can. In one swishing arc, the baseball bat comes up from behind me and over my head and on to the head of the ugly fucking robber. It clobbers him square on the top of his skull, which makes a low 'dink', like the sound of a cracked bell in one of them old church places, and he collapses to the floor as if, well, someone just smacked him around the fucking head with a baseball bat. Which they have – me, I smacked him over his fucking head with a baseball bat. Fucking Jensen Interceptor dishing it out for a fucking change rather than getting clobbered first.

He's on the floor and his eyes are half-open, and so is his mouth, and he's going 'gerrrrrrrrrrrggggggggghhhhhhhh'. And as he's moaning down there, the blood starts to roll out from under his hair and pour down his face and drop off the end of his nose. It's dark, dark blood, and lots of it too. It spreads out across my floor.

Me, I'm standing there, all huff-puffing and going 'hergh, hergh' with each breath out, still holding the baseball bat, thinking about the way the bat jerked in my hand when the fatter and heavier end hit the robber on his fucking head.

He's sort of all in an upright pile on the floor, like a MagicJoints puppet suddenly out of battery power, so I push him over so he's like lying down, and he's still going 'geeerrrrrgggggghhhh' and everything, and I goes through his pockets, still going 'hergh, hergh', trying to catch some breath and calm down. I was calm for the hitting, but now the surges of all the biochemicals are giving me the shakes and thumping and my hands are shaky-shaky trembles, out of control.

Inside his coat it's warm – nasty other-person warmth. Putting my hand in there feels all intimate and weird. I'm close to him, and I'm touching him. I dig into the pocket there and find his ID. I picks it out, delicate, as if he's going to wake up cos he feels he's getting fucking robbed, but it's shaking as it comes out of his overcoat, in my hand all quivery. I opens up the ID. As soon as it came out of his pocket I can see he's gov; there's the official crest on the wallet. And inside it tells which department: he's Security Department. He's got the same ID tagger that Brock wears. He's a fucking spy. Same as me.

He's gone quiet, and the blood that poured so fast to start with is slowing, just drooling out now. He's still breathing, his bottom lip vibrating with it, spraying little needle-spurts of his blood each time he breathes out, like a tiny hole in a hosepipe spraying the water out. It's going all over the place, the blood, all up the white woodwork from his mouth and pooling all over the fucking floor out of his head, his hair all gooed up in it.

I'm not sure what to do, so I goes to the bedroom and gets my emergency stash of boris. It's in the med-storage section by the autolight (latest model, from the German designers Wad).

Straight away I get stuck in, feeling that I need it – and deserve it – after everything what's happened. The happy feeling off the boris isn't the same as usual, instead there's like a panic feeling, with everything inside all revving in the wrong gear, the blood rushing around in there like down the water-splash ride at Starfucks. It's like I'm running and running when, in fact, I'm just sitting on the edge of my bed holding on to my knees and trying to breathe properly. I'm still going 'hergh, hergh' and the strangle in my throat is back, making me go 'ack, ack' again. I'm in a bad way, fucking totally freaking out. Maybe it's the fucking electric brain chip. I feel like I need to talk to someone, someone who'll calm me down and remind me that everything's OK and not as bad as it seems. Cos it seems fucking bad right now, what with me having caved a gov spy's skull in and him bleeding all over in the hall, and the fact that he had been sent to do my place over cos the gov are totally fucking after me cos they know I'm in with Fyodor, nicking stuff from the archives, and I'm their fucking brain experiment gone out of control.

I want to talk to Claire. She'd make it better. Just hearing her voice would make me feel like things aren't as bad as they seem, and that there's going to be a time when what's just happened will be well in the past and forgotten. But as I think about her, and about what's happening now being forgotten, I start to think thoughts I haven't had before. I start to think that all that's been happening since I got mixed up with Miskin and the department and Reg and his bombing and everything, all this is stuff that's not going to be forgotten. It's not like it's another night down at Starfucks, where one night you have threesome-sausage, another night you go for fours-up, and it goes on and on, night after night, until you forget which night was which, and it doesn't really matter anyway cos it's all just another night down Starfucks. All that's just filling time, all fucked off of the boris and laughing and doing it. It's not real, is it? If you can't remember much about it, it's not real. But all this Reg/Claire/Martin Martin stuff, which right now has resulted in a fellow spy probably bleeding to death in my pad, this isn't silly stuff that'll get forgotten. This is real big trouble. And suddenly I feel scared.

I stand up. Stars shoot through my brain and I hear crackles and fizzes like squibs. My hands are hot and moist. A breeze comes in through an open window and hurrs across my face, making me feel all the sweat shapes over my eyes, down in front of each ear, in the crease under my chin, the back of my neck. And still there are red water rapids spilling around inside me, through all the veins, pumping and pumping.

Suddenly, I hear another noise. This snaps me out of it. I go into the hall. The gov spy is still lying there, quiet. He hasn't moved. The blood has spread out and it's still and shiny, like a dark repulsive mirror. The front door is gaping wide open, and standing there, framed by the doorway, staring at the collapsed and bashed-up body of his pal, is another gov spy. His mouth is open, like he's trying to figure out what he's seeing. What he's seeing has made his legs turn to wood, and he just stands there. He sees me, and points at his mate. Then his other hand starts groping towards his coat, trying to tuck inside it. He's going for his heat. In a holster, hiding under his normal work clothes, which could fool you into thinking he was just some civil servant or business bloke, he'll have a hot piece of gov-issue metal, fully fucking loaded with flesh seekers, all ready to burrow into my brain like a lead maggot at high fucking velocity.

So I turn and run. Three paces gets me into the bedroom, another four at full stretch and full speed get me to the open window and I'm up on the ledge in one jump.

Even if I wanted to, I can't stop myself from falling. There's not enough of the ledge for me to stand on, and as soon as my heels hit it, it slips away from under me, like it's the building falling backwards away from me, not me launching out of the window of my twenty-nineth floor flat.

There is no pain. I close my eyes as the falling begins and I imagine that instead of me being the one thing in the universe that at that moment is going against the laws of nature, everything else is. So it's not me falling, but the rest of London falling away from me, and me just floating in mid-air, in the same spot. The rushing of the air in my face – coming so hard that it forces its way into my mouth, making it billow out like a flabby farting ballon – feels like the commotion caused by so much concrete moving around so fast, as if the city has a metal rod passing through it, like those footballers on the olden-days table games, and someone has just smacked their giant hand down on all of south London, and the whole place is tipping up.

The angle of the nation is adjusting itself to avoid me getting hurt. Big things are happening for Jensen Interceptor.

Twenty-nine

AT FIRST, I'm not sure where I'm at. I'm still; it's quiet. I am comfortable. I am on my back, surrounded by softness. I am in bed. A bed. Not my bed. A bed in a small room. Through my eyes, everything is smeared, greased over and needing a bottle of It's Greezy Auntie to clean itself up. I move my head from side to side, slowly, as if I think I can sweep the smear away by wiping my face on thin air. It doesn't really help. My head flops back into the pillow. I'm not very well. A bit fucking Uncle Bill. I'm trying to say something.

I hear a voice. I sort of recognise it, but, you know, it's no one I know, if you know what I mean.

'Who the fuck are you?' says the voice. I lift my head, I'm feeling well out of sorts, and there's a small commotion going on in my belly; it's a ploppy pit, like porridge boiling, or quicksand, like out of a jungle show, and it bubbles and rises up, making me gasp gas. 'Arp!'

'Jensen Interceptor,' I manage to say, answering the question that got asked, but feeling a full-on quease, like I might spew here. I can't see, I'm dizzy as fuck; it's taking all the effort there is inside me just to keep my head up and tell this person who I am.

'It's Jensen Interceptor,' says I again, and it feels like I'm trying to talk with my head in a bucket of mud. As well as these two words, there's dribble coming out my mouth. My head feels half-paralysed, like when they make your gob numb at the oralist.

My inquisitor, I can just make him out – he's a fuzzy shadow in the light coming from the window behind him – he is sat by my bedside. He's blurry around the edges and I have to squint to look at him. The light hurts.

'Well, that fucking clears that up, then,' says the black shape.

'Yes . . .' I say, but the effort is too much, and my lights go out again, and I'm into a blackness the likes of which I've never seen before.

I hear snoring. Loud, open-mouthed, wheezy fucking old-trampy snoring. It's only after I hear it for the third time that I realise it's me who's snoring, ripping my own blanket of sleepy silence. But it's a sick sleep I'm having. Sick in, like, a totally sick way, cos I know, even in my sleeping, where I have heard this voice before, and how it is that I have heard these very words before. I've heard it all cos I have been here before, and I have seen (or should I say Seen) all that has happened just now. I was standing in this very room, looking down on Martin Martin in his hospital bed when it happened. He'd just thrown his major wobbly at the TV studio; he'd gone all mental and shouted at the Jackson bloke and his granddaughter, the two stupids. I'd been there too, at the studio. I was floating above the audience of smelly olds; I'd seen Martin Martin collapse to the floor and spew blood; I'd watched Devlin Williams go all panicky nutbags and then stuff unconscious lolly-headed Martin Martin into his fast car; and I'd followed Devlin Williams' zoomy motor to the hospital, this hospital. I stood in the corner of this very room, and Devlin Williams saw me. He said, 'Who the fuck are you?' and Martin Martin said, 'It's Jensen Interceptor.'

In my sleepy sickness of bosh-headedness, the idea comes in like a tiny splinter of glowing diamond, sharp and bright and hard and piercing my brain with its rays of light:

I am Martin Martin.

As time passes, I get to feeling stronger. But I am not fully in control of the body of Martin Martin. I'm not used to the way it moves or its weight. Everything I try to make it do seems to require more puff and hardness than I've got to give. So my efforts to move around knacker me out, and I knock things over. Martin Martin's tongue is bigger than Jensen's and my mouth feels blocked up by it, and it's not only his tongue what's bigger than I'm used to, if you know what I mean. Not that Jensen's ever had any complaints in that department, mind you.

I am in a place I do not fully understand, where people speak in ways that sound difficult and strange, like they're putting it on for a history show. Nurses tend to me and witter on in peculiar voices, all like, 'Ooh, the state of the buzzes these days, took me ages to get in today,' and 'Did you see the prog on the teevee last night? That PM, eh? Har! har!', and rubbish like that, but their attention is kind. I gaze at them without talking, rolling MM's big tongue around in his mouth, and they continue their nursing and their wittering. Devlin Williams comes and goes. I hear him ask the nurses how long it'll be till he can take me out of here, and I hear the doctor, in her large-and-in-charge voice, tell Devlin Williams that there's nothing clinically wrong with me and that it's probably just overwork, stress, burning candles at both ends, nervous exhaustion, all I need is a good rest.

I can't tell you how long all this fucking stuff goes on for, cos I'm random, in and out of it, flickering on and off like a broken street light, flashing between darkness and light with an aching head, like it's been kicked in like a fucking football, and heavy, heavy limbs.

But during all this twilight of half-life and half-death, Martin Martin's life and the contents of his head are mine. I totally fucking know what Martin Martin has done, and I know what he will do. I know how he began, and I know how he will end. My knowledge of MM is all in, like, little fucking bits; some of it is proper thinking, memories and that, the rest of it feels like some sort of instinct, like a fucking tiger in the fucking jungle. I mean, it's not as if you go around thinking, 'I am who I am' all the time, is it? You just go on what seems right and natural, and that's who you are, just like a tiger or a monkey or a fucking marmoset. So I am, like, MM. I just am him, so all I have to do is, like, fucking be, yeah?

In my recovery sleep, I can see the kids at Martin Martin's school; they're all fucking calling him names like 'tosser' and 'Joey' and 'spaz' and fucking words like 'spacker' and 'nobber' and 'git', all because he's weirdy-woo and different, and I can feel his pain and loneliness about not having any little pals to run around with.

I can See how he came to be on the TV, after years of thinking he was just a mental case, good for nothing except working total shit jobs in petrol stations and pushing around metal baskets on wheels at huge food markets, trying to keep the voices in his head quiet.

I know how Devlin Williams came to find Martin Martin and offer him work on his show, where Martin Martin would contact the dead for money and fame. At first, he wanted none of it, but his basket-pushing life was total fucking shitbags and he wanted out. So he took the job on the TV and life got better, even though he never could keep a girl, cos the girls would freak out cos Martin Martin's special brain skills were always too much for them. When a girl put Martin Martin inside herself at sexy time, her head would fill with images she didn't want to have and so she would leave and never talk about it again.

Also, I feel the last few moments of Martin Martin's disaster show on the TV. He was doing his thing, looking around for someone dead to communicate with, someone who needed to say hello/goodbye to their mum and dad or their sister or husband. And that's when he bonded with Emile Henderson, who came out of the dark wet earth in France, and joined Martin Martin.

In my sicky dreams I am Martin Martin. And so I am also Emile Henderson. And I am also Jensen Interceptor. The three are together as one; Martin Martin, Emile Henderson and Jensen Interceptor.

Holy fucking fuck, eh?

Thirty

'LISTEN, MARTIN, what in the name of fuckeration has been going on?'

This is Devlin Williams talking to me. We're in his van with all the studio stuff in the back. His TV van. He got fed up in the hospital, me in bed all spoogle-brained, murmuring and gibbering, and made what he called an executive fucking decision to remove me. He took me out the hosp in a chair with wheels, shoved me in the back of his van, and now he's driving me through the streets of London, shouting at the traffic and people outside. He's like, 'You CYANT!' and 'Get out my FACKIN' WAY!' all the time. Me, I'm all wrapped up in a blanket, as flat out as can be managed on the back seat, between the front, where Devlin drives, and the back, where all the screens and that technical stuff for making shows is. My head is leaning against the window of the van, bonking against it every time Devlin drives over a bump. I'm fucking dizzy with it, and pukey too.

I keep looking up to the sky to see if there's anyone up there, floating around, looking down at us, following us. I wonder if some other Jensen Interceptor is up there, like I was up there before, zooming through the air and Seeing all this, while this Jensen Interceptor, who has become Martin Martin, is down here, all fucking wibbly-wobbly in the back of Devlin's tin van.

'Martin! Concentrate!' shouts Devlin. I haven't answered him from before, and he's getting adge. Proper adge seems to be Devlin's normal. But his voice comes to me sluggish. It's treacly and sounds unreal. I can see his eyes, all sleepless red round the edges, framed in the little mirror he keeps squinting at.

'Martin, I've kept quiet about what's been going on because I wanted you to get better. I didn't want to be bothering you after your collapse. Are you listening to me?' His eyes keep staring at me in his little mirror, but cos his head's facing forwards for the driving, I can't see his mouth move. It's like his googly eyes in the mirror are doing the talking.

I manage to sort of burp a sort of a 'yes' noise, to let him know that I am listening to his googly eyes, and so he carries on.

'I'm getting a lot of heat, Martin. The network wants to know why their expensive new production has been postponed, and they want to know when you'll be back at work. I keep telling them you just got a bit ill. That's right, isn't it Martin, you just got a bit ill, didn't you? Bad flu, or too much of the old sherbert, yeah?' The motor stops at some traffic lights and Devlin drums the steering wheel with the palms of his hands. He looks over his shoulder and smiles at me.

'Too many late nights? You just needed a good rest. That's it, eh?'

I don't say anything. I just look at him. The words he's saying stream into me really slow. He turns around and keeps talking, craning his neck to see if the light has changed from stop-red to go-green.

'Look, I understand, Martin, I really do. There's nothing I like more than a bit of charlie of a weekend.'

The lights change, and Devlin makes the motor move fast into the clear road ahead. 'But you've got to hold it together when you're at work, yeah? But never mind, no harm done and . . .'

I go 'Hmmm,' cos it's the only noise I can make.

Devlin stops talking. It's quiet, apart from the racing of the engine and the 'dip-dop, dip-dop' noise that comes every time Devlin turns off one road and on to another one.

There's a new tone in Devlin's voice when he speaks again. Like a bit frightened, and quieter than before.

'Listen, Martin, seriously . . . I just make telly programmes, yeah? You know the score, don't you? I make the telly programmes, I sell them to the network, I get money, I give you money, everyone's happy.'

He pauses again.

'You do what you do really well. When we did our first show together and I watched you doing your psychic stuff I thought to myself, 'Now there's a showman; he could be a star." I liked the way you were with all them old cretins you spoke to. It seemed like you really were communicating with their dead ma or whatever. You gave 'em just enough to make them believe in you. And they went away happy, yeah?' Devlin is cut off cos he has to stop all of a sudden. Someone must have pulled out in front of him.

'YOU FACKIN' CYANT!' he shouts, and I'm thrown forward against the front seats as the van stops and goes 'beeeeeeep!' really loud. People in the street look around. One of them catches my eye and looks shocked. I think it's the dribbling.

'Nobhead!' shouts Devlin, and we manoeuvre the motor past whatever it was that made him fat-welly his brakes.

'But I never said I believed in it,' Devlin carries on. He's all shrugs and waving his left hand around as he drives on. 'I never said I never believed in it neither. The audience believed in it, and that was good enough for me. You knew that, didn't you? It was showbiz, yeah? But with an edge. Do you get my point?'

'No,' I says, cos I don't. I'm feeling worse, dizzy and sick with all the jerking around in the back of this van. I keep eyeing the sky, still on the lookout for Flying Jensen, cos I'm hoping there's someone up there who's looking out for me. But there's nothing up there. Just sky and clouds and the long thin spews that come out of the arse-end of jet airplanes.

'What I mean, Martin,' pipes up Devlin again, 'is, well, is it real? All your psychic stuff? Is that real? Because I'm not sure any more. I thought I knew what it was all about, but I'm not . . . I just don't know.' Devlin stops talking again. There's something on his mind. Then he comes out with it: 'What happened in the studio, Martin? What was all that shouting about? It didn't sound like you at all. That's not how you do your thing, is it? And what did I see in the hospital room yesterday? You knew, didn't you? I saw something, someone, and you knew who it was, didn't you? You said his name. Then he disappeared. He just disappeared, Martin. Like a fucking . . . ghost.'

'Jensen Interceptor,' says I, and with a smile too, even though I'm all head spinning and gut rumbling, and with MM's horrible big tongue in my head.

'That's it! Jensen Interceptor! That's what you said!' Devlin's excited.

'What the fuck happened at the studio, Martin? What's been going on? What was all that guff about the war? Who's Jensen Interceptor?'

Poor old Devlin. Always the panicking. Thinks he's all in control, but he's got no idea. Not even half an idea. He thought MM was just showbiz, like a magic trick done for kiddies.

'Martin, I've got to know, are you for real? Cos there's some very strange things happening and I'm feeling a little bit nervous, and I don't like it.'

'For real,' says I, with a nod. Still no Flying Jensen up above.

'Prove it,' says Devlin, staring at me in his little mirror. 'Tell me something that only I could know.'

'You're forty-two years old,' says I.

'Thirty-five,' says Devlin, with a little wag of his finger, telling off.

'Forty-two,' I repeat, cos I know I'm right and that Devlin Williams is lying.

I can See everything I need to See about Devlin Williams. There he is: I See him when he was a tasty teenager, muscles and tight T-shirt, wanting to kill his dad, cos his dad's an old drunkie and gets punchy when he's all boozed off his knackers, thumps his wife and his kids. He bashes them around when he gets back from the pub, so they are all totally scared of him all the time. The way he growls at them in the mornings with his bad head; the way he freaks them by doing weird shit, like eating cat food out of a tin with a fork – horrible. They totally fucking hate him, but they've never done nothing about it. They never even talked about it. They're too scared to even talk about it, almost like they think he has special powers. He's got no special powers. He's just a thick bully.

Devlin's poor old mum, always worried, went first. She died of the cancer and Devlin was so angry about it that he wanted to kill his old drunkie dad, who got more punchy and drunkie as his wife got more ill and thin and in pain and dying. Devlin thought his dad should have got the cancer stuff choking his throat up, not his poor old mum. And so one day, after his mum went in the ground to be seen no more, in a right old proper rage, Devlin Williams smacks his dad in the chops at the breakfast table. One punch. Just like that. No warning. He never said nothing like, 'I'm going to smack you one in the chops now, you old fuck, for what you did to me and Mum and Sis.' He was just sitting there in his old quiet rage, not scoffing his brekky, glaring, staring down at the table.

The old drunkie dad, always miserable since his wife copped it, even though he hit her and totally fucking monstered her while she was alive, he took this punch in his face like he'd been expecting it. He was thick and horrible, but not so thick that he didn't know somewhere deep in his slow fucking head that his big son hated him and that one day he'd get back what he'd given out for all those years. The thwack that Devlin gave his dad put him off his chair and on to the floor, and he took his breakfast with him – splashy milky-cornflakes mess all over.

But the dad had nothing to give back no more. The dad was all tired and old and had had enough. No more punches to dish out to his angry boy, so he lay there all bloody and tired and old and fucked and said nothing and did nothing. Devlin Williams walked out the house and he went to London and forgot all about his punchy old dad and his mum what died from the cancer in the throat. He left it behind and he became a new boy in London.

His punchy drunkie old dad lived another five years, but Devlin never spoke to him again, and when his old punchy dad's liver rotted inside his guts and finally did for him, Devlin never went to his funeral neither. He just got drunk on the night he found out his dad was dead, and made all his mates uncomfortable about it cos it was like he was celebrating, but drunk and angry celebrating, like he was more angry than he'd ever been.

All this I See, just lying there, propped up a bit in the back of Devlin's studio-on-wheels. I lean forward, holding on to the back of Devlin's seat to help pull me up. I don't have much fucking strength, I'm still dizzed and stomachy, feeling MM's nausea.

'You popped your dad in the face over breakfast,' I says into Devlin's ear, and I fall back, gasping with the effort. I close my eyes. The tyres squeal, the motor makes a violent lurch and we stop. The motor just sits there with me and him in it. No one around. No one sees.

Devlin says 'Fuck,' quiet and whispery.

Then he starts the engine and we're off again. He doesn't say anything else for the rest of the journey, and he drives real careful too, which suits me.

*

'A thousand channels, all of it cack.'

This is Devlin Williams again. We got back to his house in one piece and we're looking at the TV in his house. It's a house like Reg's, only bigger and nicer and more new. I'm still not saying too much, cos it's still tricky getting control over Martin Martin's body, and anyway, there's not much point in talking, cos I know where we're headed. It's like a fucking chain reaction, popping and fizzing, and I need to pop and fizz along with it. Mind you, the only thing popping and fizzing is MM's guts, worse than when I yagged up the bolly naze all that time ago, when I first met Claire and the little Italian.

Devlin's holding a remote control for his TV, and the channels go by – flick, flick, flick, flick – and he's saying that all of it is rubbish. It's only him that can make TV progs worth watching, he's saying. He's in way over his head and is going a bit mental. I told him something only he knew. And he knew it was only him that knew. All the others involved – Mum, Dad, Sis – they're all gone, in that order. He's never told no one. He knows that. It's his big secret. A fucking proper one.

Not only that, he saw Jensen in the hospital room. He totally saw a ghost from the future, so half his circuits are burnt-out. He'll believe anything. So now he's on instinct, and he just wants to save himself and his money. MM is Devlin's boy, so he's trying to look after him. But he doesn't know that MM is not exactly MM any more.

But he does know that MM has got some big skill that he doesn't understand, and he knows that he can sell that skill, that the people who make the TV progs will love it, and that millions of people will watch. Devlin might be working with only half a brain, the other half blown by seeing Jensen Future Ghost, and by seeing Emile slip into the proceedings in the studio, and by the little slice of secret Devlin info I gave him, but the half of his brain that's left is the half that can get things done. He can make deals, and he can put shit together. He can make us all a lot of cash, he says. This little orphan boy – a bit like me actually, and a bit like MM, and a bit like Emile, whose mum got blown up in their house while he was in France in the big war – he's trying to make everything OK for himself with money. I haven't got the heart to tell him he'll never get to spend any.

I'm still feeling well dodgepot, even though I'm not bad enough for the hospital any more. But Devlin's in a hurry to sort everything out and get his show back on the road.

'Gotta get the show back on the road, eh, Martin?' he keeps saying.

While I lounge on Devlin's comfy old-skool seater, all wrapped in a blanket with choccies and a mug of tea, Devlin runs about the house. He's chit-chatting like buggery on the little phone thing that he carries around with him, and it's ringing all the time, trilling out piercy horrid little tunes, which make me jump every time. He's sorting shit out, boasting and bullshitting about MM, pulling off deals with wankers and fucks and putting together his big plan. He's not wasting any time.

'We're going to get you on *The Barbara James Show,* prime time, mainstream, not the poxy cable rubbish we were doing before,' he rants at me in between phone calls. He's marching up and down, getting in the way of the TV so I can't see the shows. 'By the end of the weekend, we're going to have landed you the biggest fucking deal in TV history, and you, my strange friend, will be a proper superstar.'

I say nothing, of course. I just let it happen. I just have to wait for the bullet to hit Devlin.

'Next year,' Devlin says, pointing at me with his eyes popping out of his head, a bit deranged-looking, 'you'll be doing a show a day in Vegas for a million spuds a pop. You are going to be fucking huge. You are going to . . . Change. The. Fucking. World.' He says this with the sound of wonder in his voice, like he's realising it as he says it. Then his phone rings again, and he claps it to his lughole and he's all like, 'Peter, Peter, give me a fucking break! I can't hire a pot to piss in for 10K. It's got to be 40. I fucking need 40!' and all that. Actually, he's a fucking cool bloke is Devlin Williams. Shame about the bullet ending him in his, like, prime. I know he's still pumping off his money gland, thinking about how much of it he's going to stick in his pockets after he makes MM a star in Vegas, but he can't help it. That's what he does, it's how he blots out his dead dad and his dead mum and his dead sis.

Underneath that, he is the one looking after MM. There was no other fucker worried about poor old MM when he was in the hospital. He might have been proper fucked up for all anyone knew. But no one gave a shit about MM being in the hosp, cos MM didn't have no fucking mates, not even a stupid tosspot he never really liked but hung around with anyway, like fucking Fyodor. No one liked MM. He freaked them all out in the end. But not Devlin Williams. Devlin stuck with MM and brought grapes into the hosp like a normal mate's s'posed to. So fucking Devlin's OK by me. Even if I do know his game.

*

The day after the day before. Me just twenty-four hours out of the hosp, but feeling better and able to move MM's big old body around without knocking stuff over so much. I'm burping less and have spent all day listening to Devlin Williams getting into double-frantic mode. His little phoney thing is biddley-biddley all day long and he's cutting off all his conversations fast, just a few words before he's pressing the red button, already thinking about the next thing. He's total adge cos he's managed to get me invited on to a show on his TV. It's *The Barbara James Show*. Every time he says her name it comes out, like, with a golden glow around it. He obviously thinks she's the bollocks and totally loves her. She's just a person on the TV, but she's important and the show goes out to all the TV machines in the country as it's being made. When she says something, the people hear it at the same time. It's 'live', which, I suppose, means it's not dead. And this is important, says Devlin, cos it means that if I tell her about something I can See and then it all comes true, then the whole nation will know that I am what I say am, and they will follow me anywhere, give me everything they've got just to hear me say things. And, Devlin says, ten per cent of everything is a fuck of a lot of moolah.

So he's on the phoney about the motor to take us from here to the studio where they make *The Barbara James Show*, about the time we have to be there, about the fucking fruit and sandwiches that'll be there for us, about the money. And he's telling everyone who'll listen that they're going to be blown away by MM and what he's able to tell you.

'It'll be the most amazing thing you'll ever see,' he keeps saying. He's calling all his mates, all his half-famous pals and powerful chums who write for papers and mags and that, and he's telling them not to miss MM on the TV with Barbara James. He talks to Jimmy, who's Mr Fucking Showbiz at Sky; that twat Freddie at ITN; Joolz at AP; Marcus at the *Times* colour sup; Sally at the *Guardian*, who knows Peter at the *Observer*, who is fucking Adrian, who writes for Australian *Rolling Stone*. Jimmy Mr Fucking Showbiz from Sky wants to do an interview there and then, but Devlin says no.

I'm ready for it. I know what to do. There's kind of no choice now. Devlin Williams has no choice in what he's doing, and he can't change what's coming to him. He can't stop that bullet. It's already got his name on it, it may as well be engraved into its shiny fucking case, even though the bloke who's going to be doing the shooting doesn't even know it yet.

Thirty-one

'DON'T FUCK this up, Martin.'

Shiny lights are bright on Barbara James' face and she's looking good. She's out there, about to talk to her crowd of Friday-night idiots, and they're all beaming, excited about being so near to where all the TV action is, so close to famous Babs they can sniff her and see the lines around her eyes. Me and Devlin are by the side of the stage, looking out to where Babs is stood talking into the camera and saying hello to the audience at home.

Devlin's giddy with it. He's been on the outside of the big-time scene for too many years now, and this is where he's always wanted to be, on the inside, where the big boys and girls make their TV, not the sort of shit TV Devlin knocks out. He knows it. And he doesn't want tonight going wrong, so he's telling me not to fuck it up.

'Good evening, and you're very welcome,' says Babs to the cameras and the crowd.

'She always says that,' Devlin hisses in my ear. I can hear the smile in his voice. 'It'll be carved on her fucking gravestone,' and he chuckles. He's loving it. 'She's bigger than Parky,' he says, like he wants to kiss her where it tickles.

'Tonight,' says Babs, smiling at a camera, 'my guests include explorer and television-documentary maker Ralph Jellings, just back from an arduous expedition to the South Pole, where he lost three toes to frostbite.' Here, the crowd of eager stupids clap, but only cos a bloke who works for the show starts clapping his hands above his head behind the cameras, so the TV audience can't see. The audience is waiting to hear the next famous person Babs is going to introduce.

They're a bit disappointed with the explorer bloke with his manky old feet.

'Also on the show is the leader of what he claims will be a new force in British politics, the Democratic Union Party, Sir Geoffrey Perkins.' The bloke clapping his hands above his head puts his whole body into trying to get the crowd excited, but they can't really be arsed to get stuck in and so there's just a sort of embarrassed slippy-slappy noise. They're right to not be arsed too, cos I saw him earlier, and he's a dandruffy old twat with hair coming out of his nose who hates foreigners. Proper dimwit.

'We have the latest indie sensations from New York playing live, Man, Controller of the Universe.' There's a bit more enthusiasm for them. Saw them earlier too. Hairies boshing baggies of boz or some-such in the bogs. Some things never change, then.

'But first, may I introduce someone whom we're assured has some truly amazing powers: Mr Martin Martin . . .'

Devlin says, 'Right, this is it, on you go. Good luck!' And he shoves me towards the stage. The shove puts me slightly off balance as I start walking. I'm still trying to get it together when the lights hit me, like the sun bashing your eyeballs when you throw open the curtains at midday after a night on the fuck at Starfucks – harsh. I can just see the clappy bloke totally going for it, trying to get them up for a bit of MM action, even though most of them haven't got a clue who MM is. I'm a bit unsteady on MM's legs from the shove, but I manage to get on course and make for the sofa that I'm supposed to sit on. As I approach, Babs is looking at me, welcoming. Her face is fixed in a big smiley, but I can see in her eyes that she's worried.

I sit down, and I stare out into the darkness beyond the dazzling lights. I squint, but I can't see nothing. I hear a few gigglies out there, though, so I gives them a big smile, just like Babs, and just like Devlin told me to. I've never been on a show before. So far, it's a good laugh.

'So tell me,' says poor old Babs, and I can feel her thinking about her career in the back of her mind, about how she trained to be a jour-nalist, serious and that, and how she thinks all this TV shit-celeb rubbish is below her – especially the shit celeb in front of her now, who she thinks is just some billshitter nob off a crappy little TV prog – but how she thinks that the money's too good to walk away from it, 'you claim to have a very special gift, don't you?' She makes it sound like she's interested. She's a professional.

'That's right, Barbara,' says I, just like Devlin told me. 'Say her name,' he kept telling me before we even got here, 'make it look as if you two know each other.' So far, it's going fucking great, according to plan and everything.

'You claim that you can contact people who have died, is that right?' says Babs.

'That's right, Barbara,' I says, and there's some more little gigglies and a couple of coughs from beyond the hot, hot lights. I look out at the audience, still dark behind the dazzle, and they murmur like the sound of a moaning wind building up. There's a bit of a moaning wind building up in my downstairs too. I still haven't got full control of MM's groany innards and they're starting to react to all the tension of being live on the TV.

'And how does this gift manifest itself? How does it work?' asks Babs, ignoring the quiet but building babble from the audience.

'It manifests itself by me seeing and hearing things in my head what no one else can hear. I just sort of see what's what,' I reply.

'And how old were you when you first realised you had this gift?' says Babs.

'I first realised I had this gift,' I says, repeating the question like Devlin told me to if I'm not sure how to answer it, 'when I was twelve.' Then I remember that Devlin said I should use her name as much as possible, so I says 'Barbara' again, but she was just about to start talking when I says it, and her mouth was already open, and cos of the gassy trouble brewing downstairs, it sort of comes out like 'Burp-ara'. Poor old Babs. She can't help it, she reacts to my little escape of wind, just a bit, but enough to make the audience even more squirmy and freaked than they already are. They heard the belch too. I can feel there's all sweat starting to drip-drip down my head and gathering above my top lip. I'm trying to smile, reassuring, but I think it might be looking like a mad grin, like you'd see on some boozy monghead who's about to piss his pants. Babs is looking like she wants it hurried up and over as soon as. So she cuts to it:

'Well, we've been told that you're really quite something when you're on form. Obviously, many people won't believe a word of it,' she looks out at the audience and gives them a little smile, and they burble some more, this time a happier noise, glad that Babs has taken control.

'It all seems a bit too much like a silly old Victorian parlour game – faked photographs of fairies at the bottom of the garden, ectoplasm and seances,' she says. 'Can you convince us here and now, on live television, that you really can communicate with the dead, and that they tell you things the rest of us don't know about? Will you give us a demonstration?' Babs looks amused, sly, as if she knows I'm about to make a fool of myself in front of all her audience, who are now like her pals, all waiting for MM to splutter and go red with all his imagined stupidness of dead people talking to him.

'Yes, Babs, I'd be delighted,' I say, another thing Devlin told me to say. But I don't know what my demonstration is going to be until it's coming out my mouth:

'There is a man, he is in charge of a very big business, and he has been telling some very big lies. It's all going tits up.'

'Oh come now!' says Babs, almost laughing, and making her audience all let loose with their wet laughter, 'that's not much of an insight, is it? You could be talking about anyone!'

I keep going, I ignore the laughing and the whispery 'this Martin Martin is just a twat'-type stuff that's going on in the audience. In my head, I can see the man I'm talking about. I can, like, totally fucking See him, yeah? He is drinking glasses of golden booze and retching – 'ack!' – with every slug he puts down his gob. It's the same hot booze I drank with the eel trampy. He's drinking, angry and desperate. He knows he can't hold off what's about to happen. He's about to get rumbled big time, him and his lot of crooked bosses and politicians, all lying and bullshitting so they can keep the huge company going when it's actually shit-out of ideas and money, fucked on its arse. The man is sitting in a motor – a big one, leather seats, well expensive – drinking his burning booze. The motor is parked high up on a road where there's nothing. No lights, no other motors, just sheep and grass and dark. The only light around is the glow coming from the controls of the motor, blue like ghosts. He is far away from London, far away from anywhere.

It is a lonely place with giant lakes. The man is crying and banging his head on the steering wheel. There's music coming out of speakers in the motor – a big orchestra playing moody music that fits with the miles and miles of hills and the straggly little trees hanging on to the ground, being blown sideways by the wind. There's a tube poking in his window, and there's all tape around it, sealing it. The tube snakes droopy out of the window and round the back of his big, smart motor. The other end of it is stuck on the exhaust pipe. The motor is running. His name is . . .

I look up at Babs. She's looking at me, scared now. I'm not sure if I've been talking out loud or what. Maybe I have. The whole studio is quiet now, as quiet as up there on the hills where the man is, where the man is killing himself.

'His name is Billings. Steven Billings. Sir Steven Billings,' I say. Babs looks like she's had a whack on the bonce. Her mouth opens and shuts but no words come out.

'There's more,' I say, and this time I just come right out with it. 'That little girl who's missing –'

'No,' says Babs, slowly, like she's having a bad dream where nothing can stop what's happening from happening (and she's right, nothing can stop what's happening from happening – it really is happening, and as soon as it's started happening, it's already happened).

'She's dead. A man killed her. Arthur Penroody. 38 Pilmer House, Neckinger Estate, London, SE16. She's still there. He's still there.'

I can See Penroody in his little hovel. Cracks in the windows and curtains closed for years. Dirty, dirty man. Inside his head is like total fucking scrambled-eggs mush, with dreams and reality mixing all the time so he can't tell which is which. He's watching his TV, but not this, he's not watching MM on the TV telling everyone that he killed that little girl. Even if he was watching MM on the TV with Babs, he wouldn't have noticed, cos in his head is all mess and shouting all the time, put there by the man that did him when he was a kiddy, just after the big war, the same big war when Emile got his head spaded in by Jackson.

'You cheap bastard.' This is Bab's voice, angry. There is shouting in the audience now. Babs has stood up. She pulls her microphone wires and bits of equipment stuff off her and throws it all on the floor and walks away, fast. There's more noise out beyond the dazzle, where the audience are. I can hear more angry voices, men, shouting. There's the clattering of seats being pushed back and feet stomping. The clappy bloke from earlier steps out on to the stage and starts trying to calm things down, asking people to stay where they are, that transmission has been cut, that everything's OK and not to make it worse by panicking or reacting, but there's some bruiser blokes wanting to do some damage to poor old MM. Just cos he told them the truth, they're out to kick his fucking head in.

I stand up, and right next to me is Devlin Williams. He's putting his arms around my shoulder and is pulling me away from the slowly advancing mental boot boys.

'Fucking hell, Martin,' he goes, 'isn't this all a bit familiar?' and he's starting to run, still holding me around the shoulders, making me scarper with him. We bump past shocked-looking people from the programme, who all stare at us as we run. They're like statues, caught up in the action of everything what's going on and finding that there's nothing they can do except look. They can't believe it. They're like Babs, stuck in the bad dream where they're all paralysed while bad stuff goes on around them. Devlin keeps pushing and pulling me, and we knock things over as we run down a corridor out the back of the studio, heading towards the emergency exit. A trolley with plates of sand-wiches goes over and smashes on the floor, sharp little bits of plate flying up around our feet as we go. When we get to the emergency exit at the end of the corridor, Devlin boots the metal bar and two doors burst open and bash against the walls.

The air is cold, we're out in the car park. Devlin, still hanging on to me – my legs all floppy and trying to run in time with his – is pointing some little gizmo thing at his motor. He presses a button, and his van goes 'woop! woop!' and its orange lights flash. He opens the back door of the van and shoves me in. I fall in, all sprawly in the back, where all the wires and screens and bits are. Devlin jumps into the driver's seater, starts the engine and, with all squealy wheels, he drives the van at top speed out of there. I roll about on the floor, all the equipment towering over me.

I can't help glancing out the window at the sky, but it's all dark up beyond the burning of the street lights, just like the darkness that was beyond the brighty-white dazzle of the lights in the studio. Even if there is a Jensen Interceptor up there, floating around above all the action, watching MM go through all the TV madness again, getting bundled into a motor by Devlin again, I can't see him. I can't See him neither.

I feel tired. I close my eyes. The van's rocking and lurching soothes me like a baby in a pram. The van's engine is screaming. Devlin is right giving it some fucking welly through the streets of London. I feel like something is about to happen. Something that I can't control. I'm hot and sweaty and I'm breathing fast, like I'm about to spew. I have a hotness in my brain. I clench my eyes shut to try to make it cool down, but it won't go away. The pressure is building up.

Devlin's phone rings. I try to stand up in the back of the van, which isn't easy. It's like being on a boat in a storm at sea, swaying from side to side. Devlin is trying to drive and talk on his phone at the same time.

'Jimmy! Yes mate . . . I know . . . I told you so . . . Spectacular . . . Really? *Really?*' Devlin closes his hand around the phone and looks at me.

'Is it Jimmy Mr Fucking Showbiz from Sky?' I ask.

'Yeah,' says Devlin. 'He says you were off the fucking dial back there, mate. Spectacular, he says. Wants an interview. Willing to pay good money for five minutes on the phone. Up for it?'

I shake my head.

'Jimmy says it's all kicking off at that paedo's house you talked about. It's turning into quite a story.'

I stare out of the window, ignoring him. There's a burning sensation in my head.

'Listen, Jimmy, I'll call you back,' says Devlin to Jimmy Mr Fucking Showbiz from Sky. When he cuts the phone off, it rings again. Devlin looks at the name that comes up on the screen and then takes the call. The conversation goes much like the one before.

'Hello, mate . . . Yeah . . . I know . . . I just heard . . . I don't know . . . I'll get back to you, yeah?' As soon as puts the phone down on the passenger seat, it rings again. This time he pulls over, and we spend half an hour parked at the side of the road, Devlin taking one call after another. Everyone is ringing about me. All his mates in the biz, everyone he's ever known, everyone he's ever given his number to, they're all calling. Nearly all of them work in TV or for the papers and they all want to talk to me. He says he'll call them back.

Eventually, he switches the phone off.

'Right, you,' he says to me, over his shoulder. 'Let's get home, and try to sort everything out. You've really fucking put the cat among the pigeons, you know. The police checked out that address where you said the kiddie was. Turns out what you said was right. It's turning pretty nasty over there. There's a mob outside the house, throwing stones. The police are there, but it might get out of hand.'

I think about the crowds outside Arthur Penroody's house: I can See them in my head. I feel an urge to be there.

'Let's go there,' I say.

'What? Why? Are you *mad*?' says Devlin.

'I want to go there. Come on. 38 Pilmer House, Neckinger Estate. I want to see what's happening.'

Devlin looks at me, and he knows he has to do as I say. He's slightly afraid of me now. He tut-tuts and shakes his head all the way there, driving carefully and muttering to himself.

When we get to the Neckinger Estate, we park on the side of the road. There are already seven vans like Devlin's parked along the road in front of us. They've all come to see the trouble. Further down the street, there is a crowd. Women with beefy arms crossed and geezers with bottles and hoods. There are kids on bicycles, hanging around the edge of the crowd, rocking their cycles backwards and forwards, laughing at all the commotion that's kicking off. They're excited. The whole crowd is excited, there's a crackle in the air, a buzz of total fucking nastiness about to blow up. A thin line of police separates the crowd from the house. The crowd is jeering and pushing and shoving, as if it's one big beast moaning and pushing against the bars of its cage, hoping that the bars will fall down and it will be able to escape and go on a rampage of revenge.

Around the crowd, there are little clusters of telly people, groups of four or five with a camera. All the cameramen are hunched over, squinting through the lens, pointing at any action they can find, or at a TV presenter who is talking into a microphone. The cameras have bright lights attached to them, and they flash whiteness in large pools, adding to the thrill and strangeness for the fucking hyped-up twats in the crowd. And all the vans are throbbing, their engines running, also bathed in white light. Thick wires run along the gutters. Up in the air, there's a helicopter. It's shining a huge light down on the crowd too. Devlin looks up.

'Fucking hell,' he says, 'it's the Sky chopper. I bet Jimmy's up there.' And he fishes out his mobile phone and dials a number.

'Jimmy?' says Devlin. 'Is that you up there in a fucking helicopter over the paedo's place? . . . You nutter! Yeah? . . . Really . . . Well, look . . . I'll ask, yeah, but I don't think you'll get any joy, not right now.'

Devlin asks me if I want to talk to Jimmy Mr Fucking Showbiz from Sky. I tell him no.

'Sorry mate,' says Devlin, and turns his phone off again.

Down on the ground there's an atmosphere like a carnival, or like when Sheeba Twosort made her appearance at the Surrey Quays Hollywood Bowl and the crowds were shoving to get a better view of her, and she was all bathed in the bright lights of the show people.

But this lot aren't here for Sheeba or any film star or pop star or anything like that. They're here cos of Arthur Penroody, the mad fucker who has killed a child. They want to break him into bits. There's the sound of smashing glass. Someone has thrown a bottle or a rock at the house, and it makes a hole in a window. The police trying to hold the crowds back look pale and nervous. The sound of sirens fills the night air, and the camera crews with their white lights all swing around to point at the police vans that are arriving, three of them, with metal grilles over their windscreens. Fucking, like, loads of coppers get out, dressed in helmets, holding long sticks and see-through shields. They look a bit like the copper/soldiers I Saw shoot the caff lady's man in the fucking head. They stand off to one side and stare at the mob, which stares back at them. Some of the coppers in helmets file around to join the ordinary, scared-looking coppers who are between the mob and the house. The tension cranks up another notch. It's all getting well fucking lairy. You can't see the faces of the new coppers. Their uniform makes them look like robots. They are tooled up and ready for some proper headkicking action. And so is the mob.

'Fucking hell,' Devlin keeps saying. When we arrived, he said it. When the bottle went through the window, he said it. And when the copper/soldiers arrived, he said it. Each time, he says it with more feeling.

'Fucking hell,' he says again. He can't take his eyes off the scene. He's even smiling.

'Let's go, Devlin,' I say. I've seen enough. I want to see something else now.

'OK,' says Devlin, and he starts the engine. 'If we stick around here, the van'll probably get smashed up. It's getting pretty bad out there. Let's go back to my place.'

'No,' I say.

'No?'

'No. I want to see the other man. The man in the car who is killing himself by the big lake.'

'Billings? The energy-company bloke? He's *killing* himself?' says Devlin.

'Yes. He's killing himself in a car near Lake Windermere,' I say. I've never been there. I don't know where it is. The words come out of my mouth without me thinking them up first.

Devlin's shoulders slump when I say Lake Windermere.

'Martin, do we have to? It's fucking miles away.' He looks at his watch and points at it. 'It'll take us fucking hours. Literally, I mean, it must be about 300 miles.'

I don't say anything. Devlin stops talking. He's just looking at me with his hand in the air, pointing at his watch. He gives up protesting, like I knew he would.

'We should call someone,' says Devlin. 'Let the local police know. Maybe they can get to him in time, stop him killing himself.'

'There's no point,' I say. 'He's already dead.'

'Why do you want to see him, then?'

'I don't know. We need to get out of London. We need to be somewhere we can't be found. Baaaarp!'

Devlin winces when I belch.

'There are some important things I have to do,' I say to Devlin.

Devlin starts the engine and we turn around in the road, leaving the mob to their night of fun.

'What? What do you have to do, Martin? Haven't you done enough?' says Devlin.

'I've not really got started, yet,' I say. I feel like I don't have to think any more. I don't have to worry about fucking nothing. I just have to act on instinct, follow the instructions that come out my fucking head, and everything will fucking happen like it's supposed to.

'Whatever you say, Martin,' he says.

'Yeah,' I say.

No one notices us leave.

Thirty-two

WE'RE SOON on the motorway, leaving the bright lights of old London town behind and heading off into the dark night along the orange-lit strip of tarmac. The only sounds are the whoosh of other motors passing us and the drone of our own engine.

'It's going to be a long night,' says Devlin as he pulls into a petrol station to buy fuel and food and drink. He gets out and puts fuel in the van and buys stuff from the shop. I watch him walk into the shop and wander about inside, picking up bits and pieces. When he gets back to the van, he plops a fucking huge great bag full of stuff to eat on the seat between us.

'Help yourself,' he says, and we pull out on to the motorway and drive and drive and drive. The white lines of the road keep coming until it's difficult to tell whether we're travelling along the road or if we're still and the road is moving under us.

After a couple of hours, the inside of the van is warm, and I'm feeling sleepy. Devlin hasn't said much since we stopped for petrol. He reaches for the van's radio and switches it on.

'I need something to keep me awake,' he says.

A man's voice, warm and rich and fruity, comes through the speakers in the van.

'It's midnight, and here are the news headlines. There is unrest in the streets of south London tonight, as crowds have gathered outside a house where it has been alleged the missing schoolgirl Celia Green has been murdered. Missiles have been thrown and riot police are trying to contain the disturbance. Our Home Affairs correspondent, David Reeve, is there now. David?'

Then David Reeve comes on the radio.

'Yes, Peter. Crowds began gathering here, in this quiet housing estate in south London, shortly after an extraordinary television broadcast earlier in the evening. A guest on the BBC's *The Barbara James Show*, a self-styled 'television psychic' known as Martin Martin, said, during a live interview, that a man living at this address was responsible for the abduction and, he claimed, murder of a child. Within half an hour of that broadcast, crowds began gathering outside the address Mr Martin had mentioned, and alarmed residents called the police. We now have something of a stand-off between a crowd of around 200 people and riot police. The police have effectively sealed off the entire area, and have been escorting forensic teams in and out of the house over the past two hours, which is fuelling rumours out here, as you can imagine.'

'What are the police telling you, David?' says the fruity voice.

'Not very much, Peter. What they will say is that they have arrested a sixty-three-year-old man and that he is currently being held at Tower Bridge police station, where he is helping police with their enquiries.'

'Are you able to confirm that this is in connection with the missing girl Celia Green?'

'Well, the police are remaining tight-lipped about that, but I can tell you that the coroner is in attendance at the address here in south London.'

'Thank you, David,' says the fruity voice, 'and we'll keep you updated with that story as it develops.'

Devlin leans over and turns the radio off.

'Maybe I don't need the radio on to keep me awake,' he says. 'Fucking hell, Martin. Looks like you were on the money, then.'

'Eh?' I says. 'What money?'

'I mean, you were right. What you said on Barbara's show. It was accurate.'

'Yeah,' I says. 'I know. Why else would I have said it?'

'So,' says Devlin, 'Lake Windermere. A bloke in a car? Dead, you say?'

'Yes.'

'The police will have found him before we get there. They'll have people out looking for him, now they know that what you said about the old paedo was true. And if not the police, the local media'll be out looking for him.'

'They haven't found him yet. They don't know he's killing himself. I didn't tell them that. I didn't tell them where he was, did I?'

We keep driving.

The sky is starting to get light when we pass Kendal. I direct Devlin. I don't know where we are, or where Billings is, but when we come to junctions, I just go 'Left' or 'Right' or 'Straight on'. The right way to turn is in my head when I need it. The monkey instinct straight out of my fucking brain, information ready for me when I need it. Devlin just obeys me, which is the right and proper thing for him to be doing.

Eventually we turn on to a small lane. We're high up. Ahead of us, on the left, is a picnic area.

'Left,' I say, when we arrive at the picnic area. We pull into the picnic area, and there is a motor parked there. A big posh green one. There's a tube attached to the exhaust pipe, and it runs around to the window.

'Fucking hell,' says Devlin.

He stops the engine and gets out of the van. I stay in the passenger seat and watch as Devlin walks over to the motor. He goes up to it slowly, as if it might explode if he makes any sudden movements. The windows are all steamed up, grey and solid. Devlin tugs at the driver's door handle. He makes a little jump backwards as he opens the door and loads of smoke comes out. Devlin starts wafting his hand around his face. He reaches inside and switches the engine off. Devlin straightens up and looks over at me.

'He's dead, all right,' he shouts across the picnic area.

I nod back at him and he comes back to the van. He gets into the driving seat. He brings the smell of the cold and the stinky car fumes in with him. He's shivering with the chill of the dawn and the freak-out of seeing a dead body.

'What now?' asks Devlin. Poor old Devlin. He's all messed in the head by what he's seen thanks to Martin Martin. He thought the world worked in one way, and now he's seeing that it works in another fucking way altogether, and none of it makes any sense to him any more. All he knows is that Martin Martin knows more about everything than he does.

'Let's get out of here,' I say. 'Find somewhere where we can sleep. Then I want to use all this stuff in the back. Can you make it work?'

'What, the OB gear?' asks Devlin.

'Yeah,' I say.

We drive for another half an hour, and find an isolated little nook in some trees, well off the main roads, and pull up. We are both tired, and almost as soon as Devlin switches the engine off, we are asleep. The sun is up, and the sound of birds all tweeting makes for a peaceful and relaxing slumber. There are no dreams.

When I wake up, Devlin isn't next to me in the driving seat; the engine is running and I hear voices in the back of the van. I can hear the clickety-click sound of typing too. Devlin has been tinkering with the screens and wires and knobs in the back of the OB van, and he has the TV going. I twist around in my seat so I can see the screen he is looking at.

'I've got the gear working. Check this out,' says Devlin. And he shows me the screen of the machine he's typing into.

'You've made news all over the world. Look at this, it's the CNN website.'

I can see a headline. It says:

'DID MAN PREDICT POWER CO. COLLAPSE AND CHILD MURDER ON UK TV?'

And there's a picture of MM off of the TV below it.

On one of the screens, there is the BBC. A man sits at a desk. He looks serious. Behind him is a piccie of MM, that is me, with the words 'PSYCHIC CHAOS' under it. The man is talking:

'Sir Steven Billings, CEO of the Oxxon Energy Corporation, was found dead in his car in Cumbria this morning. The car was parked near Lake Windermere. In the hours since his death was announced by police, the share value in Oxxon, the world's largest energy company, which controls oil pipes under the Caspian Sea and across the Middle East and employs more than 50,000 people worldwide, has plummeted.'

The TV bloke's voice is stern and down for that bit, but it changes for the next bit, he goes higher and sounds like he might even think it's funny, or like he's asking a really long question:

'This is a dramatic new twist to the story that has been dominating headlines overnight: Martin Martin, the television psychic who claimed on live television last night that he knew the whereabouts of the murdered schoolgirl Celia Green. Mr Martin, who is known for his cable-channel show, *Spectre vs Rector*, was on *The Barbara James Show* to promote his new series, *Martin Martin's on the Other Side*. But last night's broadcast fell into chaos when Mr Martin not only suggested that Sir Steven Billings had been involved in a systematic cover-up of Oxxon's accounting procedures, but gave the name and address of a man he said had killed the missing schoolgirl Celia Green.'

Devlin sighs and shakes his head. His leg is bouncing up and down as we watch the TV.

'David Reeve is there now. David?' says the BBC bloke.

On the TV, the pic of MM behind the newsreader is replaced by moving pics of a bloke holding a microphone to his mouth. It's David Reeve. He was there last night, talking on the radio too. He's standing outside the house where the madman killed the little girl. He's got his finger in his ear cos there is all sorts of racket and commotion going on. There's a fire truck there with blue lights spinning, and there are loads of people all shifting around, being held back by rozzer-coppers with their arms outstretched.

'Well, Jonathan,' says David, sort of shouting, 'extraordinary scenes here in south London. Police have set up a barrier around the house, effectively sealing off the entire street, and forensic teams have been in and out of the house all through the night. Angry crowds have been building up throughout the night and at about three in the morning it seems that a Molotov cocktail – or some other kind of improvised incendiary device – was thrown into the house by someone in the crowd. The flames spread very quickly. The fire brigade arrived, but their efforts were hampered by the angry crowd, who appeared to want the house to burn down. The house is now gutted, and tension remains high, both here and on the nearby Eveline Lowe Estate, where there have been sporadic outbursts of violence throughout the night.'

Back to the newsreader chap, Jonathan, in the studio, sitting at his desk, comfy in the studio, looking up at his mate Dave on the screen.

'And any news on the man police arrested last night?' he asks.

'Yes, Arthur Penroody was arrested here last night and taken to Tower Bridge police station, and he has since been charged with murder. The police also removed a body last night, and we have been told that this is, indeed, the body of Celia Green.'

In the background, behind shouting Dave or David, the crowd is shouting also. The police are having a hard time keeping it together. It's getting hairy there.

'Why did you have to mention a paedo?' says Devlin, not looking at me, but still staring at the screen. 'The power company bloke is one thing, but you didn't need to add the whole paedo thing, did you? I mean, it's impressive, but fucking hell, Martin. Paedos? What a shitstorm.' And he slowly shakes his head again. I say nothing, but keep staring at the TV and dunk my bix in my fizzy drink from the bag of goodies Devlin bought last night. I slurp it up.

Devlin jabs a button on the remote control and we're on another channel, looking at another bloke in another studio, who's in the middle of telling us about another load of trouble.

'. . . burned to the ground. And trouble is also simmering as queues build up outside petrol stations. Prices have started to rise in the wake of the news that the troubled energy company Oxxon is on the verge of collapse. Trading in its shares was suspended this morning, and employees turned up to work this morning to find themselves locked out of their buildings. Police have been called to the London and New York headquaters of the company, where disgruntled employees have been gathering and tempers are flaring. Oxxon was created eleven years ago and soon became one of the most successful energy companies in the world by trading futures in energy like any other share, until its gambles in international energy markets had become larger than the value of its core business. Oxxon employed over 20,000 people in more than forty countries –'

Click. Devlin changes channel again. There's a stupid in the street with a microphone being pushed in his face. His eyes are burning cos he's pissed off and excited that the telly has chosen him to talk to. There are more people behind him going 'Woourgh!' and 'Oi! Oi!' and jumping up and down trying to get themselves seen by the camera. They're pulling faces. Big men, and boys too. Some women, but not many. The stupid with the microphone being pushed in his face is saying:

'Stands to reason, yeah? It's disgusting what they do. We won't have it around here. We're showing them. If the government aren't doing nothing about it, then we will.' And then a big shout goes up, 'Yeah!', from the crowd and it makes the telly sound go distorto-crackly.

Click.

An American voice:

'. . . in England. He appeared on a live television chat show, where he told the nation that Sir Steven Billings, the CEO of Oxxon Energy, the biggest supplier of domestic electricity in the States and the largest oil company in the world, had been lying about his company's accounts. Billings was found dead in his car later that night. In the same broadcast, Martin Martin shocked viewers when he gave the name and address of a man he claimed had murdered a young girl Celia Green. The little girl had been missing for more than a week and the story had been dominating the news in England.'

Click.

'. . . leave the meringues to cool off and harden in the oven, because at this stage they are still rather sticky to the touch –'

Click.

'Only forty-nine ninety-nine –'

Click.

'Suicide of Sir Steven Billings –'

Click.

'. . . worried about the knock-on effect of this scandal? Will the economy go into free fall at the news that –'

Click.

'. . . protection of children. We have been let down by the agencies responsible for keeping tabs on these monsters –'

Click.

'. . . burning down of a mosque in Leicester. Ivan, are the police saying whether there is any connection between this and last night's broadcast?'

Click.

'. . . so who exactly is Martin Martin? James Western has this report on the mysterious man at the centre of the storm.'

Devlin doesn't flip the channel. He wants to see what they're saying about me and about him. There are pictures of Martin Martin on a TV show. The titles come up: *Spectre vs Rector*. Martin looks younger, a bit fucking surly, like he doesn't really want to be doing no TV progs, but here he is anyway. And over these pictures of MM's early TV days, James Western tells us what he has found out since MM became the most famous person in the world about twelve hours previous.

There's a noise outside, making it difficult to hear the TV. Devlin presses the remote control so the sound goes louder. The sound is above us now. It's a chop-chop-chop sound, a long deep noise, like 'burrrrrrrrrr'. It keeps getting louder and swirling around. Devlin pushes the volume up higher on the TV. Now the TV is really fucking loud:

'MARTIN MARTIN FIRST APPEARED ON TELEVISION AS A GUEST ON THE DAYTIME CABLE SHOW *SPECTRE VS RECTOR*. A SELF-STYLED 'PSYCHIC', MARTIN WOULD APPARENTLY CONTACT DEAD RELATIVES OR FRIENDS OF PARTICIPANTS IN THE SHOW PASSING ON ADVICE FROM 'THE OTHER SIDE'. HE WAS, PRESUMABLY, THE 'SPECTRE' PART OF THE PROGRAMME'S TITLE. THE 'RECTOR' WAS THE REVEREND DAVID WATTS, THE BAPTIST MINISTER OF THE HACKNEY MISSION, WHO WOULD GIVE ADVICE FROM A CHRISTIAN PERSPECTIVE. THE SHOW WAS JUST ONE OF THE MANY GIMMICKY PSYCHIC SHOWS BURIED IN THE DAYTIME SCHEDULES OF COUNTLESS SMALL CABLE CHANNELS.'

The TV is so loud that it's nearly drowning out the swirling chopping noise. Devlin doesn't seem to hear the noise outside, he's transfixed by what he's seeing. He's proud. His show is being talked about.

'*SPECTRE VS RECTOR* RAN FOR TWO SEASONS, AND WAS DUE TO BE REPLACED IN THE NEW AUTUMN SCHEDULES WITH A NEW SHOW FEATURING MARTIN MARTIN AS THE MAIN ATTRACTION. DURING THE FILMING OF A PILOT FOR THAT NEW SERIES, IT SEEMS THAT MARTIN MARTIN HAD SOME KIND OF SEIZURE AND VERBALLY ABUSED A

MEMBER OF THE AUDIENCE, ACCUSING HIM OF MURDER.
WE SPOKE TO A MRS GENTLE WHO WAS IN THE STUDIO
AUDIENCE THAT AFTERNOON –'

'Oh fuck,' says Devlin, 'here we go.'

On the TV there comes the face of an old lady: wrinkles, hat and
glasses.

'IT WAS TERRIBLE,' says the old, 'WE WAS THERE TO SEE
THE PSYCHIC, YOU KNOW, TO COMMUNICATE WITH THE
OTHER SIDE AND THEN THIS FELLER, HE'S SUDDENLY
USING TERRIBLE LANGUAGE AND SAYING THAT THIS
OTHER FELLER HAD MURDERED HIM, AND THEN HE
COLLAPSED AND WAS SICK AND SHOUTING. IT WAS
FRIGHTENING. IT SHOULDN'T BE ALLOWED, YOU KNOW.
YOU DON'T EXPECT THAT SORT OF THING, DO YOU? I
MEAN . . .'

Back to James Western:

'THE RECORDING ENDED WITH THE AUDIENCE
ESCAPING THE STUDIO EN MASSE AND MARTIN MARTIN
BEING RUSHED TO HOSPITAL BY HIS PRODUCER, DEVLIN
WILLIAMS. DEVLIN WILLIAMS HIMSELF IS NO STRANGER
TO CONTROVERSY, HAVING BEEN RESPONSIBLE FOR
MANY TELEVISION SHOWS, OFTEN ADDING UNEXPECTED
AND EXTREME TWISTS TO ESTABLISHED FORMATS AND
COMING UP WITH THE LIKES OF *ALONE*, A SHOW WHERE
ONE MAN WAS LOCKED IN A SMALL ROOM ON HIS OWN
FOR TWELVE WEEKS AND SUBJECTED TO PSYCHOLOG-
ICAL EXPERIMENTS IN A BID TO WIN £12,000; AND THE
QUICKLY CANCELLED *HOMELESS*, ANOTHER REALITY TV
SHOW WHERE TWELVE HOMELESS PEOPLE WERE PUT IN
A HOUSE TOGETHER. VIEWERS WERE INVITED TO VOTE
TO EJECT ONE HOUSEMATE A WEEK UNTIL A WINNER
EMERGED, WHO WOULD THEN BE GIVEN THE KEYS TO
THE HOUSE. THE SHOW WAS PULLED OFF THE AIR AFTER
ONLY TEN DAYS, WHEN THE BROADCASTING AUTHORITY,
OFCOM, RECEIVED OVER A THOUSAND COMPLAINTS
FOLLOWING AN ON-SCREEN FIGHT WHICH ONLY ENDED

WHEN A FIRE WAS STARTED AND THREATENED TO
ENGULF THE ENTIRE HOUSE.'

'He's making that sound worse than it was,' says Devlin, like he's
in a dream or a trance, still staring at the screen and sounding slightly
hurt, not really talking to me or anyone. Just saying it with his, like,
gob. He's still not hearing the bashing and whirring going on all around
us. It's like we're in the middle of a fucking massive storm, but outside
there's no rain or wind. It's a helicopter.

'Devlin,' I say. I want to tell him that there's a helicopter above us.

'Shh!' says Devlin. 'I want to see this.'

Up above, it's all thump-thump-thump, chop-chop-chop in the air;
great blades thwacking the sky, the noise of it coming in and out,
like when Bammer Rhymes stamps on his phasing machine and the
sound goes inside out and whooshes around your head – like the
biggest hit of boz you ever did – bursting your brain, and the crowd
go fucking mental and cheer and stamp and shout and throw themselves around.

Thump-thump-thump!

'WE GATHER THAT MARTIN MARTIN SPENT SEVERAL
DAYS IN A LONDON HOSPITAL RECUPERATING, AND WAS
DISCHARGED SOMETIME LAST WEEK. DEVLIN WILLIAMS
THEN CONTACTED *THE BARBARA JAMES SHOW* AND
SECURED A BOOKING FOR HIM TO APPEAR LAST NIGHT.
A SPOKESMAN FOR THE SHOW SAYS THAT THEY DID NOT
KNOW IN ADVANCE WHAT MARTIN MARTIN WAS PLAN-
NING TO DO, OTHER THAN MAKE SOME PSYCHIC PREDIC-
TION OF A GENERAL NATURE. THEY SAY THAT THEY HAD
SEEN PREVIOUS SHOWS FEATURING MARTIN MARTIN AND
CONSIDERED 'HIS ACT', AS THEY DESCRIBE IT, TO BE A
HARMLESS BIT OF FUN. THEY COULD NOT HAVE KNOWN,
THE SPOKESMAN WENT ON, WHAT MARTIN MARTIN WAS
INTENDING TO SAY. BARBARA JAMES HERSELF IS NOT
CURRENTLY AVAILABLE FOR COMMENT, AND THE BBC
HAVE ANNOUNCED AN URGENT REVIEW INTO GUIDE-
LINES FOR LIVE PROGRAMMING IN THE FUTURE.'

Devlin, he's hypnotised by it all. He flicks the channel again. This time there's a shaky view of the tops of some trees. Through the trees, you can just glimpse the top of a van with all aerials on top of it.

'Hold on,' says Devlin, 'that's us!' and he stands up too fast and bonks his head on the roof of the van. He leans across to the front of the van, winds down a window and sticks his head out. The chopping of the chopper suddenly booms into the van, together with a blast of cold air. I look at the TV and the camera up in the helicopter switches to its telephoto lens, zooming in fast on the window where Devlin is leaning out. I can see him on the TV, looking up at the camera in the helicopter, and the voice on the TV shouts:

'THERE'S SOMEONE AT THE WINDOW, IT IS EITHER DEVLIN WILLIAMS OR MARTIN MARTIN HIMSELF. IT'S A BIT DIFFICULT TO MAKE OUT THE FEATURES FROM UP HERE, BUT I THINK THAT'S DEVLIN WILLIAMS. YES, YES IT IS. DEVLIN WILLIAMS HAS APPEARED AT THE WINDOW OF THE VAN.'

Devlin comes back inside and closes the window, shutting out some of the intense chopping.

'Fucking hell,' he says. 'It's the boys from Sky in their fucking helicopter.'

'Is it Jimmy Mr Fucking Showbiz from Sky?' I ask.

'Probably,' says Devlin.

'Call him,' I say. 'Tell him I'll talk to him.'

Devlin switches on his mobile phone. It immediately starts beeping. He ignores the beeping and dials a number.

'Jimmy?' says Devlin when he gets through. 'Is that you? Are you up there in that fucking helicopter? OK . . . yeah . . . well, the phone's been switched off. I did tell you he was something special, didn't I? Listen. I can give you an exclusive. Martin says he wants to talk. I'll pass you over.'

Devlin hands me the phone. I tell Devlin to start driving. As the engine starts, I put the little phone thing to my ear.

'Hello? Hello?' I hear.

'Is that Jimmy Mr Fucking Showbiz from Sky?' I say.

'Er, ha ha, yes, this is Jimmy. You're live on air Mr Martin.'

The van starts moving. I can see we are moving on the screens in the back of the van. We turn left on to the road.

'Where to, Martin?' Devlin shouts over his shoulder as we pick up speed. I cover the phone with my hand.

'Head back to London,' I say.

'Oh fucking hell,' says Devlin under his breath, and, on the TV in front of me, I watch the van come to a halt and reverse back down the road into the picnic area, and then turn right on to the road. The heli-copter follows us.

'Listen to me, Jimmy Mr Fucking Showbiz from Sky,' I say, and I hear my own voice come out of the TV, all double slap-back echo. I pick up the remote and shut off the sound. I lean back in my seat in the back of the van and close my eyes. Images start to swell up in the darkness and there's that deep tired feeling coming over me. The sound of the van's engine and the chop-chop-chop of the helicopter above us all swirl together and mush around. I press the phone to my head, lodging it there with my shoulder. Then I reach out and start typing on the keyboard of the internet machine.

I speak and I type, my eyes are closed.

I start to See things.

I See. . .

. . . a man with a machete; he is cutting into the flesh of another man. There is blood pouring from him. There are hundreds who are being killed with machetes all around. A red stream runs from the piles of slashed corpses and flies are settling on the dead men already. The man I See is named Bagosora.

. . . a woman named Jones, Mathilda Jones, she is stealing money from an old person in a care home in Birmingham. She helps herself from a drawer in the old woman's bedside cabinet. She steals from many of the old people who trust her.

. . . Jane Curtis has a tube of chocolate sweets, the chocolates are covered in a shell of coloured sugar. She is wondering how many sweets there are in the tube and what colours they are; there are twelve red ones, ten blue ones, six orange ones, ten brown ones, five green ones and five yellow ones.

. . . Anue Amorim of Brazil; your grandfather was a Nazi war criminal. Your father knew this.

. . . Peter Johnson, married to Joanne Davis, 34 Staymer Street, Bournemouth. Your wife is going to leave you.

. . . next Saturday's Championship football results will be Barnsley nil, Ipswich Town one; Coventry City two, Burnley one; Charlton Athletic two, Crystal Palace three, Hull City nil, Queen's Park Rangers nil; Norwich City two, Sheffield Wednesday one; Preston North End nil, Leicester City three; Sheffield United two, Cardiff City nil; Southampton nil, Stoke City two; Watford Town one, Wolverhampton Wanderers three.

. . . a child named Patrica in Akron, Ohio, is choking on a diamond ring.

. . . lightning strikes near a lake in Buffalo, New York. It hits a small shack, which burns. No one is hurt, but three naked people, two female, one male, see it.

. . . there is a fault at a factory in Taiwan producing batteries for computers. They will make and distribute over a million batteries before the fault is discovered.

. . . a bomb is about to explode in the Turkish town of Marmaris.

I wake up and I'm on the floor of the van. It's still moving. I can still hear the chop-chop-chop above us. My head is hot and sore from where the phone was pressed against it. The phone is on the floor, next to my head. I pick it up. Jimmy Mr Fucking Showbiz from Sky isn't on the line any more. I must have cut him off.

I dial a number. I don't know what number I am dialling, I just press the buttons automatically. I get the answering machine. I say:

'My name is Martin Martin. Listen to me. Call the police. The newsagent is being robbed.'

I dial again. I can't stop.

'Hello?' says a voice.

'Janet Hargreaves,' comes out of my mouth.

'Yes . . .' says Janet Hargreaves.

'My name is Martin Martin. Listen to me. Your cancer has gone.'

I press the red button. I dial again.

A voice comes on the line.

'Yes?' it says.

'Jackson?' I say.

'Yes . . .' says the voice, hesitant. 'Who is this?'

'You murdering bastard. Your time has come.'

These words are coming from my mouth, but I am not in control of them. They come from elsewhere. Maybe they're coming from the electric fucking chip. Maybe they're coming from Martin Martin's brain. Maybe fucking Emile's brain. I don't fucking know. I just fucking do it.

'Listen, I don't know who you are, but you'd better leave me alone.'

'You know who I am,' I say.

'You're that freak off the telly, aren't you? I've been watching you. You're in that van. The police are on to you.'

'You know what I say is true,' I say. 'Everyone knows what I say is the truth now, don't they? I've said so much. I've told the world. And next I'm going to tell them about you. There's no one left to avenge the death of Emile Henderson, Jackson. But those women, remember them? The ones you murdered when you drove your lorry? Do you remember what you did? I can see what you did. I'll tell them. I'll tell those poor women's sons what happened to their mums. I'll tell them where they'll find the remains so they can give them a decent burial. And I'll tell them it was you. I'll tell them what you did and how you did it. I know what you did. You're next, Jackson. I'll tell Jimmy Mr Fucking Showbiz from Sky all about you next. Jackson, you know what to do. Use a gun. Put it in your mouth. It won't hurt. If you wait until those poor sons of those poor women come after you, that will hurt.'

I end the call to Jackson. Everything feels to me like when you're sick with the pukes and you get the wibbly fucking wobblies and one minute you're all fucking hyper and excited and up for it, and the next you're fucking weak, like a little kitten, and boo-hoo. Every time I make a call, it's like I'm reaching for the bucket to hurl into, each time it's like a big vom from the bottom of my fucking soul. Like: 'Erp – Oi! Mrs Woman in fucking wherever the fuck it is you live, your fucking husband's a fucking burglar!', and it leaves me panting and wanting it to, like, fucking stop, but then there comes another lurch from my innards, from my fucking brain innards, and out comes another bit of puke: 'Bluergh! Dave fucking Bloke in Sunder-fucking-land, you will be hit by a fucking bus on Thursday whether you fucking like it or not.'

I look on the TV screen. Our van is still there. It's on a motorway now. There are other vans and motors driving alongside us. There are like, loads of fucking people leaning out of the window and cheering, punching the air and taking photos of our van. There are motorbikes too, swerving around in between the cars and vans, slowing up and then going faster, overtaking, buzzing around like a load of flies chasing a fucking turd on the move. Behind them, there are lorries. Great big lorries that tower over the cars and vans and motorbikes. They honk their horns and they sound like ships at sea. Big, honking fuckers. Every now and then, I get a glimpse of the copper cars with their blue lights flashing and their headlights flashing too. They are trying to get closer to us, but there are at least thirty vehicles between us and them and they won't let the police near us. They can't even get past the lorries. And behind the police are OB vans, more fucking telly people, following Martin Martin down the motorway at top speed. Up above, there are two helicopters; one with Jimmy Mr Fucking Showbiz from Sky, the other a police helicopter. It is a proper procession of fucking mental fucking madness.

I turn up the sound on the TV in the back of the van. On comes a voice:

'. . . a series of startling claims which have led to further distur-bances on the streets across the country. Martin Martin's prophecies, broadcast live from a mobile phone to a television-news channel, have resulted in violence on an unprecedented scale. Reports are also coming in that Martin Martin has been making dozens of personal calls to individuals. He also appears to be using a laptop computer inside the well-equipped van to keep a kind of blog and to send emails to other individuals. The blog is being accessed by hundreds of thousands of people all over the country, so that even when the television-news channel he is talking to censors the names Martin Martin mentions, all the information is still freely available on the internet. One of the more astounding and inflammatory lists Martin Martin has posted looks like a rundown of all the burglaries committed in Newcastle in the last seven days, with the names and addresses of the victims given alongside the names and addresses of the people Martin Martin claims to be responsible for the burglaries. That list alone has resulted in widespread violence in Newcastle. He has also posted a list of politi= cians who, according to Martin Martin, have been taking drugs, which makes for interesting reading. And all the while, these unprecedented scenes are unfolding on the M1 motorway, where Martin Martin is currently being tracked by police as he heads towards London. The police have been unable to contact him or, indeed, stop the vehicle he is travelling in. This is because, as you can see, Martin Martin's vehicle has been joined on the motorway by a large convoy of supporters, who have surrounded the vehicle and refuse to allow the police to get any closer. They are treating Martin Martin as some kind of messiah. And, it has to be said, in the space of twelve hours he has told more truths than any other leader seems capable of. He really is a remarkable man.'

Then we see a copper in a hat looking serious and stern; just his head and shoulders.

'We would ask those members of the public who are travelling on the M1, they might be listening to this on their radios, to please pull away and allow the police to take care of the situation. This is a poten- tially very dangerous state of affairs, and we don't want to see anyone getting hurt. We need to speak to Mr Martin about some serious alle- gations he has been making, and I would add that impeding the police in our attempts to talk to Mr Martin could result in a charge of perverting the course of justice.'

I close my eyes.

Out of the TV, I hear all the talk about what Martin Martin's up to, how I'm the centre of a storm.

'There is increasing clamour for the government to do something about Martin Martin,' says a voice on the TV. 'His broadcasts are creating havoc across the country. Earlier, I spoke to Harvey Jeest, Conservative MP for Sutton and Cheam.'

A new voice comes on: Harvey.

'Martin Martin can't be allowed to libel and slander people willy- nilly, making these outrageous and unsubstantiated claims. Quite apart from his wholesale trashing of perfectly decent people's reputations, we are seeing summary justice being meted out by packs of vigilantes on our streets. Who will he accuse next? And of what? This is not how law works in this country.'

'But isn't the problem here the fact that it has become apparent that Martin Martin's predictions, or claims, whatever you want to call them, are turning out to be true?' says the interviewer.

'We have a system of law in this country based on the fundamental right to be tried by a jury of one's peers, not to be accused of crimes without any investigation, evidence, or the consideration of mitigating circumstances. That is not the kind of society we have or, I hope, want. To see people being killed – and, let me remind you, that is what we are seeing – on the hearsay of some television psychic, of all people, is obscene. The widespread chaos being caused by this irresponsible and frankly insane behaviour must be brought to a halt, and the principal players – I mean this Martin Martin character and his acolyte Devlin Williams – need to be stopped, and they need to be stopped immediately. And that crackpot minority which is treating Martin Martin as some kind of messianic solution to the ills of the world, they should take a look at the result of Mr Martin's work – all this violence and hatred he has unleashed – and ask themselves if this is the kind of society they wish to be a part of. The last thing we need is yet another crackpot extremist spouting nonsense.'

The voices off the TV start to swirl and fade, and I can See all this mess and chaos and stuff they're talking about. It's cranking up, like the big noisy bit at the end of an exciting car chase where all the violins and tubas and drums are skrieking and whining and banging so your nerves are all fucking jangled up and you're gripping the arms of your seater and your knuckles are white.

With my eyes closed, I can See what's happening all over the fucking country. I can smell it too; a stinky reek coming off old Blighty, the awful pong of rubber burning, motors with all their windows smashed in, fire peeping out from under them. It's dark down there now, but the cities are burning orange. Orange from the street lights and the lights on the motorways, orange from the flames that dance up the side of big buildings that have been torched. Shops are smashed and there are people running in and out of the holes in the big windows, like rats in and out of their burrows, or bees in and out of their hive, helping themselves, coming out with their arms wrapped around big boxes: stuff they've nicked. The coppers' choppers are all in the sky, shining bright white light down on the people running around the streets and in and out of the shops. And from inside the choppers, the coppers shout through amplifying machines.

'Stay where you are, do not move!' and all stuff like that. But they're being ignored, and some people even stop to look up and flip the choppers off, like, 'Fuck off, chopper coppers!'

Everything's getting done in. Chip shops, pet shops, the lot. The angry crowds around the petrol stations have lost it, and the mobs around the houses where the local weirdos live have grown and they've attracted more people, ones who can sniff all the electric air and the vibe and love the trouble. They're out for nicking stuff and breaking stuff and fighting, trying to push police vans over, setting fire to parked cars, lobbing stones through windows just because there are stones and there are windows to lob them through.

A man with blood coming from his old bald head, blood that has spread blobby on to his white coat, is sweeping up the glass that has sprayed all over his shop floor. His face is sad. He is a chemist. His shop won't ever open again and he won't be a chemist no more. The stone-throwers have moved past his shop and are doing in shops half a mile up the road now. They're fucking loving it. They're having the night of their lives.

I pick up the phone again. I dial the number nine, then another one, then another.

A voice comes on.

'Emergency Services. Which service do you require?'

'My name is Martin Martin,' I say, the words coming out of me like another vommo, streaming out, no control from me.

'Emergency Services. Which service do you require?' says the voice on the other end.

'Accidents will happen, eh?' I say, and hang up.

And then Devlin lets out his shout. His little yelp of death. I see the small hole in the windscreen where the bullet came in. Devlin is slumped forward. He has let go of the steering wheel. I brace myself for what I know is coming.

The van veers to the left, and then more violently to the right. There is a noise – 'WHUMP!' – as we hit the central reservation. Then there is a moment of calm, the van is fucking totally flying in the air, with the sound of the engine racing, wheels spinning, no longer gripping tarmac. Then there is another crash as the van lands on its side and all the TV screens shatter and come away from where they've been attached. I am aware the van is rolling over and over because glass from the screens is flying all around and cutting me up; big sharp lumps of it are forced deep into my flesh. I am tossed around like a little fucking dolly. I have no control over Martin Martin's body as it gets all smashed up and sliced and fucking broken up into bits. I feel no pain. I relax and allow the damage to come to me, like when you close your eyes after a cloud passes and the sunshine comes.

Thirty-three

ALL THESE fucking holes. Holes in heads, put there by fucking bullets or with a spade. Plugholes with time running down them like swirly tornados in the water, sucking houses and cars and people, like me – fucking Jensen – down with them, slurping them all down like a big greedy monster. Plugholes like the one in my fucking Dermo Shower, with the water coming up the wrong way and flooding my fucking spank flat and fucking my life up. They're all like big secret holes in time, like time's a big cheesy lump the size of the universe, with me scampering about inside it like a mouse. I just can't tell where I'll be popping up next.

Well, when I pop up this time there is sun on my face. It is warm. Maybe it is too warm. The skin of my face feels hot and tight across my skull.

Those are the first things I can feel: hot sun, stretched face.

Next, my chops. They ache. Throb, throb, throb. With every pump of the blood around my bod, the pain comes in my gob.

After that, the feeling starts to come in the back of my head and on the backs of my hands. There's pain, sharp and scratching, snagging its horrid broken nails along my soft brain. But the pain's coming through heavy, a deep-hurting ache in the head, bulging. All this pain; it's like the treble and bass of pain.

I am flat on my back. I try to move, and when I move, it's like my arms and legs are connected like a puppet's. I move a leg, dragging it across whatever it is I am lying on, and an arm moves. And my head too, it shifts involuntarily with every other movement. And, when I move, there is a scraping sound. Like gravel. Like I am lying on a thin layer of crunchy gravel, and that gravel is on a layer of something else, something softer than pavement, but still hard. Hard and hot under this hot sun, sucking up the sun's rays into itself and frying whatever sits on it. Which at this moment is fucking me, Jensen Interceptor.

Then I have the whole fucking graphic equaliser of pain. Every little layer of pain has been tuned to play in perfect harmony with the other. If it didn't hurt so fucking much, I'd be impressed. Out of my sore mouth comes my little moan:

'Ohhhhhh!'

I squirm about some more, as if that's going to make the fucking throbbing and the hurt stop. The gravel scratches and grinds away at me, noisy and dry and stinging, especially on the back of my head. I can taste blood, so I try to spit it out – 'Ptui' – but it just loops around like nasty gummy jelly and sticks to my sun-baked cheeks. My lips are cracked and hard.

I turn my head to one side. I can feel the gravel against my cheek, digging in and leaving its little dents in my face. Fucking gravel. Through my squinty eyes fighting the bright sunlight and the blue, blue sky, I can see a shadow or a silhouette. It looks like a frozen black explosion from a firework; a fat zoom up, then the bang and splatter of sparks and stuff at the top. But it's not a firework. I wouldn't be able see a firework on a sunny day like this. It's a palm tree, like they have in Miami and all them fucking hot places like that. Am I in Miami or Hawaii? The only time I've ever seen fucking palm trees is when they had them at the opening of the Baker Street Starfucks, which was all, like, a Hawaii theme with hula girls and cocktails and surfboards and all that kind of grass-skirt shit. The other place I've seen these spiny-spikey trees is on the roof of the Old Bank. The flat roof opposite and below my bedroom window. The roof where the girls sunbathe on hot days, all covered in lotion and with their whoppers on show, getting baked, like I am now.

I turn my head the other way. I am too hot, and it's like there is steam coming out of my mouth, and every move I make is slow. The bits of gravel stuck to my face, some drop off as I slowly turn. In front of me, on this side, is a wall. A small wall, three feet high. On the other side of that wall, I now know, is the Rotherhithe Sky Tower. And there will be my open bedroom window, from where I leaped like a mad nutter, when behind me there was a gov spy about to pump off a flesh-seeking bullet in my direction.

The time has come to get upright, so I push myself up. I can't be that badly hurt if I can move. And all this pain to, that means I'm not paralysed. I can feel all of me hurting like buggeration and rotten fuckery. I struggle up so I'm sitting, my body leaning against the wall. I peep over.

There, above me, is my bedroom window, gaping open. The curtain is moving from side to side in the slight breeze. I can just about make out my wall-mounted speaker system. I see no agents.

This is it. I am back. A little scraped and bruised, perhaps, but not fucking done in. The agent's gun must have let rip with its fucking nasty techno bullet; it must've punched through the window as I flew, but it couldn't find me. With no flesh for it to seek up there, 300 feet in the air, it must've just given up and dropped to the ground. Me, in my hurry to escape, I made it to this roof. I didn't stop running when I got to the window, I just flew through it and I fell where the second agent couldn't see me – behind this wall.

My head doesn't just hurt on the outside, where the skin's been rubbed beefy-raw by the gravel. It hurts deep on the inside; it's that little electro pebble or nugget stuck in there. It just sits there, cold and dark, annoying my brain and hurting me, like a stone in my shoe, but too deep to itch it away. And now, it is just a cold dead lump in my head. I don't fucking know if I'm seeing the idea of Martin Martin or actual Martin Martin. Martin Martin told me not believe in the the idea of him. But how the fuck am I supposed to tell the fucking difference, eh? And anyway, the Martin Martin who told me that was full of Emile fucking Henderson, wasn't he? I fucking ask you.

Oh, fuck it. Just fucking fuck it.

I get up. Everything hurts more. My clothes are all ripped and bits of cloth are stuck hard to the cuts and dried blood around my knees. I shuffle towards the palm tree, the gravel scraping under my shuffling. Next to the palm tree, there's a little water fountain for drinking from. I make my hot face wet and moisten my lips. I drink and drink until it starts to feel like my stomach will pop. I cup handfuls of water and pour them over my head, purifying myself, getting all the dust damped down. I push my hair back and start to feel better. I can focus now, and I can see the door that will get me off this hot roof that saved my bacon from a death plunge. Soon I will be down to the street, where I will be able to get to Reg's place and to Claire. I feel pulled there, as if a big magnet is dragging me.

'Good grief, Norfolk, what the hell happened to you? Come in, come in. Oh, Norfolk, what happened?'

It's Reg, and he's pulling me into his flat, his arm over my shoulder, holding me up, holding me like me and him are brothers. When I got to Reg's neck of the woods, I couldn't get any further. I couldn't find my way to Claire's, and so it was Reg's door I found myself in front of, all fucked up and in pain and nearly passing out cos of it all. Bleeding too.

'Don't worry, you're safe now. Everything will be OK,' he's saying as we get up the stairs.

I sit at the table in his front room.

'What have they done to you, Norfolk?' he says, hovering over me.

I think about his question, but I can't answer it. I open my mouth, but there are no words. My eyelids are droopy.

Reg goes to a cupboard, and he brings out a box with a red cross on it. He sits me down by the window and looks at my face and my head.

'Oh dear, Norfolk. You are in a bad way, aren't you? Let's get you patched up, old man.'

'Yeah, cheers Reg,' says I. A brown glass bottle comes out of Reg's medi-kit. Then a big wad of fluffy cotton wool. He pours some liquid out of the bottle on to the fluffy cotton wool and starts patting bits of my face with it. It stings like total fucking agony.

'Oooargh!' I shout.

'Don't worry, Norfolk,' says Reg, 'we'll soon have you cleaned up, and you'll feel better.' The stuff he's dabbing all over me makes a hospital smell. The blobs of cotton wool soon get all drenched in blood, and Reg chucks them in the bin, pulls out some fresh ones and starts all over again, tipping the bottle and cleaning me up.

While he does his nursey bit, he's all, like, talking away, about this and that, about Claire, about how he can tell she likes me, about all sorts of old cobblers. He talks about when he was young, about how he got duffed up once, and how the smell of the stuff in the brown bottle reminds him of it, cos someone had to clean him up, just like he's cleaning me up now. He half-laughs to himself, and then he shrugs his shoulders and shakes his head.

'That was a long time ago,' he says.

'Yeah,' I says. 'When you was a fucking student, in a pub.'

Reg stops cleaning my bashed-up face and says something. But thoughts are blanking my ears out. I'm looking at the floor, but I'm not really seeing what's there. I'm seeing different to what's around me. I'm staring at a book. An old tatty book with brown edges all stained and fanned out. A ghost book. A book what's not there at all, but I can see it anyway. I can't read the title. The book has been read and reread so many times that white cracks and lines run down the spine, and they've wiped out what was written there. I look closer, and I see the name of the book on the cover: *Martin Martin's on the Other Side*, by Reginald D. Rankin.

I suddenly get the feeling again. Not the scrapey achy-breaky feeling from all the violence that has been done to my bod thanks to the old death plunge on to the roof of the Old Bank, although that's there, right enough; and not the pukey yag-up feeling, although there's plenty of that too. No, it's the swimmy feeling in the head that comes as the scenery's changing or someone dead's about to pop up and start chit-chatting with me. It's like when I talked to the lush caff lady and I Saw her story and how the gov fucked her lover over, shot him in his head – it's that feeling.

The hard little pebble lodged in my brain is lighting up again. Reg's gaff totally melts away, like sticky spoodge, and the room spins out and darkens until it's disappeared. The stone in my brain is glowing and warm, and it's telling me a story. It's Reg's story. Reg's life long before I met him, back when I was doing the FGs about food recognition and all that.

Here's Reg, all young and not beardy, skin on his face rubbery and not papery like it is now. He's in a class with loads of other young people in funny old clothes. They're nearly all wearing little tops with short sleeves, the girls and the boys, and on the chest there's writing or a picture, or both. They're all listening to a bloke talking. Well, not all of them are listening, but Reg is. He's listening like he's hearing really top info, stuff that's important. The bloke, the teacher, he's crapping on about the gov, all sorts of types of different govs I've never heard of, like anarkee and fashism and hollygarky.

And here's Reg later on, with others, in a small room thick with smoke off the big cigs that are getting smoked and lit by candles. Shit music coming out of shit tinny little speakers and the big cigs are being passed around and they're talking. They're all clever boys, long-word merchants – arse-bound, as Fyodor calls them, meaning they've got their heads up their own arses.

Reg says, 'Look what they did to Martin Martin,' and his hand is a fist shaking as he says it.

Another boy says, 'Oh, Reg, you and Martin Martin!'

'Yeah,' says another, 'conspiracy theorist. You just cloud everything over when you talk about that rubbish.'

'But it's not rubbish, Dave,' says Reg. This Dave, he looks over at his mate and shakes his head, like this is stuff from Reg they've all heard before.

'It was twenty years ago, Reg,' says this Dave. 'Those riots were caused by fuel shortages when Oxxon collapsed. And Oxxon collapsed because it was run by a crook. It was a minor outbreak of mass hysteria. There was a lot of tension in the air back then. Bombs going off on crowded trains, political uncertainty, countries facing each other off like it was 1939 all over again. It was the sort of thing that happens on those very rare occasions when the plebs find out how the world really works and they panic for a day or two. They all soon settle back into watching telly and buying things and forget all about it. Like when turkeys freak out. Have you ever been in a turkey shed when they all go bonkers?'

'No,' says the other boy, not really interested.

'Quite a racket, I can tell you. It's like one of them has mentioned Christmas and they all start going out of their minds with fear. But it always stops almost as soon as it starts, and they all get on with being turkeys. Those riots were all over in a few days. That dodgy psychic chap had nothing to do with any of it. It's not meaningful, Reg. You should know better.'

'You call yourselves scholars!' says Reg. He's getting a bit hysterical-turkey himself now, his voice croaky and high and whiny. 'Those riots lasted for weeks,' he says, starting to shout. 'Unrest continued for a year. It was a *revolution*. It was ruthlessly crushed and it's all been forgotten. It's all there for you to read about. It's logged in the computer archives. There's *hours* of footage from the BBC, the news bulletins, the live reports – you can actually watch the van they were driving crash on the motorway. You can see the police helicopter leave the scene when the van crashes. It's all there. Come with me, I'll *show* you it.'

'Oh God, Reg, really,' says one of Reg's mates, his voice all fucking bored with the fucking boredom of it all. 'Yes, let's all troop down to the archive and hunker around a little screen and watch lo-def films of a car crash that happened years ago. Maybe after that we can all sit around and enjoy a couple of hours watching the war in the Balkans or the collapse. Or maybe we could watch the tanks on the streets of Gdansk in 1988. Oh, no wait, I've got an idea, let's check out the trial of Saddam Hussein! That'll be fun!'

'All your Martin Martin stuff has been forgotten, Reg,' yawns another one of the boys, 'because it was just a load of oiks running around setting fire to kiddy fiddlers' houses, and because later in the year the whole world had other, rather more important issues to concern themselves with.'

'Yes Reg, minor issues like China wading into the war in the Middle East and the collapse of the American empire.'

'The break-up of the EU.'

'Lights out over Europe, Reg – you know, *real* history? Important things?'

These clever fuckers, all ganging up on poor Reg. They've obviously already told him they think he's an idiot a hundred times before.

'Reg, we've heard it all before. It's like all that Holy Grail crap everyone was banging on about for a while back then. If it wasn't one load of old bilge everyone was getting in a lather about, it was another. And if you insist on writing your dissertation about it, you'll fail your degree and live a life of crushing poverty surrounded by oiks. You'll wear cardigans with holes in the elbows at best, and at worst you'll be aimlessly pushing a supermarket trolley around filled with old plastic bags and tripping over your beard. Mark my words, Reg, old boy. Don't be so bloody stubborn. It's ridiculous.'

'It's not ridiculous. It's . . .' Reg struggles for the word and then finds one, 'important.' No one says anything. They just look amused. 'Don't you see?' Reg continues. 'The power elites and their mind games have always been able to shut down the population when they needed to. It's what they do best. It's what they exist to do!'

Reg's mates look at each other, laughing in their eyes at Reg and his ranting.

'Look,' he says, crazy with how he's being giggled at and totally not taken seriously, 'in 1914, the country was on the verge of revolution; the working classes were organising against capitalism, and then the Great War broke out, and the working classes were sent out to die in their millions in mud and filth. Very bloody convenient.'

'So the First World War was organised by the British government to quell some stroppy miners? Is that what you're saying, Reg?' asks one of the boys.

'It's not that simple, but that's how it works.'

'Tell me this, Reg, how did the government manage to get rid of any evidence about Martin Martin? If he was so important, why isn't there more material about him? Where are the books? The historical records? Why is it that anyone who is sensible agrees that the Martin Martin episode is nothing more than a freakish little weekend of madness along the lines of raining frogs or crop circles?'

'Because the power elites dictate who is "sensible", they set the terms for the debate, they run the media and they marginalise anyone who doesn't agree with them. You'll be rewarded professionally for your work about China, Dave, because it fits in with the propaganda system. You'll have a glittering career, tenure at some university, all the rest of it. I'll be set aside and laughed at. I won't get published; I'll be considered a crank.'

'Yep. That's what they said about Erik Von Daniken,' says this Dave, and he laughs, and the other boy laughs too.

'Hitler's diaries!' says the other boy, and there's more laughing.

'Oscar Kiss Maerth!' says this Dave.

The other boy: 'Cheats! Liars! Frauds!'

Now they're laughing so hard they can hardly sit up.

Once they calm down, the other boy starts talking to Reg, realising that maybe they've gone too far teasing him. They are his mates, after all. It's not as if they don't like him, and they can see he's angry.

'Listen, Reg,' says the other boy, being nice now, 'it's not that we think you're a crank, although you've never been quite the same since you volunteered for those medical trials, and we're not saying that the whole Martin Martin thing didn't have some kind of conspiracy behind it, like JFK or, oh I don't know, men on the moon if you like, it's just that if you want to get ahead, you ought to concentrate a little more on the miracle of modern China.'

This Dave: 'Ah yes! Now then, Reg, there's something upon which it would be worth concentrating your considerable intellectual skills. My dissertation's already got a publisher, you know. I think I'll call it "Communism and Capitalism: The Miracle Alliance". I'm going places, Reg. The world needs on-message political philosophers. But you're headed nowhere with this absurd obsession of yours. Why don't you just drop it, and get on board and join the team for the big win?'

The other boy nods his head.

'Reg, just because the government said Martin Martin was a sordid little charlatan, it doesn't automatically follow that he *wasn't* a sordid little charlatan,' says the other boy. 'Defending a long-dead self-promoting television psychic isn't going to do your career any good whatsoever, Reg. This university isn't a place to beaver away at crackpot theories. It's preparation for you to join the elite.'

'That's right,' says this Dave. 'And so you can have a fuck-off big house and a load of wonga in the bank.' And with that, this pair of Reg-baiters start their honking laughter again.

Reg just stares at the floor. I can see his ears are red. He's well angry, fucking had enough, but the boys think he's embarrassed. They think it's a joke. But it's not a joke.

Poor old Reg, the shunned apostle.

So here's Reg again, I'm Seeing him still, but the boys have melted away and it's later on. Maybe later that night, maybe it's a year later. He's tippy-tap typing away on a computer, his face is blue-lit off the screen, his eyes are bulging as he tippy-tap types. There are bits cut out of newspapers, all yellowed and stacked up. There are pages and pages of stuff written by Reg, sheets of it covered in his scrawl. Some bits are connected to other bits by arrows, other clumps of Reg's scribble have circles drawn around them with exclamation marks, lots: !!!!! On the wall there are more papers, pinned and stuck by pin and sticky.

I can see the words Reg is writing as they appear across the screen:

Of this much we can be sure: Martin Martin was born in London towards the end of the twentieth century, and he died thirty-three years later, on his way back to London. What is less certain is how he died, and why.

Reg stops typing after that, and rubs his chin with his palm. It makes a raspy sound. Reg needs a shave, his young-man beard is poking through. He carries on typing.

I propose that life on earth changed when Martin Martin came among us, and that his death was murder. I believe that he was sent here for a reason, and that the authorities became nervous of his powers and the message he was going to share with mankind. His authority would have sapped the authority of the state, which would have withered and died as the individual's power grew to outstrip it.

They knew that it was within Martin Martin's power to see through their lies. Systems of government across the world would have collapsed if ordinary people everywhere had instinctive, truthful knowledge of their real motives.

No more wars fought for oil. No more power elites lining their own pockets at the expense of starving millions. No more prevaricating over safeguarding the future of the planet from the catastrophes of global dimming. Imagine a world witnessing the dismantling of the military-industrial complex. A world would have emerged where a truly compassionate connection would have sprung up among all people, and evil-doers would have been weeded out and destroyed, betrayed by their own thoughts.

And it is for that reason Martin Martin was executed. That's right: executed. Just as the Russian vine will entangle its host plant and strangle it to death, so the creeping, silent tendrils of secret government reached around the neck of Martin Martin and snuffed him out.

Martin Martin was murdered by the government of the United Kingdom. And this happened here, in England, a democracy which has no death penalty, not even for convicted murderers of children – a heinous crime, which the government attached to Martin Martin in their desperate attempts to besmirch the public's memory of him forever. After all, who wants to remember a paedophile with anything except contempt? It was the perfect ruse.

Reg stops typing again and this time runs both his hands through his hair. Then he's off again.

Martin Martin had an important message for mankind. He was going to teach us to communicate, to reach each other's true natures, to see all the pain and suffering behind each person's eyes, and also the joy and the love there. Eventually, Martin Martin's teachings would have led all of mankind to a joyful union that would have abided for all time. It would be this final nexus that would halt the appalling cycle of violence that humanity is doomed to suffer.

Again Reg stops. He writes in bursts. This must be his book, or the beginnings of it: *Martin Martin's on the Other Side*. He stops, chews the inside of his mouth or the end of a pen, and just stares off to one side of his computer screen, waiting for inspiration to strike. Then he types again, in a hurry.

But the government was the judge for its own cause, and like a machine programmed to save itself at any cost, it turned on its own people. This blank-eyed, soulless creature we call government, bereft of morality, convulsed in autonomic self-preservation at the threat to its stability as posed by Martin Martin. Like a parasite sucking at its host, it sensed danger, perhaps even its own destruction. And so, with no thought for the greater good, long having abandoned any notion of serving mankind, this swollen parasite struck down the comparatively weak Martin Martin with the venom of its deadly lash, and, in doing so, set back mankind's chances of living in peace and harmony for who knows how long. It was a tragedy on a scale we cannot start to process.

Reg is on a roll now, and he's not stopping.

Martin Martin had a rare gift, and he proved his possession of this gift for all to see. Not for him the easily misunderstood homily or gesture. No, Martin Martin set out to prove what it was he had to offer. He had much to teach, and he needed to let mankind know that his message was the one true message, not a confusion of ancient symbols and stories misheard and retold, degenerated over centuries of schism and lies. Martin Martin was about to share the ultimate gnosis, the special knowledge that would see the chains of bondage finally fall away from humanity for all time.

For Martin Martin knew that all time happens simultaneously, that all possibilities exist at all times together. There is no future or past, but one constant present, which stretches across the cosmos and embraces all. In the face of this indisputable truth, our earth-bound squabbles would have melted away, revealed to even the most devout warrior as petty and pointless.

So why, you might ask, if Martin Martin was in possession of such an awesome vision, did he not know his own death was imminent? How could a being so blessed have allowed something so mundane as a car crash to end his life? Martin Martin was man and beyond-man in one; he existed in hypostatic union; two natures in one person. He was fully man and fully God. It was the man who was killed that night. And with Martin Martin dead, the world was able to accelerate unimpeded on its path to madness and destruction, war and conflict, the engine of the enslavement of the many by the few.

Man cannot kill God.

But God knows he tried.

And now I See Reg a few days or weeks later, getting socked in the face by a thuggie little fucker. Just duffed up random, for no good reason, not even for his wallet, just for fucking fun, outside a boozer where Reg had been having a quiet drinkie and reading a book and having a think about everything, not bothering no one. I grant you, Reg did look like a loon-bag freak when he was young, and sitting there in the pub reading a book with a big fucking beard and fucking stupid specs, totally bumming the cool noisy pub vibe, making the girls all feel uncomfortable, which is no good when you're trying to get in their knicks and see what they have to offer, and they're wanting you to get in there too, and they want you to see their goodies on offer and all that – top fucking banana, yeah? Maybe I'd have given him some fucking gyp too. But not proper nasty like what the thug gave Reg for no good reason. Kick, bash, slap, 'Fucking students' and all that. 'Hur hur hur,' goes the thug, and scarpers off, and Reg is all on the fucking pavement, his first kicking making him silly in the head, and blood coming from his mouth, a tooth booted or punched out of it.

And then he's getting all sorted out with stinging clear liquid out of a brown bottle by a nice boy back at university, a boy who likes Reg but who Reg thinks is a fucking moron. The boy's not a fucking moron, he's just a nice boy who likes Reg and helps him out when he needs it with the stingy liquid out of the brown bottle.

And now Reg is helping another boy, another boy what's been all duffed and smashed and fucked up. He's dabbing with the stinging liquid out of the brown bottle, and he's remembering the boy who helped him all those years ago. And the boy he's helping now, – that is me, Jensen fucking Interceptor, Norfolk from fucking Norfolk – can remember what Reg remembers.

And suddenly I'm back with Reg, in Reg's gaff. He's kind of looking bonkers. There's been too many weird things happening for him; everything's going fast when it never went anything but slow. Until I showed up, that is.

He's dabbing away at one of my ears, really rubbing hard, not really concentrating. It's hurting.

'Reg,' I says. And then there's a weird sensation around the ear. It suddenly feels cold around the lughole. I put my hand up to it, and Reg is holding something in his hand.

'What on earth?' he says. He's got like disgust and surprise on his face.

I look at the little scrap of pink he's holding in his hand. It's an ear. Reg looks at the ear, and then back at me and where my ear still is, where he was rubbing. He's got the Makeover Team's ear in his hand. His rubbing made it fall off. My Makeoever Team disguise is falling apart. Not exactly a fucking surprise, considering what I've, like, fucking been through.

'I can explain, Reg,' I say.

'What the . . . ?' says Reg, backing away from me.

He moves back towards the same cupboard he got his medi-kit out of. He keeps his eyes on me, still holding the horrid little wobbly ear. His face is still like a fucking mask of horror, and now there's suspicion coming into it too.

'It's OK Reg, nothing to worry about. It's not like, you know, it's not a disguise or anything! I'm not a fucking spy or nothing! Straight up!'

Reg says nothing. He chucks the ear on the ground, and scrabbles behind him, opening the cupboard door. The ear splats on the floor, like a little scrap of raw chicken. Reg pulls out a tin, the sort you might see biscuits in. He needs his two hands to place it on the table. He sits opposite me and opens the tin. I have to squint to see what's there. Inside I can see the lump of explosive that Reg showed us before. Now it has wires coming from it.

'Don't you move, Norfolk,' says Reg. I'm feeling hot and sweaty. The pain of all my scuffed flesh joins up with this horror feeling that I've been totally rumbled by Reg. He's fucking sussed me now; the cat's out of the bag and all that, well, half-out anyway. All this is turning into a burning sensation all over my body, like I'm glowing with fire.

I feel like I'm going to be sick. It's a nausea rush from the pits of my guts. I get to my feet and stagger across to the window. I gulp air from the window but the pukey feeling doesn't go away. I feel so dizzy and mushed in the bonce that I might fall over at any moment.

'Don't move, Norfolk,' says Reg. 'I have the detonator. I'll kill both of us . . .'

Inside my head, the electro chippie jumps and jolts. Or is it my memory? What was it that Martin Martin told me? A fucking dangerous moment with Reg? Go for the pocket where the detonator is? The left? Whose left? Reg's left or my left?

In my head, I see the nights I've had at Starfucks, and all those times when I've nestled in the warm boobies of the Starfucks girls and watched the action. Off my nuts on boris and laughing and giggling like a baby, Fyodor gurgling and acting like a child, falling over on the ice and knocking the mountaineer over. Playing, like in a nursery while the grown-ups take care of the serious business. Starfucks: it's like being in the Duncan-Smith soft room, strapped up and needled into calmness.

There's a crashing sound. Three big thumps, then a kind of splintering. And then a shout, loud and croaky. The shout goes:

'Stop!'

It's a girl's voice.

Reg is at the table, frozen to the spot, not fucking mad frozen, but just like he daren't fucking move frozen. He's got the bomb on the table, and his hands are on it.

'Take your hands away from the bomb, Reg,' says the voice. Straight away I realise it's Claire. I look at her. She's in the doorway; she's kicked the fucking door right off its fucking hinges, and it's hanging back against the wall. I can actually smell wood. She's holding a gun and it's pointed straight at Reg.

'Claire!' I says. If I wasn't feeling weirded out and fucked up before, which I totally fucking was, I am now. I can hardly see through my nausea and pain and the shock of seeing Claire holding a gun, pointing it at Reg's head. She looks like she's off a show about, like, fucking detectives or something.

'Shut up, Jensen!' she shouts at me, not even looking at me. She doesn't let her eyes off Reg, who's still standing there, staring with his gob wide open.

Reg looks at me.

'*Jensen?*' he says.

'Oh shite. Ooh fucking shite' says I, my mind popping with all the, like, fucking total meaning of what her calling me Jensen, like, fucking means, and a noise starts up deep in my skull, the same kind of clanky fucking whirring I heard when my fucking Dermo Shower packed up.

'I know who you are, Jensen,' says Claire, still with her big fuck-off gun in her hands, its muzzle solid as a rock, Reg's head in its sights. 'But I need you to be quiet for the moment.'

Reg looks back at Claire.

'Claire?' he says. The fuses are blowing behind his eyes. I can almost see the smoke coming out of his ears. 'What are you doing? Norfolk? What's she talking about? Claire . . . put the gun down. What's all this about?' he laughs, chuckles, but not cos it's funny.

'Step away from the bomb,' says Claire.

'I can't do that, Claire,' says Reg. He knows bad shit is coming down on him, and all he's got to hold it off is his fucking bomb.

They look at each other in silence for a few moments; she holding the gun, he holding the bomb.

'Claire?' I says.

'Will you shut *up*, Jensen!' she says again. That's, like, totally not like the Claire from before, telling me to shut up like that. This is a new Claire. With a big fuck-off gun. The hurt in my brain starts up again. I get a sort of death feeling, like maggots crawling around in my head, and a stench too, a rot stench.

'Ohhhh . . .' I say. I hold my head and drop to my knees.

'What they did to you, Jensen,' says Claire, ' it just wasn't right. It's put me in an impossible position. But Reg, seriously, you've got to step away from the bomb, or I will have to shoot you.'

'I'll detonate it,' says Reg. He's sweating. So am I.

'Ohhhh . . .' I says, the throbbing aches in my head are swelling up some more.

'Who is he, Claire? Who is Jensen?' says Reg. 'And who are you?'

'Never you mind, Reg,' I wail. 'Don't you go listening to Claire. She must've gone fucking mental or something. She's talking mental, yeah?'

'Jensen, I told you to keep quiet,' she says. 'His name is Jensen Interceptor, Reg. He works for the government. He's a spy.'

'What?' says Reg. He's right proper out of it now. He doesn't understand anything, except that he's got a big bomb and Claire's got a big gun.

'I'm so not a spy!' I shout. I don't really know why. I suppose cos it's like all my careful undercover work is totally fucking unravelling and I'm trying to keep it done up nice and tight. But the hurting and the sickness is weakening me, and I can't really think of any decent lies to say.

'I'm on your side!' I try to shout, but it's feeble, and it's not really true, cos I don't think I'm on anyone's side. I can see that I'm not on Claire's side or Reg's side. No one's on Jensen's side. Not any more.

'I really liked you, Jensen,' Claire says. 'They shouldn't have put that chip in your brain, Jensen. That was wrong. But I wouldn't be here now if it wasn't for the chip.'

She's still looking at Reg, pointing the gun at him. Reg can't believe what's happening to him. Everything he thought was true and right is disappearing down the fucking plughole with a big slurp, getting all mashed up and belching back up with all bits of shit in it, just like my poxy Dermo Shower.

'I want you to know, Jensen, that the times we spent together, they meant a lot to me. I really cared about you. I still do, Jensen.' All this she says still holding the gun up.

I'm on my knees on the floor, feeling like I'm going to vom up everything inside me, all my guts and my throat and my fucking brain too.

'You too, Reg,' says Claire. 'I care about you too. Really, I do. That's why this has to stop. As your caseworker, Reg, I'm pleading with you, step away from the bomb. It's all got to stop. You need some medication and a stay in hospital. Come on now.'

'I'd like to go to hospital,' I moan.

'Jensen, *please*,' says Claire. 'This is a very dangerous situation.'

That reminds me. Reg and a dangerous situation. Just like what the Emile Henderson Martin spook told me when I chased him all the way to old Rotherhithe. That proves it. The chip isn't putting this in my head. I was told this would happen. I had to beware Claire and to go for the left pocket, where Reg has the detonator.

But whose left? Fuck! Fuck! Fuck! His left or mine? Cos, like, his left is my fucking right, so what if I go for my left, and it turns out that the detonator is in his left?

Reg and Claire are staring at each other. Only I can stop this. Emile/Martin Martin told me. It has to be me. The only chance for it all to stop is me.

The fucking throb in my head feels like I'm getting bashed over and over by fucking trampy Gizza Kwid, like I'm smacking my head on the table in the Italian restaurant again, like the Makeover Team blokes are opening up my skull and filling it with their fucking red-hot electro chippies until they're coming out my eye sockets, like I'm jumping out the fucking window of my flat and I'm falling head first on a hard gravel flat roof, like it's me getting thwacked around with a baseball bat instead of the cunt who was robbing my fucking gaff, like my brain is the little hard pea rattling around all mongovered. I feel like I'm on the way out, on my knees, wanting everything inside me to come out, all the poison out of me, all the fucking electro chippies out. Get it all out.

I make my move. I spring like some kind of jungle fucking cat right at Reg. I go for my left. The other left was too confusing. I'm hoping that if I get to the hand holding the detonator, he'll drop it, and we'll all be OK; Reg can go to a retraining camp and get all needles and drugs and get sorted out, and I'll get mended, and me and Claire will get it on and, like, live together and have fucking babies and she'll go around my spank gaff putting all, like, fucking flowers and shit in vases and asking me if I think they look pretty, which they fucking will, all right?

The explosion happens before I hear it.

The heat of it and the smell of it before the noise of it. Suddenly, there is no air to breathe, and there is just a hot white flame.

I can't believe the fucking bomb has gone off. And yet, at the same time, I totally know that the fucking bomb has gone off.

The explosion pushes the windows out of the building and a load of Reg's old stuff goes out with them, all shredded up. The furniture is now in sticks and cloth and flying balls of flame.

There's the familiar smell of hair burning and chemical explosion.

There's also the smell of flesh burning. I've never smelled it before, but I know exactly what it is.

I see Reg go up with the explosion. His head goes up, not attached to his body, the mouth gaping like a fish's as it spins around. The rest of Reg's body jerks up and his arms wave.

The explosion lifts me and throws me out of the hole in the wall where the window was just a moment earlier. I'm going like a rocket, fire pushing me into the sky.

That's it. Me out of a fucking window again. Unconscious before I hit the ground again. Just the sound of glass hitting the concrete and the echo of the roar the bomb made.

I never even got to feel better after the last time I flew out of a window. Cuts on top of cuts. Burns on cuts. Bones broken that were probably already broken.

Thirty-four

BET YOU weren't expecting me to come around after that one, eh? I'm like a cat, yeah? Fucking nine lives, yeah? Another explosion, another fall, another bullet, but I keep coming back. I survive them all. I always pop up again. Like a cork bobbing around on a huge dirty great big fucking ocean.

This one took a long time to recover from, though. Getting blown the fuck up with a bomb is a major hardcore fuck-up, yeah? So there was a totally huge stretch in the hosp, with nurses coming and going, with doctors looking at me through special glasses, and with all machinery attached to me.

I was out of it most of the time. Off my chump on pain-killing jib-jabs, juice coming into my veins from a bag up on a pole next to the bed. The machines were all going 'blip, blip, blip' and the docs and the nurses were like more spooks, drifting around in poor old Jensen's cracked noggin, doing mad things and making me all confused in the brain. Like, I'd see a bloke in a white coat and specs, leaning over me and looking all concerned, and then he'd turn into Claire, as if she was standing over my head (with me peeking up her skirt, having a good long and happy deckers at her lovely knicks and what's under them – my own personal *Porn Disco*). But then I'd see Miskin or Brock, and I wouldn't be feeling so happy. And sometimes I just kept seeing Reg's head spinning around and around, like it was in space, with bits of mush flying off it, and spurts of blood sploshing all about the place. The Reg's-spinning-head scene would stop and repeat, as if it was on some fucking loop, and then it wouldn't be Reg's head no more, but Claire's. And I would moan and moan, but I couldn't move, and I'd get all fucking drenched with blood and bits would hit me in the eye – bits of Reg and bits of Claire; little scraps of the flesh off Reg's neck or one of Claire's eyeballs would bounce off my cheek, all soft and squishy and wet and vile. The right proper fucking horrors, I tell you. And then I'd have that dream about Miskin again, the one where he's eating the eels when they're still alive, with all bits of the eel-innards goo stuck in his horrid teeth, and then that would change into him eating Reg's head with fucking Brock stood by like a waiter, and Reg's head served up on a silver dish with salad and stuff around it. Reg's horrible cooked head and Miskin grinning and dribbling and tucking in, and me feeling like I'm going to puke my load all over the table, sweating and dizzy. Reg's head dream, over and over. Nasty.

There was one time when it felt like I'd come around. I looked to one side and sat right there was Miskin. He was eating grapes and flicking through a magazine. He glanced up from his mag and saw that I was looking at him. I was well fucked up. I thought that this was some kind of replay of that time when it was me waking up in a hospital and Devlin Williams was eating grapes and I was MM and MM was me and all that mad shit.

I tried to sit up to see what else was going on in the room. Any other ghosts or spooks hanging around? Would there be another Jensen Interceptor lurking in the fucking corner, visiting from the past or the future or something? Or perhaps Martin Martin, all bashed up from his death in the van full of TVs? Or maybe Emile fucking Henderson, with his head all smashed in, still trying to get his revenge. I'd had enough of that lot. I didn't want to see any of them ever again. I didn't want no more trouble off any of them. I didn't want no more fucking getting smashed and bashed and not knowing who's who and what's what and who's after me. I didn't want to see Reg suddenly back to life, just so I could watch as he goes towards blowing himself up all over again with his stupid fucking bomb. Know what I mean?

But there was no one else around. No spooks or spectres. Just Miskin and his mag and his grapes.

'Jensen Interceptor!' says Miskin, trying to sound jolly, but it not really suiting him, a smile on his face like it had been painted there by someone rubbish at painting. 'Our little hero! How are you feeling?'

Fucking hero? Aren't I the bloke who he's been trying to bump off, sending agents around my gaff to fuck me up with flesh-seeking bullets? How can Jensen Interceptor be the hero if it was Jensen Interceptor who was receiving nicked info out the Archive Facility off of Fyodor?

'I'm feeling a bit fucking shithole, Miskin, to tell you the truth,' I says. And then, just in case, like, I say, 'Sir.'

'Yes, well, I'm not surprised,' goes Miskin, putting his mag down and spitting out a couple of grape pips with his little red tongue. 'You've been in the wars, haven't you? Still, all's well that ends well, eh Jensen? You're on the mend, and our leaky toilet has been rather publicly mended.'

'Reg?' I ask. 'My special project – all sorted?'

'Reg?' says Miskin. 'Well, Mr Reginald Rankin most emphatically has not been mended, has he? He's blown himself into small pieces. And he nearly took you with him. Hmm, Reg and his little gang of loonies. Health Department operatives had an eye on them for us. But you sorted that one out for us too, didn't you? Sort of a two-for-the-price-of-one deal. Very neat, very cost-effective. A little cell of terrorists eliminated, and our leak problem nicely plugged. Our leaky *in*convenience, so to speak . . . ha ha!'

I look at Miskin, blank.

'Government papers going walkabout from the Archive Facility, all the fuss in the media, fights in the inter departmental refectory, threats of funding cuts?' he says, like he's dropping hints. I get that feeling in my stomach, like when you're in the express lift at the department and you go from the twenty-sixth floor to the ground floor and the lift goes all the way down in one.

'Eh?' I goes, sort of trying to bluff it out.

'Your silly pal,' says Miskin, smiling, looking nasty.

'You mean Fyodor?' I says.

'That's him. Your little friend Fyodor. Leaky Fyodor. Tut-tut. Naughty Fyodor. Still, that's all solved now. Fyodor is off somewhere, paying the price for his misbehaviour, and we at the Security Department have sealed the leak in a dramatic coffee-shop arrest, thanks to your undercover work.'

'Me?' I say, shocked.

'Yes, Jensen,' goes Miskin, sounding all patient, using his talking-to-a-stupid voice. 'Your investigation led us to him, we were able to arrest him in the process of passing over sensitive government documents. Part of our massive and carefully orchestrated covert operation.'

'Massive?' I says, still bewildered by what Miskin is trying to tell me, and, like, not getting it.

'We'd been suffering leaks for some time, so we placed 63,000 government employees under surveillance. There were about 4,000 of them leaking in one way or another. Another 1,000 were pilfering: posting fraudulent expenses claims, walking out with government property, bloating their fuel allowances, all that kind of thing. It's going to keep the media in stories about the Security Department's sterling work on behalf of the nation for months. Anyway, turned out one of the leakers was Fyodor. Case solved. Well done, Jensen. Well done, Brock, for recruiting you, and well done, Miskin, for masterminding the entire operation, and doubly well done for foiling a major terrorist bomb plot along the way. And in such dramatic fashion too, Jensen. Very media friendly. Reminds everyone that the government's battle with terrorist forces is keeping everyone safe.'

He helps himself to another grape and pops it in his gob.

'Sixty-three fucking thousand?' says I, cos like, fucking hell, yeah?

'That's right, Jensen.' says Miskin. And then: 'Jensen, are you being dense again?'

The Security Department was investigating 63,000 people. I mean, that's, like, fucking pretty much *everyone*.

'But why was Fyodor leaking stuff?'

'Oh, I don't know. To help you with your investigation of Reg, I expect,' says Miskin, like it's the most obvious thing in the world to say.

'He was helping me do gov biz, wasn't he?'

'Yes, he was.'

'So surely that was all right, yeah? I mean, he was helping the Project, wasn't he?'

'Yes, he was,' says Miskin. He sighs.

'So he wasn't that leaky, was he?'

'Leaky enough, Jensen,' says Miskin.

'Yeah, but not proper leaky, eh? He was just a little leaky. He was like a fucking leak you make by sticking a pin into a tube. You'd hardly notice a leak like that.'

'Still, Jensen, a leak's a leak, isn't it? The Security Department is nothing if not thorough. A small leak left unattended will, inevitably, become a larger leak. And, in time, that tiny little leak will become a flood. And then we will have a very serious problem indeed. And we can't afford to let it become a serious problem. Best to nip it in the bud, and be seen to be nipping it in the bud, so the public understand that there are some things going on that need nipping in the bud: leaks, leaks about terrorists, terrorists. It's all sensitive information. There are reasons why the government has to keep things secret, and it's events like this which remind the public that this is the case.'

'I don't get it,' I say.

'Let me put it this way, Jensen,' says Brock. 'The government had a problem with documents leaking from the Archive Facility, yes?'

'Yes.'

'So it becomes the Security Department's job to investigate and plug that leak, yes?'

'Yes.'

'So we investigated the leak, discovered the source of the leak and we fixed the leak, yes?'

'Yes.'

'And so the citizens of this great nation can sleep easy in their beds, knowing that they are being protected by their government, yes?'

'Yes.'

'But 63,000!' says I. 'That's everyone!'

'It's ongoing, Jensen. The investigations never stop. Mark my words. Best we all behave ourselves, eh?'

'And so what happens now?' I ask.

'Index-linked funding increases are secured for the Security Department for another five years, the ambitious Major Funding Initiative goes ahead and there is no question of our fine department being broken up or having to deal with budget cuts. Unlike some other departments I could mention.'

My empty gaze makes Miskin sigh again.

'Jensen,' he says, 'look at it like this. If you were, say, in the business of mending broken toilets, which situation is more advantageous to you? One where there are no broken toilets, or one where there are many broken toilets?'

'I suppose the more broken toilets there are, the busier I'd be,' I say, pondering his weird question.

'Now imagine this: if you were in the business of both making toilets *and* mending them when they leaked, would you create toilets that never leaked?'

'Erm, well, no,' I stutter, 'You'd want the toilets to start leaking at some point, cos then you could mend them.'

'That's right,' says Miskin, smiling now and relaxing back into his chair. 'And it's the same with security. It's in our interest to have an ongoing security situation. We exist in order to monitor the ongoing security situation. If there was no ongoing security situation, there'd be no need for the Security Department. If there were no leaky toilets, there's be no need for you to fix them, Jensen. And then where would you be?'

'Out of a job?' I venture.

'Precisely!' says Miskin, and he reaches for another grape.

'But I don't understand. I thought we were all part of a team; Unity and Success and all that. You know, where does Fyodor fit in with that?'

'Everyone has their orders, Jensen.'

I stare at Miskin.

'Fyodor was looking after you, Jensen. That's what he was doing. You were one of his. He went a little too far, though, and so you had to look after him for us. And you did. He had a caseload of twenty. The pressure got to him. It often does. There's an internal review into all that going on at the moment, looking into whether we ask too much of our agents. I expect we'll have to change our procedures as a result.'

'Fyodor was a spy too? He was spying on *me*?'

Miskin sighs again when he sees me looking confused still.

'Do you like football, Jensen?' he asks.

'I prefer watching the monster trucks,' I tell him, 'but yeah, football's all right.'

'A football team plays against another football team, and it is important for every player on the team to win. They pull together as a team in order to win. But for each of the eleven men in the team, there are are more waiting to take their place. They're on the sidelines, limbering up, training, getting harder muscles, learning how to run faster, becoming tougher. They want the team to win, but they want to take the place of a man on the team. They fight each other for a place. They battle for supremacy, and yet they are on the same team. Yes?'

'S'pose,' I say.

'It's the team's manager who must foster this competition. Only the manager knows the overall strategy. Everyone else can only guess at it. It's the manager who pits player against player in psychological battle. They are pawns in the manager's game, unaware that they are being strengthened and tested. Sometimes, though, Jensen, a player gets a broken leg, and he's out of the game, a career-ending injury. It happens all the time. Sometimes that's the cost of playing the game at the highest level.'

'And Reg?' I says, my mind spinning with all this info, trying to sort it the fuck out in my head.

'Reg too. He played his part. Suffered rather more than just a broken leg, though, didn't he?' Miskin laughs when he says this. Then he goes on: 'Reg's little bomb plot, thwarted by Security Department special attaché Jensen Interceptor, who bravely put himself in danger to save society from harm. You're the brave defender, Jensen, who went in for a dangerous tackle to save your team from an attack on goal. You took the striker out, but you got your leg broken in the process. You're out of the game now, Jensen, I'm afraid. It was front-page news for days, though, and the media has been closely following your recovery too. There have already been three shows about you, Jensen. Very popular. And the PM has just announced a large increase in the security budget, with full support from the public. Quite right too. These deep-undercover operations are very, very expensive.'

All through this, I'd been craning my aching neck a couple of inches off the pillow, trying to take in all this football stuff what Miskin was laying on me. I couldn't keep my head up any more. It fell back into the pillow, and I found myself staring up at the ceiling with images of

n up by Reg's fucking bomb, all bits of her sprayed everywhere
ned up later by mongs from the Sanitation Department, cleaning
lood and the flesh and the mess, the sort of cleaning up that no
person wants to do. And I come awake and boo-hoo and shout,
it would be the needles and the pills again, and I'd feel better.
the three months of unconscious mending, there was the rehab.
nd weeks of hobbling about on sticks, then swimming, then
rubber balls and squeezing them. They put metal inside to hold
ogether that got blown up by the bomb. There are screws and
new joints made from plastic and rubber in me now. And I'm
d up. Lumpy red-raw all over my back, not smooth like I used
t not my face. My face is like it was, back to old Jensen's face;
py face of Norfolk the trampy geezer from Norfolk is gone

football players in my head, all diving around and tackling each other through muddy green grass, the thumping sound of their boots in my ears, a bone getting snapped in a leg and him with the snapped leg getting taken off on a stretcher.

So all what I'd been through, it was all like some kind of fucking show? They made me do what I did so they could catch Fyodor? But Fyodor was already in on it? The whole thing was a set-up to make it look like the Security Department has got its shit together? Mending leaks it had created in the first fucking place?

Miskin's head pops into my view of the ceiling.

'You see, conflict is the engine of progress, Jensen.' He leans in, closer to me, like he's going to tell me something very, very important. Something he believes in, like Reg believed in Martin Martin. His eyes go like blue steel when he talks. Fucking scary.

'Conflict is in the soul of us all, raging to escape. All you have to do is harness it, like splitting the atom, and you'll have enough energy to propel yourself into the future. Imagine all the energy of all the people of our great nation, united in conflict, urging ourselves on to greater achievements. Even those pitched against this system, our machinery of conflict, like Reg, it brings out the best in them too. As they define themselves in opposition to our machine, Jensen, they rail and they harness their own inner conflict. That becomes the energy that drives them. And that energy feeds our energy. We are all a part of the big conflict machine. Reg, Fyodor, you, me. We all play our part. That is the way of the universe. Violence, splitting apart, coming together, and splitting apart again. Destruction and creation, kept in balance by those of us called to the task. It is as inevitable as it is beautiful. But the balance is vital. We must hold the balance of power. If the balance tips in the other direction, away from the state and towards the likes of Reg, well, then we're in trouble.'

After this speech from Miskin, I was feeling as dizzy as when I was slipping through wormholes and getting all muzzed up about MM and Emile and Jensen and all that. It didn't make any sense to me, and at the same time, it sounded like the truth.

Miskin gets up to leave.

'It's been nice chatting with you, Jensen,' he says. And he reaches down to shake my hand.

There were still a couple of things bothering me. For one, the blokes in my gaff that time, from the department. One of them, I'd clobbered with my baseball bat. The other, I'd scarpered from and jumped out the window.

Miskin looked confused for a moment when I mentioned this to him. Then the light of realisation switched on in his eyes and he laughed.

'Oh yes, that's right! Brock's maintenance boys. Oh, Jensen, that was priceless. Still, they should have let you know before letting themselves in to mend your shower. You weren't to know they weren't rotten burglars, were you? I think one of them had a headache for a few days, well, a month or two, perhaps, but I believe he's fine now. No permanent damage. Well, not particularly serious damage anyway. The other was desperately worried when you jumped out the window and disappeared into the clouds, not to be seen again until you were scraped off the pavement outside Reg's flat after the bomb.'

'What about the chip in my head?' I ask.

'A chip?' says Miskin. 'I'm sorry. Jensen, you've lost me there. A chip?'

'I was told I had a chip in my head.'

'And who told you that, Jensen?' says Miskin, after a few moments of quiet.

'Martin Martin.'

'Right-oh,' says Miskin, suddenly happy and sounding sympathetic. 'Of course he did. You really have suffered, Jensen. You've survived a bomb attack. I wouldn't set too much store by any notion you might have that long-dead people have been visiting you and putting ideas in your head. There's a good chap.'

'Claire told me about it too. Before the bomb went off,' I say, a bit sulky.

Miskin is silent again for a moment.

'Like I said, you've survived a bomb attack, so I don't think any of us ought to take too seriously anything you think is true, eh? And I don't have to tell you that much of the information you came across as part of your extraordinary investigation is highly sensitive, classi-

fied. So don't go around telling anyone, eh? Jensen. After everything you've seen, you wo leak would you? That really would be no goo would take an extremely dim view of that, as

'And Claire?' I asks, the one big question.

'Claire. Yes. The mental-health worker. S Health Department from the Security Departm the poor, running self-help groups and works A solid source of information, behaviour-mon should read her reports one day, Jensen. You' you can tell she had a soft spot for you. Sp community. Yes, shame that. Collateral damag have felt a thing. Now then, I must leave. I c Get well soon. Cheerio.'

I close my eyes. I fall asleep, exhausted.

I was waking up more often after Miskin vis had been to see me, but because I was mendin where I'd been. I preferred being awake to th I was asleep, I'd be off in the world of Reg's-h eels and all that mucky shit. I'd wake up co trembly. Then the docs would come along into my veins, or give me a needle, or pills i

I only found out how long it took for me like, better. They probably tried to tell me b to hear anything. I was three months uncon It took that long just for the burns and the

There were flashes of memories of Cla byes time. I always dreamed that she was would be, sitting there looking concerned reading a book, or sleeping in the half-ligh was nothing to worry about. And then the Claire were all happied up in the sunshin had a baby, a baby girl called Rose, and e we'd remember the girl with the hops koto then I'd come around some more and Claire

got blo and cle up the normal and the Afte Weeks holding the bits bolts an all scar to be. B the stro now.

Thirty-five

THIS NEXT voice is a voice in my ear, shouting all hot and croaky from too much boris and trying to make itself heard over the loud music. Me leaning against the bar, off dreaming, not concentrating:

'Hoy! Hoy! If it isn't old Jensen Interceptor! Fuck me!'

Here it is, then. Out of hosp, all patched up and as right as fucking rain, getting some tasty snifter up me and trying a new drink at the new Starfucks in Peckham. The music's biff-biff-biff – well fucking loud. Some new nationcore shit out of Africa, yeah? Mad shit, but all the fucking rage with all like necklaces and stuff you can wear while you listen to it. Going down a fucking treat with the trendy fuckers and all the cunts and teenies. Everyone's all decked out in fucking leather necklaces and rocking the nationcore. It all blew up while I was all fucked up, so I never saw it coming, but it's fucking right fucking on it, yeah? Love it.

But, you know, it's fucking weird, right, sitting in Starfucks. Like, I keep expecting to see fucking Fyodor come out the bogs with his cock hanging out and laughing like a fucking drain, or to see him fall down the stairs again all off his nut and dressed in a toga. But he's not here, is he? Nowhere to be seen, old Fyodor. Gone, gone, gone is Fyodor. And I kind of fucking miss him, yeah? Now I'm here in Starfucks, I remember how always it was me and him what did all the Starfucks fun together, and how we'd get right done in, and he'd talk me into more and more, until I was so fucked up I didn't know which way was up, and we'd end up back at my place throwing all, like, food and shit at each other and laughing, and then we'd pass out in bed.

But all that's gone, and now I'm here alone, feeling the new boris brand (they call it Boris Intense, and it kind of fucking is, but I'm an old hand, yeah, takes something fucking well special to burst my bubbles).

Here's a thing, right: as I think about all Fyodor and that, I find it's getting more difficult to remember any more details than just that me and Fyodor had a fucking good laugh and that he was fucking funny. The harder I concentrate, the more difficult it gets. I can't even see his face proper no more. He always did look a bit like Mackie Garage off of *Monster Trucks*, and now when I think of Fyodor and try to picture his face, all I can see is Mackie Garage getting all excited and shouting about the *Monster Trucks* action. It's probably the medical-grade gear they pumped into me at the hospital. And the B-19s. All the stuff to sort my brain out once and for all, so I wouldn't get all moody and weird and go fucked up in the head about getting blown up and shit like Claire getting all torn to bits by Reg's bomb in front of my face.

Anyway, yeah, right, so I was sat at home, the spank pad up the Rotherhithe Sky Tower (all that's fixed up proper now; all the water is gone, new floors and a fucking new Dermo Shower, thank you very fucking much), and, you know, I just couldn't think what to do or where to go. I suppose I miss Fyodor. And Claire. But I'm on these fucking well-monster pills. They don't even have a fucking proper name, just B-19s. They keep me on the straight and narrow, feeling all right, keeping it together so it's all, like, together.

You should have seen the fucking stack of *Monster Trucks* shit that had piled up while I was all out of it and bashed up off of that explosion. There was, like, weeks of it. It would have taken me years to watch it all, yeah? And anyway, the whole *Monster Trucks* thing has moved on. There's *New MT Extreme* now, where the trucks are all stripped out. They're pretty much like big fucking cages on wheels. And the drivers are chained into their seats with all locks and shit so they can't get out, and the trucks are twice as big as before. And they've got all these gouging knife things sticking out of them, and they drive into each other and try to fucking all slice each other to bits or force each other into pits of flames, shit like that. So now there's *New MT Extreme*, old *Monster Trucks* just looks kind of old and lame and really shit and like, why was I ever into it in the first place? Fucking modern shit is so much cooler than fucking old shit. It's really cool that new shit comes along that's fucking way better than the old shit, yeah? Can you imagine if that's not what happened and everything stayed the fucking same all the time? Fucking boring, yeah? Shitbags.

Erm, right, so there I was, at home, kind of bored with all my *Monster Trucks* stuff and thinking about deleting it all and, like, not fucking bothering to watch it, like ever, yeah? And I thought, 'Fuck this for being bored, I'm going out.' So I put on some neat clothing, shaved and all that stuff so I'm poncified and looking good and hit the streets.

Thing is, once I was out, I couldn't think where to go. All the places around the Sky Tower are for food and shops and that, and I didn't fancy trekking up west. I'd heard about the Peckham Starfucks refurb, so I decided to check it out.

So there I am, on my fucking tod, the new nationcore clanking away, the girls offering it up but me not really up for it. I'm just taking it easy at the bar, thinking about other things; about Fyodor, but forgetting him while I'm thinking about him, like watching water seep down into the ground after rain, or like when the music fades out and there's nothing left no more where once there was loud beats but suddenly it's gone and you can't remember the tune to whistle or sing to yourself, even though while it was playing you were like, 'Yeah! This is the fucking best shit fucking ever, yeah?'

And then there's this voice.

'Hoy! Hoy! If it isn't old Jensen Interceptor! Fuck me!'

I turn around to face this voice bothering me. I can't recognise who it is, but I know I know him. It's dark, and the new boris is confusing things. The nationcore isn't helping, and the serum in my veins from the hospital is making things sort of out of focus in my brain.

'Sorry, mate,' I says. 'I don't know who you are.'

'Yeah, well,' says the bloke, 'hardly fucking surprising is it? You've been right fucked up, yeah? I seen you on the shows and in the mags and fucking everything. I said to everyone who'd fucking listen, which was fucking hardly anyone, the cunts, "I know that bloke! We was mates! You should have seen him off his fucking trolley on the klear haze in the bogs! Smacked his fucking head into the mirror!" They was the days, eh? Old fucking Jensen Interceptor.' And he grabs me in a big hug, like he's my long-lost brother or some such.

Something's tickling away in my head, but I still can't place this dozy fucker. He sees my face still with no light on behind the eyes.

'Basic-skills training? Gibson? Remember?'

Fucking Gibson! It's fucking Gibson! The twat off the basic skills (protection) course what I went on before everything kicked off. Fucking Gibson, who mucked about like a mong and didn't take the course serious. Fucking Gibson, who dosed me up on his mad klear-haze powder and that little vial of stuff that made it go off double big time and sent me doollaly! Gibson's fucking funny. I remember him now, and here he is in front of me, large as fucking life, hugging me to his chest, his suit all pressed up into my face, him slapping me on the back and going, 'Fucking Jensen Interceptor, eh? Fancy bumping into you again! And you, all fucking famous!'

'Yeah, fucking great!' I says to Gibson.

'Amazing, what you been through and all that,' says Gibson. 'What's it like getting blown up?'

I shrug. I been asked that a lot of times since I got out the hosp and found out that I was like a fucking mini-celeb.

'It hurt,' I says to Gibson, who laughs until there's snot coming out his fucking nose, like I'm the funniest fucker he's ever met.

'You're fucking funny,' he says. 'Let's totally, like, hang out, yeah?' he says.

And so we do. We get proper messy as the night goes on. But we just sit there at the bar, Gibson listening to me tell him about how fucking society works, how Unity and Success is all about harnessing the conflict. I tell him about how Dermo Showers are made to pack in.

'Oh, the bollock!' he shouts when I tell him this. 'I've got a Dermo 04.'

'Nah,' I shake my head, 'You don't want an 04. You should go for the 54. The 04's always going to fuck up every three months; the quarter valve on them is made of crappy plastic and snaps well easy.'

The Dermo 54 is total shit too, as it goes, but I'm not about to tell him that. One thing at a time. He's got to serve his apprenticeship, yeah? Just like what I did. He needs to learn bit by fucking bit.

I decide to go home. Gibson gives me his card.

'If you want to hang out again, call me, yeah?' he says.

It says 'Gibson Stratocaster, Social Studies Section'.

'Cool name, mate,' I say, cos I didn't know he was called Gibson Stratocaster before.

'Yeah,' he says, 'ta. But it's not as cool as yours, is it? You're fucking well cool.'

'Yeah, well,' says I. 'See you.'

It's funny, but in the old days there would have been no way I'd have left any Starfucks without having filled my boots. But without Fyodor there, it kind of seems pointless.

When I get home, I stick the big screen on and settle down to get into some decent *Porn Disco* action, but I just don't seem to be able to get up for it, yeah? I just get to feeling sleepy.

As I half-watch the porn, arse and tits and cock all over the place, I get to thinking that everything that went on before seems like it didn't really happen. Which is fucking handy when you think about it. I mean, who wants to go around thinking about what happened last year, or ten years ago? If you thought about all the things that have happened before, all the bad things, all the killing and the piles and piles of corpses and bones and human dust under our feet, you'd go mad. Look at Reg. What good did it do him, all living in the fucking past like that? If you've done bad things, just forget about it and move on. What happened yesterday happened yesterday. You need to be thinking about what's happening right now, or tomorrow, maybe. The same goes for the future. There's no use in thinking about that too much either. Leave all the thinking to them that know how. You'll be rotting flesh under the ground soon enough and then none of it will fucking matter one bit, nothing you did or said.

Which means there's only now. Now's the place. Not stuck in the past like the Martin Martinists, still all angry and mad as mumbles over something that happened ages ago and which makes them go around causing all the explosion trouble.

I doze off on the seater. I got a new seater when I got out of hosp, to fucking cheer me up and that. A Spinoza, direct from the factory. It totally fucking matches my suit which I had made up by Spinoza's personalised-design service, which is fucking well cool.

I wake up on the seater and look at the screen. The lights have stopped flashing about, there's just a still image up there. As soon as I look up at it, it disappears into a blur of static and the screen flashes to black, but I saw who it was up there on the screen.

It was Martin Martin. Trying to pull me back. But I'm not going. I don't want no scrambled brains and bombs again. I've had enough of all that. I close my eyes, and I feel the sleep come up over me like a big black fucking wave out of a big black fucking ocean.

Acknowledgements

My heartfelt thanks to:

My agent, Antony Topping at Greene & Heaton, whose willingness to help me goes beyond the call of duty, I'm sure.

Christopher Dawes, aka Push, my first ever editor and mentor.

Will Francis at Greene & Heaton for some excellent input, and Elizabeth Cochrane, also of Greene & Heaton, for her work on my behalf.

My editor at Jonathan Cape, Dan Franklin.

Alex Bowler at Jonathan Cape.

Steve Appleton and Paul Thompson of Worldnet Productions, whose varied skills and constant support have been very important.

My father, and my brother, Rick.